Wildburn

Edith Moss

Published by Edith Moss, 2024.

This is a work of fiction. Similarities to real people, places, or events are entirely coincidental.

WILDBURN

First edition. November 12, 2024.

Copyright © 2024 Edith Moss.

ISBN: 979-8230400721

Written by Edith Moss.

Chapter 1: In the Line of Fire

The heat presses in from all sides, a tangible weight that clings to the skin and suffocates the air. My eyes burn from the smoke, but it's not enough to cloud my focus, not enough to stop me from pushing forward into the madness of it all. My boots sink into the soft, ashy earth with every step I take, each movement a reminder that the fire is a living, breathing thing, and it's hungry.

I glance back over my shoulder, where the fire line breaks open in a torrent of flames, thick and hungry, tearing through the trees with a roar that seems to echo the fury in my chest. But it's the figure standing between me and the line of fire that catches my attention, more than the blaze itself.

He's got that rugged look, the kind that should be reserved for those men who've spent their lives outdoors, breaking the rules as if it's second nature. His dark hair is matted with sweat, eyes sharp as they lock with mine. He stands there like a mountain, unmoving, his body angled in a way that leaves little room for anyone else to pass. I try to skirt around him, but he shifts, blocking me with ease, as though he knew I was coming the moment I started moving.

"Not this way," he says, voice low and steady, though there's an edge to it. "You'll get yourself killed."

I stop, the tension thick enough to cut through. There's something in his gaze, something that burns with the same intensity as the fire behind us. He's not wrong. The way ahead is a firestorm waiting to swallow anything in its path, but I'm not one to turn back.

"You don't know what I'm capable of," I snap, taking a step forward, my boots crunching against the charred earth. His jaw tightens, a muscle twitching as he watches me, calculating.

"Don't be stupid," he counters, his voice hardening. "This is no place for bravado. It's not about what you can do. It's about getting out alive."

"Isn't that the point of every job we do?" I fire back, the words sharper than I intended. But the anger is real, a frustration that's been building since I first heard the rumors about him. The rookie smoke-jumper. The one who doesn't follow orders. The one who's already had too many close calls and doesn't seem to care. Everyone warned me to watch out for him, that he'd get someone killed. But what do they know? What do I know, for that matter?

He holds my gaze for a moment longer, the silence stretching between us, thick and uncomfortable. Then, without warning, he shifts to the side, his stance more relaxed, as though he's decided to give in, just this once. But even in that, there's a sense of danger, like he's letting me take the first step into something that could go horribly wrong, and he's just waiting to see if I'll make it.

I don't hesitate. I move past him, my boots hitting the dirt with a rhythm that matches my pulse. The air around me shimmers with heat as I plunge forward, pushing through the thick smoke that chokes my lungs and fills my eyes with tears. But I keep my focus—there's no time to waste, no time to second guess. The fire is unpredictable. It's changing every second, growing, evolving, and I can't afford to fall behind now.

Behind me, I hear him follow, the faint rustle of his gear a constant reminder that he's still there. I don't need to look back to know he's close, too close for comfort, and I don't like it. I don't like the way his presence lingers in my mind, a distraction I can't shake off. The fire's crackling roar almost drowns out the sound of his boots, but the thudding of my own heart is louder, a reminder that we're both walking into the unknown.

Ahead, the trees are consumed by flames, their branches snapping and crackling with each gust of wind. The fire is a living thing, a beast hungry for destruction, for chaos. The air is thick with the scent of burning wood, the sting of smoke lingering in the back of my throat. I push forward, my hands reaching out to steady myself against the heat, the surge of adrenaline coursing through me, quickening my steps.

Then, the sound of the crackling fire shifts, a sharp, unnatural noise that freezes me in my tracks. A tree, already weakened by the flames, is starting to topple. I don't have time to think. I dart to the side, adrenaline surging through my veins as the massive trunk crashes down where I was standing just moments ago. The shockwave from its fall sends a cloud of embers swirling in the air, and I hear a grunt behind me—a curse, followed by the unmistakable sound of boots scrambling to avoid the same fate.

"Careful!" he calls out, his voice strained. "Don't get too close!"

I don't have to turn around to know he's there, his breath heavy, his presence looming just behind me like a shadow. My focus snaps back to the tree, now blocking the path. The fire's spread faster than I thought, its reach hungry, its unpredictability something I should've expected but didn't. This isn't a time to be cocky, not a time to show off.

I know what I need to do. The fire line is ahead, but it's thick with smoke and danger. The best way to break through it is to fight fire with fire. I reach for my gear, unzipping the pouch on my waist and pulling out the flare gun. It's a simple tool, a last-resort option, but it's better than nothing.

I take aim at the base of the tree, the flickering flame of the flare lighting up the smoky air as it streaks through the sky. The flare hits the ground with a burst, igniting a controlled burn just far enough to allow us to pass. It's risky, but it's our only shot.

"Follow me," I call over my shoulder, my voice hoarse from the smoke. "And stay low."

He doesn't argue. Not this time.

The flare pops, bursting into the air like a star gone wild, its tail of orange trailing behind it. I don't wait to see if it does its job—because it will, I've seen it work a thousand times before—but I'm already moving, feet digging into the earth, body low and bent under the weight of what's coming. The fire is relentless. It's like a beast, wild and unpredictable, and right now, I'm the one foolish enough to stare it down. But I've done this before. I've survived it before.

Behind me, I hear him follow. His presence is a weight I can't shake, heavy and unyielding. He's still close, close enough to make my skin itch with something that feels dangerously like tension. There's no room for tension when the earth is about to crack open and swallow us whole. Still, the quiet hum of his footsteps makes me aware of every inch of space between us. It's too much space. I can almost feel him breathing down my neck, but it's not a comfort. It never is.

"Your flare's going to burn out soon. You're not getting through this way," he calls, his voice cutting through the thick air, gruff and unyielding.

I don't stop. I don't even flinch. The fire behind me is already making its claim on the forest, and I can't let it take another step forward. I've seen it happen. I've watched fire swallow everything in its path without mercy, without hesitation. That's why I do this—because I won't let it take what matters.

"Then I'll find another way," I mutter, more to myself than to him, but he hears me anyway.

"You can't outrun it," he says. It's not a challenge. It's a fact. And somehow, that makes it worse. I don't need his warnings, don't need his help, but every time he speaks, it's like a reminder of how out of my depth I am. The fire's crackle grows louder, its roar shaking the very air, and the wind picks up, thickening the smoke, pushing it forward like a living thing.

I squint into the haze ahead. The trees around me are already beginning to bend under the heat, their leaves curling and shriveling before they turn to ash. I push through the wall of smoke, my breaths shallow but steady, feeling the heavy weight of my gear pulling at me with each step. I know I'm a heartbeat away from exhaustion, but that's not a luxury I have right now. There's no room for weakness.

But then, a sudden crack—a snap—and I'm falling forward, catching myself just before I hit the ground. My hand meets something wet and slick with mud. The floor of the forest has changed. It's soft, too soft, and it gives beneath me, threatening to pull me under. A swamp? Not now. Not here.

I glance back, hearing the unmistakable crunch of boots behind me. He's right there, his outline barely visible through the smoke, moving with a speed and precision that speaks of experience. I can't help but watch him, even for the briefest moment, as he cuts through the haze like a blade through cloth. He's efficient. But he's not me. He's not here, in the same space, not in this mind.

"Don't stop. It's not safe," he warns again, though his voice has dropped, low and steady now. It's not so much a command, but an observation, as if he's been tracking me for miles and already knows what I'll do. And yet, I can't seem to pull myself away from the way his words linger in the air, hanging there as if waiting for something—some sign that I'll listen.

I push through the muck and debris, my boots sinking further with each step. The ground is shifting, soft in places, treacherous in others. I hate it. It's unpredictable, like everything else right now. If I slip, I'll be caught, and there's no telling what that could mean for me. The fire, the smoke, the heat—nothing about this makes sense, and it's driving me to the edge. But that's what I do. I get close to the edge, close to losing myself, and then I find a way out. I always do.

The thudding of my boots is the only sound in the world that matters now. The fire has its own rhythm, its own beat, but it's not enough to drown out the steady drum of my heart. My chest tightens as I move further, the air thinning, each breath harder than the last. I can't see past the smoke anymore, can barely make out the shapes of the trees, their silhouettes sharp against the blaze. But still, I move.

"You really think you're going to outrun this?" The voice is too close now, almost a whisper, but it cuts through the crackle of the flames with sharp precision. The words seem to flicker, and I turn just in time to see him come into view, right in my path. How did he get here so fast?

"What part of 'don't stop' do you not understand?" he asks, the sharpness of his tone leaving no room for argument.

I raise an eyebrow, pulling myself to my feet, trying to shake the last of the damp earth from my hands. "Maybe I just don't like being told what to do," I reply, my voice laced with something I can't quite place. Maybe it's defiance. Maybe it's exhaustion.

"You're stubborn." It's not a question; it's a statement. And I can't argue with it. I am stubborn. It's a trait that's kept me alive in this job, and I'd rather die with my pride intact than give up.

"I'm not stupid," I shoot back. "I know when to stop."

But as I say the words, I realize something—something that's been niggling at the back of my mind. He's not backing off. He's not just here because I'm too stubborn to listen. There's something more to this. Something more to him. And in that moment, the flames don't seem so dangerous compared to the fire smoldering between us.

I push forward, the crackling blaze now roaring on all sides, the weight of the heat pressing in, suffocating the air. My heart pounds in rhythm with the steady thrum of my boots, each step taking me further into the chaos. I don't dare look back, not even for a second. The fire demands your full attention or it will swallow you whole. Every inch of my body is attuned to the rhythm of the flames, the wind pushing them faster, hotter, but I keep moving. My hands sweat in my gloves, my gear feels heavier with each passing second, and the smoke wraps itself around me like a second skin.

But still, he's there. I don't have to turn around to know. His presence is a constant pulse at the back of my mind, a reminder that I'm not alone in this fight, whether I like it or not.

I hear him before I see him—a sudden rustle in the brush, the sharp snap of a branch underfoot. He's catching up, his breath harsh through the mask, and for a split second, I wonder if he's just here to make sure I don't do anything too stupid. He's got that way about him—the kind of man who watches you from a distance and then swoops in to fix the mess you've made of it.

"You're pushing it too far," he calls, voice low but insistent. The wind shifts, carrying his words straight to my ears, and it takes every ounce of my strength not to turn around and snap at him. I don't need a lecture. Not now, not when the fire's eating its way through the trees like a voracious beast.

"I'm not stopping," I say, through gritted teeth, my voice strained under the pressure. "This is what we do, right?"

There's a pause—just long enough for the words to hang heavy in the air between us. Then, almost reluctantly, his shadow falls beside me. He's moved up, right alongside me, his breath coming as quickly as mine.

"Yeah, but that is not what we do," he mutters, jerking his head toward the rising wall of fire ahead of us. It's a molten sea now, crackling and hissing, threatening to consume everything in its path. The wind has shifted again, pushing the flames back toward us.

I glance up, a mix of dread and determination flooding my veins. I know it's bad. I can feel the heat intensifying, the air growing thick and sharp, almost as if the flames are aware of my every movement. But I don't stop. Not for him, not for anything.

"You're going to get yourself killed," he says again, a note of something too close to frustration in his voice. Maybe it's just the heat, or maybe it's me—him having to chase me down like some reckless kid, always one step ahead of danger. He doesn't know this fire the way I do. Doesn't know the terrain, doesn't know the way it shifts and twists, the way it plays with you until you're too far in to see the way out.

"I'm not dead yet," I throw back, but the words feel thin, insincere even to me.

A huff of a laugh escapes him, sharp, mocking. "You're a piece of work, aren't you?"

I don't know whether I'm supposed to be offended or impressed by the way he sounds. Either way, I don't let it stop me. I force myself to breathe, to focus on the fire, the rhythm of the fire, to ignore the heat that's crawling under my skin. This isn't about him or about anything else. It's about surviving this, and nothing else.

"Where's the drop zone?" I ask, trying to keep my voice steady. My mind is racing, calculating the odds, the wind direction, the shift of the flames. I need a plan, and fast.

He doesn't respond immediately. Instead, he pushes forward, glancing around, clearly assessing the danger, the way any experienced jumper would. His face is set in that grim expression I've seen too many times.

"We're too far," he finally says, voice hard. "We won't make it."

I freeze, the implications of his words slicing through the thick smoke like a blade. He's right—if we don't make it past the next ridge, we won't have enough time to escape. The fire's moving faster than we anticipated.

But I'm not one to take defeat sitting down.

"Then we make our own drop zone," I say, voice calm now, a plan taking shape in my mind.

He stops short, looking at me as if I've lost my mind. I don't blame him. It's crazy. It's reckless. But it's the only option we have left. I can see it now, the way the fire lines are folding in on themselves, closing in tighter, pushing us toward the cliffside where the fire can't follow.

"You can't be serious," he says. "That's suicide."

"And what's your plan?" I shoot back, turning on him. "Wait for a rescue team that's never going to show? Hope the fire dies down before it takes everything we've worked for?"

His eyes narrow. "You think I'm just gonna sit back and watch you do something stupid?"

"No," I say, meeting his glare. "But if you're going to try and stop me, you'd better move fast."

I turn back to the fireline, feeling the heat now like a living thing behind me, but there's no time to second-guess. No time to think about what could happen. Only what will happen.

And then, just as I step forward, the ground beneath my feet shifts—a loud crack and the unmistakable rumble of something massive breaking apart. A tree, one that had been standing only seconds ago, falls toward me, its branches snapping like broken bones in the night.

I freeze, just as the world tilts sideways, and then I hear it—the unmistakable sound of him shouting my name, but the rest is lost in the crash, the thunder of the tree's fall, the roaring fire... and the deafening silence that follows.

Chapter 2: Heat of the Moment

The sharp click of my boots echoed down the long, sterile hallway, each step a rhythmic reminder that I was tethered to something I couldn't quite shake. It had been a hell of a night, the kind that left the air thick and charged, like a storm waiting to crack open. We had spent hours fighting the flames, watching them lick and claw at the sky, until it was nothing but ash and the stench of smoke curling through our pores. There were murmurs about the fire being set on purpose, and while the rest of the team gossiped behind closed doors, I couldn't bring myself to care. Not yet.

Instead, I found myself looking for him.

Mason Hale was a presence. A force of nature all on his own, standing in the center of the chaos with the calm of someone who'd seen it all. His face, always unreadable, was the kind of handsome that made people second guess their own reflection. But it wasn't just his looks, not really. It was the way he carried himself, shoulders straight and back like a man who knew every single thing about everyone around him—but kept it hidden behind an impenetrable mask of professionalism.

The room was heavy with the stench of sweat and burnt wood, the kind of scent that clung to you for hours, no matter how many showers you took. The air was thick with adrenaline and unspoken tension, the sort that could snap if you weren't careful. I hadn't meant to cross his path. Not tonight, not after everything. But there he was, just standing there, eyes sharp, dark, waiting. I couldn't move past him, couldn't look away.

His stare was like a rope, pulling me closer despite every instinct telling me to step back. I tried to breathe through it, to keep my face neutral, but the more I stared, the harder it became. There was a tension between us, something that I couldn't define, something that had started to form the moment I walked into the room. Mason didn't speak, didn't need to. His silence wrapped around me like a thick fog, making my thoughts muddled and slow.

I watched as he leaned against the doorframe, arms crossed in that disarmingly casual way of his, and I swore I saw a flicker of something behind those dark eyes of his. It wasn't amusement, exactly. It was a challenge. One that he didn't have to voice, because I knew what it meant. It was the same thing he always did. He made you feel like you were playing a game where you didn't even know the rules, but somehow, you still couldn't stop playing.

I shifted my weight, eyes flicking to the rest of the team, who were scattered around the debrief table, murmuring to each other in tight circles. They were still rattled from the fire, still pulling at the edges of their nerves. But Mason? He didn't flinch. Not when they mentioned arson. Not when the chief barked orders. He was a rock in the center of a storm.

But I knew better than to be fooled by that smooth exterior. Everyone had a breaking point. Everyone had something that they kept buried beneath all those layers. Something they didn't want anyone to see. And with Mason, there was always something that made my heart beat a little faster, something that made my skin prickle with warning.

I forced my gaze to the table, even though I knew better. I shouldn't have been thinking about Mason Hale at all, not in the middle of the debrief, not when everything was hanging by a thread. But when I felt his presence shift, when I heard the slightest exhale of air from his direction, I couldn't help myself. I wanted to know what was behind those eyes. What was buried in that impenetrable calm of his.

"You're not worried?" I asked, my voice sharper than I intended, cutting through the murmur of voices around us.

Mason's lips twitched, just barely, but he didn't answer right away. Instead, he stepped a little closer, the air between us thickening, like a magnet pulling me in. His body heat was almost tangible, a steady hum that vibrated in my bones. "Worried?" he repeated, his voice low, almost contemplative. "About what?"

I couldn't help the tension that coiled in my chest at the sound of his voice. It was too smooth, too certain, like he had the answers to questions I hadn't even thought to ask yet. I wanted to take a step back, but my feet remained frozen. This was ridiculous. We were supposed to be focusing on the fire, on the investigation. Not whatever this was between us.

I swallowed, trying to ignore the flutter of unease creeping down my spine. "About the fire," I said, struggling to keep my tone level, my heart rate steady. "About whether or not it was intentional."

The corner of Mason's mouth lifted again, but it wasn't a smile. It was something else, something darker, a flash of something dangerous that made my pulse spike in an instant. "We'll find out soon enough," he replied, his eyes never leaving mine. There was a finality to his words, a certainty that chilled me more than the night air. "But in the meantime, you're more concerned about me than the case, aren't you?"

I felt my heart stop for a beat. Of course he'd noticed. Mason always noticed. He had a way of seeing right through you, peeling back all the layers you thought you'd hidden.

I opened my mouth, searching for something clever to say, something that would deflect the heat of his gaze, but no words came. Instead, I just stood there, caught in his orbit, the rest of the world fading away.

I wasn't sure who was more dangerous. The fire, or the man who stood before me, knowing exactly what it was doing to me.

The hum of the fluorescent lights overhead was the only sound as I leaned against the conference table, my fingers drumming absentmindedly against the cold wood. My heart still thudded in time with the adrenaline of the night's fire, but it wasn't the fire that kept me awake now. It was Mason. Always Mason.

He hadn't moved since our brief exchange, still standing by the door like some immovable object, his presence pulling at the corners of my attention. Every time I tried to focus on the debrief, his quiet, watchful gaze would find its way back to me. It was maddening, the way he did it. No words, no gestures—just the unspoken weight of his gaze that turned every mundane moment into something full of potential danger.

I could feel the others in the room trying to act normal. It was like they knew Mason too, knew the kind of force he could be when he decided to show his teeth. They'd all been there long enough to understand the subtle shifts in his demeanor, the way he only spoke when he needed to, and even then, his words had the sharpness of a blade. But no one else seemed to be as affected by his silent observation as I was.

I bit back a sigh, glancing around the room. Mark and Sophie were huddled over a map, murmuring about possible leads, while Detective Lopez sketched notes into his battered notebook, his brow furrowed in concentration. It was a typical debrief, full of the necessary details that we'd all forget by tomorrow. And yet, with Mason's presence hanging over me, nothing felt typical anymore.

The fire was suspicious, no doubt about it, and the rumors of arson were enough to keep everyone on edge. There were so many ways this could go, so many paths we could follow to uncover the truth. But the longer I stood there, the more I realized something: it wasn't the fire that would keep me up tonight. It wasn't the case. It was Mason. The way he watched me like he could see through every layer I wore, like he could sense the uncertainty crawling beneath my skin.

I pushed myself off the table, pacing a few steps in the cramped room, hoping the motion would distract me, but my eyes always found their way back to him. When his gaze finally flickered down to the papers in front of him, his posture relaxing just a fraction, I felt an unexpected pang of relief. But it was fleeting, vanishing the moment he looked up again. The same unspoken challenge was in his eyes, the same deep knowing that made me question if I had any control over this situation at all.

"Everything alright?" Sophie's voice was soft, almost too soft for the tension in the air, but I caught the flicker of concern in her eyes.

I nodded, forcing a smile. "Yeah, just... tired. It's been a long night."

She didn't look convinced, but she didn't push either. Sophie was good at reading people, but she also knew when to let things slide. I appreciated that, though it didn't do much to ease the tightness in my chest. I had a feeling she knew more than she was letting on about the strange undercurrent between Mason and me, but I didn't feel like airing that dirty laundry. Not now.

Lopez cleared his throat, cutting through the moment of silence. "We'll need to get a team out to the scene in the morning. Someone should go through the building and the surrounding area for any signs of tampering."

It was the kind of plan that seemed both necessary and painfully obvious. I could tell Lopez was already lost in the details of the investigation, his mind ticking through the list of possibilities. But there was something about the way Mason shifted slightly, the faintest ripple in his composure, that caught my attention.

His eyes never left me as he spoke. "I'll go. I'll check the scene myself."

The words hung in the air, loaded with an intensity that made the room feel smaller. It was like he was offering something, but not quite. Like he was making a promise without making a promise.

I swallowed. "I'll go with you." It wasn't a question. It was more like I had no choice.

He didn't answer right away, but his lips curved into the faintest of smiles, as if he'd been expecting me to say exactly that. The heat between us simmered under the surface, palpable, even in the midst of all the chaos surrounding the investigation.

Mason glanced at Lopez, who gave a brief nod of approval before turning back to his notes. There was something about the exchange that seemed almost too effortless, too practiced, as if Mason had already decided on the course of action, and everyone else was just following along.

The door shut behind us with a quiet click, and for a moment, I thought I could breathe again. The space between us, once thick with unspoken words, now felt heavier, as though the absence of the others made it easier for the tension to settle in.

We walked in silence through the empty hallways, the sound of our footsteps muted on the polished floor. The building, once buzzing with the frantic energy of the fire, was now eerily quiet. Even the faint hum of the ventilation system seemed too loud in the silence. I could feel Mason just behind me, his presence a constant shadow, and I couldn't decide if it was comforting or unsettling. Probably both.

Outside, the air was cool, the breeze carrying the faintest remnants of smoke from the burned-out shell of the building. I could already see the faint glow of the crime scene tape, the glow of the flashing police lights still flickering in the distance. The smell of charred wood still lingered in the air, an acrid reminder of the chaos we'd fought through earlier.

Mason's hand brushed mine as he passed by me, a fleeting touch that shouldn't have mattered but did. I didn't look at him, but I felt the heat of it all the same.

"You seem distracted," he said, his voice low and rich, pulling me back from the edge of my thoughts.

I didn't answer right away, unsure of what to say, unsure of what he was even asking. Instead, I focused on the scene in front of me—the twisted metal, the burnt remnants of what had once been a building. The investigation. The case. All the things I should be paying attention to.

"You ever wonder why we're drawn to things like this?" I finally asked, my voice softer than I intended. "The chaos. The destruction. It's like... it's like it finds us, not the other way around."

Mason didn't answer at first, and for a moment, I thought he wouldn't. But then he spoke, his words carefully measured. "Maybe it's because it's easier to face fire than whatever burns inside of us."

It wasn't the answer I expected. But then again, with Mason, nothing ever was.

The crime scene was nothing like what I had expected. After all the weeks of preparation, the countless hours of surveillance and strategizing, standing there now felt like stepping into a ghost story. The air tasted metallic, thick with the remnants of burnt wood, and the dim glow of the lights from the police vehicles made the scene look like something from a nightmare—a place where too many things had been lost.

I tried to focus on the task at hand, on the scattered debris and the way the ashes still seemed to whisper with the scent of fire. My brain told me to pay attention to the evidence—the scorched remnants of a place that had once been full of life—but my body was rooted in something far more unsettling: Mason's proximity.

He was only a few steps behind me, his shadow falling across the ground like something out of a bad dream. I could feel the weight of his presence even if I didn't dare look at him directly. He moved silently, like a predator, and I wondered if he knew exactly how this—this strange dance between us—was making me lose track of everything else.

"You're quiet," he observed, his voice breaking through the silence like a sudden thunderclap.

I didn't look at him. I couldn't. Not now. His words were like the wind shifting, and I hated that I could feel it in my bones before it even happened. "I'm focused," I said, more to convince myself than him. "Trying to see things clearly."

"Mmm." He wasn't buying it. "Funny how clarity is hard to find when you're looking at the wrong things."

I resisted the urge to roll my eyes, but it wasn't easy. "And what do you think I'm looking at?"

He stepped closer, just enough to make my pulse hitch. "What you're not looking at," he said, a slight edge to his voice that I couldn't ignore.

I caught the subtle shift in his stance, the way he moved just a fraction closer. I was trying to focus on the aftermath of the fire, but every part of me was hyperaware of the way he stood there—his hands tucked into his jacket pockets, his jaw tense, his eyes narrowed like he was trying to decipher a puzzle only he could see.

I couldn't stand it. I needed to regain control of the situation. This wasn't about us. It couldn't be.

The sharp crack of broken glass broke through the tension like a sharp knife through cloth, and I jumped slightly. Mason's eyes flicked to the sound, his posture instantly shifting from casual to predatory. His focus was so razor-sharp it made my breath catch.

"Stay close," he ordered, his voice a low, urgent murmur. It wasn't a suggestion.

Despite the cold air, I felt a flush creep up my neck. My mouth opened to protest, but the words wouldn't come. Instead, I just nodded, and it felt like I had just sealed my fate in that simple movement.

The area around the fire was still being combed for evidence, the flicker of flashlights cutting through the dark like a steady pulse. The faint glow from the police vehicles created long, eerie shadows that stretched out across the wreckage, casting everything in an ominous light. The building had collapsed in on itself, leaving behind a skeleton of twisted metal beams and charred remnants of what had once been a place of life. Nothing about it felt normal—nothing about the scene made sense.

I hadn't even realized that Mason had stepped forward until he was already knee-deep in the debris, crouched down next to a patch of ground where the earth had been scorched and cracked open by the fire. His movements were deliberate, measured. He was scanning the area, his fingers gently brushing the blackened earth, and I couldn't help but wonder what he was seeing.

It wasn't until he looked up at me—his expression unreadable—that I realized I'd been holding my breath.

"There's something here," he said quietly, his gaze holding mine with an intensity that stole my breath away. "Something... off."

I wasn't sure if he was talking about the fire, the scene, or us. But I couldn't shake the feeling that whatever it was, it was far worse than anything I could have anticipated.

"Off?" I echoed, my voice a little too sharp, a little too uncertain.

He nodded slowly, his eyes flicking back to the spot where he had knelt. "The fire doesn't fit. It's too... calculated."

My stomach churned at his words. "Calculated? You think someone set it intentionally?"

He didn't answer right away. Instead, he stood, brushing off his hands with the same cool precision he brought to everything he did. His gaze lingered on me for a beat longer than necessary, and

I could see the storm brewing in his eyes. "I think we need to be prepared for a lot more than we're seeing here."

Before I could ask him what he meant by that, his eyes darted over my shoulder, focusing on something just out of my view. His body stiffened, and I followed his line of sight instinctively. But by the time I turned, the figure was already disappearing into the shadows, a brief flicker of movement that sent a chill running through me.

Mason cursed under his breath, and before I could ask, he was already moving, swift and silent. "Stay behind me," he ordered, his voice a low growl.

I didn't have time to argue. Not that I would have anyway.

The darkness of the alleyway ahead swallowed the figure whole, but Mason was relentless. He didn't hesitate, didn't question. It was like he was chasing a ghost, his footsteps sure and steady as he moved forward, following the trail left behind by the figure in the night.

I hesitated for just a moment, uncertainty flooding me, but then I followed him. My heart thudded in my chest, adrenaline spiking again as I moved to keep up with his rapid pace.

We reached the alley, the air thick with tension, when suddenly Mason stopped, his hand coming up to still me. He was listening—waiting for something, some sign.

A crack echoed in the distance, followed by a faint rustling sound. My heart raced, my breath shallow, and I almost didn't notice the figure reappear in front of us, shrouded in the dark.

But when they turned around, my stomach dropped. It wasn't just any person. It was someone I knew.

And what they were holding made everything inside me freeze.

Chapter 3: Smoke and Mirrors

The morning light was thin, hesitant as it stretched over the town, casting long shadows that seemed to twist and shudder under the weight of last night's events. I sat on the porch, cradling a mug of coffee that was more warmth than substance, the steam rising in delicate spirals before it vanished into the chill. The scent of scorched wood still clung to the air, thick and acrid, like it had etched itself into the very fabric of the day. There was something unsettling about it, that lingering burn, like it wasn't quite finished.

A sudden knock on the door broke my reverie, sharp and insistent. I didn't need to check to know who it was. A glance through the window confirmed his silhouette, leaning casually against the frame. Of course, it would be him. I had almost forgotten he existed after last night's chaos, and now, here he was, back again like a puzzle piece I hadn't asked for but was determined to find its place.

"Coffee?" I asked, my voice laced with more sarcasm than I intended.

He shrugged, pushing the door open before I had a chance to invite him in. I didn't bother with a response—he wasn't the type to ask permission anyway.

I knew the rules by now. He walked in like he owned the place, making himself at home as if he'd always been here, and I, well, I was the one scrambling to keep up. But this morning, I didn't feel that familiar unease—the dissonance between wanting to know more and fearing what that would mean.

"What do you want?" I finally asked, setting my mug down on the counter, letting the silence stretch between us.

He was looking at me, studying me with those unnerving eyes, like he could see right through me. "I was hoping you could tell me why everyone's so nervous about the body they found this morning."

I blinked, momentarily caught off guard. A body? Who? I hadn't heard a word about it.

"What body?" I asked, forcing the words out as if they weren't foreign in my mouth.

He smirked, that same lazy, arrogant curve of his lips that always made my insides twist. "You've been keeping your ear to the ground, haven't you? Haven't heard the news?"

I hated that he was right. I didn't need to ask. I knew now, in that brief moment of hesitation, what he was getting at. The fire. The strange happenings. The town. Of course, it would all connect somehow, but I hadn't been prepared for it to happen so quickly.

"Someone's dead?" I repeated, though the question seemed pointless.

He nodded, the shift in his expression just enough to show me that this wasn't just some passing curiosity for him. "Found near the burn site. And you know what they're saying. It wasn't an accident."

I swallowed, the reality of his words finally sinking in, the chill of fear creeping down my spine like the slow slide of a knife. For a moment, I felt lightheaded, dizzy from the weight of it all. It wasn't supposed to be like this.

"You think it's connected to the fire?" I asked, my voice almost a whisper.

He didn't answer right away, but the flicker in his eyes told me he already knew. He'd figured it out—whatever it was. And he wasn't about to let me off the hook so easily.

"It's a little too perfect, don't you think?" His tone was light, but there was a sharp edge to it now, something guarded that hadn't been there before. "A body found after the fire. Too clean. Like someone's trying to make a statement."

I stared at him, watching his every movement as he moved to the window, his back to me as he surveyed the empty streets outside. There was something in the way he held himself, tense but controlled, like he was always waiting for something to happen. Or perhaps something to break.

"So what's your theory?" I asked, leaning against the counter, crossing my arms in a move that was meant to be casual but only emphasized how unprepared I felt.

He turned to face me, his eyes narrowing ever so slightly. "My theory? I think you know a lot more than you're letting on."

I froze. The accusation hung in the air like a taut wire, humming with the weight of his words.

"Don't look so surprised," he said, his voice low, almost mocking. "You've been following this story for longer than anyone realizes. Haven't you?"

I blinked, but there was no denying it now. His words were pointed, and they hit harder than I expected. I had been curious—no, more than curious—about the fires, about what had really been going on in the town. But I wasn't about to admit it. Not to him. Not yet.

"You don't know what you're talking about," I said, trying to sound confident, but even to my own ears, it came out too weak.

"Sure I don't," he replied with a wry smile, the kind of smile that made me want to throw something at his head and laugh at the same time. "But here's the thing. You and I are in the same boat. We both know more than we should, and neither of us is talking. Yet."

He stood there for a beat, letting the tension stretch like it was some kind of challenge. Then, almost as if to break the silence, he added, "You'll be seeing more of me, whether you like it or not."

I wanted to say something, anything that would cut through the air, but the truth was, I wasn't sure if I was ready to know the answers. And I definitely wasn't sure if I could handle whatever it was he was trying to tell me.

I didn't trust him, not entirely. But something in me wanted to. And that scared me more than I cared to admit.

"Don't think I'm going to make this easy for you," I said, but my words felt hollow, like they meant nothing.

He chuckled, his gaze unwavering. "Who said anything about easy?"

And just like that, he was gone.

I didn't expect him to come back. Not like this. There was a bruise in my mind from the way he'd left—like a door slamming shut without a sound. But the next morning, the world was different. The air was thicker, like something had happened in the night, and the weight of it was pressing on everything.

The whispers started as I stood by the fire pit, half-distracted, watching the last remnants of smoke curl lazily into the bright sky. It was too still this morning, no birds calling, no cars rumbling by. Just the strange, muffled hush that always seems to settle over a place after tragedy, when the air itself seems to hold its breath.

I caught a glimpse of a man walking past my window. Tall, broad-shouldered, his hat tilted low enough that I couldn't quite make out his face. But I knew him. No one had seen him before the fire, but now, after the body, no one seemed to care.

I grabbed my coat and stepped outside, feeling the crisp bite of the morning air seeping through the fabric. The town was quieter than usual. It always seemed to hold its breath after something happened. I had grown used to the small-town dynamic of news traveling faster than lightning, but this felt different. There was something more urgent in the silence.

As I made my way toward the burn site, the scent of charred wood still hung in the air, and I could taste it on my tongue. The smell was too fresh. Too recent. It didn't feel like something from days ago—it felt like it was still happening. Like the fire hadn't gone out at all, but had merely shifted its shape and taken on a new form.

I turned the corner to the clearing where the fire had been, and that's when I saw them—two officers standing near the edge, a yellow tape marking off the area. And the body, lying there, still and cold as the first frost. His face was partially obscured, but I knew immediately that it wasn't just another casualty of misfortune. This man had been deliberate.

There was a whisper in the back of my mind, something I couldn't quite put into words, but the second I saw the way his hands were positioned, the stark lines of his body, I knew—this was no accident. The burn site had attracted attention for a reason, and now this man's death made it all the more dangerous.

A rustling noise behind me jerked me back from the gruesome scene, and I turned just in time to catch a familiar figure emerging from the shadows of the trees.

"You're looking for answers again, aren't you?" The voice was low, familiar—just enough to send a shiver down my spine.

I swallowed, but the taste of ash was still on my tongue. He stood there, hands in his pockets, looking like he belonged to this place in ways no one else did. He wasn't scared. Not of this town, not of me, not of whatever lay just beyond the edge of the forest.

"What do you know about this?" I asked, my voice tight.

He took his time responding, his gaze lingering on the body as though he were inspecting a piece of furniture, rather than a life cut short. Finally, his lips quirked into that same infuriating half-smile.

"I don't know much. But I think we both know it's connected." His words were careless, but the way he said it made my chest tighten.

"How?" I couldn't stop myself from asking. There were too many questions, too many things that didn't add up.

He glanced at me, his gaze sharp. "You don't know it yet, but you've been watching the wrong fire."

I shook my head, confused. "What does that mean?"

"You've been looking at the burn sites—the charred remnants, the heat, the smoke. But there's a story beneath that," he said, his voice dropping lower, almost a whisper now. "A story that goes deeper than flames."

His words hung in the air, dense and heavy, and I couldn't help but feel like I was being pulled into something bigger than I had anticipated. I took a step closer, not sure if I was braver for it or simply more foolish.

"Why do you keep saying things like that?" I challenged, my voice louder now, desperation creeping in. "What is it that you know? What aren't you telling me?"

He looked at me then, really looked at me, and for a brief moment, I caught the flicker of something else in his eyes—something deeper. Something guarded.

"You don't want to know," he said, his voice rough now. "But you're going to. You're in this now whether you like it or not."

I took a step back, a coldness seeping into my bones that had nothing to do with the weather. My gut twisted, but I couldn't help but feel an odd pull toward him, like he had just unlocked a door I hadn't known was there.

"You're still a stranger to me," I said, more to steady myself than anything else.

He cocked an eyebrow, that damn half-smile tugging at his lips again. "Strangers are just friends you haven't made yet."

I didn't know what to say to that, so I didn't say anything at all. The silence stretched out between us, thick and uncomfortable, and for the first time, I realized how much of it was a game for him. He was playing a game, and I was the pawn.

A vehicle pulled up behind us, the crunch of gravel under tires slicing through the tension. I glanced over my shoulder to see the officers stepping out of the car, their eyes flicking between us. The man was already taking a step back, fading into the shadows with a kind of fluid ease that made me wonder how much he'd been holding back all along.

Before he disappeared completely, he looked over his shoulder, and for a second, his expression softened, just enough to make my pulse quicken. "Be careful," he said, his tone suddenly serious.

Then, he was gone—vanishing into the trees like he had never been there at all.

I stood there for a long time after, the silence of the burn site pressing down on me, heavy as stone. Something was wrong, something was off, and I couldn't quite grasp it yet. But I would. That much I knew for certain.

The wind picked up in the afternoon, kicking dust through the town like it had somewhere to be, and the scent of something burnt still clung to the edges of the day. I was back at the diner, my fingers tapping impatiently against the chipped porcelain mug, the kind that probably cost pennies but somehow felt like they'd seen a hundred years of secrets and bad coffee. It wasn't even noon, but I could already feel the weight of the day pressing on my shoulders. Whatever had happened this morning, with the body by the fire, wasn't just the latest chapter in this town's odd little history—it was a tipping point. A moment when everything could go wrong.

Or, I thought, maybe everything had already gone wrong, and we just hadn't realized it yet.

I couldn't shake the feeling that the stranger—whatever he was, whatever he wanted—was tied up in this mess. He was too much of an enigma, too well-versed in playing games with people's nerves. He'd said something, something that felt like a dare. I didn't think it would come to anything, but the pit in my stomach said otherwise.

"Cynthia!"

I jerked my head up, my thoughts scrambling as I realized someone had called my name. It was Rachel, her round face all rosy-cheeks and concern, eyes flicking over my shoulder toward the door.

"The new guy's here again," she said with a grimace, as though the mere mention of him made her uncomfortable.

I followed her gaze, already knowing who she meant. He stood just inside the diner, his hands in his pockets, looking like he'd walked out of a noir film and into the middle of our quiet little town. The air seemed to shift with his presence, like he was pulling all the weight toward him without even trying.

I didn't know why I still couldn't quite place him—he wasn't like the rest of us, not even close. But there he was, as if he belonged here, as if we all should've been used to him by now.

"You're really going to let him in?" I asked Rachel, my voice low enough not to carry.

She rolled her eyes, clearly annoyed. "It's a free country. Unfortunately."

I couldn't help but smirk at her tone, but it didn't last. He was already headed our way, and I had a sudden, overwhelming urge to stand up and walk out of the diner. But instead, I sat there, rooted to the spot, watching him get closer.

"Morning," he said when he reached my table, his voice like dark honey—smooth, rich, just the slightest bit dangerous.

"Not for me," I replied, trying to ignore the flutter of something in my stomach.

He slid into the seat across from me without waiting for an invitation, his eyes catching mine in that way that made me feel like I was being peeled open and studied in the worst possible way.

"I think you're looking for answers in the wrong places," he said casually, like we were discussing the weather.

I blinked, the words hitting me square in the chest. "What's that supposed to mean?"

He leaned back in his seat, his lips curling into a smile that barely touched his eyes. "It means, you're not asking the right questions. You're so focused on the fire, on what's been burned, you're missing what's been left behind."

I didn't say anything at first, but I could feel the tension building, the weight of his words sinking deeper into my chest. There was something about him, something about the way he spoke with such confidence, that made it hard to ignore. It was like he knew more than he was letting on, and yet, he was still dangling the answers just out of reach.

"So, what should I be asking?" I finally said, unable to keep the challenge out of my voice.

"You're asking about the body, aren't you? The one they found by the fire. But that's not the part you need to understand," he said, his tone quieter now, more intimate, as though we were the only two people in the room. "You need to figure out why he was there in the first place. Why he wasn't burned with the rest of it."

I froze, the breath catching in my lungs as his words settled in. My thoughts scrambled for some kind of explanation, some thread to pull on, but nothing came. It didn't make sense.

"That's..." I started, but nothing followed. The words were too big, too twisted to fit into anything neat.

"Think about it," he urged. "The fire's not the point. It's what's missing that matters. And you're not seeing it because you're too focused on what's in front of you."

I stared at him, my mind whirring. I hated that he was right, but it was becoming painfully clear. I wasn't looking for the right things. There was something else, something buried deeper than the charred earth, and I had been too blind to see it.

Before I could respond, he stood up, brushing the front of his jacket with the kind of casual grace that suggested he was always in control.

"Figure it out," he said with a nod, his voice a soft edge of finality. "Before it's too late."

And just like that, he was gone, slipping out of the diner like he'd never been there.

I stayed frozen for a long time, staring at the empty seat across from me, feeling the weight of his words gnawing at the edges of my thoughts. There was something I was missing—something important—and I had no idea how to even begin untangling it.

I looked at Rachel, who was watching me with an unreadable expression. She knew better than to ask what was going through my mind.

But before I could speak, the door swung open again, this time more forcefully. A tall man in a uniform stepped inside, his eyes scanning the room. When he spotted me, his face went pale.

"Cynthia," he said, his voice shaky. "You need to come with me. Now."

I didn't hesitate. I didn't need to ask why. Because in that moment, I knew whatever was happening, whatever game was being played, it had just escalated. And I was already too deep to get out.

Chapter 4: Through the Flames

The air is thick with smoke, curling like the very breath of a dragon, and the sky above has been swallowed whole by the flames. I've fought fires before, but this—this is something else entirely. The mountain's bones are cracking as the fire swallows it whole, climbing, crawling, devouring everything in its path. It's as if the earth itself is burning with a rage that has no explanation. I try not to breathe too deeply, but the air is so dry that even my lungs are beginning to protest.

"Stay close," his voice comes through the crackling fire, sharp and low, with an edge that cuts through the chaos. His words are a command, not a suggestion, and for reasons I can't quite name, I obey.

I don't have to look to know he's there—his presence is an invisible weight on the back of my neck, pulling me in, grounding me in the madness. And, of course, he's the last person I need to be thinking about right now. Focus. Focus on the flames, the escape route, the fact that the only thing standing between us and a swift, fiery death is our training and luck. But somehow, in the middle of the blaze, my thoughts keep circling back to him.

His name is Callum, a man as enigmatic as the fire itself. I can't tell you much about him, except that he's always been here. Always close by, watching, observing. He has that quiet intensity, the kind that makes you feel like you're a piece of an elaborate puzzle he's just about to solve—and not in a good way. Maybe it's the way he moves, deliberate, measured, always two steps ahead. Or the way he doesn't seem to care about anything, except the job at hand. There's a tightness to him, an impenetrable wall behind those sharp, stormy eyes. It's not like he's rude. No, Callum is polite, professional, like a man who never lets himself feel anything. I guess I've always assumed that's what made him so good at his job. Until now.

He shifts next to me, his body blocking my view of the fire, but not the heat that presses against my skin. The flames leap at us, almost mocking our desperate dash through the smoke-filled air. It's terrifying, in a way that makes you question how much time you have left to breathe. But, somehow, there's comfort in the space between us. A strange, electric hum that I can't quite shake. I'm just about to tell him to stop looking so damn serious when his hand brushes against mine.

The contact is brief, a momentary flicker of warmth, but it sends a jolt up my spine. His fingers—rough, calloused, familiar—linger for just a heartbeat too long. And then, he's gone. His hand, just as quickly as it arrived, disappears into the dark.

I swear, for a moment, my heart stops. Not out of fear of the flames. No, this is different. This is something deeper, an unsettling realization that lingers even as I force myself to focus on the fire raging before us. There's no time to examine the sudden spark, the undeniable tension that has crackled in the air between us. We're running, dodging flames, our every step a battle against the fury of nature. And yet, that brief touch—that tiny, fleeting moment—sticks with me.

"Come on, move!" he growls over the roar of the fire, his hand shooting out to grab my arm. The strength in his grip is undeniable, but there's something else there too—a softness, if such a thing can exist in the middle of a wildfire.

I don't say anything, not because I don't want to, but because the words get lost in the heat of the moment. Instead, I just let him lead, my feet pounding the earth behind him. His pace is steady, and though it seems like we're barely escaping the flames, he's confident. Too confident. Almost like he's been here before.

I try not to let that thought linger. It's absurd. But the look on his face tells me something I can't quite place. It's as if he's running from something—and maybe that something is just as dangerous as the fire itself. I catch a glimpse of his face just as the orange light flickers across it. His jaw is clenched, eyes narrowed as if they're focused on a spot far beyond this inferno.

I open my mouth to ask him what he's thinking, but the question dies before it's fully formed. Because, just as quickly, he turns, his eyes locking with mine for the briefest second. That look—sharp, almost too intimate—sets my heart racing in a way that has nothing to do with the fire.

Before I can process it, we're back in motion. He pulls me roughly to the side, away from a wall of flame, and I don't even have time to brace myself. My body slams against his, and for a moment, it's not the heat of the fire I feel, but the heat of him. His chest, hard against mine, his breath warm and quick. I pull away instinctively, but his grip on my arm doesn't loosen. It's like he's holding me together, like he knows something I don't.

"Stop thinking," he mutters, his voice almost drowned out by the crackling and hissing of the fire around us. "We get through this, and then we talk."

He lets go of me as quickly as he had before, and I'm left standing there, heart pounding, the air buzzing with the energy between us. And just like that, we're back in motion, running again, but this time, something in me shifts. Maybe it's the fire, the smoke, or maybe it's the wildness in his eyes, but I know that whatever happens next, this—this feeling—has only just begun.

The smoke is a suffocating blanket, a thick gray fog that settles into the creases of my lungs. The crackle of the flames is deafening, an almost living thing, hungry and insatiable. The fire leaps from one tree to another, the jagged, wild dance of its destruction mesmerizing in its fury. Each gust of wind sends a fresh wave of heat rushing toward us, and with each passing moment, I can feel the mountain itself giving way. We're running on instinct now, with no room for hesitation. The edge of the cliff is closer, but it doesn't seem to matter. We'll outrun it. We have to.

Callum is ahead, his long strides eating up the uneven terrain as if it were a smooth path, his focus unyielding. The way he moves—there's an elegance to it, despite the chaos. It's a strange kind of grace, like he's not just moving through the world but in control of it. The fire at his back seems almost like an afterthought, as if it can't touch him, as if nothing ever could.

But I know better.

I know that beneath that hard exterior, behind those dark eyes that always seem to be calculating something, there's something else. I've seen it before. Brief glimpses—when the moonlight catches his face in just the right way, when his guard falters for a second, and I see the weight he carries. It's like a shadow, hanging just out of reach. I don't think anyone else notices, but I do.

And I can't help but wonder if it's not just the fire that haunts him.

I stumble slightly as a branch catches my foot, and he's there, moving so fluidly that I barely see him turn to grab me before I hit the ground. His hand is like iron around my wrist, his grip firm and sure as he yanks me upright. His gaze flickers to mine, just for a second, and that's when I see it. The fleeting vulnerability, the softening in his expression, before it's gone again, replaced by that hard, distant look.

"You okay?" he asks, his voice still low, almost muffled by the firestorm surrounding us. His tone is clipped, controlled. But there's something in the way he says it—something that makes my heart skip a beat.

"I'm fine," I say, brushing myself off, though I'm not sure if I'm convincing him or myself. "Just a little off balance, is all."

The words hang between us, but before either of us can say anything more, the ground shifts beneath our feet. The fire rages around us, but now, the smoke thickens, and the air is heavier, more suffocating. Something's wrong—there's a sharpness in the air, an almost tangible feeling of impending doom. It's not just the fire that's a threat anymore. It's the mountain itself, as if it's finally had enough of our attempts to tame it.

"Move!" Callum shouts, grabbing my arm again, this time pulling me with a sense of urgency I can't ignore.

We start running again, the sound of the fire growing louder, closer. It feels like the flames are chasing us now, like we're the hunted rather than the hunters. But something is off about the way the fire is moving, something that I can't quite put my finger on. It's... too controlled, too deliberate. The way it spreads, the way it leaps from one tree to another—it's not random. It's as if someone—or something—is guiding it.

I glance over at Callum, trying to catch his eye, trying to make sense of the tension in his jaw, the grim set of his shoulders. He's not reacting the way he should. Most people would be panicking by now, but not him. He's too focused, too intent on getting us out, and yet... there's something about the way he's moving that feels like we're heading toward something. Not away from it.

We make it to the edge of the clearing, where the fire's reach is at its peak, the orange glow illuminating the sky like a warning, like the eye of a storm. It's there, in the glow of the fire, that I see it—the shadows moving at the edge of the trees. Not the usual wildlife fleeing the blaze, but something more deliberate. Something human.

I stop short, my breath catching in my throat. "Did you see that?"

Callum's eyes narrow, scanning the trees, his face unreadable. "See what?"

I point toward the flickering shadows, but by the time he looks, they're gone. Only the crackling fire remains, spitting embers into the air.

"Must have been the wind," he says, though there's no mistaking the edge in his voice. He's not convinced.

I open my mouth to protest, but then I hear it—footsteps, soft but deliberate, crunching the dry earth behind us. It's not the wind this time. Someone's out there, and they're coming closer.

"Get down," Callum hisses, pulling me down beside a cluster of rocks that offer a small measure of cover. His body presses against mine, shielding me as he reaches for the weapon at his side.

I'm frozen, heart pounding, my mind racing. The fire is already a threat in itself, but this—this feels like something worse.

The footsteps grow louder, closer, but still there's no sign of who or what is coming toward us. Callum's breathing is slow and steady beside me, and for a second, it feels like the world has stopped. The fire rages on, but in this moment, we're both suspended in time. My skin is prickling with the weight of the silence, the intensity of the moment.

Then, without warning, he turns his head to me, his lips just inches from my ear. "Stay quiet," he murmurs, the heat of his breath sending a shiver down my spine. "We're not alone."

The words hang heavy in the air, and I know, deep down, that whatever happens next, we're not just fighting fire anymore. We're fighting something much darker.

The quiet is suffocating, stretching between us like a taut wire ready to snap. I can hear my own heartbeat thumping in my ears, the only sound in the oppressive silence that has settled over the forest. Callum's body is a hard, unyielding presence next to me, his breath steady despite the chaos raging around us. The fire crackles in the distance, the mountain's anger only held at bay by the flimsy safety of the rocks we've hidden behind. But now, it feels like the fire is the least of our concerns. It's the shadows creeping closer that have my stomach in knots.

My pulse races as I glance at him, his jaw tight, eyes scanning the trees with a sharpness that sends a chill down my spine. He's always been the stoic one, the one who handles everything with that calm detachment, as if nothing ever fazes him. But right now, there's something more than caution in his eyes. There's an urgency, a flicker of something darker—something that says this isn't just another fire for him. This is personal.

"Do you hear it?" I whisper, not daring to make a sound too loud. But the words are out before I can stop them.

Callum's gaze flickers toward me, the corner of his mouth twitching slightly. "I hear it," he mutters, his voice low and gritty. "And I don't like it."

The sound of footsteps crunching against the dry earth grows louder, closer. It's not the quick, panicked scramble of someone fleeing the fire. No, these steps are slow, deliberate—almost like they know exactly where they're going. I strain my ears, but there's nothing else. No rustling leaves, no wind to cover the sound. Just the ominous approach of whoever is out there, stalking us through the smoke.

I want to ask who it is, what it means, but I don't. I know better than to question Callum when he's in this mode. He's trained for moments like this, for the unknown lurking in the dark. He doesn't need to explain himself, and frankly, I'm not sure I want to know the whole truth. The truth is always more dangerous than the lie you're living, and right now, my only job is to survive.

My breath catches in my throat as the shadow shifts again, moving between the trees just outside the circle of light cast by the fire. There's something hauntingly familiar about the shape of it, like I've seen it before. My mind flashes to images I can't quite pin down—whispers from the past, faces I've forgotten. The fire, the smoke—it's all too much, too many unanswered questions spinning in my head.

A voice, deep and gravelly, cuts through the air, and I freeze.

"You two are making a lot of noise for people trying to hide."

I whip my head toward Callum, but he's already on his feet, moving silently like a predator in the night. I follow, my legs trembling beneath me, but I force myself to stay low, to move with purpose. There's no time for fear, not now. If there's one thing I've learned about Callum, it's that he's not the kind of man who gets caught off guard. And if he's taking charge of this situation, I know there's no escaping it. We'll have to face whatever it is together.

We move silently through the trees, ducking low to avoid detection. The fire's glow paints everything in hues of red and orange, casting eerie shadows that twist and warp as if the forest itself is alive. My mind races as I try to make sense of what's happening, of why the fire feels more dangerous than it should. But I can't shake the feeling that it's not just the fire threatening us. There's something else out there, something we've yet to face.

Callum holds up a hand, signaling me to stop. He motions for me to stay behind him as he steps forward, his movements fluid and precise. I can barely make out his form in the flickering light, but I know his every move is calculated. There's a quiet intensity to him now, an edge I've never seen before. The kind of edge that tells me he's not afraid of the fire. He's afraid of something else.

I creep forward, trying to stay out of sight, trying to keep up without making a sound. My heart thunders in my chest as I inch closer to the clearing where the shadowed figure waits. It's not just one person. There are more. At least three, maybe four, all of them moving like they belong here. The forest is their kingdom, and we're the trespassers.

Callum raises a hand, and I freeze, my blood running cold. He motions for me to stay back, his fingers pressing lightly to his lips.

I want to argue, to demand what's going on, but I don't. I can see it in his eyes—he's got a plan. A plan that doesn't involve me charging in recklessly.

I hold my breath as Callum moves forward, closing the distance between himself and the figures in the clearing. His eyes narrow, his posture tense, and for the first time, I see it—real fear. Not fear of the fire, but something else. Something that's been haunting him, lurking in the background of everything he's done.

"Callum..." I whisper, but he silences me with a sharp look.

He's not just trying to survive this. He's trying to stop something.

The figures in the clearing seem to sense his presence before I can. One of them steps forward, tall and broad, with a face hidden beneath the shadow of a hood. I can't make out the features, but the air shifts, thick with the weight of recognition, of something dark.

Callum moves again, his hand reaching for something at his waist. The sudden flash of steel in the dim light is a reminder of how dangerous this moment is.

Then, the figure speaks, their voice cutting through the smoke-filled air with chilling clarity.

"You should have stayed away, Callum."

I don't know if it's the fire crackling or the blood rushing in my ears, but I swear my heart stops. And then—nothing. The silence is deafening, suffocating. Whatever comes next, I know we're past the point of no return.

Chapter 5: Whispers in the Ash

The air was thick with the scent of smoke, heavy and suffocating as it clung to every surface, to every breath. The fires had begun two weeks ago, at first a flicker in the distance, a warning of something that might burn away. But now, they were closer—closer than anyone cared to admit. The trees seemed to be shrinking into the horizon, their trunks charred and blackened, reaching toward the sky like the twisted fingers of a lost soul. And the camp... the camp was alive with whispers.

I heard them, of course. You'd have to be deaf not to. They crept through the cracks of the walls, through the rustle of the trees, through the stares that lingered too long. "Accidents," they called them. A slip of the flame, a gust of wind. But the more the fires spread, the less it felt like coincidence. The whispers were louder now, sharper. "Someone's doing this on purpose."

It didn't help that people were starting to look at me differently. They always did. There was something about being the one who could do things, who could sense things, that made people uneasy. They didn't trust what they didn't understand. So when the fires came, when the first crackle of destruction lit up the night, I became the subject of every unspoken conversation. I caught it in the way they stared at me, in the way their voices dropped when I walked by. It was there, even in the way they turned their backs as I passed.

But it wasn't just the others who were watching me. He was, too.

I'd been aware of him the moment he stepped into the camp. He was the sort of man whose presence rippled through a room like a stone dropped into a pond. He didn't need to speak for you to know he was there. His eyes—those cold, assessing eyes—seemed to pierce through to the core of everything. And his silence spoke louder than any words.

His name was Noah, though I didn't know if that was the name he'd been given at birth or the one he used to survive. Either way, it fit. There was something about him that felt like a storm on the horizon—foreboding, untouchable, yet with the potential to destroy everything in its path. He wasn't like the others in camp, the ones who clung to whatever comforts they could find in the ashes of their lives. He moved with purpose, his boots always sharp on the ground, never a moment of hesitation in his steps.

It was the way he looked at me that unsettled me the most. It wasn't just suspicion—it was something deeper, something that flickered behind his eyes when he thought no one was looking. Something broken. Something desperate. For a moment, I thought I'd imagined it, the softening of his features, the subtle shift of his posture, but it was there, like a brief, flickering light in the shadows. And then just as quickly, it vanished, replaced by that cold, impenetrable mask he wore like armor.

It was as though the closer the fires came, the more he studied me. He started to ask questions, and not the kind of questions anyone would ask in passing. No, his questions had weight, a demand for something I couldn't offer. His voice was clipped, sharp like a blade cutting through the smoke. "What do you know about the fires?" he'd ask, his gaze unwavering, drilling into me as if he thought I held all the answers, as though I could somehow end them with the flick of my wrist.

I didn't know who was setting them, but the idea that he thought I did—well, that twisted something deep inside me. I could have backed down, told him to go ask someone else, but I wasn't that kind of person. I wasn't afraid of him. Not really. I'd survived worse than his sharp words, his cutting gaze.

But the thing that bothered me wasn't his suspicion. It was that flicker of something more—something that seemed to pull me in, even as he tried to shut me out. Every time I pushed, tried to get closer, to ask the right questions, that mask would snap back into place. Silence. Thick, suffocating silence. It was like trying to speak into a void, to reach something that wasn't there.

I could tell he was holding something back—something important. The way he'd dart his gaze away when he thought no one was watching, the way his hands clenched into fists whenever someone mentioned the fires. And the more I watched him, the more I realized how well he hid behind his walls. But everyone had a breaking point, and I was going to find his.

The tension in the camp was palpable, like a string pulled too tight. People were nervous, and when they weren't talking behind closed doors, they were casting furtive glances in every direction. The smell of burning wood was constant now, a reminder of how close the flames were, how much we were all standing on the edge of something. The air was heavy with fear, with suspicion. It was a pressure that seemed to build with every passing day, until it felt like it might all come crashing down at once.

Noah's questions grew sharper. "You know something," he'd say, his voice low and demanding. "What are you hiding?" There was a bite to his words now, a challenge that made my heart beat faster, but I didn't back down. I couldn't.

And just when I thought I might have him, just when I thought I'd finally cracked his cold exterior, he would retreat. Like a shadow slipping from my grasp, his walls would go back up, leaving nothing but that unsettling silence in his wake.

I started to wonder if I was the only one who noticed it—the cracks in his armor, the way his eyes would soften before he buried them again. If I was imagining it, or if it was something real.

The fires were getting closer. And Noah? He wasn't the only one who had something to hide.

It was the small things that unsettled me most about Noah. A fleeting glance, the tilt of his jaw when he was deep in thought, the way his breath would catch just before he spoke. The subtle things, the ones that felt like they could break you if you weren't careful. He was an enigma wrapped in a layer of distrust, and every attempt I made to figure him out seemed to bounce off the walls he'd built around himself. I'd seen it before—people who wore their solitude like a cloak, afraid of anything that might unravel them.

But there was something else, something that gnawed at me as much as the smoke in the air. He wasn't just watching me. He was studying me, like he was looking for something in me that he hadn't found in anyone else. It wasn't paranoia, or at least I didn't think it was. It was the way his gaze lingered too long when I was in the same room as him, the way his fingers would tap rhythmically on a table whenever I spoke, as if measuring the weight of my words.

I tried to ignore it. Tried to push the thought aside. We were all here for the same reason, after all—survival. In a place like this, you didn't make friends. You didn't get attached. But somehow, Noah had become something I couldn't shake, even when I told myself I wasn't interested in the mystery he posed. Even when I reminded myself that his questions weren't friendly; they were calculations, probing for weaknesses.

The rumors were getting louder, too. Not just the fires—those had their own set of theories. But there was talk of someone moving through the camp at night, stealing food, slashing tents. There were no names, no faces. Just suspicion, thick and sticky, like sap that clung to the trees. And each time I overheard someone muttering about it, I'd catch a flicker of movement at the edge of my vision—Noah, his dark eyes sharp and unwavering. It was as though he, too, had begun to feel the weight of the whispers.

One evening, as the sky bled into hues of orange and pink, I found myself walking alone to the water's edge. The camp was quieter than usual, the usual hum of activity subdued, as if everyone was holding their breath. I knew Noah was somewhere nearby. I could feel his presence even before I saw him, like a shadow just out of reach.

I wasn't sure what had pulled me to the water. Maybe it was the need for space, a breath of fresh air away from the suffocating weight of all the questions that seemed to follow me. Or maybe it was because, in all the chaos, I'd started to wonder if Noah might have the answers I wasn't willing to admit I needed.

I knelt at the water's edge, dipping my fingers into the cool liquid, watching the ripples spread outward. The sound of the river was calming, a gentle reminder that there was still something untouched by the madness surrounding us.

"You always come here when you think no one's watching."

The voice was low, familiar, and it made my heart jump in my chest. I didn't need to turn to know who it was. He had a way of sneaking up on me without a sound, like a storm creeping across the horizon, inevitable and unstoppable.

I straightened, fingers still trailing in the water, and then glanced over my shoulder. Noah stood a few feet away, his arms crossed over his chest, eyes studying me with that same unsettling intensity. His jaw was tense, the lines of his face drawn tight as if he were battling with something he couldn't quite name.

"I wasn't hiding," I said, trying to keep my tone casual, but the words came out sharper than I intended. "Just... thinking."

He raised an eyebrow, his lips pulling into a faint, amused smirk. "Thinking, huh?"

I shrugged, though I could feel my heart rate quicken under his gaze. There was something about the way he looked at me that made it impossible to keep my thoughts straight. "You don't always have to be so suspicious," I added, testing the waters. "Not everyone's out to get you."

His eyes narrowed, and for a moment, the air between us felt thick, like the storm before the rain. "I'm not the one hiding anything, am I?"

I didn't answer immediately, though I knew he was pushing me, trying to provoke a reaction. But I wasn't about to give him the satisfaction of seeing me flinch. The question hung there, heavy and thick like smoke, and I knew it wasn't just about the fires anymore. It wasn't even just about the camp. It was about something deeper. Something between us.

"Is that what you think?" I finally said, my voice barely above a whisper. "That I'm hiding something?"

For a moment, Noah didn't respond. He just stared at me, those dark eyes of his unreadable, like a puzzle I couldn't quite solve. His lips pressed together in a thin line before he took a step forward, closing the distance between us.

"No one is who they seem to be, not here," he said, his voice low but full of an edge that made the hairs on the back of my neck stand up. "Not even you."

The words hung in the air, and I could feel a knot tightening in my chest. What was he trying to say? That I was hiding something? That we all were?

I wanted to push him, ask him what exactly he thought he knew. But instead, I stayed quiet, my fingers still trailing through the water, its coolness a strange comfort against the heat of the moment. I could feel him standing there, waiting, but I wasn't sure what for. His gaze didn't waver. It felt like he was waiting for something from me, something more than just answers.

And in that silence, I realized something. He wasn't just suspicious of me. He was scared. He didn't trust anyone, not even himself. It was like he was trying to protect something, but I couldn't figure out what.

"So," I said finally, my voice breaking the stillness, "what's your theory, Noah? You've been watching me. Do you think I'm the one setting the fires?"

For a moment, he said nothing. Then, he took a deep breath, like he was steeling himself for something. His gaze flickered to the horizon, where the last slivers of sunlight dipped behind the trees.

"I don't know," he murmured, almost to himself. "But I'm starting to wonder if the real danger isn't the fires at all."

The air was thick, the oppressive weight of it pressing down with a stifling silence, broken only by the occasional crackle of the fire or the murmur of voices low enough to avoid detection. The camp was on edge, a taut wire ready to snap. People were looking over their shoulders more often now, eyes darting like birds sensing the approach of a predator. No one trusted anyone, not fully. We were all shadows now, waiting for the moment when the darkness would swallow us whole.

I was no exception. Noah's words had been a puzzle that refused to be solved, a riddle I couldn't quite crack. The fires were one thing—clearly someone, or something, was behind them—but Noah was starting to feel like something else altogether. His presence had been unsettling from the start, but now, with the added weight of his suspicions, it felt almost suffocating. Every glance he gave me held more than a simple question. There was an edge to it, a sharpness that sliced through whatever pretense I'd been clinging to.

I had never been good at pretending, not for long anyway. The game of denial was something I had grown tired of, especially here. But there was something else about Noah's gaze that made me want to get closer, to unravel whatever had him so tightly wound. I could feel it in the way his shoulders tensed whenever I was near, the subtle shift in his posture when our paths crossed. It wasn't just suspicion. It was more—something buried deep, something I couldn't reach but could almost taste, like smoke on the air.

The campfire crackled loudly that evening, flames dancing in a way that seemed almost too eager. I found myself drawn to it, the warmth offering a false sense of comfort in a place that had none. The circle of people around it shifted nervously as the embers burned low, their faces flickering in the dim light. It wasn't the campfire that held my attention, though. It was Noah, standing just outside the ring of light, his profile sharp against the darkened sky.

I hadn't realized how much I'd been watching him until I caught the faintest hint of movement—his hand, the one that had been resting on his belt, twitching as if he was about to reach for something. For a brief moment, I thought he might be reaching for his knife, or perhaps something more. But then he paused, his fingers curling into a fist at his side.

I could almost feel the tension between us, the magnetic pull of something unsaid. But as always, he was quick to shut it down. His eyes flicked toward mine for a split second, then he turned, disappearing into the shadows beyond the firelight without a word. I stared after him, a mixture of frustration and something else swirling in my chest. It was as though he was daring me to follow, daring me to find out what he was hiding.

I didn't follow him immediately, though I knew I would. There was something in the air tonight, something different. I could feel it in the hairs on the back of my neck, the thrum of anticipation in my blood.

When I finally stood and made my way toward the edge of the camp, it was as if the very earth had been holding its breath. The camp was quiet, too quiet, the usual chatter replaced by an eerie stillness. Even the wind had died down, leaving only the rustle of trees in the distance to keep me company. I found Noah near the old storage sheds, his figure barely visible in the dim moonlight.

He was standing perfectly still, his back to me, as if waiting for something. Waiting for someone.

"You like being alone, don't you?" I said, stepping closer, my voice cutting through the silence. It was meant to be casual, to throw him off balance, but the words came out sharper than I intended.

Noah didn't turn. Instead, his shoulders stiffened, and for a moment, I wondered if he'd heard me at all. But then he spoke, his voice low, almost too soft for me to catch.

"I'm not alone," he said, his words trailing into the night air, as though he were speaking to himself more than to me.

I paused, trying to decipher the meaning behind his words. "You think someone's out here with us?"

His head tilted slightly, but he didn't face me. "Maybe," he murmured, "or maybe I'm just waiting for the right moment to see who's going to show up next."

The hair on my arms stood on end. There was something in his tone, something deliberate, like he knew more than he was letting on. He knew something about what was happening in the camp, and I had the sinking feeling that I was about to find out just what that was.

"What are you talking about?" I asked, my voice steady despite the unease spreading through me.

For a moment, he didn't respond. His silence hung there, heavy between us, thick and suffocating. I could feel the weight of it pressing against my chest, making it harder to breathe. And then, almost too casually, he said, "The fires are just the beginning. Something worse is coming."

I froze. The air seemed to tighten around us, a tangible tension that made my skin crawl. His words didn't make sense. The fires had already taken so much—what could be worse?

"Worse than the fires?" I asked, though the question felt pointless. I didn't want to know the answer.

He turned then, and for the first time, I saw something—something raw and unguarded—in his expression. It was fleeting, gone before I could make sense of it. But it was enough to make my pulse race, enough to send a chill racing down my spine.

"I've seen the signs," he said quietly, his gaze locking with mine. "You're not the only one with secrets here."

The ground seemed to tilt beneath me, as though the world itself were shifting. Before I could speak, he was moving again, his steps quick and purposeful.

"Stay away from the fire tomorrow night," he added over his shoulder, his voice low but filled with an unmistakable urgency. "It won't be what you think."

And then he was gone, disappearing into the shadows like a ghost.

I stood there, alone in the darkness, his words echoing in my mind, louder than the sounds of the night. Something worse was coming. The fires were just the beginning.

And as the cold wind began to stir again, I realized that I might have just walked right into the heart of whatever was coming next.

Chapter 6: Dangerous Sparks

The first tendrils of morning light barely touched the horizon, painting the world in streaks of pink and gold, when the call came. The kind of call you dread in this line of work—urgent, clipped, and filled with an unsaid threat. The fire was out of control.

I didn't need to hear more. I grabbed my gear, barely acknowledging the rough handshake of my supervisor as I pushed past the others, my boots hitting the cracked concrete with the familiar rhythm of urgency. It felt like any other day until I noticed him standing there, arms crossed, his eyes already locked on mine. Caleb, always quiet, always observant, and today, for reasons unknown even to me, he was going to be my partner in this mess.

"Thought you'd be leading the charge today, Kincaid," I muttered, tightening the straps on my jacket, avoiding his gaze. The fire was far too close, the smoke already thick enough to taste, and I wasn't in the mood to do any small talk.

He smirked, a slow, deliberate pull of his lips. "And here I thought you were tough enough to handle it solo. Guess I'll just be the backup."

His voice was the kind of low growl that could either comfort you or make you second-guess your decisions. Right now, it did a little bit of both.

We didn't speak again as we trudged through the underbrush, the air already thick with the scent of scorched earth. The fire was a beast, raging in the distance, and the smoke rolled across the land like a living thing, choking the sky, turning daylight into dusk. It wasn't the kind of blaze that could be tamed with a few quick sprays of water. No, this was the kind of inferno that would eat everything in its path, not caring for anything in its wake—just as ruthless as the storm that had ignited it.

The crunch of our boots in the dirt was the only sound that cut through the chaos of crackling flames and the occasional hiss of trees collapsing in on themselves. Caleb was close behind me, his presence a constant shadow at my back. I could feel his eyes on me, the weight of his attention lingering longer than it should. I didn't want to acknowledge it, but the way he moved with me—silent, calculating, and just a touch too close—pulled at something inside me, something I couldn't quite name.

The heat hit first, like a slap to the face, making my skin prickle with discomfort. The air shimmered with the intensity of it, waves of burning energy curling around us, the scent of it all—pine, dry grass, and the undeniable tang of something alive being reduced to ash—cloying in my lungs. I reached for my radio to check in with the others, but the static was relentless. Our team was out there somewhere, but we were alone in this thick, suffocating silence.

I turned back to Caleb, ready to make a snarky remark, but the words died on my tongue when I saw him—his jaw set tight, eyes squinting against the smoke, hands steady despite the panic that gripped the rest of my gut. He was the kind of person who didn't crack under pressure, a fact that both unnerved and drew me in. There was something about his stillness, the quiet strength he carried, that made me want to break it. To ask him why he'd signed up for this. To question why someone like him would be out here with me, instead of leading his own team, safe and sound, away from the madness.

"How much farther?" My voice came out strained, and I instantly regretted it. But Caleb didn't seem to mind. He stepped forward, his eyes narrowing as he scanned the fire.

"Not much," he said. "Just beyond this ridge. But we need to stay sharp."

I nodded, swallowing down the lump in my throat, not sure if it was the smoke or something else. We kept moving, our steps quickening as the fire raged closer, the noise of it loud in our ears now. There was no telling how bad it was out there, but it was clear the situation was escalating fast.

We reached the top of the ridge just as a gust of wind sent a fresh wave of heat across our faces. My skin stung from the sudden onslaught of fire-breath, and I barely had time to shield my eyes before a snap of flame erupted from a nearby tree. Caleb reached out, pulling me back just in time, his hand gripping my arm with a fierceness that made my pulse spike.

His touch lingered a moment too long before he let go, his breath ragged. "Don't make me have to save you again."

I couldn't tell if he was teasing or if the words were meant to mask something else, something darker. He was always so hard to read, his emotions wrapped in layers of calm that almost made him unreadable, but in that instant, when his fingers had brushed against my skin, I felt something else—something that felt too much like the heat around us, too consuming to ignore.

We were so close to the heart of it now, the fire leaping and cracking in the distance, the sky an angry orange. And then, as if on cue, the radio went dead. I glanced at Caleb, who was already scanning the horizon, his jaw working in tense silence.

"We're on our own," he said quietly. "It's just us now."

It wasn't a reassurance. It was a warning.

With no radio, no backup, and no clear way out, I felt the weight of it settle in my chest. I wanted to say something, anything, to break the suffocating tension between us, but the air was thick with smoke, thick with heat, and thick with something else—something that had nothing to do with the fire at all.

I took a step forward, the ground beneath me shifting, and when I looked up, Caleb was closer than before. The space between us, already too small, vanished in a heartbeat. He didn't speak, didn't move at first, but I felt his eyes on me—intense, searching.

And then, in the midst of everything, he reached out, his fingers grazing my cheek. It was slow, deliberate, the heat of his touch almost unbearable against the fire that raged around us.

For a heartbeat, the world seemed to still. The fire, the smoke, the chaos—they all faded away. It was just him and me, standing on the edge of something that felt too dangerous to acknowledge.

But then he pulled back, shaking his head, his eyes darker than the smoke around us.

"Don't." His voice was rough, a warning, or maybe a plea, but it wasn't enough to erase the tension crackling between us.

And as we turned back to face the flames, I couldn't shake the feeling that the fire wasn't the only thing we had to survive today.

The smoke was thicker now, swirling in angry plumes that seemed to rise from the ground itself, as though the earth was exhaling its own rage. We moved through it with purpose, but each step felt like wading through thickening molasses, the heat pressing against my skin with an oppressive weight. The fire had spread faster than anyone anticipated, and now it was a beast—uncontainable, untamable, just as dangerous as the unspoken tension between Caleb and me.

He was still close, too close for comfort, but I couldn't find it in me to push him away. His presence, solid and unwavering, felt like the only thing keeping me grounded. But the way he moved, how he hovered just behind me, his hand brushing against my back when I stumbled over a piece of debris—it was more than just professional caution. He was watching me, tracking my every move, as though he knew something I didn't, as though he could read every flicker of doubt that crossed my mind.

I had always thought of Caleb as a man of few words, someone who didn't waste time on pleasantries. But in the thick of this inferno, with everything around us on the verge of collapsing, I couldn't shake the feeling that there was more to him than the calm exterior he so carefully constructed. Beneath it, I suspected, was something raw, something dangerous.

"Careful," he murmured, his voice low and tight. The air around us crackled, the fire a constant roar in the background, but his words sliced through the noise with precision. "Don't step there."

I glanced down just in time to avoid a jagged piece of rock sticking up from the ground, its sharp edge hidden beneath the smoke. I hadn't even seen it, but Caleb had. He always did. His eyes, alert and sharp, missed nothing. It was a quality that unnerved me, that made me feel as though there was no space left for secrets between us.

"Thanks," I said, a little breathless, trying to shake off the sudden feeling of vulnerability that came with his proximity. But instead of stepping back, he followed me closely, his pace steady and unhurried, as though we weren't walking through a battlefield.

We pressed on in silence, the only sounds our labored breathing and the crackling fire, until I noticed a change in the air. The wind had shifted, carrying the heat of the flames toward us. I could feel it in the sweat on the back of my neck, in the way the temperature surged, as though the world itself was closing in.

"We need to move faster," Caleb said, his voice a sharp edge. He was right, of course. The fire was getting closer, its orange glow now visible just over the next rise, creeping toward us like a living thing with a mind of its own.

I turned to say something, but before I could, the ground beneath us trembled with the weight of a nearby explosion. The shockwave sent a ripple through the air, and I barely had time to grab Caleb's arm before he was thrown off balance. For a moment, time seemed to stretch, the world spinning around me as I caught my breath.

His arm shot out, wrapping around my waist to steady me, and for the briefest of moments, I felt his chest pressed against my back. His heartbeat, steady and fast beneath his jacket, seemed to echo in the space between us. I could feel the heat of his body, his breath hot against my ear.

We stood there, frozen in place for a heartbeat longer than necessary, as if the fire had taken away every other thought but the one that had suddenly become too loud to ignore—the one that swelled between us, burning hotter than the flames just beyond the ridge.

I pulled away first, breaking the moment before it could go any further. "We can't stay here," I said, trying to sound composed, but the words came out more rushed than I intended. "The wind's changing. The fire's coming."

He nodded, his jaw clenched, eyes narrowed as he scanned the horizon. But when he spoke, his voice was softer, almost too quiet, as if he were contemplating something far more dangerous than the fire we were running from.

"I'm not leaving you out here alone, Kincaid," he said, his words deliberate, as though each one held more weight than the next.

I opened my mouth to argue, but the heat from the fire pressed in around us, suffocating, relentless. There wasn't time for back-and-forth. I needed to focus, needed to push past the part of me that wanted to collapse into the comfort of his promise, to give in to whatever strange pull was growing between us. I knew better. This was not the place for distractions, and Caleb was the last person I should be distracted by.

Still, his words stuck with me, like the lingering taste of smoke on my tongue.

We moved forward, faster now, our footsteps synchronizing as we climbed over the next ridge. The fire was closer, the crackling of burning wood louder, and the sky above us had turned a sickly orange, as if the sun itself were being swallowed by the flames. I kept my eyes ahead, but my mind kept returning to Caleb—the way he moved, the way his gaze never strayed far from me, the way he seemed to anticipate my every move. It wasn't just his physical presence that kept me on edge. It was the unspoken understanding between us, the way his eyes could flicker with something far more dangerous than the fire itself.

But I couldn't afford to think about that now. We were on borrowed time.

We reached the edge of a clearing, and for the first time, I allowed myself to breathe, my chest rising and falling with the effort. The smoke was thick here, but the fire hadn't reached this far yet, and for a brief moment, I thought we might be safe. But then the ground beneath us trembled again, and the trees nearby exploded in a shower of embers, their towering figures splintering apart with a sound that rattled my bones.

I looked at Caleb, who was already pulling me forward, his hand firmly gripping my arm. His jaw was set in determination, his eyes scanning the clearing ahead. He didn't speak, but the way he moved—protective, urgent—spoke volumes.

We had no time to waste.

We kept moving, the fire looming ever closer, its roar now a constant in the background, a reminder that we were on borrowed time. Caleb's grip on my arm tightened, his fingers digging into my jacket as if the world could fall apart at any second—and maybe it would. The air was thick with smoke, the heat almost unbearable, and I could taste the bitterness of it on my tongue. There was no escape from it, no easy way out. We had no radio, no backup, and no clear path forward, only the orange glow of the flames and the crackle of destruction.

"You know," Caleb said, his voice surprisingly light for the situation, "I've had better first dates."

I shot him a quick glance, surprised by the humor in his tone. It didn't fit with the urgency of the moment, but it was the first thing that made me feel like we weren't entirely doomed. "First date? You're not even buying me dinner first."

He grinned, the kind of grin that almost made the fire's heat bearable, even as it threatened to swallow everything around us. "Guess I'll owe you one," he said, voice soft but tinged with something else—a quiet intensity that somehow made the danger surrounding us feel personal.

I didn't know why, but I let the moment hang there between us, his words a strange comfort in the madness. His usual stoic demeanor, always guarded, had cracked, and for a split second, I saw the person behind the hardened exterior—someone who knew this wasn't just another fire, and that whatever we were facing now, it was more than just smoke and flame.

We rounded a bend, and I froze, every instinct on high alert. Ahead of us, the fire was stretching across the land like a living thing, its tendrils snaking through the forest, burning everything in its path. The trees were mere skeletons now, their once-great trunks reduced to charred remnants, smoke spiraling into the sky like some kind of terrible omen. The flames leaped higher with each gust of wind, reaching for the sky, as if hungry for something more.

Caleb stopped beside me, his body stiffening. "This isn't good," he murmured, eyes scanning the horizon, calculating. I knew what he was thinking. We had two choices: try to outrun the fire, or find a way to stay ahead of it and hope we could make it to a safer zone. Neither sounded particularly appealing.

"Yeah, no kidding," I muttered, tugging at my collar, the air almost too hot to breathe. "What do we do now? Keep running straight into the fire?"

His lips twitched, the smirk not quite reaching his eyes. "We improvise."

I didn't question him. In a situation like this, improvising was all we had left. And in truth, I wasn't sure if I trusted anyone else to lead me through this madness. Caleb moved with the kind of purpose that made me feel like I could keep going, even when every muscle in my body screamed for me to stop. His focus was razor-sharp, the danger of the fire and the threat of being completely isolated in the wilderness not even flinching him.

He tugged me forward, his hand warm against my back, guiding me around a cluster of burning trees. My heart pounded in my chest, the rhythm of it syncing with the crackle of the fire as it consumed the world around us. Every few steps, I glanced over my shoulder, expecting the worst—the fire creeping up behind us, snapping at our heels, devouring everything in its path.

The world was a hell of heat and smoke, and for a while, it felt like we were running from the fire and everything else that had ever mattered. The sound of Caleb's breath beside me, the steady cadence of his steps, was the only thing keeping me grounded in reality, even as everything else felt surreal.

The wind picked up, shifting again, and suddenly, the fire was no longer behind us. It was in front of us, too, a wall of flame that seemed to leap toward the heavens. There was no way around it now.

Caleb swore under his breath, but there was no panic in his voice, only a calm urgency. "This way," he said, tugging me toward a narrow ravine that cut through the landscape like a natural divide.

We dove into the ravine, the walls steep and jagged, forcing us to scramble down on hands and knees. The fire roared above us, a living, breathing thing, but down here, we had a brief moment of respite. The air was heavy, thick with smoke and the smell of burning wood, but we weren't completely consumed yet.

I could hear Caleb's breathing, his heavy footsteps behind me as we climbed deeper into the ravine, the world narrowing around us. The walls were slick with moisture, a natural spring somewhere deep in the earth. We kept moving, and for the first time in what felt like forever, I felt a flicker of hope—a tiny spark of possibility.

Then, the ground beneath me shifted.

The earth trembled violently, and before I could react, I felt myself falling, tumbling down into the darkness, my breath stolen by the drop. A split second of pure terror. Caleb's shout followed me as I fell, but his voice was distant, fading into the chaos above.

My heart hammered in my chest, and I tried to reach for something, anything, but the world was spinning too fast. Then everything went black.

The last thing I heard before the darkness claimed me was Caleb's voice, his tone no longer calm but frantic. "Kincaid!"

And then... nothing.

Chapter 7: Burning Secrets

The fire crackled and popped, its glow casting shadows that danced across the worn canvas of the tents. It had been a long day, but I couldn't shake the sense that something was different, something had changed between us. I could feel it in the air, thick and taut, like the space just before a storm. His presence beside me was a constant hum, a vibration that somehow both grounded and unsettled me. I didn't want to acknowledge it, but my mind kept pulling at the threads of the moment, weaving a tapestry of possibilities. His gaze lingered longer than usual, a touch too intense, as if he were waiting for me to say something—or perhaps, more troublingly, for me to not say anything at all.

We were still deep in the throes of work when the others started packing up. I could hear the rustle of papers, the shuffle of boots across the dirt, but none of it could drown out the tension that had settled between us. It wasn't just the quiet—no, it was the unspoken words, the ones I couldn't bring myself to ask.

I glanced at him from the corner of my eye, noticing how his jaw tensed as he hunched over his notebook, scribbling furiously. There was a flicker of something in his expression, a storm hiding behind those pale blue eyes. I swallowed the knot that had formed in my throat. My frustration flared, the silence between us gnawing at me like an open wound.

"Why are you avoiding me?" I blurted, not sure where the words came from, but there they were, out in the open. The air shifted, a sudden stillness enveloping the campsite. His head jerked up, locking eyes with me, but there was no warmth in his stare, only a cool hardness that I wasn't used to seeing.

"I'm not avoiding you," he said, his voice clipped, too controlled. It was the kind of response I would expect from someone who had spent years building walls around their heart.

"Then why does it feel like I'm invisible to you?" I shot back before I could stop myself, leaning forward on the makeshift wooden desk, my fists clenched against the splinters. "What's going on with you? You've been different since we got here. I thought we were—"

"Stop." He interrupted, his voice suddenly raw, cutting through the tension like a blade. "You don't know anything about me."

I froze, taken aback by the force of his words. The rawness in his tone shook me, and for a moment, I regretted pushing him so hard. But then, I realized that I wasn't going to back down. If he wanted me to stop, he was going to have to give me a reason why.

"I know enough," I said, softer now, but firm. "You're hiding something, and I want to know what it is."

For a long moment, he didn't speak, and the air between us felt like it might snap, a taut wire stretched too thin. He exhaled sharply, as though weighing the decision to open up, and then, with a sigh that seemed to carry the weight of years, he put down his pen and leaned back in his chair.

His gaze drifted toward the fire, the light flickering across his face, and I watched the shadows in his features soften, just a little. "I didn't think you'd care," he muttered, almost to himself.

I bristled at the implication. "You think I don't care?"

"No," he said quickly, his eyes meeting mine. "I think you're too busy trying to figure out your own mess to notice mine." His words stung more than I expected. "It's not your problem."

But it was. Everything about him had become my problem the second I started questioning his every move. I hadn't expected to care this much, but here I was, caught in his orbit, unable to look away.

"Don't do that," I said, my voice tight, fighting back the hurt. "Don't shut me out like that. You think I haven't noticed the way you keep everything locked up? You think I'm blind to the fact that you're running from something?"

He stiffened, the muscles in his back pulling taut, but he didn't respond. I could see the walls rise in front of him, taller and thicker with every passing second. It was clear that whatever he was running from, he wasn't ready to talk about it. And yet, I could sense the ache beneath the surface, the quiet desperation.

"I'm not running from anything," he said finally, but the words lacked conviction. "I just don't owe you an explanation."

For a moment, I considered letting it go. I could walk away, let him bury his secrets, and pretend it didn't matter. But the thought of retreating into silence, of losing the chance to understand him, gnawed at me.

"Maybe not," I said quietly. "But that doesn't mean I'm going to stop asking."

His gaze flickered back to the fire, his fingers tapping against the edge of the table in an unconscious rhythm. I could see him fighting with himself, trying to decide whether to continue this strange dance we were engaged in. It wasn't until the fire crackled again, sending a shower of embers into the night sky, that he spoke.

"Fine," he said, his voice so low I almost didn't catch it. "I'm not who you think I am. I never was."

I leaned in, sensing that he was on the verge of saying something important. His words hung in the air, thick with meaning, but before I could press him further, he stood abruptly, the chair scraping across the dirt floor. "I'll tell you another time," he said, his tone final, closing the door on whatever it was he had been about to share.

I watched him walk away, the shadows swallowing him whole, and for a long time, I sat there, the unspoken truth heavy between us, just out of reach.

The next morning, the cool air hung heavy with the scent of pine and earth. The camp had returned to its rhythm, a hum of boots crunching over gravel, the shuffle of papers and maps being spread out on picnic tables. I could feel the eyes of the others on us—subtle glances, whispered exchanges—but no one dared to speak of it aloud. Not that I could blame them. If they knew anything, it was that sometimes it was better to leave things unsaid.

I tried to focus on the task at hand, spreading out the maps, mentally tracing the route we needed to follow for the next phase of our project. But it wasn't the plans or the charts that were occupying my mind. It was him. The way his silence had been louder than any words he might have spoken. The strange heaviness that still clung to the air between us, a fog that refused to lift.

I glanced over at him. He was standing at the edge of the camp, his back to me, arms folded as he stared off into the distance. It was a sight I had seen a hundred times—his brooding silhouette, the way he seemed to exist in some other space, some other time. But now, it felt different. It felt like he was a thousand miles away, a world I couldn't reach.

And yet, as I watched him, something in me tightened—a mixture of frustration and something else, something I couldn't name. I had confronted him the night before, demanded answers. But now, there was a new question burning in my mind. Was he even aware of the way he affected me? Was he aware of the pull, the tension that crackled between us like static?

It wasn't just about the secrets anymore. It was about him, the person behind the guarded eyes and the terse replies. The man who hid behind a wall of silence but was still so profoundly... there. I hated how easily he slipped into my thoughts.

"Are you just going to stand there and stare at him all day?" a voice broke through my thoughts, sharp and amused. I turned, finding Emily standing with her arms crossed, a sly smile tugging at her lips. She was a master at reading people, and it seemed she had picked up on the shift just as quickly as everyone else.

"I wasn't staring," I protested, my voice betraying me as I cast a quick glance back at him. "I was just thinking."

"Uh-huh." She raised an eyebrow, the mischievous glint in her eye unmistakable. "Thinking about him, I bet."

I opened my mouth to protest, but the words died on my lips. There was no point in denying it. Emily had always been able to read me better than anyone, a fact I found both maddening and comforting.

"You're in deeper than you think," she continued, her tone shifting from teasing to something more serious. "Don't let him pull you in if he's not ready to give you anything in return."

I swallowed hard, the truth of her words settling uncomfortably in my chest. I wasn't foolish enough to ignore the fact that I was being drawn into something I didn't understand. Something that could just as easily burn me as set me free.

"I'm not going to chase after him," I said, the words coming out more forcefully than I intended. But even as I said them, I could feel the lie lingering in the air. I had been chasing him for days, whether I wanted to admit it or not. It wasn't just about the past, or the questions he had left unanswered—it was about the way he made me feel when he was near. The way his presence tugged at something deep inside me.

Emily didn't say anything for a long time, but her gaze softened, as though she knew exactly what I was thinking. "Just make sure you're not the one who gets burned."

I nodded, but my thoughts were already elsewhere, drifting back to him, to the way his back had been turned to me, to the way he always seemed to be just out of reach.

The rest of the morning passed in a blur, with the usual tasks filling the space between the two of us. Every time I caught sight of him, I could feel the tension building again, coiling tighter around me. But I didn't dare speak to him, not after the way he had closed off the night before. I couldn't shake the feeling that every time I tried to get closer, he would only push me further away.

By late afternoon, the camp was abuzz with the next stage of our plans. Everyone was busy preparing for the fieldwork we would be conducting in the coming days, and the distractions gave me just enough space to breathe. But I couldn't escape the feeling that I was being watched. I glanced over my shoulder, half-expecting to find his eyes on me again, but this time, when I turned, he was standing right behind me.

I startled, my heart skipping a beat, and I quickly looked away, trying to play it cool. "You need something?" I asked, keeping my voice steady.

He didn't answer immediately. Instead, he just stood there, silent, his presence as solid as the ground beneath my feet. I could feel the weight of his gaze pressing into me, making the air between us crackle with electricity.

"You know," he finally said, his voice low, "you're not as subtle as you think."

I blinked, confused, and turned to face him. "What do you mean?"

"The way you keep glancing at me. The way you keep watching me when you think I'm not looking," he said, his lips curving into something that almost resembled a smile. Almost. "I'm not blind."

A flush crept up my neck, and I quickly looked away. "I wasn't—"

"I'm not looking for answers," he interrupted, his voice suddenly more serious, more guarded. "I'm just telling you, if you want to keep pretending, you can. But it won't change anything."

I swallowed, the words hanging between us like a warning. What exactly was I supposed to do with that? I didn't know what hurt more—the fact that he seemed to know me so well or that he was still shutting me out.

He stepped back, as though the conversation was over, but I couldn't shake the feeling that we were standing on the edge of something, something volatile and dangerous. And no matter how much I tried to pull away, I knew that the moment I stepped too close to the flame, I was going to get burned.

The night was falling quickly, a cool breeze sweeping through the camp and carrying with it the scent of fresh pine and damp earth. The fire crackled softly, its light flickering against the edges of the tent. I stood by the map, my fingers tracing the route we were supposed to follow, but all my thoughts were elsewhere. In that odd, silent way he had, he was there again, haunting my mind with his unreadable stare and the unsettling way he seemed to disappear into his own thoughts, as though I weren't even standing beside him.

I had tried to move on, to focus on the task at hand, but every so often, I could feel him—the weight of his presence pressing into me. It wasn't just the intensity of his gaze that unsettled me; it was the way he closed off, shutting himself out of reach. The night before, he had said something—something that hinted at more than I had expected. But now, his walls were back up, stronger than ever.

I bit my lip, glancing over at him. His jaw was clenched, his posture rigid, as though every inch of him was on guard. And maybe he was. Maybe the closer I got, the more he had to fight to keep me from breaking through. I couldn't decide if it frustrated me or fascinated me more.

A shout from across the camp snapped me from my thoughts. The others were gathering for the evening briefing. I hesitated, one last glance lingering on him, but then quickly turned to join the rest. The moment I walked away, I could feel the shift between us. It wasn't just the awkward silence anymore; it was something more—something charged and taut, like the air just before a thunderstorm.

The meeting was a blur of details. We were preparing for the fieldwork ahead—more routes to check, more data to gather. I was still focused on the maps, half-listening to the conversation, but my mind kept circling back to him.

After the meeting ended, I found myself alone by the fire, staring into the orange glow as though it might offer some answers. My frustration was building, the knot in my stomach growing tighter. I had pushed him, yes, but why had he shut me out so completely? Was there something more? Was I just the next person he couldn't let in? Or was there something I hadn't seen, something lurking just beneath the surface that he was too afraid to face?

It didn't matter. I wasn't about to leave it alone.

Before I could think better of it, I was standing up, brushing the dirt from my pants, and heading toward his tent. The sound of my boots crunching on the gravel seemed louder than it should have been, each step dragging me closer to something I wasn't ready to confront.

He was sitting outside, his back to me, shoulders hunched. I could see the tension in his posture, the way his muscles coiled beneath his shirt. He didn't hear me coming, but when I stopped just behind him, I could feel the shift, the subtle awareness that passed between us.

"I'm not going to let this go," I said, my voice steady despite the hammering of my heart.

He didn't move at first, but then he sighed, long and deep, as though the weight of the world was pressing on him. "I told you before," he said, his voice low, "I don't owe you anything."

"That's not good enough," I shot back, crossing my arms over my chest. "You can't just pull me in and then walk away every time things get difficult."

He turned to face me, his expression unreadable. "You think I want this?" His voice was tight, as though the words themselves were painful. "You think I wanted you to ask about my past?"

My pulse quickened, my breath catching in my throat. I had been too quick to assume that this was about me—that somehow, he was being distant because of something I had done. But the truth, the real truth, seemed far darker than that.

"Maybe not," I said slowly, trying to keep my tone calm. "But you're here, aren't you? You didn't leave. You're still here, standing in front of me, which means something, whether you want to admit it or not."

His eyes darkened. "You don't know anything about me. About what I'm running from."

And there it was—the words I had been waiting for. There it was, hanging between us like a secret too dangerous to speak aloud. But before I could process it, before I could ask him to explain, he stood up abruptly, his chair scraping against the ground.

"I told you," he said, his voice a low growl, "I don't want to talk about it."

My breath caught. "Then why are you still here?"

He took a step toward me, the intensity of his gaze almost burning. "Because you keep pushing," he said, his voice rougher than I expected. "You keep pushing, and I can't stop you. But I'm not going to let you destroy me in the process."

I swallowed, unsure how to respond. I had never heard him so raw, so close to breaking. The walls, the distance, all of it—the anger, the frustration, it was all coming undone in front of me.

And then, just as quickly as it had appeared, the vulnerability vanished. The storm in his eyes faded, replaced with that familiar mask. He stepped back, the distance between us growing once more.

"Forget it," he said, his voice once again cool, distant. "You don't want to know. You can't handle it."

The words hung in the air, the finality of them echoing in my mind. I opened my mouth to say something, anything, but then the shout of one of the others echoed from across the camp, calling me back.

I hesitated, my gaze lingering on him. He didn't look at me again.

Turning on my heel, I made my way back to the fire, the unanswered questions swirling in my chest. And though the others were busy with their preparations, I couldn't shake the feeling that something was about to happen—something I wasn't prepared for.

Behind me, the night felt heavier than it had before. The secrets between us, the ones he refused to share, were pushing against the walls of my mind. And just as I thought the tension might snap, the sharp sound of something breaking in the distance cut through the air. I froze, every muscle in my body locking in place.

A voice—his voice—came through the dark. "Get down! Now!"

And then the ground shook beneath my feet.

Chapter 8: Ashes to Ashes

The wind howled through the cracks in the walls, carrying the smell of wet earth and damp wood, the scent of a place that was never quite dry. I could feel it all around me—an unease that hung in the air, like the heavy breath of something waiting to happen. The camp was quiet now, eerily so. Most of the crew had retreated into their tents, trying to escape the weight of the unknown pressing in on them. A third member of the team had disappeared overnight, just like the others. The search turned up nothing—no sign, no trace, not even the faintest footprint. Just the hollow, oppressive silence of the forest surrounding us.

We were deep in the wilderness now, far from civilization, in a place where the trees whispered secrets no one wanted to hear. The only thing we had left to cling to was each other, but that fragile bond had been tested time and again. The tension was palpable, seeping into every conversation, every glance. The unspoken fear that someone—or something—was picking us off, one by one. And yet, there was a strange comfort in that. In the idea that whatever was happening was happening to all of us, and that meant none of us were entirely alone.

I was walking back from the clearing where we had last seen the missing crew member, the forest floor slick beneath my boots. The sound of distant footsteps behind me had me turning, and I saw him—Jack. His eyes were shadowed, his jaw tight as if holding something back. He was a seasoned investigator, a man who had seen more than his fair share of dark things, but tonight, there was something raw in him, something fragile that I hadn't noticed before.

He moved toward me with a kind of quiet urgency, as if every step took effort. He pulled me aside, out of earshot from the others, and his voice, when it came, was barely above a whisper. "You feel it too, don't you?"

I nodded, not trusting myself to speak. What was there to say? We all felt it—the creeping dread that had taken hold of our minds, the feeling that something, or someone, was watching us from just out of sight. The tension had reached a breaking point, and none of us were immune to it.

"I don't know what's going on here," he said, his voice a little hoarse, as if the words were tearing at his throat. "But I've got a bad feeling. A feeling that whoever or whatever is doing this is getting closer. Maybe closer than we think."

His words settled over me like a thick fog. I couldn't remember the last time I'd felt my heart race like this, my instincts screaming at me to run, to get out of this place before it was too late. But there was no escaping. The forest wasn't just a place we were trapped in—it was a part of us now. It had its claws in us, pulling us deeper into its grasp.

Jack's eyes searched mine, as if looking for some sign that I understood what he was trying to say. There was no bravado left in him, no shield of confidence. Just a raw, naked fear that mirrored my own. The realization hit me hard—this was no longer a simple mystery to solve. This was survival.

"Listen," he continued, his voice steadying, "I think we need to work together. We're stronger that way. But I'm not sure how much longer any of us have before it all falls apart." His gaze flickered over my shoulder, a sharp glance as if expecting someone to be standing there. But there was nothing—only the silence of the night. "I'm not saying I trust everyone here, but you..." He trailed off, the words unsaid hanging between us, thick and uncomfortable.

I crossed my arms, the chill from the air creeping into my bones. "And what, you think we'll solve it if we stick together? You think there's some sort of logic to this madness?"

He gave a quick, almost humorless laugh, his eyes darkening. "I don't know. Maybe. But we have to try." There was something in his gaze now, something that made the hairs on the back of my neck stand up. Was it desperation? Or was it something darker?

I didn't know if I could trust him. The truth was, I wasn't sure I trusted anyone anymore. Not since the first person had disappeared. The unanswered questions gnawed at me—why had they gone? Where were they? And most haunting of all, who was next?

"You're not the only one with questions," I said, taking a step closer, my voice low. "But what if this is bigger than we think? What if it's not just about us? What if we're being used?" My words felt hollow even as I spoke them, but there was a kernel of truth in them. It wasn't just the crew that was at risk anymore; it was everything we were trying to uncover.

Jack shifted, his posture changing—tense, guarded, like a man who was suddenly realizing the full weight of the situation. "I don't think we're being used. I think we're being hunted."

His words echoed in my mind, haunting in their simplicity. Hunted. It was the only explanation that fit. But who, or what, was doing the hunting? And why?

The silence between us stretched, and for the first time since all this started, I felt the flicker of something deeper, a connection that neither of us was willing to acknowledge yet. An unspoken bond, forged not by trust but by the shared fear that had brought us together. He was right about one thing—we had to stick together, because if we didn't, there was a real chance we wouldn't make it out of here.

"I don't like this," I muttered, more to myself than to him. But Jack heard it, and his lips twisted into something that could have been a smile. A smile that held no warmth.

"Neither do I," he said quietly, his eyes flicking back to the camp, where the others were still huddled in the growing dark. "But we don't have much of a choice, do we?"

The firelight flickered in the center of camp, casting long shadows that seemed to stretch and twist as if they had a life of their own. We huddled around it, trying to pretend the world outside was normal, trying to fool ourselves into believing the sudden disappearances were just a string of unfortunate coincidences. But none of us were fooling anyone—not even ourselves. The tension was too thick, hanging in the air like smoke, choking out any semblance of peace.

Jack and I lingered on the edge of the circle, just far enough from the others to speak without being overheard. His eyes were locked on the fire, but I could feel the heat of his gaze, could feel the way he was studying me, sizing me up. It made me uncomfortable, and yet there was something about it that drew me in, like a magnet pulling against my will. He was the kind of man who made you question things, even when you knew you shouldn't. And right now, with the camp on edge, and the unsolved mystery of the disappearances hanging over us, I found myself questioning everything—my thoughts, my instincts, my own sanity.

"Do you believe in coincidence?" Jack's voice cut through the quiet, soft but with a sharp edge.

I turned toward him, the question hanging between us like a dare. His lips twitched, almost imperceptibly, as if he were amused by my reaction. It was unsettling how calm he seemed in the face of everything that had happened. Most of the others were either too scared to speak or too tired to even bother trying to hide their fear. But Jack, he was different. He wore his fear like a second skin, but it didn't stop him from looking at the situation with a cool, calculating eye.

"Depends on the kind of coincidence you're talking about," I replied, my tone a little sharper than I meant it to be. But I wasn't ready to admit that I was just as unsettled as everyone else, maybe even more so. "What exactly are you getting at?"

He shifted slightly, eyes still on the fire. "These disappearances... they don't add up. People don't just vanish. Not like this. Not without leaving some trace behind. Something's wrong, and I think we both know it."

I didn't say anything at first. I wasn't sure what to say. It felt like there was a part of me that already knew what was happening, a part of me that was willing to bury that knowledge as deep as I could. But Jack wasn't the type to let things slide. His gaze finally met mine, and the weight of it felt like a question I wasn't ready to answer.

"You think we're being hunted?" I asked, my voice barely above a whisper. It was the only thing that made sense, the only explanation that fit the way the tension had been building, growing thicker with every passing hour.

His expression darkened, a flicker of something—anger, fear, or perhaps a mix of both—flashing across his face before it was quickly masked by his usual calm. "I don't know. I want to believe we're just dealing with bad luck, but..." He trailed off, his eyes narrowing. "You heard what the others were saying. People have been here before. People who went missing without a trace. People who never came back."

I felt a chill race down my spine, the reality of his words sinking in like a stone. This wasn't the first time a team had disappeared in this place. There were whispers—rumors—that this forest had a way of swallowing people whole, taking them without a trace and leaving only memories. And now we were caught in the same web. I had hoped it was just superstition, just something to keep people on edge, but now? Now I wasn't so sure.

"I don't know if I can keep pretending this is all a coincidence," I said, my voice barely audible. I wasn't sure if I was speaking to Jack or to myself at this point. "This place... it feels wrong. And I don't mean just the missing people. I mean everything. The air. The trees. The way it all seems to close in on you, like it's watching. Waiting."

Jack's gaze softened for a moment, as if understanding what I was trying to say, but then he straightened, shaking his head. "You're not the only one who feels it. I've been here too long to ignore the signs. There's something happening in these woods. Something we can't see, something we can't fight. But we have to keep moving. We have to stay focused. Because if we don't, it'll pick us off one by one."

I nodded, not because I agreed, but because it was the only thing to do. Jack was right. We couldn't afford to fall apart. We had to keep our heads, no matter how much the fear gnawed at us from the inside out.

He turned to face me fully now, his expression hardening. "I need you to keep your head on straight. We need to trust each other if we're going to get through this. If we're going to get out of here alive."

I looked at him, really looked at him, and for the first time, I saw the weight of what he was carrying. He wasn't just afraid of the forest, or of whatever might be lurking out there. He was afraid of something else—something much more personal. I didn't know what it was yet, but I could see it in the way his jaw tightened, in the way his hands flexed at his sides as if he were holding onto something he wasn't ready to share.

"Alright," I said, my voice steady despite the way my heart was hammering in my chest. "I'll trust you. But you need to promise me something."

Jack raised an eyebrow, as if surprised by the shift in my tone. "What's that?"

"You need to promise me that we're in this together. No more secrets. No more running off on your own. Whatever's happening here, we face it as a team."

He held my gaze for a long moment, the firelight dancing in his eyes. And then, just when I thought he was going to say something that would make everything worse, he nodded.

"Agreed," he said, his voice firm, but there was something in his eyes—something that made me wonder if, in the end, we were both just trying to outrun something we couldn't name.

The night pressed in around us, thick and heavy, as if the forest had gathered itself to listen. The camp had been reduced to hushed voices, the crackle of the fire, and the occasional rustle of someone shifting in their sleeping bag, too afraid to truly sleep. It felt like the air itself was pregnant with secrets—heavy, suffocating. I wasn't sure how much longer I could stand it, the silence, the waiting. Waiting for something to break. Something to give.

Jack and I had become an uneasy alliance, two strangers bound by shared fear, and a growing suspicion that none of us were as innocent as we had once thought. The others had retreated into their tents, but the tension in the camp had only escalated since the last disappearance. Whispers were being passed in the dark, and there was no longer any attempt to keep the fear at bay. Everyone knew something was wrong, but none of us had the answers. And as for Jack? He was no longer the enigmatic investigator I'd met at the beginning of this trip. He was a man undone, unraveling before me, but his resolve was still strong. Stronger, perhaps, than anyone else's.

"Can we trust them?" My voice came out softer than I'd intended, the question hanging between us like a rope stretching over an abyss.

Jack didn't answer immediately. He didn't need to. His eyes, cold and calculating, flickered to the shadows where the others slept, his jaw working in thought. Then, without a word, he reached into his jacket pocket and pulled out a small, weathered notebook. I watched as his fingers gripped it tightly, his knuckles going white.

"They're not who they say they are," he muttered, almost to himself. His voice was lower now, and his eyes met mine with a sudden intensity that sent a shiver down my spine. "None of them are. But that's not the worst of it."

I swallowed, trying to push down the rising panic that threatened to choke me. "What's worse than not being who they say they are?"

Jack hesitated for a moment, and I felt the pull of the moment, like a weight settling on my chest. "You ever heard of a place called Gray Hollow?"

I frowned, trying to place the name. It was familiar, like a half-remembered dream, but it didn't immediately click. "Sounds like a ghost story."

He nodded, his expression grim. "It's more than that. It's a place people disappear into. A place where time doesn't work the way it should. Where the forest... chooses its victims."

The words settled over me, slow and heavy, like cold water filling up a cup I hadn't realized was there. The forest. Gray Hollow. The disappearances. Was it possible?

"Jack, are you—" I started, but the sound of movement cut me off. We both turned, instinctively, the hair on the back of my neck prickling. Someone was coming out of their tent. It was too dark to see clearly, but the figure was unmistakably tall, a shadow that moved like a man but was something more, something unnerving.

Without thinking, I stepped closer to Jack, and he instinctively put a hand on my arm. His touch was light but firm, as if grounding me in this moment of increasing uncertainty.

"Stay calm," he whispered, his breath warm against my ear. "We don't know who we can trust."

I nodded, but my heart was pounding, louder now than the distant winds rustling through the trees. The figure stepped closer, the crunch of dry leaves underfoot echoing in the silence. And then, just as quickly as it had appeared, the shadow darted back into the darkness, vanishing from sight.

"Who the hell was that?" I whispered, my voice thick with suspicion.

Jack didn't answer right away. His eyes were narrowed, scanning the camp, the surrounding darkness. When he finally spoke, it was with a quiet certainty that made my stomach flip. "That wasn't one of us."

My heart dropped. "You're sure?"

He didn't answer, but his silence was all the confirmation I needed. The unease in my chest blossomed into full-blown dread, and I found myself backing away, unconsciously seeking the relative safety of the firelight. It felt like something had shifted, like we were no longer alone in the camp.

"We need to check the perimeter," Jack said, his voice low and steady. He was already moving, slipping into the shadows without hesitation, a man who had learned how to disappear in the dark.

I hesitated for a split second, torn between following him and running for cover. But the fear that had been growing inside me—this deep, gnawing terror—pushed me forward. I couldn't stay here, not while whatever was out there was moving among us. We had to get answers.

I followed Jack, trying to keep my steps quiet, as if the forest itself was listening. The night seemed to close in around us, the darkness swallowing every sound, every movement. I could hear my own breathing, sharp and shallow, as we moved deeper into the trees.

And then, just as I thought we might have reached the edge of the camp, the air shifted—something heavy, almost electric, prickled in the stillness. My heart raced, and I glanced over at Jack, only to see him frozen, his body taut with some kind of warning.

"Do you hear that?" His voice was barely audible, but I heard it all the same—his words trembling like leaves in the wind.

I listened, straining against the dark. A distant sound, a whisper, maybe more than one. Too soft to be a voice, but close enough to feel like it was meant for us.

Before I could respond, the crack of a branch snapped through the air—loud, too loud, right behind us.

We spun, adrenaline surging. My heart thudded in my chest as I searched the darkness, my breath ragged in the silence that followed.

And then, out of the blackness, I saw it.

A figure. Taller than any of us, hunched, moving in the shadows like it belonged there.

I froze, not sure whether to run or stay. Jack reached for my arm, his grip tightening, but his eyes never left the thing in the woods.

"What the hell is that?" I whispered, barely able to keep my voice from shaking.

Jack's answer was a whisper I'll never forget.

"It's not human."

Chapter 9: Scorched Hearts

The heat was oppressive, a wall of scorched air that clung to everything. It was early afternoon when the fire broke free, winding its way through the dry underbrush of the valley like an insatiable serpent, crackling and hissing as if the very earth had been angered. There was no warning, no whispered breeze or distant smoke that might have tipped us off. One moment, I was walking along the trail, listening to the soft rustle of leaves and the chirp of birds in the canopy, the next, the world was ablaze.

I didn't know why I was so surprised—wildfires were a regular visitor to these parts, and by now, I'd learned the rhythm of their unpredictability. But this one was different. The fire wasn't content to just burn through the lowland brush; it was climbing, hungry for more, licking at the sky. My breath caught in my throat as the sharp scent of burning wood filled the air, thick and suffocating, like the earth had caught fire from the inside out. There was no time to think, only to move.

My hand instinctively found the radio at my side. "This is Madison. Wildfire near the east ridge. I'm going in to assess the damage."

"Understood," came the crackling response from the station. "Stay safe, Madison."

Safe. The word sounded like a joke. There was no safety here, not with the wind whipping the flames into a frenzy. I glanced around, scanning the perimeter of the camp, my heart slamming against my ribs. The fire was moving too quickly. I didn't know who had gotten caught in its path, but I was damn sure not letting anyone burn without a fight.

I grabbed my pack and started running toward the woods, knowing the direction where people might be. The smoke stung my eyes, and my lungs protested the sharp, acrid air. The forest, usually so welcoming, now felt like a maze of danger, with every step feeling as though it could be my last. The closer I got to the heart of the fire, the more I could feel the heat on my skin, the searing, unforgiving heat that made the very ground tremble underfoot.

Then, through the smoke, I saw him.

Jared.

His silhouette emerged from the haze like a ghost. His face, always so hard, was covered in soot, his eyes narrowed against the smoke. He moved with a kind of purposeful grace, like he had been forged for moments like this. And yet, as much as he looked like a man prepared for battle, I could see it—the crack in his armor, the hesitation in his step.

"Jared!" I shouted, though the wind nearly swallowed my voice.

He didn't hear me at first, too absorbed in his task. I forced my way through the trees, desperate to get closer, to reach him before it was too late. The air was thick with heat and urgency, and as I pushed forward, I saw something that stopped me cold.

Jared, the man who had built his entire persona on being unshakable, was faltering. His left leg buckled beneath him, and for a split second, I thought he was going to collapse into the smoldering earth. Without thinking, I bolted toward him. My fingers brushed the side of his arm as I reached out, my grip firm as I steadied him.

"Don't you dare," I muttered, the words sharp with a mixture of fear and frustration. "You're not going down like this."

He didn't pull away.

For a moment, the world seemed to quiet around us. The crackling fire, the rush of my breath, the heat—everything faded to the background as our eyes locked. I saw it then, in the depths of his stormy gaze—a flicker of vulnerability, of doubt. It was gone in the next instant, buried beneath his usual stoic mask. But it was enough. Enough for me to wonder if I had been right all along about him.

Jared nodded once, his jaw tight. "I'm fine," he muttered, brushing off my touch as if it were nothing. But I felt the weight of his words more than any force of nature.

"I don't care," I snapped back. "You're not fine, and I'm not leaving you behind."

He glanced at me, his expression unreadable. "You should be. This is too dangerous."

"I'm not running away. Not this time."

A spark of something—whether frustration or admiration—I couldn't tell—flashed in his eyes, but before he could respond, the roar of the fire grew louder, as if in agreement with my stubbornness.

"Come on," he said, his voice low, commanding. "Stay close."

And for once, I did as he said.

We moved as one, side by side, pushing through the thick smoke, our lungs burning with every step. There was no time for words now. Just the sound of our boots pounding against the scorched earth and the crackling inferno that threatened to consume everything in its path.

I could feel him, close enough to almost reach out and touch, but I didn't. Not yet. There were more important things to focus on—survival, for one. But the tension between us was palpable, like an electrical current that charged the air. Every brush of our arms felt like an unspoken invitation, each glance heavier than the last.

The fire was relentless, but so were we.

We came across the first group of survivors—three hikers, caught in the blaze, too stunned to move. Jared was already pulling them toward safety, barking orders, his every movement efficient, precise. He was a machine, cold and calculated, a far cry from the man I had once known. And yet, beneath that hardened exterior, there was something deeper. Something that made me wonder if the walls he had built around himself could ever come down. If they could, would I be the one to tear them down, or would the fire consume us both first?

But for now, there was only the fire, only the fight for survival. And Jared.

Always Jared.

We worked through the smoke like shadows, our bodies moving in tandem, driven by a shared sense of urgency. The fire loomed over us, a beast that had found its voice and was now roaring with an insatiable appetite. Each breath I took felt like it was filled with shards of glass, scraping against my lungs as the fire danced at the edge of my vision. Jared was in front of me now, cutting through the forest with purpose, his every move methodical. But I could tell he was struggling—just slightly, though, as if he was trying to bury the weight of it under his usual impenetrable exterior.

His face was a portrait of controlled determination, but I noticed the way his shoulders were drawn tighter than usual, like he was holding something in—something heavy that had nothing to do with the inferno threatening to swallow us whole. It was a small thing, barely perceptible. The kind of thing that would have passed most people by, but I saw it. And I couldn't help but wonder if it was that damn fire—if it was messing with his mind the way it was messing with mine.

The group of hikers we'd rescued had finally been cleared to safety, but the danger wasn't over. The wind had picked up, pushing the flames westward, faster than we could move. Every few seconds, I glanced over my shoulder, trying to gauge the fire's progress, my pulse hammering in my throat.

I knew we needed to keep moving, but I couldn't shake the feeling that something was wrong with Jared. Not physically, not really. It was more than that. His gaze was distant, like he was fighting a battle with some invisible enemy, one that wasn't the fire at all. I could see it now—the way his jaw clenched, the way he seemed to draw inward, like he was fighting to hold onto something in his past that I wasn't supposed to know about.

"Hey," I said, my voice quieter than I meant it to be. "You good?"

He didn't immediately answer, which was typical of him. Jared wasn't much for talking when the world was on fire, literally or metaphorically. But when he did respond, his tone was flat, distant. "I'm fine."

I didn't believe him. And I didn't think he believed himself, either. But there was no time to push it. The fire wasn't waiting for either of us to figure our stuff out.

We trudged forward, the heat unbearable now. My clothes were sticking to my skin, and sweat pooled at the small of my back. I wiped my forehead with the back of my hand, my focus divided between the fire and keeping Jared in sight. The crackle of the flames was a constant in the background now, a pulse that seemed to echo in my own chest.

And then, a burst of wind swept through the trees, and the fire took a new turn. The direction of the flames shifted suddenly, and the sky above us darkened, as though the world itself had decided it was done playing nice.

"Madison!" Jared's shout was barely audible over the roar of the fire, but I heard him. Barely.

I turned to find him standing still, his back to me, his body rigid. The fire had surrounded us, and the escape routes had dwindled down to almost nothing. He looked over his shoulder, and for the first time, I saw something in his eyes that wasn't just determination. It was something else—something raw.

"Jared, move," I urged, stepping forward, the urgency in my voice sharp. "We can't stay here."

But he didn't move. Instead, his shoulders dropped, and for a moment, I thought he might collapse again, this time for real. It was like all the tension, all the stress he'd been holding in, was finally too much. His breath came in short, labored bursts, and for the first time in as long as I'd known him, Jared was showing signs of vulnerability—real, unfiltered vulnerability.

I was frozen. Not out of fear, but out of something else. Something I wasn't sure I understood. I was used to him being the rock, the steady hand. But this? This was new, and it was shaking something loose inside me.

"You don't have to do this alone," I said before I could stop myself, the words tumbling out like I'd been holding them back for years.

His eyes flicked to mine, and there it was again—the briefest crack in the walls he'd built. It was gone before I could touch it, before I could even think about reaching for it, but for a heartbeat, it had been there. A flicker. A breath. A moment where Jared was just as human as the rest of us.

"I'm fine," he said again, but it was quieter this time, almost like he was trying to convince himself.

I didn't respond. There was nothing to say to that. I had never known Jared to be so... uncertain. It was like the fire had forced something out of him, and it was rattling him in ways I didn't understand.

We continued, slowly now, the air growing thicker as we moved deeper into the trees. My eyes stung from the smoke, and my breath was coming in short, painful bursts. The fire was creeping closer, and I knew we didn't have much time left before we would be trapped. I had no idea how we were going to get out of this, but for some reason, the weight of Jared's silence seemed even more suffocating than the smoke.

"We need to go," I said, grabbing his arm. This time, he didn't pull away.

He looked at me, really looked at me, his gaze searching, like he was trying to figure something out—something that had been lurking between us for far too long. His jaw tightened again, and for a second, I thought he might finally say something. But instead, he just nodded.

"Yeah," he said, his voice barely a whisper.

We moved forward again, the fire licking at our heels, but there was something different in the air now. Something that had shifted between us, and I wasn't sure if it was the fire, or the weight of everything unsaid that hung in the spaces between us.

The fire roared louder now, a guttural, living thing, eating up the forest as if it were starved for years. The world around us seemed to shimmer in the haze, a twilight realm where time had slowed and stretched, bending under the weight of smoke and heat. Every step I took felt heavier, the earth beneath me hard and unforgiving, yet the intensity of it was almost comforting. It was a distraction, a reason to focus on something other than the knot forming in my chest. And that something wasn't the fire.

It was Jared.

We kept moving, but now it was different. Every time my hand brushed his, every breath I took in the thick air, every fleeting glance shared between us, the tension built. Not just from the heat of the fire but from whatever this thing was between us. He was still distant, but there was something almost tangible now—an understanding that neither of us could ignore. It was like we were walking along a razor's edge, balancing between survival and...

something else. Something that, if we were to face it, might destroy us just as much as the fire was threatening to.

I caught sight of a fallen log, charred and blackened, just ahead of us. The fire was creeping closer, and we had little time before it would trap us here.

"Jared, we need to go—now," I said, trying to shake him from his trance. He hadn't said a word in minutes, hadn't even looked at me, and I was beginning to wonder if I had lost him somewhere along the way.

He glanced at me, his eyes briefly locking with mine before he looked away. That fleeting moment of connection was enough to send a strange, shivery warmth down my spine. But there was no time to indulge in whatever strange emotions were stirring inside me. There was only the fire, relentless and savage, its heat licking at the edges of the trees.

"I know," he muttered, the sound of his voice low and rough, like gravel sliding across stone. It was the first time I had heard any emotion in his tone since we started this madness together. But it didn't last long. He was back to his quiet self again, the one who refused to let anyone in.

We reached the edge of the clearing just as the fire's roar grew louder. The sky above was a canvas of orange and red, the smoke swirling in a thick, suffocating cloud. And then, just when it seemed like we had reached safety, I saw it. The wind changed direction again, sending a fresh gust toward us, and the fire surged forward, pushing us back toward the trees.

"Move!" Jared's voice was sharp, snapping me out of my stupor. He grabbed my arm, dragging me behind him as the blaze caught the wind and spun, clawing at the ground with ferocity. My heart pounded as I ran, the air too hot, too thick to breathe properly. It felt like we were trapped in a furnace, the world closing in around us.

The ground trembled underfoot as the fire swept toward us with terrifying speed. Jared didn't let go of my arm. His grip was unyielding, like a lifeline. He was pulling me toward something—toward safety, I hoped—but I couldn't quite see where we were going anymore. The fire had obscured our path, and all I could do was trust him.

"I can't—" I began, but before I could finish the sentence, Jared was already dragging me to the side, pushing me toward a narrow path between two massive rocks. I stumbled but caught my footing, the urgency in his hands driving me forward. We weren't going to make it. I knew it. The fire was right behind us, too close, the heat almost unbearable.

"I said, move!" His voice was tight, but there was something else there now—something that cut through the chaos. Was it desperation? Fear? It was hard to tell with him, but it made my pulse race in a way I hadn't anticipated.

I didn't dare look back. The fire was a wild thing now, snapping at us like it could reach out and grab us at any moment. My legs burned, my lungs ached, but we were still moving, and that was all that mattered. We rounded the corner of the rocks, and I collided with Jared's chest as he stopped abruptly.

"Where—where are we?" I gasped, my breath shallow, my legs unsteady. I glanced over my shoulder, my heart skipping a beat as I saw the fire creeping up, its tendrils reaching for us, a hungry beast.

"This way," he said, his voice harsh but clear. He pulled me with him, the strength of his grip like steel, his movements fast and sure. But there was no clear path now, no sense of where we were going. It was just survival.

The landscape was changing—no longer a familiar forest, but a place I didn't recognize. The heat was unbearable, my skin prickling with each step. I was beginning to feel the edges of panic, the fire too close, the air too hot. And still, Jared kept pulling me forward, his eyes set in a grim line, focused, as if he knew exactly what he was doing. I wasn't sure I did.

And then, just when I thought there was no way out, we came upon a sudden drop.

Jared stopped dead in his tracks, his body tense, his jaw set. I didn't see it at first, but when I stepped closer, I understood.

A cliff.

We were standing at the edge of a steep drop, the ground below looking like a jagged mouth ready to swallow us whole. The fire was too close now—its heat scorching my back, the flames roaring like a hungry animal, reaching for us, making it feel like the earth itself was about to burn.

"Jared, what do we do?" I asked, my voice rising in panic.

He didn't answer. Instead, he stepped back, eyes scanning the area around us, as if searching for an answer that didn't exist. And then, without warning, he turned toward me.

"You're going to have to jump."

I froze.

"Jump?"

Chapter 10: Under Fire

The camp was a cacophony of tension the moment I walked back through the rusted gates. It hung in the air like smoke, thin and choking, curling around every conversation, every sharp glance. A handful of soldiers stood in huddled groups, their voices low but their words sharp. I had barely set foot inside the main tent when the whispers hit my ears—accusations heavy with suspicion, murmurs of betrayal. There was no mistaking it. They were all talking about him. About Nathan.

I had known it would happen. A team like this, bound by nothing but the edge of survival and a shared secret, was always a powder keg waiting for a spark. But the air felt heavier today. The investigations, the questioning—it was all becoming too much. And Nathan, usually so impenetrable, was unraveling right before my eyes. His dark eyes, once filled with a quiet confidence, now seemed darker, like an endless pit. He stood at the center of it all, silent, a figure of suspicion, and the worst part? He didn't say a word in his defense.

I tried not to notice how his gaze lingered on me every time I entered the tent. It wasn't the way he looked at the others—blank, calculating—but the way he watched me, like he was waiting for something. Like he was waiting for me to speak, to do something to prove I hadn't lost the thread of loyalty that had once tied us together. The truth was, I could feel the pull in my chest, that undeniable tug between the man I thought I knew and the person he was becoming in the eyes of the team.

For all his silence, for all the accusations, I couldn't help but wonder if they were wrong. Nathan had never given me a reason to doubt him. Sure, he was closed off, distant, always with that shield of indifference around him, but was that enough to turn on him now? To throw him to the wolves of suspicion without any real proof?

I had seen soldiers come and go in this hellhole, people whose hearts and minds had twisted under the pressure. But Nathan—he wasn't like that. Or so I wanted to believe.

When they finally cornered him, dragging him to the center of the camp like a guilty animal, I couldn't help the sick feeling that curled in my stomach. His eyes met mine then, briefly, before they were forced to the ground in submission. And that look—raw, desperate—shook me. He wasn't fighting back, wasn't defending himself, and I knew in that moment that something deeper was at play.

The tension reached its peak when I caught a glimpse of the commander, his weathered face a mask of cold judgment. It was clear he had already made his decision. Nathan was the suspect. The whispers that had started innocently enough were no longer innocent—they were accusations, each word another stone on the pile that would eventually crush him.

But before the moment could settle into something worse, Nathan's voice cut through the chatter, low but undeniable.

"I'm not the one who did it," he said. It wasn't a plea, just a statement. His eyes flickered toward me again. "I didn't do it."

I didn't know whether to trust him or not, but I couldn't look away. Something in his voice—the rawness, the exhaustion—stirred something in me. A part of me screamed to believe him, but another part, the part that had learned to trust only evidence and reason, told me I was being a fool.

I knew I had to decide.

When the meeting dispersed, I lingered behind, hesitant. My fingers curled into fists at my sides, fighting the urge to storm over to Nathan and demand he explain himself. But he didn't give me the chance. Without a word, he caught my gaze and motioned with a slight jerk of his head toward the far edge of the camp.

I followed him, each step a drumbeat of dread in my chest. The farther we walked, the more the sounds of the camp faded until only the soft rustling of wind and the crunch of gravel underfoot filled the space between us. I tried to keep my face neutral, but my thoughts were spiraling, a storm of questions I didn't know how to answer. Why wouldn't he speak up? Why wasn't he defending himself?

Finally, we stopped under the shadow of a large, dilapidated truck, its tires long deflated, the metal shell pockmarked with the scars of time. Nathan turned to face me, his face a mask of grim resolve. For the first time, I noticed the exhaustion in his eyes, the hollows beneath them that spoke of sleepless nights and grinding fear.

"I didn't do it," he said again, this time his voice softer, almost pleading. "I know what they think, what they're saying. But I didn't. I can't explain it. But I'm not the one who betrayed us."

His words hung in the air like an open wound, raw and bleeding. I wanted to reach out, to reassure him that I believed him, but I couldn't. Not yet.

"Then why won't you defend yourself?" I whispered, the words slipping out before I could stop them. "Why are you just standing there, letting them accuse you? You could say something—anything—to clear your name."

Nathan's gaze softened for a moment, the hardness in his features faltering. He took a step closer, his voice low, the words coming out like gravel.

"Because it's not about me anymore. It's about you," he said, his words a punch to the gut. "They'll turn on you if you defend me. They'll think you're in on it. I'm not asking you to take my side. I'm asking you not to make it worse."

For a long moment, the silence between us felt like an abyss, a chasm that neither of us could cross. His words, his trust, weighed heavy on my chest. I hadn't realized until now how much I had come to rely on that trust. How much I had come to rely on him.

The decision was mine, and I knew it. I didn't have answers. I didn't have proof. But I had to trust my instincts, my gut, and I couldn't walk away from him now.

"I'll stand by you," I said, my voice steadier than I felt. "Even if it costs me everything."

He looked at me then, really looked at me, and for the first time in days, I saw a flicker of something—hope, maybe, or gratitude. Whatever it was, it was enough to make me feel like I had just made the most dangerous, important decision of my life.

The weight of his trust settled heavily on my shoulders, a burden I hadn't anticipated. I had spent so long carefully guarding my heart, building walls so high that no one could get through. But Nathan? He had found the cracks, slipping in silently until there was nothing left to protect. He had seen past my armor, and now, in the stillness of this camp overrun with suspicion, I realized I was holding something of his—a piece of his soul, fragile and raw. And I wasn't sure I knew how to keep it safe.

The days that followed blurred together in a haze of uncertainty. My mind swung between the endless loop of doubt and loyalty, a pendulum that refused to stop. Every time I glanced over at Nathan, sitting in the corner of the makeshift campfire, his posture stiff but his eyes restless, I was faced with the same question. What if he wasn't telling me the whole truth? What if I was falling for a lie?

The investigation, it seemed, was less about finding the truth and more about forcing someone to take the fall. The team—my team—had turned against him in a way I hadn't expected. Their voices were filled with accusations, their faces contorted with distrust. It wasn't even subtle. It was a blood sport, and Nathan was the prey.

I tried to stay distant, tried to keep my emotions in check, but it was impossible. Every word they said about him felt like a slap to my chest. A part of me wanted to scream at them to stop, to remind them of who Nathan was before this mess. But I kept my mouth shut, listening as they dissected his every move, every action. They talked like they knew him—like they had ever really known him. They had no idea.

But there was something else, something more insidious brewing beneath the surface. It wasn't just the accusation of betrayal that stung; it was the way they spoke about him as if he was no longer human. It was as if they had already written him off, like he was a character in a story whose fate had been sealed. And maybe, just maybe, that was the hardest part to swallow—how easily they discarded him.

I couldn't bring myself to speak against them, not when I felt my own suspicions gnawing at the edges of my resolve. I had to wonder: If I was wrong about Nathan, what did that make me? Was I just as blind as they were, a fool chasing after someone who had no real interest in me?

That's when he came to me again, his footsteps soft against the dry dirt, his presence as undeniable as the storm clouds that had begun gathering on the horizon. He didn't speak at first, just stood there, his silhouette outlined by the flickering campfire, casting long shadows over his face. When I looked at him, really looked, I saw the toll it had all taken on him—the hollow eyes, the tension in his jaw. He wasn't just under fire from the team; he was under fire from everything around him.

I forced myself to keep my breathing steady. "You need to talk to them," I said, the words rough in my throat. "You can't keep hiding behind silence. They need something—anything—to believe you."

He shook his head slowly, as though the very idea of explaining himself was too much to bear. "You think I haven't tried?" His voice was raw, jagged, like broken glass. "I've told them over and over that I didn't do it. But they don't want the truth. They want a scapegoat."

I bit my lip, feeling the sting of his words. He was right, of course. But it didn't make it any easier to stand by and watch him sink further into the quicksand of their suspicion. "So, what are you going to do? Let them tear you apart?"

Nathan's laugh was bitter, lacking any trace of humor. "What choice do I have? You think I'm going to stand up and tell them my life story? I'm not a saint. I never claimed to be. But I didn't do what they think I did."

His words hit me harder than I expected. There was something in his tone, a crack in the armor that made me want to reach out, to pull him into the safety of the only place left that could offer comfort—the space between us. But I held back, unsure if my own feelings had any room to grow in the wreckage of this camp, where trust was as fleeting as the wind.

I stepped closer, drawn by the intensity of his gaze, the heat of his presence. "Nathan," I said softly, almost to myself, as if trying to convince myself as much as him. "If you didn't do it...then who did? You don't just get accused like this without something to go on. The evidence—"

He cut me off, his hand shooting out to grab my wrist. His grip wasn't painful, but there was something urgent in the way he held me, something that sent a shiver down my spine. "Don't talk about evidence. I've seen how it gets twisted, how people who are desperate will do anything to survive. They'll sell their souls to clear their names. I'm not doing that."

For a moment, neither of us spoke. I could hear my heartbeat thudding in my ears, a constant reminder that this—whatever this was between us—wasn't just about the investigation anymore. It was something bigger. Something I wasn't sure I was ready to face.

"You're asking me to take your word for it," I said, my voice a whisper, my heart threatening to beat out of my chest. "You want me to believe in you, when all I have are your words and my own feelings."

He didn't hesitate, his eyes locking onto mine with an intensity that almost made my knees weak. "Then believe in me, damn it. Believe in me when no one else does."

And that was the moment everything shifted. The choice wasn't just about loyalty anymore. It wasn't just about whether I should stand by him or protect myself. It was about who I was willing to become in the process—someone who would sacrifice everything to hold onto a truth that might not even exist.

I closed my eyes for a brief second, swallowing down the knot in my throat. When I opened them again, Nathan's face was right in front of me, his breath warm against my cheek. "I'm not asking for redemption. I'm asking for a chance."

And somehow, I knew—deep in my bones—that this was no longer a question of what I could lose. It was about what I was willing to risk.

The weight of his trust was almost too much to bear. I could feel the pressure of it in my chest, an invisible hand squeezing the air from my lungs. I wasn't sure when it had happened, when the delicate dance of camaraderie had shifted into something deeper, more complicated. I had spent so much time pretending I didn't care, convincing myself that I was immune to whatever it was that made him stand out from everyone else. But here, in the quiet moment between us, it was impossible to deny it any longer. I cared. More than I should. And now, that care was threatening to tear everything apart.

The days crawled by with an unsettling slowness, each one weighed down by the growing tension in the air. I could feel the eyes of the others on me, their unspoken questions heavy on my back. They were waiting. They were watching. And maybe, just maybe, they were hoping I'd choose the easy way out—stay silent, avoid picking a side, let the storm pass over me.

But I couldn't. Not anymore. I couldn't stand by and pretend that Nathan was the enemy. Not when I saw the way he looked at me, his eyes soft with something that might have been gratitude, or maybe something else entirely. I didn't know if he was asking for my loyalty or my belief, but either way, he was asking for something from me, and it was all I could do to keep myself from giving it to him.

The camp had grown quieter in the past few days, the once-lively chatter now replaced by hushed conversations and furtive glances. The soldiers, who had once been a united front, were now divided into factions. Some of them were still loyal to Nathan, unwilling to believe the worst. But more and more, I saw the others turning away from him, their doubts growing like a cancer. It wasn't hard to see who they blamed. It was all so neatly laid out—Nathan was the odd one out, the outsider. The perfect scapegoat.

I hated them for it. For reducing him to a symbol of something darker, something they could point to and accuse without ever truly understanding him. But I couldn't stop it. I couldn't make them see what I saw. I couldn't make them understand that Nathan wasn't the monster they thought him to be.

The tension was unbearable. The days felt like they were closing in on me, suffocating me with their weight. I found myself retreating further into myself, even as I clung to the small slivers of hope that Nathan's silence wasn't guilt, but something else. Desperation? Fear? A knowledge that the truth might not save him, that nothing could save him but the choices we made next.

One evening, as the sun dipped low in the sky, casting long shadows over the camp, Nathan found me again. It wasn't like the last time—there was no urgency in his movements, no frantic desperation in his eyes. Instead, there was something more calculating, something darker. His face was unreadable as he approached, and for a moment, I wondered if I had imagined the softness in him before.

"I need you to come with me," he said, his voice low, devoid of the usual warmth.

I glanced around, my heart beginning to race. "Where?"

"Away from here. Just for a little while." His eyes scanned the camp, landing briefly on the soldiers scattered around the fire. "It's not safe. Not anymore."

A sharp pang of dread shot through me, but I didn't ask questions. I didn't need to. It was clear he wasn't asking for permission, and if I hesitated, I knew it would only make things worse.

I followed him, heart pounding in my chest, as we slipped through the shadows of the camp, avoiding the watchful eyes of the others. Every step felt like an act of defiance, a rebellion against the very loyalty that had once been my anchor. But with each step, the weight of my decision grew heavier. Nathan had asked for my trust, and for better or worse, I had given it to him.

We didn't speak as we walked, the silence between us thick with unspoken words. The camp seemed to grow smaller as we moved further from it, the sounds of our footsteps muffled by the soft dirt beneath our boots. Soon, we were deep enough into the forest that the only thing that remained was the sound of the wind in the trees and the distant hum of the camp behind us.

Nathan stopped suddenly, his hand reaching out to grip my arm. I looked up at him, startled by the force of his touch, but he was staring ahead, his expression tense.

"Something's wrong," he said quietly. "I'm not the only one who's been watching, and I'm not the only one who's being hunted."

I opened my mouth to speak, but the words died on my tongue as a rustling sound interrupted the stillness of the forest. My pulse quickened, my senses on high alert.

Nathan's hand tightened around my arm as he pulled me into the shadows, his body a shield between me and whatever was coming. The rustling grew louder, closer. The unmistakable sound of footsteps crunching through the underbrush, the unmistakable sound of someone—or something—moving with purpose.

"Nathan..." I whispered, my voice trembling.

He didn't answer. Instead, he reached into his jacket, his fingers brushing against the cold metal of a weapon, his movements quick and practiced. I knew then—this was no longer just about proving his innocence. This was about survival.

I heard it then, a voice breaking through the dense underbrush, low and gravelly. "You're not going anywhere, Nathan. Not this time."

My breath caught in my throat as I recognized the voice. I had heard it before—more than once. The camp's commander. The one who had once believed in Nathan, trusted him. But now, his voice dripped with something else—something darker.

The footsteps were getting closer. Nathan's grip on me tightened, pulling me even deeper into the shadows.

"We need to go," he muttered. "Now."

And just as he started to move, I felt it—something sharp against my neck, cold and unforgiving. My breath hitched as the world seemed to freeze around me. Nathan turned, his eyes wide, and for the first time, I saw fear in them.

The commander's voice came again, this time closer, mocking. "Did you think you could outrun me, Nathan? Did you think I wouldn't find you?"

And then, everything went black.

Chapter 11: Into the Inferno

The air was thick, smothering, as if the mountains themselves had decided to press in, suffocating the world. My boots crunched over the underbrush, but the sound was drowned by the roar of wind and crackling leaves. There was a tension in the space, a thick hum between us, the kind that gripped the chest and made it hard to breathe. My hand brushed the rough bark of an old oak, the feeling of its jagged surface almost grounding me. The forest was both familiar and alien in the dusk, every shadow a threat, every whisper of the breeze a warning.

"You're sure this is the right way?" I asked, my voice barely rising above the wind, trying not to sound like I doubted him. But I did. I couldn't help it.

He didn't look at me when he answered, his focus sharp, eyes scanning the terrain like a man who had learned to read danger in every shifting branch and footfall.

"I'm sure."

A brief answer, typical of him—efficient, to the point, and unsettlingly calm. He moved ahead without hesitation, each step purposeful, as though he knew the mountain's pulse in a way I couldn't possibly understand. His every movement was calculated, the grace of a predator, but there was something else there too, a kind of restless energy that made the air crackle. His name was Lucas, and though I'd known him for months now, I still couldn't say I knew him. Not fully. And I wasn't sure if that made me feel safe or terrified.

The lead we had followed, the cryptic hint of something buried deeper in the mountains, had brought us to this remote part of the world. The more we pushed into the wilderness, the quieter the world seemed. The trees were thicker here, gnarled limbs reaching overhead like old men's hands, their fingers twisting and clawing into the sky. The sound of water had long since faded, and we were left with nothing but the creaking of branches, the low hum of unseen creatures, and the occasional snap of a twig underfoot.

Suddenly, a burst of heat washed over me, making me flinch. I stopped in my tracks, confusion clouding my senses. It wasn't just the heat of the day or the oppressive weight of the air—it was something else. Something raw.

Before I could even speak, the world exploded into chaos.

Fire.

It roared to life in the distance, a wave of orange and red that rippled through the trees like some monstrous serpent. The wind caught it, sweeping the flames higher and closer with a malevolent speed. My heart lurched, and panic twisted through my chest. The blaze was far too large, too fast to be natural. Someone had set it. Someone who knew we'd be here.

"Run!" Lucas's voice cut through the panic, sharp as a whip. "Move, now!"

My legs froze for a heartbeat, but his hand was already on my arm, yanking me forward. The ground beneath my boots seemed to disappear, as though the mountain itself was being consumed by the fire. The scent of burning pine mixed with the sharp bite of smoke, filling my lungs with each desperate breath. I felt the heat licking at my skin, the air so thick I could taste it, but I didn't look back. Not yet.

Lucas didn't let up, pulling me through the brush, moving with a terrifying certainty. His movements were effortless, as though he were dancing with the flames instead of fleeing from them. I tried to keep up, but I was stumbling, my legs tangling in the underbrush, and every few steps, I could feel the scorching breath of the fire at my back, urging me to move faster, to survive.

A sudden crack overhead made me freeze, my heart hammering against my ribs as a branch splintered and fell, narrowly missing us. I gasped, but Lucas's hand was on my waist, guiding me, his grip ironclad. His face was set in a grim line, eyes scanning the horizon, reading the storm of chaos unfolding around us. His jaw was clenched, but his body didn't falter.

We reached a ridge, and for a moment, the fire seemed to pause, as if it were contemplating its next move. But it was only an illusion. The flames swept forward with a hungry roar, and I realized that if we didn't move again, we'd be trapped.

"Climb," he said, already hauling himself up the steep incline.

There was no hesitation in his voice, no room for doubt. I followed him, scrambling up the ridge like a frightened animal, my breath coming in ragged bursts. Every inch felt like an eternity. The fire was right there, too close, too hot. It pushed us higher, closer to the jagged rocks that formed the mountain's spine.

Finally, we reached a narrow outcrop, the edge of a cliff jutting out like the last sliver of safety. I collapsed against the rough stone, gasping for breath, my heart still racing in my chest. The flames were below us now, but they hadn't given up. They clawed at the mountain, hungry for more.

I turned to Lucas, my chest heaving, eyes wide. "What the hell just happened? Why is this fire chasing us?"

For the first time in what felt like forever, he looked at me, really looked at me. His eyes—dark, intense—held something there, something almost vulnerable. But it was gone as quickly as it came, replaced by that cool, unreadable exterior he wore so well.

"I don't know," he said, his voice low, controlled. "But we're not safe yet. There's someone else out here."

I felt the hairs on the back of my neck stand up. Someone else?

Before I could ask more, he stepped closer, closing the distance between us. There was no warning, no lead-up. He simply pulled me into him, his arms strong, his body warm against mine. The heat of the fire seemed to dissolve in the intensity of that moment, the world narrowing down to just the two of us, suspended on the edge of a cliff with nothing but the echoes of danger around us.

And then his lips were on mine. The kiss was urgent, desperate, a release of all the tension that had built between us from the first moment we'd met. I kissed him back, not caring that it didn't make sense, not caring that everything was wrong. It was the only thing that felt right.

The air tasted like smoke and burned my lungs with every breath, but the kiss still lingered, the warmth of it a stark contrast to the inferno at our backs. I pulled away, but the taste of him—rich, dangerous—was still on my lips, and I couldn't shake the feeling that something had shifted between us, that something far darker than fire had ignited.

The flames roared like a living beast, creeping up the cliffside, forcing us to move again. But my feet were rooted to the ground, my mind still spinning with the intensity of the moment. He hadn't let go of me. His hand was still resting on the small of my back, his fingers pressing into the fabric of my jacket as though he couldn't bear to let me out of his reach. I couldn't say I blamed him. I wasn't sure I wanted to be free either.

"Lucas—" My voice was breathless, strained, but it barely rose above the crackle of the fire below us. "You're not answering me. What the hell's going on?"

His jaw clenched, but he didn't pull away. Instead, he stepped back, his eyes scanning the horizon like they were searching for something beyond the flames, something that only he could see. His hand fell from my back, but the absence of it felt like a loss.

"Not here." His voice was steady, controlled, but there was something beneath it—something tight, like a rope ready to snap. "We need to move."

I didn't argue, though I wasn't sure I could have managed more than a few words. The fire was closing in, the air thick with smoke, and my lungs were starting to ache from the lack of clean air. I followed him as he moved to the edge of the outcrop, his movements smooth, confident. Like he wasn't even concerned by the blaze creeping closer, like this was just another day.

As we moved, the mountain seemed to shift beneath us. The ground felt more unstable now, as though the earth had been waiting for something to break. I kept my eyes fixed on his back, on the way his shoulders moved with a purpose I couldn't quite grasp. Every step seemed to carry some weight I couldn't touch, and I was starting to realize that the man I thought I knew—the one who had been my partner in this strange, dangerous world—wasn't the person I had believed him to be.

We found a narrow ledge just above the treeline, where the mountain curved inward, sheltering us from the worst of the fire. Lucas crouched down, his face hidden by the shadows of the jagged rock, but I could feel his eyes on me, even without seeing them.

"You've got questions," he said, his voice rough, like he'd been grinding the words against something hard. "And I'm not going to lie to you anymore. Not now. But you need to listen first."

I didn't trust myself to speak. Part of me was still reeling from the kiss, from the way it had made everything feel different, like the air had been scrubbed clean, only to reveal all the raw, jagged edges I'd been avoiding. But there was something else in his words, something urgent and sharp that cut through my thoughts.

"Someone set that fire," he continued, his words slow, deliberate. "Someone who knew we'd be here. Someone who's been watching us, waiting for the right moment."

My stomach churned. "Why? Who?"

He didn't answer right away, his gaze flicking over the mountainside like he was searching for an answer in the crags of the rocks. I followed his line of sight, but all I saw was the endless stretch of wilderness, bathed in the eerie light of the fire below.

"I don't know," he said finally, his voice tight. "But I do know they've been tracking us for weeks. Maybe longer. This... this wasn't just an accident. They wanted us to be alone, isolated. No backup."

I swallowed, the gravity of his words settling over me like a thick fog. I had known this was dangerous, had known there were forces working against us. But this? This was different. This felt personal.

"What do they want?" The words slipped out before I could stop them, but the answer was already hanging in the air between us, unspoken and yet understood.

"Me."

His words were low, almost a whisper, but they hit me like a blow. My heart skipped a beat, then settled back into an uneven rhythm. The fire was too far below us to reach now, but the heat still radiated through the mountain, and for a moment, I forgot how to breathe.

"What do you mean, 'me'?" I could barely get the words out, my throat dry, my chest tight. "Why you?"

His eyes finally met mine, and for a moment, I saw it—the truth. A raw, vulnerable truth that he'd been hiding beneath that cool, unreadable exterior. He wasn't just a partner in this. He was part of something bigger, something far more dangerous than I'd ever realized.

"I'm not who you think I am," he said, his voice barely a breath. "And this mission? It was never about the job. Not really."

I blinked, feeling the ground shift beneath me again, the weight of his words too much for me to process. "What are you talking about?"

Lucas stood up suddenly, his movement sharp, jagged. He turned his back on me, and for a moment, I thought he was done, that he was going to push me away again, like he had so many times before. But then he spoke, his voice low and rough.

"They're not just after me. They're after both of us."

I stared at him, the weight of his words sinking in. The truth hung there, heavy, dangerous, and for the first time since we'd started this insane journey, I understood that there was no going back. Not now. Whatever had been started in that kiss—whatever had been burning between us—was only the beginning of something much darker. Something that neither of us was ready for, but neither of us could avoid.

The air felt colder now, even though the fire below us still licked at the earth with hungry fingers. I was shaking—not from the cold, but from everything that had been left unsaid between us, and the weight of the truth that hung in the silence. I couldn't help but watch Lucas as he turned his back, scanning the horizon again, his posture tense and rigid, like he was a coiled spring, waiting for something to snap.

I wasn't sure what I had expected when he finally spoke—more lies, more deflections, more of that impenetrable mask he always wore. But this? This was different. This was something he couldn't hide, something that felt too big, too dangerous to ignore.

"They're after both of us," he repeated, his voice low, thick with a frustration that told me he'd known this for far longer than I had.

I wanted to scream. I wanted to shout that I hadn't signed up for this, that I didn't ask to be dragged into whatever mess this was. But I bit my tongue. Because, honestly, if I let myself lose control, I wasn't sure I'd ever get it back.

I crossed my arms, trying to ward off the chill creeping into my bones, though it had nothing to do with the weather. "Why?" The question sounded so simple, but I knew it wasn't. I knew it was more complicated than I could understand.

Lucas turned, his eyes meeting mine, and for a fleeting moment, I saw something crack behind the wall he'd built so high around himself. It was almost like he was trying to make a decision, weighing the risk of telling me more against the danger of leaving me in the dark.

"Because," he started, his voice rough, hesitant, "I'm not just a soldier. I'm not just a guy working a job. I'm... a target. A very specific one."

I took a step closer, my heart hammering in my chest. "A target for who? Who's doing this to us?"

He hesitated again, like the answer was something too dangerous to say out loud. And that was when I realized—he was trying to protect me. Protect me from something bigger than either of us.

"I don't know all the details," he said finally, his gaze drifting back to the fire below us. "But I know enough to understand that whoever's after me doesn't want anyone to get close. Not to me, and not to the people I work with."

I opened my mouth to argue, but the words caught in my throat. I wasn't sure what I was supposed to say. Part of me wanted to demand more answers, but another part of me, the part that had kissed him only moments ago, feared the truth. Because deep down, I knew that whatever Lucas had been hiding, whatever had been drawing us deeper into this nightmare, was about to change everything.

He looked at me then, his eyes dark and distant. "This is bigger than both of us. They're pulling strings, and I'm the pawn they're willing to sacrifice to get what they want."

I took a step back, processing what he was saying. Sacrifice? I'd never seen him like this—vulnerable, lost. And it made something cold twist in my stomach. It was like looking at a man who had already accepted his fate, and all I could do was watch.

"So, what now?" The words felt hollow, coming from me. I didn't know what I was asking for—answers? Reassurance? I didn't even know if there was a way out anymore. All I could see was the crackling fire in the distance, and the cliff-edge that separated us from what was below.

"Now, we survive," Lucas said, his voice steady again, the mask slipping back into place. But his eyes didn't lie. They never did. "That's all we can do."

I swallowed hard, my throat thick with the weight of everything that was left unsaid. "You're not going to die," I said, the words slipping out before I could stop them.

His lips twitched, but there was no smile. "I'm not so sure about that," he muttered, his voice carrying the weight of a thousand unsaid things. He took a deep breath and looked out over the mountains once more, his gaze narrowing as though he saw something beyond the haze of smoke. "There's a safe house not far from here. We can make it there. If we move now."

I nodded, trying to push the gnawing feeling in my gut aside. If he said we could make it, then I had to believe it. I didn't have another choice. "Lead the way," I said, though my voice sounded much steadier than I felt.

We started moving again, climbing along the jagged rocks that curved higher, forcing us to take each step with caution. The fire was far below us now, a growing mass of orange that reflected off the surrounding cliffs, making the world feel like it was on fire. But Lucas kept his pace steady, his focus never wavering.

And yet, as we moved, I couldn't shake the feeling that we were being watched.

I didn't say anything at first—didn't want to sound paranoid. But the feeling lingered, crawling along my spine, making my skin prickle.

I glanced at Lucas, but his face was unreadable, his attention fixed ahead. And that was when I saw it. Movement—too swift, too deliberate, just beyond the treeline.

My heart skipped a beat.

"Did you see that?" I whispered, my voice barely audible over the sound of the wind.

Lucas froze, his body going taut as he scanned the area. His hand instinctively went to his side, reaching for the weapon I knew was there, but it was clear he wasn't just reacting to a threat. He was already anticipating it.

"I saw it," he said quietly, his voice edged with tension. "Stay close. And don't make a sound."

I barely had time to register the fear in his voice before I heard the unmistakable snap of a twig behind us, followed by the unmistakable sound of footsteps.

We weren't alone.

Chapter 12: Smoke Signals

The morning fog hung thick in the air, clinging to every surface like a secret, waiting to be uncovered. I could barely make out the outlines of the camp through the haze, but the sounds were unmistakable—people stirring, pots clanging, and the low murmur of voices growing louder as they gathered, no doubt to discuss the discovery that had shattered whatever fragile peace we'd managed to carve out here. The message had been clear enough. A single phrase, scrawled in charcoal across the underside of a crate. A warning—cryptic, but with unmistakable intent. Someone among us was a traitor.

I didn't need to see it to feel the shift in the air. It was as if the ground had tilted beneath my feet, and for a moment, I was suspended in that quiet space between reality and chaos. I knew the signs well enough; I had lived through them before. The tightness in his shoulders as he stalked past me, the sharp, sidelong glances he cast in my direction as if I were the very embodiment of suspicion, his jaw tight, lips pressed in a thin line. It was too much. He wasn't just looking at me like I might be the traitor. He was looking at everyone that way—like the walls had eyes, like the very air was thick with deception. I wasn't blind to the weight of it, and neither was he.

I found him standing by the edge of the camp, his back to me, hands shoved deep in his pockets. He was trying to pretend like he wasn't affected, trying to act as if the undercurrent of distrust wasn't gnawing at him like a relentless wolf. I took a step forward, the gravel crunching underfoot in protest. It was no good. We needed to talk. The walls we had built between us were too fragile now, too cracked from the weight of everything unspoken.

"Hey," I said, my voice steady but softer than I intended. "We need to figure this out. Together."

He didn't turn around immediately, but I saw the shift in his stance, the subtle stiffening of his spine. He was going to fight it. I knew he would.

"I don't have time for that," he muttered, his words low but biting. "We've got bigger problems."

"Not if we don't fix this first. You know that. Whoever did this could destroy everything we've worked for." My breath caught slightly as I stepped closer, careful not to crowd him. He was an island in this camp, and I wasn't about to push him further out to sea. "You're not the only one feeling the weight of this."

He spun around, his eyes flashing with something sharp, something raw. There was a flicker of emotion there—more than just anger, more than just suspicion. I saw a vulnerability in the way his gaze faltered before meeting mine. Something shifted in him, and I could almost feel the walls he had built begin to crumble.

"Don't pretend like you understand," he snapped, his voice low, tight. "You haven't been here as long as I have. You don't know what it's like when everything you've built is ripped apart by the people closest to you."

I didn't flinch, didn't take a step back. Instead, I held his gaze, steady and unflinching, until the storm in his eyes began to waver. "No," I said, the word a quiet confession, "I don't know. But I know betrayal. And I know what it does to people."

He exhaled slowly, the tension in his body loosening just a fraction. "It eats you alive," he muttered, more to himself than to me. His eyes dropped to the dirt between us, as if seeking something to anchor himself to. "I've seen it. Felt it. Betrayal doesn't just destroy the person who's wronged; it destroys everyone."

I waited for him to continue, for the words that would explain the weight of that scar he carried, but he remained silent, his hands now clutching at his sleeves as if they were the only thing keeping him from falling apart. I took a step closer, my voice soft but insistent.

"You don't have to carry this alone, you know."

His gaze flicked up to mine, that brief moment of vulnerability giving way to something darker, harder. He stepped back, breaking the connection, a flicker of something almost like fear in his eyes.

"I don't have a choice," he said, voice trembling just slightly. "No one does."

There it was—the fear, the raw ache of something that had never fully healed. I could see it now, the way the past haunted him, the way every glance he cast over his shoulder was a silent echo of something lost.

Before I could say anything else, he moved away from me, his steps deliberate and quick. The rest of the camp was beginning to stir around us, the whispers growing louder. There was no escaping the fallout now. The air hummed with tension, with suspicion, and I couldn't help but feel the sharp pang of his words still echoing in my chest.

I watched him disappear into the distance, his figure swallowed by the mist, and I couldn't shake the feeling that the story we were living wasn't just about the traitor in our midst—it was about the ghosts we carried with us, the ones we tried to outrun, the ones that always found a way back.

The next morning, the camp had a different pulse to it. A buzz that hadn't been there before, a tautness hanging in the air like the calm before a storm. I could feel it under my skin, like the subtle shiver of an impending change. The whispers had grown louder, almost as if the very earth beneath our feet was speaking to us. They said it was just a coded message—scratched on the underside of a crate—but the implications hit harder than any bomb could. A traitor. One of us. Someone willing to throw us all under the wheels of the very machine we were trying to build.

I didn't have to search far to see how deeply it was affecting him. He was there, like always, standing at the edge of the clearing, but this time, his posture was different. Gone was the steady confidence, the quiet strength he usually exuded. In its place, something else flickered—an unease that clung to his movements, to the set of his jaw. He was watching everyone, his gaze darting from person to person, as if expecting each one to crack and reveal their darkest secret. Even me. I felt it, the weight of his gaze on me, like I was suddenly the one under suspicion.

He didn't approach me, not at first. It was as though the invisible line between us had grown tighter, more constricting. I could see the questions in his eyes. The doubt. And I hated it. For all the tension and the silence between us, I had always thought there was a bond, some unspoken understanding that ran deeper than anything else we might have shared. But now, it felt as though that understanding was starting to unravel, thread by delicate thread.

And then, when the camp had settled into a rhythm, he found me.

It wasn't anything grand—no dramatic confrontation. He didn't even say my name. Just a sharp gesture, his hand slicing through the air, a silent summons that sent my heart racing. I could see it then—how tightly he was wound, how badly he wanted to say something but was too afraid of what it might be. The way his eyes were flicking to the ground, to the trees around us, anything but to my face. He was battling with something. And I wasn't sure if it was just the betrayal he feared or if there was more.

"Are we doing this, then?" he asked, his voice rough, as if he'd been up all night rehearsing the words in his head, trying to make sense of them.

I didn't answer right away. I couldn't. I wasn't sure how to even begin.

"Doing what?" I finally said, trying to sound casual, trying to keep my voice from betraying the nerves gnawing at my insides.

"You know what I mean." His eyes flicked up to mine, searching. "Is it you, or not?"

I wasn't sure what I expected—maybe a little more restraint, a little more effort to disguise the storm swirling behind those dark eyes. But no. The truth was out in the open, raw and jagged. He was looking at me like I might be the one responsible.

I could feel the tension in my chest tighten, the heat of it creeping up my neck. "I'm not the one," I said, my voice sharper than I intended. "But I'm not the only one either."

There was a beat of silence, and for the briefest moment, I thought he might actually say something, might crack open whatever was so tightly sealed inside him. But he didn't. Instead, he took a breath, exhaled sharply, and looked away. I wasn't sure if he was trying to hold it together for both of us or if he just couldn't stand to look me in the eye anymore.

"You've got no idea what this does," he said quietly, his voice quieter than before, but that tension still pulsing through it, thick and heavy. "Betrayal isn't just something you recover from. It stays with you."

I frowned, watching him closely. "I know what it's like to feel like you've been stabbed in the back," I said, my voice softer now, measured. "But there's a difference between knowing it and letting it control you. You can't keep living in the past, in whatever this is, if you want to move forward. None of us can."

He was silent for a long time. Long enough for me to wonder if I had gone too far, if I'd said something that he couldn't take back. But then, with a single sharp exhale, he spoke again, his voice rougher, as if the words had been grinding against his throat.

"Tell me about yours," he said, his eyes snapping back to mine with an intensity that made my chest tighten. "The betrayal. Who was it?"

I took a step back, caught off guard by the question. I didn't want to go there—not now, not with him. Not like this. The thought of opening that door, of letting him see the wounds I'd never quite healed, made my stomach twist. But there was something in the way he asked, something raw in his eyes that made me pause. Maybe it wasn't just me who had a past, who carried scars. Maybe we were both trapped in this cycle of unfinished stories, of pain we couldn't outrun.

I swallowed hard. "A friend," I said quietly, my eyes slipping to the side, focusing on the distant trees. "Someone I trusted. They sold me out. Left me out in the cold."

He nodded slowly, as though processing my words. "Sounds familiar."

I couldn't help it. I snorted, a harsh sound that surprised even me. "It's always familiar, isn't it? Like we're all just replaying the same damn scene."

His lips twitched, the ghost of a smile on his face before it vanished, replaced by that tightness. "Yeah," he said, his voice quieter. "But it's never quite the same, is it?"

I didn't have a response for that. Not yet, anyway. There was too much between us, too much unsaid, too many things we hadn't quite figured out. But I felt it then—the shift, the crack in the walls. Whatever had brought us here, whatever fire had been smoldering in the background, was starting to burn a little brighter. And I wasn't sure where it would lead us, but I knew this: It wasn't over. Not by a long shot.

Chapter 13: Blaze of Deception

The heat clung to my skin, relentless and smothering, like a cloak of fire itself. I felt the sweat trickle down the back of my neck, the smell of charred wood and the bitter tang of smoke curling in the air, a constant reminder of the danger that had been following me like a shadow for weeks. We were closing in on something, a truth that felt colder than the flames. But it was a truth I could no longer ignore, not when every moment seemed to burn brighter, hotter, until I was sure we were all just going to crumble to ash.

The team had been working in overdrive, fighting fires, investigating the cause, but with each new blaze, I felt the walls closing in. Something wasn't right. I could smell it on the wind, feel it in the way we moved, the way our conversations danced around the real issues. And now, standing in the smoldering remains of a fire that had just been contained, the world suddenly seemed too quiet, too still, as if even the air was holding its breath.

"That's the fourth one this month," Luke's voice broke through the heavy silence, his words tight, like the muscles in his jaw. He had been distant lately, all sharp edges and unreadable expressions, though I couldn't blame him for it. He had a job to do, and I was becoming too much of a distraction. But I couldn't just leave him to face this alone. Not after everything we had uncovered, not when I knew, deep down, that the threat wasn't just the flames. It was something—or someone—closer, hidden beneath the surface, waiting to strike again.

I glanced over at him, noting the way his broad shoulders tensed as he surveyed the charred remains of the building, his fingers twitching near the holster at his side. The flicker of tension between us was palpable, thicker than the smoke still hanging in the air, but it wasn't just the fire that was consuming us. It was the unspoken words, the truth we both knew but neither of us was brave enough to face. His eyes were always on the horizon, on the next danger, and I couldn't figure out if it was because he was avoiding me, or if he was avoiding what we might become if we allowed ourselves to sink into the chaos around us.

"You still think it's arson?" I asked, breaking the silence. The words felt heavy on my tongue, a challenge I didn't want to ask, but couldn't stop myself from voicing.

He didn't answer right away, instead taking a long, deliberate breath as he ran a hand through his dark hair, now sticking to his forehead with sweat. His brow furrowed, a slight twitch in his jaw that only added to the tension that coiled tighter with every passing second. "I'm not sure anymore. The fires... they're too precise. Too controlled. It doesn't feel random."

His gaze met mine, and I saw the flicker of doubt there, the same flicker that had been in my mind since the first fire broke out. Something wasn't adding up. The burns were too clean, too intentional. And the timing—it was always at the most inconvenient moments, when we were stretched thin, when we couldn't afford to waste time on a single errant spark.

"You're saying someone on the team is behind this?" I asked, trying to keep the surprise out of my voice, though my heart had started to beat faster. The thought was almost too much to bear. A member of our own team, someone we trusted, was playing a game with fire, and not in the metaphorical sense.

"I don't know." He exhaled sharply, frustrated. "But I don't like the way things are lining up. We've got leaks—people who are supposed to be on our side, but they're... they're not. They're sabotaging everything. I've seen the way some of them look at me. It's not just the usual suspicion. It's something else."

My stomach churned at the realization. We were surrounded by enemies, but I never thought they would come from within. The people I had been working alongside, who I thought were just doing their jobs, might have been feeding us lies from the start. It was almost too much to process, like standing in the heart of a wildfire, knowing there's no escape but to run straight into it.

"Then we need to figure out who's behind it," I said, my voice coming out more determined than I felt. "We can't let this go any longer."

Luke turned to face me fully then, his eyes locking with mine in a way that made my pulse skip. For a moment, there was nothing but the heat of the fire behind him and the quiet weight of the words he wasn't saying. His expression softened, just slightly, but I caught it. The vulnerability that crept in when he thought no one was watching. I wasn't fool enough to think he didn't feel the same pull between us, but this—this was different.

"I need you to stay out of it," he said quietly, his voice low and fierce, a stark contrast to the smoldering chaos around us. "This isn't safe. You're not ready for what we might find."

I swallowed, the words like ash in my throat. "I'm already in it, Luke. I'm not going anywhere."

For a long moment, we just stood there, staring at each other, the world holding its breath between us. Then he sighed, long and defeated. "Fine. But I'm not going to hold your hand through this."

I grinned, the corners of my lips curling up despite the weight of what we were facing. "Good. I don't need you to."

We both knew the stakes now. We were walking a fine line, and the closer we got to the truth, the more dangerous it became. Each piece of the puzzle was falling into place, and the picture it was forming was far darker than either of us had imagined. But there was no turning back. Not now. Not when the flames were getting closer, licking at our heels, threatening to consume everything we had left. And in that moment, despite everything, I couldn't shake the feeling that, whatever happened next, we'd burn together.

The morning light filtered through the slats of the firehouse blinds, casting long shadows across the room. My coffee had gone cold again—its bitterness now an afterthought as I focused on the stack of papers in front of me, a jumbled mess of incident reports and photos. Each page seemed to tell the same story, but there were gaps, pieces missing. I could feel it, like a low hum beneath my skin, the growing certainty that the truth was buried somewhere in these files, waiting to be uncovered. And yet, every time I thought I was getting close, I found myself slipping further into the dark.

Luke was pacing the length of the room, his boots heavy on the worn floorboards, eyes narrowed in that familiar, intense way he had when he was thinking. His movements were clipped, as if every second mattered, as if we were running out of time—because we were. The fires were escalating, and the whispers around the station were getting louder. Someone was pulling the strings, and that someone wasn't on the outside looking in. They were in here, with us, hiding behind the faces I had learned to trust.

"So, what's your theory?" I asked, though my voice felt weak under the weight of the question. My eyes flicked over to him, watching as he stopped by the window, arms crossed over his chest, staring out into the early morning mist like he was waiting for an answer that wasn't there.

He turned slowly, his face tight with frustration. "I think we're dealing with someone who's been hiding in plain sight. Someone with access to everything—every move we make, every decision we make. It's not just about setting fires anymore. It's about control."

Control. The word tasted sour in my mouth. I had always prided myself on being a quick study, someone who could read people, understand their motivations, but this—this was different. Whoever was behind this was always one step ahead. Always. And it was making me second-guess everything. Every glance. Every word. Could it be someone I had known for years? Someone I had trusted?

The door creaked open, and I looked up to see Sam, one of the newer recruits, leaning against the frame. He was young, too eager, his energy more nervous than confident. He wasn't the type to break protocol, but there was something in his eyes now that made my pulse spike—a mix of fear and something else I couldn't quite place.

"Hey," Sam said, shifting awkwardly from one foot to the other. "You need anything?"

"No," Luke answered sharply, his voice a little too tight for comfort. "We're good."

But Sam didn't leave. Instead, he stepped inside, crossing the room to where I was sitting. I could feel the weight of his presence before he even spoke again. Something was off. His breath was shallow, his hands trembling slightly at his sides, but it wasn't fear. It was something worse.

"Look, I don't know if I'm imagining things, but... I think I saw something last night," he said, his voice low, barely above a whisper. "I was cleaning up the engine bay when I heard footsteps. I thought it was just someone checking the trucks, but then I saw the shadow. It moved across the floor like it was trying to hide."

"Who?" I asked, leaning forward, suddenly on alert. My instincts were firing, telling me this wasn't just some rookie's overactive imagination. Something had shifted, and I could feel it in the air, thick and oppressive.

"I—I didn't get a good look," Sam stammered, his hands now visibly shaking. "But I know it wasn't anyone from the team. And when I went to check, the door to the storage room was ajar. I swear it was locked when I left."

Luke's posture shifted, his gaze becoming more calculating. "You sure about this?"

Sam nodded, but it wasn't the kind of certainty that made me feel better. It felt like a gut instinct he didn't fully trust himself.

"Yeah. But I didn't want to bring it up before. Didn't want to look... paranoid." His eyes darted nervously around the room, avoiding both of us, as if he expected someone to leap from the shadows and call him out.

"I'll go check it out," Luke said, already moving toward the door, his footsteps firm but fast.

I followed him without thinking. There was no way I was letting him do this alone. Not when the walls were closing in, and I could practically feel the heat of someone watching us, waiting for us to make the wrong move.

The engine bay was quiet, save for the hum of the overhead lights and the distant sound of sirens somewhere outside. The door to the storage room was cracked open just enough to send a shiver of doubt slithering down my spine. Luke stopped at the threshold, his shoulders stiff as he glanced back at me.

"You stay here," he said, his voice low, but there was a hint of something softer in it—something like caution, but also something like care.

I shook my head. "I'm not letting you do this by yourself."

We both knew that wasn't the reason he wanted me to stay behind. He didn't want me in the line of fire. But I wasn't about to back down. Not now.

We entered the room together, the faint smell of dust and oil mixing with the acrid tang of something else. Something colder. I could feel it in my bones, a creeping unease that made the hairs on the back of my neck stand on end. The storage room was mostly empty, save for shelves stacked with old equipment, hoses, and spare parts. But in the far corner, just beneath the small window that let in the faintest slivers of light, something caught my eye.

A piece of paper. Crumpled, half-hidden behind a crate of firefighting gear.

I reached for it before Luke could stop me, unfolding it with care. The words were hastily scrawled, barely legible in the dim light. But I made them out. *If you dig too deep, you won't like what you find.*

I glanced up at Luke, my heart racing in my chest. This wasn't just about fire anymore. This was about something far more dangerous.

The paper trembled in my hands, its message both a warning and an invitation. I could feel the pulse of danger humming just beneath the surface of every letter, every inked curve, the weight of the words settling like a stone in my gut. Luke, standing beside me, was already scanning the room, his gaze sweeping over the cluttered shelves, looking for something he knew he wouldn't find. The danger wasn't here; it was in the message. It was in us.

"If you dig too deep, you won't like what you find," I read aloud, my voice a little too steady, even though everything inside me screamed otherwise. The room felt smaller now, the air heavier, suffocating in its silence.

Luke's jaw tightened as he processed the words, his hands curling into fists at his sides. "It's a threat. Whoever's behind this, they know we're onto them. And they're not afraid to make it personal."

"I don't think it's just a threat. It's a warning," I said, my mind racing. "They're trying to stop us. They know we're close. Too close."

He took a step toward me, his hand brushing against my arm in that fleeting, electric touch that sent my heart skittering. "You need to get out of here, now."

I looked up at him, feeling the heat of his gaze burning through me. "You're not going to stop me."

"I'm not trying to stop you," he replied, his voice low and tight with frustration. "I'm trying to keep you safe." The words were almost too soft, too raw, as if he was saying them for the first time, as if they carried a weight neither of us had anticipated.

The silence stretched between us, thick and heavy, before I nodded sharply. "I'm not going anywhere. We're in this together. And we're not backing down now."

He didn't answer immediately. Instead, he turned away, his mind clearly elsewhere, processing the implications of the message. I could see the battle waging within him, the push and pull between his protective instincts and the undeniable tension that had been building between us for weeks.

I took a steadying breath and followed him as he moved towards the door, a step behind, but no less determined. He paused just before the threshold, eyes lingering on the darkened hallway beyond. Something about the stillness of the station felt wrong—too quiet, too watchful.

"You don't think it's someone who's already left the team, do you?" I asked, my voice tight as I caught up with him.

"No," Luke said quickly, shaking his head. "Whoever's behind this is still here. They're still in the game."

I nodded, the weight of his certainty sinking in. I had thought, for a moment, that the traitor might have slipped away, that the chaos would settle once the fire had burned itself out. But that wasn't the case. This was only the beginning.

We made our way back toward the main building, every step echoing in the hollow quiet. The station seemed to hum with an unease, the low buzz of radios and the occasional clink of gear far too loud in the empty hall. As we passed the crew room, I caught sight of Sam again. He was standing near the door, his back stiff, watching us with that same anxious intensity.

"You okay?" I asked, trying to keep my voice light, despite the sinking feeling in my stomach.

Sam hesitated for a moment, his eyes darting between Luke and me. Then he nodded, though it looked more like a reflex than genuine assurance. "Yeah, just... thinking."

"About last night?" Luke's tone was sharp, as if testing the waters, gauging whether Sam was still hiding something.

"Yeah," Sam said slowly. "It's just... it's hard to shake off. You know? The feeling that someone's watching."

I exchanged a glance with Luke, both of us sensing the unspoken weight in Sam's words. He wasn't just nervous. He was scared.

"We need to talk," Luke said, his voice even but laced with that underlying urgency. "All of us. Now."

The tension in the room thickened as the three of us gathered in the corner, away from the others. Luke's eyes were locked on Sam, but I could feel the storm brewing in his chest, ready to break at any moment. This wasn't just about fire anymore. This was about survival. And the walls were closing in on us faster than any of us realized.

"Who's behind it, Sam?" Luke's voice was low, but the edge in it was unmistakable. "You're not telling us everything. I know you saw something. And I need to know what it was."

Sam swallowed hard, his hands clenched so tight I thought he might leave marks on his palms. "I don't know. I don't want to get anyone in trouble. I—"

"Trouble's already here," I interrupted, my patience slipping. "Whoever's behind these fires isn't just playing games. They want to burn everything down. And if you're hiding something—"

"I'm not hiding anything," Sam cut in, his voice trembling with a mix of fear and defiance. "I swear, I just... I don't know who it is. I only saw the shadow. But the thing is... it wasn't just the shadow I saw." He stopped, the words hanging in the air, thick with implication.

I leaned in closer, my heart thudding in my chest. "What else did you see?"

"I saw him," Sam whispered, his eyes darting between us as if expecting someone to step out of the shadows. "It was—it was Greg."

The name hit me like a punch to the gut. Greg. The quiet, steady presence I had always trusted. A seasoned firefighter, respected by everyone. The idea that he could be behind all of this felt like a jagged shard in my chest, one that didn't belong, one I didn't know how to remove.

Luke's expression darkened, and I could see the disbelief written on his face. "You're sure?"

"I—I think so. I mean... it was dark, but I swear it was him. The build, the way he moved—it was Greg."

The room felt like it was closing in, the walls pressing in from all sides. "If you're wrong," Luke's voice was cold, too cold, "this could be the end of your career, Sam."

"I know," Sam whispered, his voice barely audible now. "But I'm not wrong. It was him."

And just as the weight of that truth sank in, the door to the crew room slammed open. The hairs on the back of my neck stood on end, the air suddenly thick with the taste of smoke again, though this time it wasn't from any fire we could put out. This time, it was from something far more dangerous.

I turned to see Greg standing in the doorway, his face a mask of unreadable calm. But the glint in his eyes? It was anything but friendly.

Chapter 14: Flickers of Trust

The sky hung heavy, thick with clouds that smothered the sun's warmth, leaving only the faintest glow that was more of a whisper than a promise. The city, normally bustling with energy, felt quieter today, as though the air itself was holding its breath, waiting for something to happen. I stood at the edge of the alleyway, the cold brick against my back, the faint scent of damp earth rising from the cracked pavement. It was the kind of place people avoided. A no-man's land of shadows and forgotten stories. A place that suited me just fine. At least here, no one expected anything from me.

There was a sound—a subtle shuffle of feet against gravel. My heart picked up, an uninvited guest of panic. For a second, I wondered if it was just the wind or if my mind was playing tricks, but the tension in the air said otherwise. I straightened, my fingers brushing the hidden blade tucked into the waistband of my jeans, my senses stretching to catch every sound, every movement.

Then, a voice, low and careful, sliced through the silence.

"You're late."

I didn't need to look to know who it was. The voice was familiar, but not in the way that comforted me. No, it was familiar in the way a storm is—something that rattles the windows and pulls at the door, but doesn't quite enter. It was his voice. Damien. The man who'd walked into my life and turned it into something unrecognizable. The man who'd turned the world upside down. I had no idea who he really was. And in a city like this, that was as dangerous as it got.

I turned to face him, watching as he emerged from the shadows. His face was more haunted than I remembered, his eyes darker, harder. But there was something in the way he moved—quick, sure, as though the world had been rewritten for him and he was the only one who knew the new rules. Something told me that, for once, I wasn't going to like what he had to say.

Damien stopped a few feet away, his presence filling the space between us like a heavy fog. I could feel the tension in his posture, the way his shoulders were slightly hunched, as though he were preparing for a fight. But it wasn't a fight I could see. It was something deeper, something unsaid that hung between us like a secret we both knew, but neither of us was willing to address.

"You got something for me?" I asked, keeping my voice steady despite the flutter of nerves in my stomach. I didn't want to ask. Didn't want to know what he might have uncovered. The truth, at this point, felt like something I wasn't ready to face. But then again, when was I ever ready for any of this?

He didn't answer immediately, just stood there, his gaze flicking to the ground as though trying to decide how much to reveal. I didn't trust him, not entirely. But right now, I didn't have the luxury of being picky.

"Something's off," he said at last, his voice grating against the silence. "More than what you've seen. This whole thing—it's not just one person. It's bigger than that."

My pulse spiked, an uneasy weight settling in the pit of my stomach. I had known, deep down, that it was too simple. Too clean. Too neat. Everything had pointed to one person, but the more I thought about it, the more it felt wrong. A conspiracy that ran this deep wasn't going to be solved by chasing shadows. It was something far more insidious. And Damien was the one who'd just put the pieces in place, even if he didn't know it yet.

"I don't understand," I said, trying to keep the edge of fear from my voice. "Who are we dealing with?"

Damien stepped closer, his movements slow and deliberate, as if weighing every word. "You think you've been following a trail.

But you've been chasing ghosts. The person you're looking for... they're just a pawn. The real players are much, much higher up."

A cold shiver crept down my spine as I absorbed the weight of his words. Higher up. That could mean anything—politicians, corporate magnates, power players who held all the cards. But one thing was clear. We were in over our heads.

I wanted to argue, wanted to dismiss it all as more of Damien's cryptic nonsense, but I couldn't. Not with the look in his eyes. He was serious. Too serious. And the desperation in his voice spoke of someone who had already seen the depth of what we were up against. He wasn't just warning me; he was begging me to listen.

"You don't get it, do you?" His voice cracked, and I saw a flicker of something in his eyes—something raw and human. "This thing? It's everywhere. It's already happening. We're too late."

I shook my head, the words too much to swallow. "What do you mean we're too late?"

He met my gaze, his expression unreadable, and for a moment, I thought I saw a flicker of something softer. Trust, maybe. Or fear. But then it was gone, replaced by the cold resolve I knew all too well. He reached for my hand, his grip firm, unyielding. And in that touch, I felt it—the surge of something I hadn't allowed myself to feel in a long time.

"Stay with me," he whispered, his breath warm against my ear. "I'll protect you. I'll get us through this."

I wanted to pull away, to remind him that I wasn't the kind of person who needed protection. But something in his words—something in the way he held me—made me pause. Maybe it was foolish. Maybe it was a mistake. But for the first time in a long time, I didn't feel like I was drowning. I felt like I could breathe again.

I wasn't sure if it was the love, or the desperation, that made me take that step forward, but I did. One step, and then another.

And as we walked into the unknown, I couldn't help but wonder—would we survive this? Or would we be consumed by the fire we had no idea we were walking straight into?

The world around us seemed to move slower, like the city had hit pause, holding its breath for something inevitable. A distant rumble of thunder teased the sky, but no rain came, only the oppressive weight of an unseen storm. It was as though the earth itself understood the gravity of what was unfolding—of what we were about to face.

Damien's grip tightened on my hand as we turned toward the looming dark silhouette of the old warehouse. The building had been abandoned for years, a forgotten relic of a past long since abandoned. Its rusty metal doors and crumbling brick walls told stories of neglect. But now, as we approached, it seemed to pulse with an energy all its own, as though it were waiting for us, for something to begin.

"I don't like this," I muttered, glancing at Damien. The words felt like they barely had the strength to leave my lips, and yet I couldn't stop them. The air around us was thick with tension, a quiet buzz that made my skin tingle with anticipation—and dread.

Damien's eyes, those dark pools of secrets I'd only begun to understand, met mine. "You should. We don't have a choice anymore. We're too far in to back out."

I stopped walking, pulling him gently to a halt. My heart pounded against my ribs, each beat an anxious whisper. "You've said that before. But this time, you're not just talking about us. You're talking about a whole lot of people. Whole systems, whole networks. This isn't some small operation. It's..." I trailed off, unable to put into words the growing horror creeping through me.

He was quiet for a moment, his gaze distant. Then, almost to himself, he murmured, "It's bigger than either of us."

The words landed between us like a stone dropped into a still pond, creating ripples that I wasn't sure how to deal with. For all the uncertainty swirling in my chest, I couldn't deny that I felt something else, something I had refused to acknowledge for too long. A thread of connection, fragile but real, pulling me toward him, pulling me deeper into this mess.

His hand brushed mine, the briefest of touches, but it was enough to spark a flash of warmth through me. It was a silent promise—one that I wasn't sure I could accept, but I wanted to. And that terrified me.

"You don't have to do this," I said, looking up at him, my voice barely a whisper. "You can walk away, you can leave it all behind. No one would blame you. Not after everything."

Damien's lips curled into something that wasn't quite a smile. It was too sharp, too jagged to be called one, but it was enough to make my heart stutter. "Not everyone," he said softly. "And I'm not the kind of man who walks away. Not when there's a chance to make it right."

A chance. The word hung between us, heavy with its own kind of danger. But before I could respond, the sound of a door creaking open broke the moment. We both turned toward it instinctively, a shared understanding passing between us. Whoever was on the other side wasn't just a source of information—they were the key to everything. The way forward. Or the final nail in the coffin.

I stepped closer to Damien, instinctively falling into the space he created between us. The world was narrowing, the distance between us and whatever waited in that dimly lit building evaporating with every breath I took.

He gave me a sidelong glance, his brow furrowed, his jaw tight. "You ready for this?" he asked, the question simple, but I could hear the undercurrent of it—everything that wasn't said, everything that could tear us apart if we weren't careful.

"No." The answer came faster than I'd anticipated, and the weight of it settled around us like a truth neither of us wanted to face.

But before either of us could make another move, the door opened wider, and a figure stepped into the light. It was a woman. Tall, with dark, slicked-back hair and eyes that gleamed with something I couldn't quite place. She was dressed in black, head to toe, her movements sharp and efficient. She looked like someone who had spent years navigating dangerous waters—and had never once fallen in.

"Didn't think you'd come," she said, her voice smooth, calculated, with just a hint of amusement.

"Neither did I," I answered, my voice sounding rougher than I intended. "But here we are."

She didn't laugh, but the slight twitch of her lips suggested she found me amusing. She stepped aside, gesturing for us to follow. "Come inside. You're going to want to hear this."

I hesitated, my gaze flicking from her to Damien. He didn't speak, just gave a short nod, and that was enough. We both stepped across the threshold into the warehouse, where the shadows stretched long and deep, swallowing us whole.

The air inside was thick with the scent of old wood and dust, the silence almost oppressive. There was no noise, no hum of electricity, just a feeling of something dark, something ancient, waiting for us in the corners.

"I'm assuming you've heard the rumors?" the woman asked, breaking the silence as we followed her deeper into the cavernous space.

Damien's expression didn't change, but I caught the flicker of something in his eyes, something that felt like recognition. "I've heard enough," he said.

"You've only heard the beginning," she replied, her voice a knife edged with something dangerous. "The person you think is behind all of this? They're just one piece of the puzzle. The true orchestrator is someone much closer than you ever imagined."

The words hung in the air, and for the first time, I felt that familiar knot of dread tighten in my chest. But now it wasn't just fear. It was the sickening realization that I was about to learn more than I ever wanted to know.

The warehouse stretched before us like an abandoned giant, its silence a hushed warning. The walls were steeped in a history of neglect, the air thick with the scent of mildew and age. Each step we took further into its belly seemed to amplify the eerie quiet, until I wondered if the building itself was holding its breath, waiting for the final act to unfold.

The woman led us down a narrow hallway, her footsteps swift and deliberate, as though she knew exactly where she was going. Behind her, Damien and I moved as one, our shared tension a heavy cloak that draped over us, making each breath feel like a labor.

I couldn't help but steal glances at Damien, whose jaw was set, his eyes scanning the shadows, his every muscle tight with readiness. But it was the flicker of something softer, more vulnerable, that caught me off guard. Something hidden in the dark corners of his expression—a flicker of doubt, of hesitation. And for the first time since I'd met him, I wondered if this was more than a mission to him. If, somehow, he was as tied to this mess as I was.

We turned a corner, and the woman stopped before a rusted metal door. Without a word, she pushed it open, revealing a small, dimly lit room. The only source of light was an overhead bulb that flickered intermittently, casting unsettling shadows across the worn floor.

I swallowed, a knot forming in my throat. "You've been here before," I said, my voice sharper than I intended.

The woman didn't answer right away. Instead, she glanced over her shoulder at me, her lips curling into a thin, amused smile. "You think this is new for me?" she asked, almost as if she were daring me to challenge her. "No. This is where it all started. This is where it ends."

I wanted to ask more, to press her for details, but the chill in the room made me hold my tongue. The walls felt like they were closing in, and I had the sudden, sickening feeling that I was standing at the edge of something far worse than I had ever imagined.

Damien's grip on my hand tightened, and I looked at him, searching his face for something—anything—to reassure me. But his eyes were distant, lost in the same sea of uncertainty that had pulled him under since we'd first met.

The woman turned to the far wall, where a large, dusty cabinet stood. She approached it with a familiarity that made the hair on the back of my neck stand on end. Her hand hovered over the lock for a moment before she twisted it, pulling the door open with a creak that echoed too loudly in the silence.

Inside the cabinet, there were stacks of papers—files, old and yellowed, some frayed at the edges. The weight of them was almost tangible, like they carried with them the full burden of the conspiracy we had been chasing.

She pulled a stack free and handed it to Damien, her fingers brushing his briefly before she stepped back. "Everything you need to know is in there. All the names, all the players. The ones who think they can hide in the dark."

Damien took the stack, his eyes scanning the top sheet with practiced precision before he tucked it under his arm. He didn't speak, his jaw clenched tighter than I had ever seen. The air was thick with the unspoken, the weight of what we were about to uncover pressing down on us both.

I couldn't stand the silence. "Who are they?" I asked, my voice barely above a whisper. "Who's pulling the strings?"

The woman's eyes gleamed, a cold, calculating look that sent a shiver up my spine. "You wouldn't believe me if I told you."

I could feel the tension crackling between us, the words hanging like a bitter taste in the air. "Try me," I shot back, my patience fraying.

She sighed, her gaze flicking toward Damien, as though she were waiting for his permission. After a long moment, he nodded.

"The person you've been chasing," she began slowly, "the one you thought was the mastermind? He's nothing. A puppet. The real person behind all of this..." She trailed off, letting the weight of her words hang in the air.

I leaned in, my heart hammering in my chest. "Who?" I demanded.

"Your father."

The words hit me like a punch to the gut. My father? The man I'd spent my whole life trying to understand, trying to reconcile with the image of the caring parent I wanted to remember, was tangled in this web of deceit? I staggered back, my breath catching in my throat.

"No," I said, the word coming out in a sharp, disbelieving gasp. "That's impossible. My father... he's..."

"He's the one who set it all in motion," she interrupted, her voice almost gentle in its finality. "He's been orchestrating everything from behind the scenes. You've been chasing shadows, but the real puppet master is someone you've trusted."

The room seemed to close in on me, the walls pressing tighter as the air thickened with a heavy kind of truth. Damien's hand moved to my shoulder, a grounding presence as my mind reeled. The sting of betrayal cut deeper than I could have ever anticipated.

I wanted to scream, to demand answers, but all I could do was stand there, my world shifting beneath my feet.

"What now?" I whispered, my voice trembling with the weight of it all.

The woman's lips curled into a knowing smile. "Now, you decide whether you're going to keep running—or if you're finally going to fight."

Before I could respond, a crash from outside the room interrupted us. The sound of footsteps pounding down the hallway reached us, rapid, insistent. Someone was coming. Someone who had no intention of letting us walk out of here alive.

The woman's smile faded, and her eyes darkened with something sharp, something dangerous. "You've got company," she said, turning toward the door. "Get ready."

I barely had time to react before the door slammed open, and the first figure stepped into the room, his silhouette casting a long shadow across the floor.

And then, in that moment of frozen time, I realized that whatever trust I'd placed in Damien, whatever hope had flickered between us, was about to be tested in ways neither of us could have anticipated.

The figure in the doorway stepped into the light. It wasn't who I thought it would be.

It was my father.

Chapter 15: Inferno of Lies

The ground beneath my boots crunches with the kind of ominous silence that feels too loud in the dark. The air is thick, not just with the scent of pine and damp earth, but with something heavier, like the storm clouds that linger in the distance, threatening a downpour. If I were anyone else, I might say the world feels still, holding its breath. But I know better. This place, this moment—it's all too volatile to be still. Even the trees seem to lean in, their branches clawing at the sky, as though they know something we don't.

I'm not sure why I agreed to meet him here, of all places. There's a part of me that would rather be anywhere else—anywhere safer. But the truth, as we both know by now, is far from safe. We've danced around it long enough. We've questioned, probed, and tried to deny it. But the lies we've uncovered don't simply disappear with a breath or a lie told well. They weave themselves into the very walls of our lives, tightening like ropes until there's nowhere left to move.

He's standing there, silhouetted against the dying embers of the campfire we left behind. I can just make out the line of his jaw, the curve of his shoulder, and the way his hands are shoved into the pockets of his worn leather jacket—like he's trying to keep the world from slipping through his fingers. I wish I could do the same. But I know better. Some things are meant to slip, whether you want them to or not.

"I didn't think you'd come." His voice is rough, like it's been scrubbed raw with too many unsaid words, too many questions that never had answers. It's not an accusation. More like a confession. Like he was hoping I wouldn't, so he could convince himself it wasn't too late to pull away.

I take a step forward, my boots steady on the uneven ground, my heartbeat a steady drum beneath my ribs. It's not fear that makes me hesitate, but something much more complicated. I've been running from this moment for so long, hiding behind excuses and half-truths. But standing here, facing him, I know this is where it all ends. The lies, the secrets, the things we've both been afraid to admit—it's time to face it all.

"I had to," I say, my voice betraying none of the nervous tremor I can feel deep in my bones. "You think I wanted to be out here in the middle of nowhere, with nothing but trees and shadows for company? Believe me, this was not my first choice."

There's a soft exhale from him, the kind that might be a laugh if the air weren't so thick with tension. "You're a terrible liar, you know that?"

I give a half-smile, though it doesn't reach my eyes. "It's not lying if I'm telling you the truth," I say, the words almost feeling foreign as they leave my mouth.

He looks at me then, really looks, and for a second, I feel like I've been stripped bare. The harsh light of the fire flickers in his gaze, and I see the storm brewing there—unspoken, unfinished. He's not just worried about the lies anymore. He's afraid of what might happen when they finally break open.

"We're in this together, right?" he asks, his voice quiet but urgent.

I nod, my throat tightening. We may not have a choice, but the truth is, I'd still rather be here, at his side, than anywhere else. "I didn't come out here to run from you. I came because we need to figure this out, once and for all. We've been dodging it for too long, and the longer we wait, the worse it's going to get."

The wind picks up, rustling through the trees, carrying with it the bitter scent of ash. It's not from the campfire; that's long since burned out. No, this is something far worse, something that has nothing to do with us and everything to do with what we're about to walk into. The lies we've uncovered are just the beginning. The more we dig, the deeper it goes, until I'm not sure what's real anymore.

"I don't want you to get hurt," he says, the words coming out as if they're heavy with something unsaid. His eyes flicker to the side, like he's trying to look away but can't. "But I can't promise that we won't. Not anymore."

The truth sits between us like an electric charge, too potent to ignore. I can feel it buzzing in my fingertips, in the pit of my stomach. The thing about lies is that they don't just deceive—they fester. And what we've uncovered isn't just a simple misunderstanding. It's a web, a labyrinth, and we're standing right in the middle of it.

"I don't need promises," I say, my voice stronger than I feel. "I need answers. We need answers. If we don't get to the bottom of this, if we don't uncover everything—then all of this, all of it, has been for nothing."

He takes a step closer, the distance between us shrinking until I can feel the heat of his presence, even in the cool night air. "You really think we can find the truth? After everything?"

"I have to," I say, the words almost a whisper, but there's a fire behind them. "Because if we don't, we're just going to keep running forever. And I'm not running anymore."

His gaze doesn't leave mine as I speak, the words hanging between us like a delicate thread, ready to snap. There's a tremble in the air, something that shifts when he takes a step forward, closing the distance just enough that I can feel his breath—a low, ragged exhale that carries the weight of all the things he hasn't said. Things he probably doesn't even know how to say. I could almost laugh at how awkward it is, but the tension is too thick for humor, too suffocating for relief. It's the kind of stillness that feels like an avalanche waiting to fall.

"I'm not asking for miracles," I add, my voice quieter this time, like I'm suddenly aware of how fragile our moment is. "I'm just asking for truth. The kind we can't hide from anymore."

He doesn't respond right away. Instead, he looks at me for a long moment, his eyes soft, calculating. The creases at the corners of his eyes deepen as if he's wrestling with the weight of my words. I know him too well to think he's not considering the consequences. There's a battle going on behind those eyes, and I'm not entirely sure whose side he's on—his, or the one he's supposed to protect. I'm not even sure which side I'm on anymore.

Finally, he speaks, and his voice is barely a whisper, as though the wind itself might carry his words away. "You're right. We can't keep pretending. But that doesn't mean it's going to be easy. You've seen what happens when people start digging too deep into things they shouldn't." He pauses, and the silence that follows is thick with the unspoken weight of his warning. "And I won't let you get caught in it."

I almost laugh at that, but the sound is too bitter for it to be anything close to humor. "You can't protect me from this, not anymore." I let the words settle between us. "We're both in this, whether we like it or not. And I'd rather go down swinging than sitting here pretending everything's fine."

The wind rustles through the trees again, this time with more force, like nature itself is trying to push us forward. We're standing on the precipice, each of us teetering between the world we thought we knew and the one that's been hiding just beneath the surface, waiting to swallow us whole. I can feel the heat of his stare, even though we're not touching. It burns with the weight of his decision, the choice he's about to make.

He reaches for me then, his fingers brushing lightly against my arm, a gesture so simple yet so full of meaning I can hardly breathe. There's no warmth in his touch. No comfort. Just a silent acknowledgment that this is it. We can't go back now. I look up at him, trying to see through the guarded expression on his face, trying to find that flicker of hope I used to see there. But all I see is uncertainty. It makes my chest tighten.

"If we do this," he says slowly, "there's no going back. You know that, right?"

I nod, but it's not in agreement, more in the understanding that we've already crossed that line. We've been crossing it for weeks. This is the moment of reckoning, the point where all our carefully laid plans and lies fall apart. I can feel the burn in my throat, the sharp edge of fear that I'm doing the one thing I swore I'd never do: expose myself to him in a way that no longer makes sense. But maybe that's just it. There's no more sense to make of any of this. The pieces don't fit together. The lies don't add up. And the truth is far messier than either of us could have predicted.

"I never wanted this for you," he mutters, his voice so quiet now it's barely there. He's close enough now that I can feel the heat radiating from him, the pulse of his heart thudding against his chest. "I wanted you safe. I wanted…"

"Safe?" I finish for him, the word tasting sharp, like a splinter under my tongue. "I was never safe. Not with all of this hanging over us. Not with the lies."

He falls silent again, but I can tell it's not because he's given up on speaking. It's because he's finally heard me. The weight of my words, the echo of my truth, hits him harder than I anticipated. For all his strength, for all his determination, the thing that's been cracking us both is the same thing we've been avoiding: the simple, unavoidable fact that we're both in too deep to get out without consequences.

"I should've never let you get involved," he says, his voice strained. The words are a confession, an apology wrapped in layers of regret.

I shake my head, stepping back from him, not because I want space but because I need it. I need to breathe without the pressure of his guilt squeezing my lungs. "You didn't let me get involved. I chose this. I chose you. And now I'm choosing to find the truth. Even if it breaks us."

The words hang between us for a moment, neither of us knowing what to say next. Then, as if on cue, the crackle of movement from the underbrush makes me tense.

It's impossible to tell if it's a squirrel scurrying or something much worse—a shadow slipping from the trees. The air turns colder, sharper, as if the very world is holding its breath. We both turn toward the sound, our hearts thudding in sync, the sense of danger suddenly all too real. It's not just the lies anymore. It's everything that's been left unsaid, lurking in the dark corners of this world, waiting for its moment. And I can feel it, in the pit of my stomach—the moment is coming.

The crack of a twig underfoot slices through the silence, sending an electric shock of tension through the air. We both freeze, my body instinctively pressing back into the shadows, hoping the darkness will shield us from whatever is coming. His hand moves to his side, fingers brushing the handle of the knife he always carries. It's not that I think he's ready to use it—he's never been that kind of man—but in moments like this, that small comfort, that piece of steel, is what keeps us grounded in the chaos.

We wait, barely breathing, as the world around us holds its breath. There's another sound, a soft rustling, followed by the unmistakable crunch of leaves. It's deliberate. Calculated. Not an animal, but something more human. My heart skips, adrenaline surging through my veins, turning my legs into lead.

"I told you," he whispers, his voice a razor edge of warning. "We shouldn't be out here."

I open my mouth to argue, but the words never come. I hear the shuffle of boots on the ground, the sharp exhale of someone in motion. It's not just one person. There's a group, their movements synchronized, methodical. I count four distinct steps.

"This is bad," I whisper, barely able to form the words. My mind races, piecing together fragments of everything we've learned. It all points to this moment, to these people. They've been following us, or maybe we've been following them without even realizing it. I can't tell if the hunter or the hunted is the one about to make the first move.

He doesn't respond. Instead, he pulls me into the nearest shadow, his body close enough to mine that I can feel the warmth radiating off him, despite the cold night air. His grip on my arm is firm but gentle, as though he's trying to protect me from more than just the danger outside.

"Stay quiet," he murmurs, his lips brushing my ear in the darkness, and I nod in response, my body instinctively leaning into his, but I can't shake the feeling that everything we've done—every decision we've made—has led to this exact moment.

The crunch of boots continues, the sound growing louder, closer. My breath catches in my throat as I glance sideways, catching a glimpse of their silhouettes, only half-visible in the moonlight filtering through the canopy of trees. They're moving in our direction. No more than ten feet away now. My pulse spikes, my heart hammering in my chest.

"Do you have a plan?" I ask under my breath, the words barely making it past my lips. I can feel his chest rise and fall in the dark, his breath steady, but his hand is trembling.

"Not yet," he says. The edge of his voice betrays the calm he's trying to project. It's a thin veneer, cracking under the pressure.

I can feel it too—the weight of everything. The uncertainty, the looming dread.

Then, out of nowhere, one of the figures shifts, his voice breaking through the silence. "You can't run forever." The words send a chill racing down my spine.

It's the voice of someone we've heard before. Someone we should have feared all along. I know that voice. It's him. The man we've been chasing, the man behind every lie we've uncovered, the one pulling the strings from behind the scenes.

"Do you hear that?" I whisper, my throat tight with the pressure of the moment.

He nods once, the movement imperceptible in the dark. "I know."

The footsteps stop abruptly. I hold my breath, trying to keep my body as still as possible. The air is suffocating, like a weight pressing on my chest, pushing the air from my lungs. The figure closest to us shifts again, his voice low, almost a growl.

"You're not going to make it out of here alive."

And then I hear the unmistakable sound of a rifle being cocked. The metallic click echoes through the trees, sharp and foreboding. My stomach drops.

"We can't fight them all," he says, his voice quieter now, edged with an emotion I can't place—maybe fear, maybe something darker. But the urgency is palpable. "We need to move."

I hesitate, torn between running and staying. The truth is, I want to confront him, the one who's been manipulating us from the shadows. But I know the odds are stacked against us. We're outnumbered, and we're running out of time.

"On my count," he whispers, his breath shallow.

I nod, even though he can't see me. I trust him—more than I should. We don't have a choice.

"One. Two..."

I count silently in my head, my muscles coiled tight, ready to spring. The sound of footsteps grows louder, closer, and just as I'm about to make my move, something shifts. A shadow flickers in the corner of my vision, a figure breaking away from the group, moving with a fluidity I can't quite place.

It's too late. Before I can react, the figure is upon us, his hand gripping my wrist in a vice-like hold.

"Got you." His voice is smooth, far too calm for the situation.

I struggle, but his grip is unyielding. The force of it sends a flare of pain shooting up my arm, but I don't stop. I can't. Not now.

I hear the sound of footsteps closing in from behind, but it's the man holding me that draws my attention. His grip tightens, and for the first time, I see the cold gleam of a knife in his other hand, its edge glinting in the faint light.

"Let her go." His voice is a low, dangerous warning, but the man holding me doesn't flinch. Instead, he pulls me closer, his body pressing against mine in a way that feels like a promise and a threat all at once.

I'm not sure if I can fight my way out of this. But I know one thing: I'm not going down without a fight. The blade inches closer, the gleam of it reflecting my fear. And then the world goes dark.

Chapter 16: Embers of Betrayal

The crackle of flames fills the air, a constant reminder of the chaos that swirls around us. Ashes fall like snow, drifting through the smoke-streaked sky, clinging to the heat that radiates from the smoldering wreckage. My breath feels heavy in my lungs, each inhale thick with the acrid taste of burning wood, a bitter reminder of the night we barely survived. We're standing on the edge of something wild, something uncontrollable, and my skin prickles as I feel the weight of it pressing in from every side. The fire isn't the only thing that's out of control anymore.

I glance to my side, catching a glimpse of him. His face is streaked with soot, his jaw set, as unyielding as the steel he's been forged from. He moves with purpose, each step deliberate, yet there's something more in his posture. Tension. I can almost hear it humming in the air between us. The silence lingers longer than it should as we work side by side, hauling buckets of water, each sloshing spill a futile attempt to douse the inferno that's still far too large for us to tame. His eyes flicker toward me, a quick, sharp glance, and I see it: the storm behind his gaze. Something is happening to him, something that I can't quite touch, but it's there, brewing beneath the surface. I want to ask him about it, but there's no time. Not here. Not now.

The crew is quieter than usual, moving in smaller groups, their eyes darting to each other when they think no one's watching. There's a palpable shift in the air, one I can't shake. Whispers twist like smoke in the wind, subtle but constant, the words curling just out of reach, enough to make the skin on the back of my neck prickle with unease. My hand grips the handle of the bucket a little tighter. They think something's wrong. They're waiting for a spark—something to ignite the powder keg we're all standing on.

I can feel it now, the crackling tension beneath the surface. I hear fragments of voices—half-formed sentences that die when I turn toward them. It's not just the fire that's threatening to consume us. It's something else. A slow burn, creeping through our ranks, poisoning us from the inside out. The weight of suspicion is a heavy cloak I can't shake, and it settles over me like a second skin. They're talking. They're all talking.

I glance at him again, the flames dancing in his eyes, lighting them up with a dangerous intensity. He's no stranger to fighting, to battling the impossible, but I've seen the cracks in his armor. Today, I see more. He's trying to hold it together, trying to keep his focus on the task at hand, but the lines around his mouth tighten, and the flicker of his gaze betrays him. Something's breaking him. And I can't figure out if it's the fire itself, or the one burning inside him.

Then I hear it—the sharp clash of voices, raised in anger. I turn just in time to see him, storming toward one of the crew members, his fists clenched at his sides. The anger is a live wire, sparking in the tension-filled air. I freeze, every muscle in my body on alert as I watch him confront someone I thought he called a friend. The man's face is pale, his hands raised in surrender, but the words are already out. The damage is done.

"You think you can undermine me, don't you?" His voice, low and guttural, cuts through the heat like a knife.

The other man's eyes widen, his mouth opening, but no words come. He's stammering, but it doesn't matter. The seed of distrust has already been planted, and I can see it in his posture, in the way he shrinks from the confrontation, as if the fire isn't what he fears most anymore. It's him. My heart pounds in my chest as I take a step forward, but it's not enough to break the tension between them. The fight is more than just words; it's the weight of betrayal settling into their bones, filling the space between them with an icy chill that not even the flames can melt.

I don't know what's worse—the fire around us or the one that's raging within him. The fury that twists his face, the tension in his every movement, it's a warning. He's teetering on the edge, and I can't help but wonder if this is the moment everything shatters.

For a moment, all I can hear is the crackle of the fire, the beating of my own heart. Then, the man he's confronting says something—just a few words, but they strike like a blow to my gut. "You're not the only one who knows what betrayal feels like." The weight of those words hits harder than any punch. It's enough to freeze me in place, enough to make my pulse spike with a sickening realization.

The fire rages around us, the heat almost unbearable as I watch the exchange. The man's words sink into me, settling in my chest like a stone. Betrayal. It's not just the flame of this fire that we're fighting. It's something deeper. Something darker. And the worst part? I don't know who's behind it yet.

I see the flash of anger in his eyes, but it's not the rage that scares me. It's the hurt. The quiet, searing pain that flickers behind it. He's struggling, trying to keep himself together, trying to hold onto the man I thought I knew. But I'm not sure if he can anymore. Not with all the doubt creeping in, not with the whispers that are eating at the foundation of everything. And it's not just him I'm worried about. It's me. It's us. Can we survive this? Or will the fire burn through everything we've fought for?

The flames lick higher, their hungry crackle drowning out everything else, but I can't shake the image of him, standing in the midst of it all, consumed by something far more dangerous than fire.

The heat of the fire is relentless, pressing in from every angle as if it seeks to consume not just the landscape but the very essence of who we are. I wipe the sweat from my brow, but it only returns, a reminder that we're no closer to getting a handle on this. The flames grow taller, their orange tongues licking at the sky, and in the midst of it, I can't help but wonder—who are we fighting for anymore? The fire? Or the people beside us? The line blurs more with every passing minute.

I glance over at him again, watching the way his fists tremble ever so slightly as he moves. It's as if he's been split in two, one part of him still the man who's stood by my side for so long, strong and steady, and the other... I don't know what it is. It's like something inside him is unraveling, but he's keeping it hidden, buried deep beneath that familiar, stony expression. He's always been a man of few words, a silent type who prefers action over conversation. But now? Now, the silence between us is deafening.

The crew keeps its distance, eyes glancing away whenever we cross paths. No one wants to meet my gaze, and I can't blame them. Suspicion hangs thick in the air, as tangible as the smoke. They think we're hiding something, I know it. And maybe we are. But it's not what they think. It's not some grand conspiracy. It's just... him. I can't shake the feeling that something's off with him—something more than just the usual frustration of fighting a battle we're not equipped to win. The kind of tension that has nothing to do with fire and everything to do with what's burning under the skin.

We've been through hell together, seen the worst of each other and somehow come out the other side still standing. But today? Today is different. I don't know if it's the heat, or the constant pressure of the fire creeping closer, but whatever is eating at him, it's spreading. Like a wildfire. And it's making its way toward me.

"Can you hurry up with that?" a voice snaps, breaking my thoughts. I turn to see one of the other crew members, a man I barely recognize anymore, his eyes sharp and distrustful. "We don't have all day to play around."

I nod stiffly, tightening my grip on the shovel, though I know he won't be satisfied no matter how fast I move. The undercurrent of animosity between us is growing, thick and choking. They're all talking behind my back. I can feel it. The whispers. They think we're part of some bigger scheme, that we know something they don't. They think we've lost control, and maybe, just maybe, they're right.

The thought makes my chest tighten, but I push it aside. This is no time to doubt. The fire doesn't care about our problems. It doesn't care about our doubts, or our insecurities, or our shattered trust. It only cares about consuming, about spreading until there's nothing left. And yet, as I look back at him, the distance between us feels more like a chasm than a mere gap in proximity.

His eyes lock onto mine for a brief moment, and I see it—a flash of something. Regret? Pain? I'm not sure, but it's enough to send a cold shiver down my spine. He turns away quickly, retreating into the smoke and the chaos, leaving me to wonder if he saw something in me, too. Something that wasn't meant to be seen.

I try to focus on the task at hand, the monotonous rhythm of digging and shoveling, of tossing dirt onto the flames, but it's hard. The air feels thick with unspoken tension, and no matter how hard I try to ignore it, I can't. It's like a cloud hanging over me, and the weight of it makes every movement feel slow, deliberate, as if I'm wading through mud.

I don't know who to trust anymore, not even myself. The fire itself is easier to understand than the emotions that are unraveling all around me. The uncertainty, the betrayal—it's like a virus creeping through our veins. I want to reach out, to ask him what's going on, to pull him aside and demand answers. But what if the answer is something I don't want to hear? What if, in the end, we're not in this together after all?

The crew is working in fits and starts now, scattering like the embers that drift up into the sky, floating away, always just out of reach. I catch glimpses of them, moving with the kind of urgency that only comes when you're running out of options. But there's something more to their frantic movements than just the fire. I've seen the way they look at each other, the tight-lipped glances, the way their hands tremble when they think no one's watching. It's fear. Fear that the fire might not be the only thing that destroys us.

My thoughts swirl in a dizzying pattern, and before I can stop myself, I find my feet taking me in the direction of him again. He's standing off to the side, near the charred remains of a fallen tree, his back to me. I can't read his posture—he's a silhouette against the fire, hard to decipher through the smoke. But there's a tension in the way his shoulders are drawn, as if he's holding something in, something too dangerous to let slip.

I step closer, my breath hitching in my chest as I take a deep breath, trying to steady myself. This is it. This is the moment I can't ignore any longer. I have to know.

"Are you going to tell me what's going on?" The words come out before I can stop them, sharp and accusing, the anger rising in my chest like a tide I can't control. I don't even recognize the voice that asks the question, but it doesn't matter.

He doesn't turn around immediately, and when he finally does, his eyes are hard. Too hard. The flicker of pain I saw earlier is gone, replaced by something darker, something that feels like it might swallow me whole. "I don't owe you an explanation," he says, his voice low, almost too calm.

I blink, the words hitting me harder than the heat of the flames. And just like that, the distance between us feels like miles.

I hear the scrape of his boots on the dry earth before I see him, and I brace myself, my fingers tight around the shovel as if it's the only thing tethering me to the ground. He doesn't say anything at first. He just stands there, the tension between us almost a physical presence, like the smoke hanging thick in the air. His jaw clenches, that tiny muscle in his cheek twitching as he looks at me, then quickly looks away.

"I don't need your help," he says, his voice rough, not quite a growl, but close enough. There's an edge to it, something sharp that wasn't there before.

I can't help but laugh, the sound too loud in the silence between us. "Really? Because last I checked, we're all still here—alive. And last I checked, you were still here too. So, what's the problem now? Is it me?"

He doesn't answer, just stands there, eyes darting toward the crew working in the distance, their movements slower now, more cautious. The heat from the fire seems to press in even tighter as I watch him. The man I've known, the one who would've stood beside me in the worst of storms, has become a stranger. Or worse—he's become someone I don't know how to reach anymore.

"Do you even care?" I ask, my voice quiet but heavy with meaning. "What happened to us?"

He takes a breath, like the question is a weight he's been carrying, and his answer is slower than I expect, like he's weighing each word. "I care. But I'm not sure what you think this is anymore."

I swallow hard, trying to keep my composure. His words cut deeper than I want to admit. "We've been through this before. And we always made it work."

"Yeah, well, maybe not this time," he mutters, his tone sharp enough to draw blood. And before I can react, he turns on his heel and walks away, not bothering to look back.

My pulse thrums in my temples as I watch him disappear into the smoke, his silhouette swallowed up by the chaos. I'm left standing there, unsure of whether to chase after him or give him the space he's clearly demanding. But I'm not sure I can stand the distance anymore. Not the kind that's physical, and certainly not the kind that's between us now.

I turn, shoveling more dirt onto the flames, my hands moving faster than they should, my mind a blur of frustration and something worse—fear. Because the truth I can't deny is that it's not just him that's unraveling. It's me too. This uncertainty, this gnawing sense that everything we've worked for is slipping away, it's a poison I can't shake.

The whispers are getting louder, no longer just rumors carried by the wind but full-on conversations happening behind my back. People are watching us—watching me—waiting for something to crack, something to give. I feel the eyes on me, the weight of them pressing in from all sides. Some of them think I know something. Some of them think I'm hiding it, whatever it is. And some of them think we're already lost.

A voice snaps me from my thoughts, a sharp bark of command that has me flinching. It's one of the senior crew members, his face grim with the kind of concern that feels like a warning. "You might want to move back," he says, his eyes flicking toward the flames. "That fire's about to break out again."

I nod, my hands shaking slightly as I drop the shovel and step back. The crew starts to gather, eyes darting toward the inferno, but even as the fire rages behind us, my mind stays firmly on him. He's somewhere out there, lost to the smoke and the heat. And I'm no closer to understanding what's happened, what's changed between us, than I was when we first set foot in this mess.

I scan the crew again, looking for something—anything—that might give me an answer. But I'm no better off. They're all acting strange now, moving in tight, secretive huddles, their faces drawn and tense. The whispers are getting harder to ignore, the undertones of suspicion louder with every glance shared between them. They're turning on each other, and I can feel the shift, the slow erosion of trust. Everyone's a suspect. Everyone's afraid.

"Hey," the voice calls again, but it's not the senior crew member this time. It's one of the younger men, a kid who's barely out of his teens. His face is streaked with dirt, his hair matted against his forehead, but there's something urgent in his eyes. "You might want to see this."

I follow him without thinking, my feet moving on their own as he leads me toward the edge of the fire's reach. My stomach drops when I see what he's talking about.

There, lying against a tree, is a body. I don't recognize the person at first, but it's clear they're not moving. The kid steps closer, his breath coming in ragged gasps. "They were one of the crew... just collapsed out here."

I swallow hard, my throat tight. This isn't just exhaustion. This is something else. The fire might be burning everything around us, but it's the quiet betrayals—the ones happening in the shadows—that are spreading faster.

We get closer, but before I can see who it is, a loud crash sounds behind me. The kid's eyes widen in shock, and I turn just in time to see a figure emerge from the smoke. He's limping, his clothes torn, his face bloodied—nothing about him makes sense. But then, as he steps fully into the light, my heart stops in my chest. It's him. It's the last person I ever thought I'd see like this.

His eyes meet mine, empty, unreadable, and the words he spits out next make my blood run cold.

"They're all going to die."

Chapter 17: Shadows in the Flames

The fire crackled, a monstrous thing that devoured everything in its path with an insatiable hunger. I could smell it before I even saw it—the thick, acrid scent of burning wood, of a world being torn apart in a chaotic dance of flame and heat. The air was heavy, thick with smoke that choked my lungs, the temperature oppressive, and yet, there was no stopping it. Not now. Not when we were this close, this close to the heart of the storm.

I hadn't wanted to be separated. We worked best together—his calm steadiness and my frantic energy balancing each other, a rhythm we'd perfected after weeks of constant danger. But tonight, for reasons I couldn't fathom, we'd been split. The team had divided us, scattering us in different directions to cover as much ground as possible. There was no time for protests, no room for debate. It was either fight or be swallowed whole.

But the distance gnawed at me in ways I couldn't shake. The fire raged around me, its orange fingers reaching higher into the night sky. The roar of it filled my ears, drowning out everything but the heat and the smoke. I had to remind myself to breathe, to keep my eyes open, to keep my head clear. But every crackle of the flames, every gust of wind that blew smoke into my face, made my heart race. The fire was an entity in itself—alive, pulsing, relentless—and every time I caught a glimpse of the swirling chaos around me, I felt like I was slipping further from control.

And then, there was the other thing. The thing that gripped me harder than any fire ever could. The thing I couldn't escape no matter how far I ran.

Him.

The seconds stretched like hours, each passing moment a heartbeat away from panic. I scanned the smoke-choked air, trying to make sense of the world that had twisted into something almost unrecognizable. I was lost in a sea of heat and ash, my eyes burning, my throat raw from the effort of breathing. Every step I took felt like it was pulling me deeper into the unknown, further away from him, further from where I needed to be.

My hand twitched involuntarily, aching for the familiar warmth of his presence, that steady comfort that had become my anchor amidst all this madness. It was stupid, I knew it was stupid, to think that somehow I could feel him through the smoke and flame. But it was as if I could sense him, that quiet pull between us, that magnetic force that had drawn me in from the very beginning.

The fire howled, a vicious wind spiraling through the charred trees, pushing me further off course. My feet stumbled over the uneven ground, my senses overloading as I tried to make sense of it all. And then, through the swirling chaos, a shape appeared in the distance, hazy and indistinct but unmistakably familiar. My pulse spiked, the knot in my chest loosening just enough to let me breathe.

It was him.

I couldn't see his face, but I didn't need to. His form was etched into my memory, his movements a quiet grace amidst the storm. I pushed forward, heart pounding in my ears, desperate to close the gap between us. The fire roared louder, but I blocked it out, focused only on him. He was there. He was alive.

As I neared, the world around me seemed to collapse, the smoke thickening until I could barely make out his outline. He didn't hear me, didn't see me—not until I was almost right on top of him. And then, when he turned, there was a moment—a beat of time so still, so impossibly fragile—that I could feel my breath catch in my throat.

His eyes locked onto mine, dark and deep, like a storm just beginning to break. In that one glance, I saw it—the raw relief, the weight of everything that had been unsaid between us. He reached out then, his hand brushing mine, and the contact was enough to send a jolt through my chest. For just a split second, I could feel everything he hadn't spoken aloud. Everything he hadn't let me see. There was something more to him than I'd realized, something buried so deep that it nearly crushed me to think about it.

I wanted to ask him then, wanted to reach into that darkness and pull the truth out of him, but the moment slipped away too quickly. He pulled back just as fast as he'd reached for me, his expression closing off like a door slammed shut.

He didn't say a word, just looked at me for a heartbeat longer before turning, disappearing back into the smoke and flame. I stood frozen for a moment, caught between a thousand questions and an even heavier sense of something lost. What had I felt in that brief touch? What had I seen in his eyes?

But he was gone, and I was left standing in the inferno, my hand still aching with the imprint of his touch.

I wanted to chase after him, to demand answers, but the fire raged around me, and there was work to be done. There was no room for softness here, no place for the feelings that had stirred within me. Not now. Not when there was a war to fight.

I turned back to the flames, pushing my thoughts aside, but the questions lingered, like smoke in my lungs—impossible to ignore.

I could feel the sting of smoke in my eyes long before the tears threatened to fall. The air was thick, cloying, wrapping itself around my lungs like a vice, making every breath feel like an act of defiance. The heat was relentless, a steady burn that scorched the edges of my skin and curled at the back of my throat. Yet it was the silence between each crackling burst of fire that felt the loudest, deafening even, as if the world itself was holding its breath.

I had trained myself to block out everything when we were in these situations—focus, focus, focus. On the fire, on the mission, on survival. But when we were separated like this, the silence grew too heavy. His absence became its own kind of noise, a hum at the back of my mind, a reminder of what we shared and what was suddenly, inexplicably, missing.

I scanned the horizon again, my eyes darting from one chaotic flare to the next, hoping to catch a glimpse of him in the smoke. Nothing. There was nothing but the inferno, a beast of its own making, roaring as if it had a soul. I had to push past the flutter of panic. There were still lives at risk—still people who needed to be saved. The fire didn't care who we were, what we felt, or whether we had someone waiting for us on the other side. It only cared that it could consume everything in its path.

My feet moved without thinking, following a path I had memorized from countless rehearsals, yet it felt different now, somehow unfamiliar. The weight of my gear seemed heavier with every step, the heat pressing down on me as though it, too, knew what I was searching for. The shadows stretched across the burned earth, twisting in strange angles, reminding me of the last time we were here—together—when the world felt less like a threat and more like a place we could still protect. A time when he'd laughed, even in the worst of it, a sound I realized I hadn't heard in far too long.

That thought snaked its way into my mind, and suddenly I wasn't sure if I was imagining it—if this whole scene was something that had played out before, if I'd just wandered into a memory that wasn't mine, but his. It would have been easy to get lost in it, easy to follow that whisper of feeling, but I had learned the hard way that the fire didn't wait for anyone's introspection.

The ground was uneven beneath me, the scorched earth a patchwork of charred remnants. As I pushed forward, I stumbled on a twisted piece of metal, the remnants of a vehicle that had been swallowed up in the flames earlier. I cursed under my breath, righting myself just in time to hear a sound above the crackling—the unmistakable call of a voice. My heart skipped in my chest, my body immediately tensing.

It wasn't his voice.

But that didn't stop me from running toward the sound, hoping that maybe, just maybe, I'd find him there, caught in the edges of someone else's fire. The smoke was still thick, still blurring my vision, but there was a new urgency now, a frantic edge to the way I moved. The voice called again, hoarse, desperate. It wasn't until I rounded a corner—where the flame seemed to leap higher—that I saw them. Two figures, silhouetted in the light of the blaze. One of them was slumped against a singed tree, eyes wide and unfocused, struggling to breathe.

Without thinking, I was on them in a heartbeat, my training kicking in, assessing the situation. The person was alive, but barely—oxygen-starved, their skin an unhealthy shade of ashen gray. I shoved my hand into my pack, pulling out the emergency inhaler I carried, pushing it into their mouth and forcing them to take a breath, then another, until their chest heaved in a ragged rhythm. I kept my focus, refusing to look around, refusing to think about the one person who should've been beside me—who always was. There was no room for distractions here, no room for anything but the job.

It wasn't until I'd helped the person up, helped them stumble to a safer spot on the outskirts of the fire, that I realized I hadn't heard that other voice in a while. I froze. The hairs on the back of my neck stood at attention as my heart skipped, and for the first time that night, I let myself look around. There was no one.

He was gone again.

The heat was unbearable now, too intense for the air to be anything but oppressive. I shoved past the doubt crawling up my spine and jogged back toward the inferno, scanning every inch of it, every shape that might hide his presence. The smoke stung my eyes, but I didn't blink. I couldn't. Not until I saw him.

It wasn't long before I found myself in a clearing where the fire had burned itself out, the earth black and smoking, a field of destruction that might as well have been a graveyard for everything it had touched. And there, at the far edge, in the shadows just beyond the remnants of the flames, stood a figure. It wasn't the same urgency I'd felt before. This time, I was angry. But the anger wasn't just for the fire; it was for him, too.

I took a step forward, my voice sharp and cutting through the silence. "You think you can just disappear? You think this is something we can handle alone?"

He didn't turn, but his shoulders stiffened, and I could tell he was struggling with something more than just the smoke.

"You don't get to pull away like that," I continued, my voice rising now. "Not again. Not after everything we've been through."

Finally, he turned. The rawness in his eyes hit me like a physical blow. There was something there—something unspoken, something I didn't understand—but it was enough to make the words die in my throat.

"You think I want to be this way?" he murmured, his voice a ragged whisper. The words were sharp, but they held the weight of something deeper—something buried too long.

I didn't know how to answer. I only knew that this moment, this ragged breath between us, wasn't the end of it. It was just the beginning.

I shouldn't have stayed. I shouldn't have let him slip into the smoke, disappearing as effortlessly as a shadow, leaving me standing there, heart drumming a frantic rhythm in my chest. But I did. Because no matter how hard I tried to block it out, the unease gnawed at me, that feeling deep in my gut, the one that whispered there was something more to this—something far more complicated than we'd ever bargained for.

The fire was still raging, its intensity unwavering, but I couldn't shake the sense that I wasn't where I was supposed to be. My hands were shaking as I adjusted the straps on my gear, too aware of the absence beside me. The silence between each flare, each gust of wind that carried ash like confetti, became suffocating. I should have been moving, doing something, anything. But my mind, that traitorous thing, refused to focus on the flames. It only focused on him.

Where had he gone? Why had he pulled away? I had felt the weight of his touch long after he'd vanished, like the echo of a sound fading too quickly. I was used to the danger, used to the smoke, the heat, the feeling of barely surviving each new crisis. But I wasn't used to the way my pulse raced when he wasn't there—when I couldn't see him, couldn't hear him.

I found myself moving, my boots crunching through the burned earth, the smell of charred wood clinging to the air. The night had deepened into an oppressive kind of darkness, broken only by the flickering light of the fire that continued its furious dance in the distance. The flames twisted, bending in unnatural ways as if they, too, were searching for something.

There was a crack in the air, the sound of something breaking, and then the unmistakable snap of a branch. I tensed, instinctively reaching for the weapon at my side. But it wasn't a threat I found. It was a figure, barely visible in the shadows, standing just on the edge of the light, so still it might have been part of the smoke.

It was him.

He was leaning against a fallen tree, his back rigid, his posture something between exhaustion and indifference. The sight of him—so close, so far—set off a strange mix of relief and frustration in my chest. My throat tightened as I took a step forward, only to be halted by a sharp, sudden laugh that rang out into the night, bitter and low.

"You really thought you'd find me out here, didn't you?" His voice, rougher than I remembered, floated toward me like smoke. I couldn't read it—was he mocking me? Or was it the weight of something heavier?

"Don't play games with me," I said, my own voice coming out sharper than I intended. My words felt foreign in my mouth, heavy with things left unsaid. "What are you doing? Why did you pull away?"

He didn't answer right away. Instead, he pushed himself off the tree, standing straighter as though the mere act of being upright had required more effort than he was willing to admit. I wanted to march right up to him, to shake him and make him explain, but something about the way he held himself kept me at arm's length. It was the same feeling I'd had earlier when his eyes had looked through me, beyond me, as if I was a passing thought, just a part of the fire to be navigated.

"I'm not the person you think I am," he finally muttered, his voice soft enough that it almost got lost in the crackle of the flames. "And I don't need you looking at me like that—like I'm someone you can fix." His words hung between us, thick with an emotion I couldn't place.

I wasn't sure what I had expected. Maybe a confession, a revelation. Something that made sense of all the half-gestures, the moments of silence between us that felt too full, too loaded with things neither of us had the courage to say. But this—this was nothing like what I imagined. His words were a punch to my stomach, leaving me breathless with the weight of them.

"You think I'm trying to fix you?" I asked, the laugh that escaped me bitter. "You think I don't know what it's like to be broken?" I took a step forward, my heart suddenly louder than the fire. "If you think I'm looking at you like I'm trying to save you, then maybe you're the one who's been looking at me wrong all along."

The silence stretched between us again, too thick, too deep. I wasn't sure if I was angry at him for keeping his distance, or if I was angry at myself for not understanding what this was—what we were. But I was tired of the guessing, tired of the heat and the smoke and the weight of the unspoken things that seemed to drag us both down.

And then, in a single, sharp motion, he stepped into the firelight, his eyes locked on mine in a way that felt too intense, too raw. "You don't get it," he said, his voice rougher than before, each word like it was being dragged out of him. "I never wanted you to know. Never wanted you to see me like this—like a damn mess. But you're here, and I can't..."

His voice broke off, the words choking on themselves. I felt the weight of them, the vulnerability in his stance, the way he couldn't bring himself to finish. He looked at me then, really looked at me, as if seeing me for the first time—and it shook me in a way I didn't expect.

I opened my mouth to speak, but before I could, a loud crack from behind him cut through the night, followed by a guttural roar. My heart lurched in my chest, a primal instinct kicking in. He turned, his eyes wide, panic flashing before he quickly masked it with a mask of calm I'd seen too many times.

The ground shook beneath us, and the fire seemed to tremble as the roar came again, louder this time, as though the earth itself had opened its mouth.

"Move," I shouted, my hand reaching for him instinctively. But he didn't move.

Not fast enough.

And then, I saw it. The massive shape emerging from the smoke, and in the split second before it lunged, everything stopped. Everything except the knowledge that we were no longer just fighting fire.

We were fighting something else entirely.

Chapter 18: Dangerous Revelations

The evening air was thick with the scent of burning pine, that odd mix of bitter smoke and charred wood, but this time it wasn't coming from the usual spring fires. It was something else—a quiet, creeping kind of heat that seemed to wrap around me, as though the very atmosphere knew we were walking through a story that wasn't our own, one stitched together with lies and half-truths. I could feel it in the hollow spaces of the house, in the corners where shadows bent just slightly too far, and in the long silences between us.

I stood in the kitchen, staring at the glass of water in my hand, watching the ripples spread out, chasing each other until they vanished into stillness. It felt like a metaphor, though I couldn't quite place it. I'd spent too many days unraveling this, piecing together things that didn't quite fit—like a puzzle with missing pieces or one where the colors bled into each other until nothing made sense. Every new detail felt like another piece of sand in an hourglass, and every second it slipped away, the truth got closer. Closer to swallowing me whole.

The sound of footsteps echoed behind me, light but sure, and I knew without turning around who it was. His presence had become a strange constant in the whirlwind of confusion, like a storm cloud you know will come but can never prepare for.

"You're quiet tonight," his voice was soft, but there was something beneath it—an edge that wasn't there before. The kind of edge that made me wonder what had happened to him in the hours when I wasn't looking.

I set the glass down with more force than I intended, the sound too sharp in the otherwise quiet room. "I'm thinking," I said, keeping my back to him. "About everything."

"Everything?" He moved closer, and I could hear the careful pace of his breathing, feel the tension in his body as if he was holding himself back from something. "Or just about the things you're too afraid to face?"

I hated that he could always see me so clearly, that he could read my mind with unsettling accuracy. But I wasn't afraid anymore, not of him anyway. I was afraid of the truth we'd uncovered, the terrible web that had been spun around us for so long.

I turned around slowly, meeting his gaze. His eyes, the color of storm clouds just before a downpour, flickered with something—fear, maybe, or regret. I couldn't decide. They didn't match the calm exterior he always wore like armor. His jaw was clenched tight, his posture too stiff, as if every muscle in his body was coiled, waiting for something to give.

"I didn't want to believe it," I whispered. "That we've been played like this. Used, even."

He took a slow breath, the air between us charged in a way that made my chest tighten. "I didn't either. But the pieces are all there, aren't they?" His voice was low now, almost as if he were speaking to himself rather than me. "The fires, the lies, the people who vanished. The connections we didn't want to see."

I wanted to look away, to avoid the truth that I had to face, but instead I found myself stepping closer. "And you think it's all connected?"

He nodded, his eyes never leaving mine. "I know it is. I've been watching it unravel for weeks now. Pieces of the puzzle are falling into place, and none of it's by accident."

I wanted to protest, wanted to throw some deflection in there, to deny it because it was easier. But the tension in the air was suffocating, and the truth was right there, too loud to ignore. It was like the world was coming apart around us, and we were just two people standing in the middle of the wreckage, waiting for the storm to hit.

"You're afraid, aren't you?" The question slipped from my lips before I could stop it, the words too soft, too intimate. I could see the way his shoulders tensed at the admission, but he didn't pull away.

"I'm not afraid of you," he said, his voice tight, but there was something in it—something I hadn't heard before.

"No," I replied. "But you're afraid of what this could mean for us. What it could mean for everything we thought we knew."

He didn't answer right away. Instead, his gaze flickered to the space between us, and I felt a strange pulse of energy, like a magnetic field pulling at me, at both of us. His hands, once rigid at his sides, now seemed to twitch, as though he was fighting the instinct to reach out.

"I didn't want you to be involved in this," he said after a long pause. "I never wanted you to know any of this. But now..." He swallowed hard, his voice dropping to almost a whisper. "Now I don't know how to keep you safe."

I took a step back, the words sinking in like ice water. "Safe?" I repeated, my voice shaking. "From what? From you?"

He flinched, his eyes momentarily closing, like I'd struck him, and for a moment, I felt a pang of guilt. But it didn't last long. Not with everything we were facing.

"I'm not the one you should be worried about," he murmured, and for a second, I could see the pain in his eyes, a raw vulnerability I wasn't sure I was ready to face.

Before I could reply, he moved closer, his hand brushing the side of my arm, sending an unexpected rush of warmth through me. He stopped just shy of touching me fully, but the air around us seemed to tremble with the weight of unsaid things, things we both knew but weren't ready to admit.

"Please, don't," I whispered, but the words felt hollow, weak. Because the truth was, I didn't know if I could resist him. Not anymore.

The space between us closed, a whisper of heat brushing across my lips. He hesitated, his breath mingling with mine, a soft, dangerous thing. "I'm sorry," he whispered, the words barely audible, but they hung there, heavy and full of something that felt too close to regret.

And then, without warning, his lips brushed mine, a fleeting, forbidden kiss that tasted like fire and ash, like everything we were about to lose.

I couldn't pull away, not even when I knew I should, because his lips pressed against mine with a weight that was too heavy to ignore. The kiss, as fleeting as it was, burned with the kind of urgency I hadn't expected—a raw, desperate energy that felt like it was pulling something from me I wasn't sure I was ready to give. The sound of my breath catching in the space between us was the only thing I could hear, louder than the chaos outside, louder than the pounding of my own heart.

He pulled back first, just a fraction, his forehead brushing against mine, as though he needed the contact, like he couldn't quite let go either. His eyes were dark, clouded with something I couldn't name, and I could feel the tension in every muscle of his body as if he were caught between a thousand different paths and none of them led to safety.

"I shouldn't have done that," he muttered, though his voice lacked conviction. The words were half a plea, half a statement, as if he needed to justify what had just happened. I couldn't blame him for that. I didn't know if I was ready to justify it either.

I shook my head, taking a step back, trying to gain some distance, even though I felt his presence pulling me in again, like gravity itself was working against me. "It's not about that," I said, my voice strained. "It's about everything else. The lies, the fires. The people who are pulling the strings and watching us burn."

His gaze flickered, an unreadable look passing over his face before it was replaced by that careful, practiced calm I had come to know so well. The kind that made him seem like he had everything under control when in truth, he was barely holding himself together.

"I know," he whispered, his voice hoarse now, worn down by the weight of all the secrets we were uncovering. "But I can't keep pretending that I'm not..." He trailed off, his words lost to the air between us.

It wasn't just the danger that hung in the air. It was the feeling of inevitability. Like everything we had been building toward—every secret, every piece of the puzzle—had led us here, to this moment, where there was no going back.

"And I can't keep pretending that I'm not..." I echoed, the words thick with everything I didn't know how to say. The kiss had been too much, too soon, and yet I couldn't quite regret it. I didn't know what it meant, what any of this meant anymore.

The silence stretched between us, heavy and suffocating. Outside, the wind picked up, the trees outside groaning in the gusts, as if they were trying to warn us that the storm was only just beginning. But this wasn't the kind of storm you could outrun. This was the kind that destroyed everything in its path, leaving nothing but wreckage.

Finally, he exhaled a breath that sounded too much like a surrender. "I don't know what happens next," he said, his voice barely more than a murmur, "but I do know one thing: I can't do this without you."

The words struck me harder than I expected, like a slap to the chest. I looked at him, at the man who had always been just out of reach, his walls too high to climb, his emotions buried beneath layers of hardened steel. But now? Now there was something raw in his eyes, something vulnerable that made my chest ache for him.

"I'm not sure I know what I'm doing either," I said, my own voice shaking now. "But I'm here. I'm not going anywhere." The truth of it settled over me, slow and steady, like the first rain after a long drought. I didn't know how we were going to get through this—this mess we'd been dragged into—but I wasn't going to leave him to face it alone. Not now. Not after everything.

He gave a tight nod, a small, pained smile curling at the corners of his lips, but it didn't reach his eyes. "Then we do this together. No more running."

I nodded, the weight of his words sinking into my bones. Running. It had always been an option, a way out of the chaos, the danger. But now, there was no escaping. There was no easy way out of what we had stumbled into. We had opened doors that couldn't be closed. Not anymore.

"Let's figure this out," I said, my voice firming, even though my heart was still racing. The uncertainty of everything loomed over us, but the bond that had been formed—however reluctantly—between us felt stronger than the fear. Stronger than anything else.

We worked together in silence after that, spreading out the evidence we had gathered across the kitchen table. Pieces of paper, photographs, maps with pins stuck in them—each one a tiny fragment of a larger picture, a picture we were still trying to make sense of. The names of people we hadn't seen in months. Places we hadn't visited in years. All of them connected in ways that didn't make sense, at least not yet. But we were close, so close I could feel it in the pit of my stomach.

"This doesn't add up," I muttered, squinting at a map of the city. There was a pattern, I could see it now, but it didn't make sense. "Why would they send us here? Why set everything in motion?"

His voice was tight, barely a whisper, as though speaking too loudly might make it all unravel. "Because we were never supposed to find out. We were always meant to be the distraction, the ones who got caught in the flames."

I looked at him then, really looked, and realized that this wasn't just about us anymore. This was about something much bigger, something that had been set into motion long before we'd ever come into the picture. And now, we were all in, whether we liked it or not. The fires were closing in, and there was no way out. Not anymore.

I felt my pulse quicken, but there was no turning back. This was it. Whatever happened next, we were both already too deep in to escape.

The night stretched on, thick and oppressive, the air heavy with the smoke of our discoveries. He was sitting across from me now, his back rigid as though every nerve in his body was still on high alert, like he was waiting for the next explosion—physical or emotional—whichever came first. The map sprawled before us was a maze of lines, names, places I didn't recognize, and connections that made the hair on the back of my neck stand up. It was too much to digest in one sitting, and yet here we were, doing exactly that.

"I don't like it," I muttered, tapping the edge of the map with a pencil, more out of frustration than any real desire to mark anything. "None of this makes sense."

He didn't respond at first, his gaze fixed on the map as though he could will it to reveal the answers. His jaw was clenched tight, his fingers fidgeting with the corner of a photograph, a picture of a man I didn't recognize but whose face was hauntingly familiar in a way I couldn't explain.

"I know," he finally said, his voice rough. "But it's the only lead we have."

I couldn't help but laugh—an ugly, bitter sound that didn't sit well in the silence of the room. "That's not reassuring, you know. 'The only lead we have.'" I shook my head. "It's like we're chasing shadows, looking for answers that don't exist."

He met my gaze, his expression unreadable. There was something unsettling about the way he looked at me, a look that felt both distant and intensely present at the same time. It made my skin prickle, but I wasn't sure if it was the tension of the situation or something else—something deeper, darker.

"You think I don't know that?" he said, his voice low, almost a growl. He leaned forward, his elbows braced on the table, his eyes flashing with something I couldn't quite place. "We've been thrown into something we didn't ask for. But now that we're here, we have to finish it."

I felt a flicker of unease coil around my chest. He was right. We were in it, whether we wanted to be or not. There was no walking away from this, no turning back to a life that didn't involve fire, deceit, and the growing sense of danger that had started to seep into every part of my world.

"I'm not walking away," I said, my words more steady than I felt. "I'm here. But I'm not going to pretend I'm not scared. We're digging into something that could swallow us whole."

He held my gaze for a long moment, his lips curling into a half-smile, though it didn't reach his eyes. "You think I'm not scared?" The words were sharp, a challenge I wasn't sure I was ready to accept. But it was there, in the tension between us, something that had always been present but never spoken. Now, with the weight of everything we'd uncovered bearing down on us, it was impossible to ignore.

"I think you've been hiding behind that armor of yours for far too long," I said, my voice quieter now, more vulnerable than I intended. "You're not the only one who's scared, you know. I don't know what's real anymore. Not when every time I think I've figured it out, I find another lie waiting to slap me in the face."

His eyes softened for a fraction of a second, the mask slipping just enough for me to see the rawness beneath. "I know. I didn't want this for you. I never wanted you to get caught up in this mess."

I almost believed him. Almost. But the more I looked at him, the more I saw the cracks in the facade, the places where the truth was beginning to seep through. There were too many things he wasn't telling me, things I was beginning to suspect, but I didn't have the luxury of asking questions that would only unravel us further.

"I didn't ask for any of this," I said, my voice shaking slightly, but I refused to let him see it. I wasn't weak. I wasn't going to let fear control me. "But here I am. And now we have to finish what we started."

His gaze flickered toward the window, the shadows outside stretching longer with the deepening night. "We're not alone in this," he said, his tone dark. "And that's what scares me the most."

My breath hitched, and I followed his gaze to the darkened street outside. The night felt different now—thicker, like the air was holding its breath. A sense of foreboding washed over me, something I couldn't quite place, but I felt it deep in my bones.

"We can't do this alone," I said, almost to myself, more for reassurance than anything else. "We need help. We need to know who's behind all of this, who's pulling the strings."

"You think I don't know that?" he snapped, his voice a little harsher than I was used to. But there was something in it, something real. A desperation I hadn't heard before. "I'm trying to figure it out. But every time we get close, it's like someone's a step ahead of us."

"Then we need to catch up," I said, my resolve hardening. I wouldn't let him do this alone—not this time. Not with everything on the line.

His eyes darted to mine, and for the first time in hours, I saw something that looked like hope flicker in his expression, a spark that burned hot and quick before it was buried under the weight of everything we had to face.

But then—there was a knock at the door. Soft, tentative, but there was no mistaking it. The kind of knock that didn't belong.

My pulse raced, and before I could say anything, he was already on his feet, moving toward the door with a fluid, predatory grace that made my stomach tighten. I reached for the handle of the drawer where I knew the gun was hidden, my fingers brushing the cool metal as I held my breath, waiting for the next step, the next breath.

He glanced back at me over his shoulder, his expression unreadable. "Stay back," he murmured.

But as his hand touched the doorknob, I heard the unmistakable sound of a voice from the other side—one I recognized, one that shouldn't have been there.

"I know what you're doing. And you need to stop."

Chapter 19: Trial by Fire

The flames weren't just licking the edges of the forest anymore; they were devouring it whole, swallowing every tree, every blade of grass, every scrap of air. The heat clung to my skin like a second layer, oppressive and unyielding, my breath coming in shallow gasps. I could barely hear anything above the roar of the fire, the crackling and snapping of branches as they gave in to the inferno. It felt like the entire world was holding its breath, waiting for something to give. Or maybe it was just me, waiting to breathe again.

"We've got to move, now," he said, his voice a sharp command, but there was a softness in it, too—a thread of reassurance woven in between the words. I could see the fire in his eyes, the urgency burning brighter than the flames around us. He was already pulling me forward, through the smoke, past the falling trees, his grip steady even as my legs wobbled beneath me, fighting against the heat and the terror that threatened to claw its way out of me.

The smoke stung my eyes, but I didn't dare close them. I couldn't afford to. Not with him so close. His presence was an anchor, a lifeline in a world that seemed to be collapsing in on itself. Each step was a gamble, each breath a silent prayer. The fire didn't care about our plans, our fears. It had its own agenda.

"Keep going. Don't stop," he urged, his hand tightening around mine.

His voice was steady, but I could feel the tremor in his grip. The same one that rattled through me with every breath I took. We were running blind through the smoke, the fire now behind us, but it was never really behind, was it? It was a shadow that stretched long across the ground, pulling at us like a force we couldn't outrun. I felt the heat on my back, a pressure that was almost unbearable, as if the flames were inching closer with every step. I had to trust him. There was no choice but to trust him.

"Where's the escape route?" My words were barely a whisper, swallowed up by the roar of the fire. I could barely think straight.

"Up ahead. Just—keep your head down," he instructed, and for a moment, there was something more in his voice, something that chilled me to the bone. He knew something I didn't.

We rounded a corner, and I saw it—a gap in the trees, a clearing just up ahead. Safety, or at least a temporary respite from the madness that had consumed the forest. But it was too close, too easy. My heart skipped a beat as we pushed forward, the weight of the moment pressing down on me, and I could feel the change in the air. Something was wrong.

He stopped suddenly, pulling me back behind the thick trunk of a blackened tree. I didn't have time to ask why before I saw it—something dark moving in the smoke, shapes too fast, too deliberate. A shadow, slipping through the blaze like it didn't even notice the fire.

"Get down," he hissed, pulling me low to the ground, his body covering mine.

I obeyed without question, my heart pounding louder than the fire. The figure emerged fully from the haze, a silhouette framed against the raging inferno. It moved with purpose, like it knew exactly where it was going—and it was heading straight for us.

"What the hell?" I whispered, my breath catching in my throat. "Who's that?"

He didn't answer. His eyes narrowed, scanning the figure's every move with a precision I couldn't begin to match. I could feel the tension in his body, coiled like a spring, ready to snap.

"We don't have time," he muttered, more to himself than to me. "If we don't move now, we're dead."

The figure continued to approach, undisturbed by the chaos around it. My pulse quickened as I pressed my face into the dirt, trying to make myself invisible. I wasn't sure if I was more afraid of the fire or the person who was calmly walking through it. But one thing was certain—I wasn't ready to find out which one would kill me first.

He didn't hesitate. In one smooth motion, he pulled me to my feet, his hand still gripping mine. We moved as one, no words, just action. He was pulling me through the smoke, weaving between the trees with the sort of precision I couldn't fathom. My lungs burned with every breath, but I didn't dare slow down. The figure was still behind us, and I could feel its gaze on my back, sharp and cold.

Just as we neared the clearing, the explosion hit. It was like the world itself had shattered, a deafening crack that sent the air vibrating around me. The blast lifted me off my feet, throwing me sideways like a ragdoll. I slammed into the ground, hard, the earth giving way beneath me as the fire roared louder in the distance, hungry for more.

The world spun, and for a moment, everything was a blur—a haze of smoke, fire, and chaos. I scrambled to my feet, my heart in my throat. The sharp sting of pain in my side told me I wasn't unharmed, but I didn't have time to process it. My eyes searched the wreckage, looking for him.

Where was he?

"James!" I screamed, my voice raw, swallowed up by the sound of the fire. My hands shook as I scanned the wreckage around me, every fiber of my being on high alert. He had to be here. He had to be.

And then I saw him, a figure moving slowly through the smoke. He was there, but not unscathed. His body was bent at an awkward angle, blood dripping from his arm. My breath caught in my throat as I ran to him, my legs weak beneath me, my world narrowing to the sight of him.

"James!" I gasped, reaching out to him, fear coursing through me like wildfire.

He looked up, his face pale, but his eyes—his eyes were still there, still sharp, still focused. "I'm fine," he said, his voice rough but steady. "Just—just get me out of here."

And in that moment, as I helped him to his feet, something in me shifted. It wasn't just the fire or the danger that had brought us here—it was the way I cared about him, how deeply it ran. I could lose him. In this moment, I realized I could lose him.

And I wasn't ready for that. Not at all.

The earth was warm beneath my feet as I crouched next to him, my hands slick with sweat and blood. His face, once so calm and collected, was now streaked with dirt and pain. Every shift of his body, every sharp inhale, seemed like it took a part of me with it. And as I stared at him, there was an unfamiliar sting in my chest, something deeper than the fear I had already felt, something that had nothing to do with the inferno roaring behind us.

"Don't," I whispered as he tried to sit up, his hand gripping the ground as though to steady himself, like his whole world was tilting sideways. "Don't try to move yet. Just breathe."

He glanced up at me, a tired, crooked smile tugging at the corner of his lips. "I'm fine. It's not—" His words caught in his throat, and he grimaced, clearly too worn out to finish the sentence. The fire around us felt like a living thing, creeping, snarling, always threatening to consume us both.

I shifted to his side, pressing a hand gently to his shoulder to steady him. His eyes flickered to mine, sharp with a mixture of gratitude and something else—something unspoken, hidden deep in the corners of his gaze. My heart stumbled in my chest, a beat too slow, too heavy.

"I don't know if 'fine' is the word I'd use right now." I tried to keep my voice light, but it came out shaky, the words tasting like too much in the air between us. The burn of the fire wasn't what made the hairs stand up on the back of my neck; it was the way his lips twitched like he was about to say something—something that could change everything.

He shook his head, wincing slightly as he did. "I've had worse. This? This is nothing."

It was a lie. His arm was cradled against his chest, the blood trickling down his hand. His face was pale, a sheen of sweat lining his forehead, but I wasn't about to tell him that. Not when he looked at me like that, like I might be the one who could fix everything, when I didn't even know how to fix myself.

"We should get you out of here." The words felt too small, too inadequate, like I could somehow patch up the cracks in the world with them. But I had no other choice. "We'll get help. I'll carry you if I have to."

He let out a breath, as if considering it, then pressed his palm against his chest, his expression shifting in that way I hated, as if he were about to tell me something I didn't want to hear. His eyes softened, and that was worse than anything—the vulnerability.

"Will you, though?" he asked, his voice low, as if he were testing something, weighing it. "Carry me?"

The air between us thickened. I could feel the heat of the fire on my neck, but it was nothing compared to the suffocating tension hanging over us. I swallowed hard, my mouth suddenly dry.

"You're not heavy," I said, but it came out like a question. Like I wasn't sure whether it was the fire or him that had me so paralyzed. "And I'm not leaving you behind."

His eyes softened even more, and I realized then that my heart was in it—really in it. There was no pretending I was okay with walking away. He had become something more than just a teammate. More than just a person in my orbit, bound by fire and chaos.

I wasn't sure when that had happened, but in that moment, I could feel the weight of it. And I didn't know if that was a burden or a blessing.

He shifted, his movements slow and deliberate, then reached out, gripping my arm gently. His voice was barely a whisper, as though speaking any louder would shatter the fragile thing between us.

"Do you ever feel like we're too close to something dangerous? Like we're not supposed to be here?" His gaze held mine, full of something I couldn't name. "Like the fire isn't the only thing threatening us?"

I froze. The question hung in the air between us, a delicate thread ready to snap.

"Is that a warning?" I finally asked, my voice steady, but my heart skipping in my chest.

He didn't answer right away. Instead, he stared at me for what felt like a lifetime, his breath shallow but steady. His hand, still gripping my arm, tightened ever so slightly, grounding us both in the midst of the chaos.

"No," he said quietly. "Not a warning. Just... a thought."

The ground beneath us seemed to shift. Or maybe it was just me. The fire that still raged in the distance felt far less menacing now compared to the fire building between us, a spark that hadn't been there before. I felt it—the connection, the raw pulse of something electric—and I wondered how much longer I could keep pretending I didn't feel it.

"Let's move," I finally said, my voice steady despite the heat creeping under my skin. I wasn't sure where this was going, but I wasn't about to stand still long enough to find out.

I stood, pulling him to his feet. He didn't resist, though I could feel the strain in his muscles as he tried to keep his balance. I was steady enough for both of us, at least for now.

"Hold on to me," I said, more sharply than I meant. I didn't wait for him to respond, didn't give him a chance to argue. He leaned against me, and we started moving, pushing our way through the thick smoke and charred remains of what had once been a peaceful patch of forest.

But we didn't get far.

There was another noise—low, rumbling, but unmistakable. Another explosion, louder this time, and closer. The ground trembled beneath us, the force knocking us sideways. We barely had time to react before the air was filled with a new wave of heat, thicker than before, rolling over us like a wave.

We tumbled to the ground again, the world going dark for a moment as my head struck something solid. Dazed, I pushed myself upright, my body sluggish and confused. My ears were ringing. My breath was shallow. But when I looked over at him, my heart dropped into my stomach. His face was twisted with pain, his breath coming in jagged gasps.

And then, as if the fire weren't enough, I realized what had really happened. We weren't alone anymore.

The figure from earlier—the shadow that had slipped through the smoke like it belonged to the fire itself—was back. And this time, it was holding something in its hand. Something sharp. Something that glinted in the flame.

And I knew, in that instant, that whatever came next, it wouldn't just be fire that threatened to burn us alive.

The world was spinning. Every inch of me felt like it had been shredded in the blast—numb, aching, and, for the briefest of moments, weightless. I could barely make sense of the world around me, the air thick with smoke and a screeching alarm that pounded in my ears, matching the frantic rhythm of my heartbeat. The ground was uneven beneath me, shifting under the pressure of the aftershock, and I couldn't even tell if I was standing or crawling.

And then I heard it—the low, guttural sound of something moving through the dirt and rubble.

I froze, breath caught in my throat. For a moment, I thought it was the fire's roar closing in again, but this was different. This was too deliberate. Too... controlled.

I turned quickly, my pulse racing, and that's when I saw him—James—his body half-draped over a fallen log, his face smeared with blood and dirt, his eyes unfocused. It didn't take long to realize what had happened. The explosion had knocked him out cold.

A flood of panic surged through me, making my heart hammer violently against my ribs. Without thinking, I was on my knees beside him, my hands reaching for his chest, his neck, anywhere I could find him.

"James?" My voice was raw, ragged, but the fear that broke through it sounded like someone else's. "James, talk to me!"

His eyes fluttered open, glazed over, but the recognition in his gaze made my chest tighten. For a moment, he just stared at me, his breath shallow, as if he were trying to process the fact that I was there. Or maybe he was still somewhere deep in the haze, struggling to break through it.

I gripped his shoulder, shaking him gently. "You're not getting off that easy," I muttered, trying to keep it light even though every word felt like a lie. "You're not dying on me today, okay?"

He gave me a weak smile, though it was obvious he wasn't entirely sure what was going on. "Dying? I'm just getting started." His voice was thick with a mix of pain and something else—something that made the air between us crackle.

His words barely registered in my brain. I was too focused on getting him out of there. "We need to move. Now."

But when I looked up, my heart dropped. The shadow I had seen before was standing just a few feet away, a twisted silhouette against the smoke, its presence so unnervingly calm that it made my skin crawl.

I couldn't see its face—its features hidden by the smoke and the distance—but there was no mistaking the way it held something in its hand. A glint of steel.

"Move," I whispered, urgency creeping into my voice. "Please."

James' hand shot out, gripping my wrist with a strength that I hadn't expected, even in his condition. His voice came out in a rasp, each word an effort. "Don't. Don't leave. It's not what it seems."

"What are you talking about?" I hissed, glancing between him and the figure.

"That... that's not someone you want to face," he said slowly, his face paling as if the mere mention of it drained the little strength he had left. "This isn't just a fire anymore, this—"

The rest of his words were lost in the sound of another explosion, much closer this time, shaking the ground beneath us. A blast that seemed to come from the very core of the earth itself.

I gasped, instinctively pulling James closer to me as the earth trembled underfoot. The figure hadn't moved. It simply watched us, standing as still as a statue. The weight of its gaze pressed against me, suffocating, like it could see straight through to my soul.

"We need to go," I said, my voice sharp, my grip tightening around James' arm. I wanted to pull him away, get us both out of there, but my feet felt rooted to the ground, unwilling to leave. That figure—the shadow—it was waiting. For what? For us? For something worse?

James didn't move. He seemed transfixed, his eyes flickering between the figure and me. His hand gripped mine tighter, and the way his fingers twisted against my skin sent a rush of warmth through my body, so starkly at odds with the chaos surrounding us. "No," he said quietly. "It's not just the fire. It's... something else. Something we didn't see coming."

Before I could respond, a sudden shift in the air made me freeze—a pressure, like the calm before the storm. The figure was moving now, the soft click of boots against charred earth ringing out in the quiet. And though my instinct told me to run, to pull James away, there was something about that presence that kept me in place, paralyzed.

James' hand slipped from mine, and I spun toward him, panic flooding me. "What the hell are you doing? We need to move!"

"I'm... I'm not sure what happens next." His voice was so calm, so utterly calm, that it sent a shiver down my spine. "But I can't—"

"I swear to God, James, you better not be doing something stupid."

He didn't answer, instead looking past me, his eyes locked onto the figure now stepping closer. Something about his face had shifted. I couldn't read it—was it resignation? Fear? But it was enough to set every warning bell in my head off.

I was about to pull him to his feet when the figure spoke—its voice a low, smooth drawl that seemed to seep into my bones.

"You've been running from this for too long, haven't you?"

The words hit like a slap. My blood ran cold.

James stiffened beside me, his entire body tensing, his hand reaching out to steady himself against me. "No," he said quickly, his voice low and strained, "we... we don't need this right now."

But it was already too late. The figure took another step forward, its face still hidden, the air around it heavier than anything I'd ever felt.

And then, before I could blink, before I could make sense of anything, it reached into the fire and pulled something from the flames—something that glowed with an unearthly light.

My heart stuttered in my chest.

"What is that?" I gasped, my voice barely above a whisper, as I stumbled back, my body instinctively trying to put distance between us.

But the figure smiled, or at least I thought it did. It was impossible to tell for sure, but the sharp, dangerous gleam in its eyes was unmistakable.

And in that moment, I realized one thing: whatever it was, we were no longer just fighting fire. We were fighting something far darker.

Chapter 20: The Scorching Truth

The air in camp was thick with tension, a smog that clung to my skin like a second layer. It had been days since the fire, but the smell of charred wood still lingered in the air, refusing to be forgotten. The heat from the inferno had scarred the land, leaving behind a landscape that felt unnaturally barren, as if the very earth had been scorched with a secret. I stood near the edge of the camp, my boots sinking into the dirt, eyes narrowing as I watched Captain Baird move around the fire. His face was unreadable, as always, but his posture stiff, betraying a faint nervousness that no one else seemed to notice.

I had to know the truth.

The fire wasn't natural. There was something about it, something that didn't add up. It wasn't just the way the flames had spread so fast, as though they had a mind of their own; it was the look in his eyes when he first spoke about it—too careful, too rehearsed. I had seen fear there, just for a moment, hidden behind the calm facade of a man used to command. And it unsettled me, gnawed at me, like a piece of glass lodged under my skin. I had to confront him, now.

With each step I took towards him, my heartbeat quickened, my pulse a rhythmic drumbeat in my ears. There was an urgency to the way I moved, the kind that only comes from knowing something terrible is about to unfold, and you have no idea how it will turn out. I didn't know if I was about to ruin everything by pushing too hard or if this was the moment when everything would finally make sense.

"Captain," I called, my voice low but firm, almost a growl. He turned at the sound, offering his usual tight-lipped smile. The kind of smile that said, I'm in control, and nothing can touch me.

But I wasn't going to let him hide behind that smile this time.

"Captain," I repeated, louder now, my frustration bubbling over. "The fires. The way they spread. You're telling me this was natural?"

He glanced around, eyes scanning the camp as though he expected to be interrupted by someone—anyone—at any moment. But there was no one. It was just the two of us, and the flickering flames between us.

"Of course, they were," he replied, his voice smooth, practiced. "It's nothing out of the ordinary. Fires happen in dry weather."

"I'm not talking about weather," I shot back, stepping closer. "I'm talking about the way it happened. The way it moved. And you," I continued, my words growing sharper with each syllable, "you were there, right? You were the first one to see it, to put it out. So why don't I believe you?"

The air felt thick, like a storm waiting to break. He shifted his weight, looking at me with those cold eyes that seemed to hold every answer in the universe, but none of them were for me. He let out a small laugh, but it lacked humor, more a deflection than anything else.

"You've got quite the imagination, don't you?" he said, his tone light but his gaze narrowing just slightly. He was trying to dismiss me, but I could see it now—the tightness around his eyes, the subtle twitch of his jaw. He was hiding something. And I was going to find it.

"No," I replied, stepping forward until there was nothing between us but the crackling fire. "I'm not imagining it, Captain. I'm seeing it. And you're lying."

The smile fell from his face, replaced by something colder. The fire seemed to flicker with the change, as if the very flames sensed it. "You've crossed the line, soldier," he muttered, his voice hardening into something that could have been a threat if he hadn't been standing in the middle of his own camp, surrounded by his men.

I didn't back down.

"You can look at me all you want," I said, my voice trembling now with the weight of all the frustration that had been building up inside me. "You can dismiss me, belittle me, but I know the truth. And I won't stop until I find it."

He took a step forward, his face inches from mine. I could feel the heat from his body, the unmistakable presence of a man who had learned long ago how to intimidate without lifting a finger. But I wasn't afraid. Not anymore.

Then, in that moment, just as I thought he would tell me to go to hell, just as I thought I would lose everything—he stepped back. And the change was almost imperceptible, but I saw it. In his eyes. The crack in the armor.

"You're right," he said, his voice now colder than the night air. "You've been asking the wrong questions." He paused, his gaze shifting to the campfire. "Some things... some things aren't meant to be known."

I took a step back, my heart racing. "What aren't you telling me, Captain?"

The words came out in a low, gravelly whisper, like the weight of a confession finally breaking through the surface of a carefully constructed wall. "There are things in my past that I wish I could forget. Things that are better left buried."

I stood there, frozen, my mind scrambling to understand what he was saying. My heart hammered against my chest, the words barely registering.

"You're not the only one who's seen the fire," he continued, his gaze distant now, lost in some faraway memory. "But you're the only one who's asked the right questions."

A sharp breath escaped my lips, and suddenly the space between us felt so much larger. It wasn't the fire crackling anymore that filled the silence; it was the weight of his unspoken past pressing down on both of us.

I couldn't stop myself. I couldn't ignore the way my pulse quickened, the way his vulnerability—his honesty—was suddenly so... magnetic. Even now, I hated myself for feeling this pull, for wanting to know more, to understand him.

But that didn't change the truth. Not yet.

"Tell me everything," I said, the words almost pleading now, desperate to understand him.

He didn't answer immediately. Instead, he looked at me, really looked at me, and for the first time, there was a flicker of something softer beneath the stone cold mask of the captain. It was regret. And maybe a little fear.

"It's not that simple," he said quietly. "Some stories, you don't want to hear. Some truths are darker than the fire itself."

The fire crackled between us, its dance of orange and yellow flickers the only thing that filled the oppressive silence. His confession hung in the air, heavy and unresolved, like smoke that refused to dissipate. Captain Baird wasn't a man who easily offered up his secrets—if anything, he kept them like a fortress, stone walls around a heart that had long ago learned to guard itself. I could see that now, his jaw clenched, his eyes far off as if looking for something in the flames that wasn't there.

I felt the weight of his words, and with it, an unexpected shift in the night air. His shoulders slumped, just barely—an almost imperceptible motion, like the first crack in a dam holding back a flood. The vulnerability in him, so fleeting and guarded, was like a glimpse of something too fragile to touch. It made my heart ache, and I didn't know why. It was a vulnerability I hadn't expected from a man like him, and I wasn't sure what to do with it. He had always been a soldier in my eyes, a man built from something tougher than human softness. And yet, here he was, unraveling in front of me like a thread pulled too tightly.

"Tell me," I urged, though I wasn't sure I was ready for whatever he might say next. "You can't just drop something like that and walk away." My words were sharper than I intended, but the frustration inside me was starting to boil over again. I hated how much he held back, hated how the mystery of him was becoming a wall I couldn't climb.

He sighed deeply, the sound so heavy it felt as though it carried years of weight. He didn't look at me when he spoke, his gaze fixed firmly on the flames as if they might offer him some kind of escape.

"Before this," he began slowly, each word deliberate, "I was stationed near a small village up north. Nothing fancy, just a post at the edge of nowhere. I was in charge of a team there, much like I am here. And like here, there were fires—wildfires, but… they weren't the same." He swallowed, his throat working visibly. "I didn't realize it at first, but something was off. The fires weren't natural. They weren't just burning the land, they were… targeting certain areas. Farms, homes, businesses—places that had nothing to do with the natural cycle of things."

I leaned forward slightly, my body drawn toward him, despite every warning bell in my head telling me to keep my distance. I'd heard about strange fires before, but this felt different. It felt like a story that was about to twist in a way I wasn't prepared for.

"There were rumors," he continued, his voice growing darker. "Whispers of something… unnatural. But I didn't believe them at first. I couldn't. And then, one night, I watched it happen. A fire broke out in the middle of a quiet field. No explanation, just there. And then it was gone. But there was something… off about the way it moved. The way it left. And I knew then that it wasn't just a coincidence."

I watched him as he spoke, his eyes distant now, the captain slipping away into something deeper, darker. It was like watching a storm roll in, and I couldn't stop myself from feeling the full weight of the tension.

"You think it was deliberate?" I asked, my voice quieter now, the question tasting like ashes on my tongue.

He nodded, once, slowly. "I don't think it. I know it. And I did what I thought I had to do. I tried to stop it—tried to fight it with everything I had. But sometimes... you realize you're fighting something you can't fight." His voice trailed off, and for a moment, the world around us seemed to freeze.

I could feel the pulse of the fire, its warmth against my skin, and yet there was a chill creeping into my bones, a shiver that had nothing to do with the temperature. The captain was telling me things no one had a right to know. And he was letting me into a part of him that, up until now, had been off-limits. It scared me. It scared me because it made me feel something I didn't want to feel.

"Who was behind it?" I asked, but the words were almost too small for the weight of my question.

He looked at me then, really looked at me, his eyes dark and full of something I couldn't name. "You don't want to know. Believe me."

I couldn't tear my gaze away. There was something in his face, some unspeakable regret that made my heart ache in ways I didn't understand. "Try me," I said softly. "I don't scare that easily."

He chuckled, but it wasn't the kind of laugh that reached his eyes. It was hollow, like the echo of something that had long since died. "You should. You'll wish you didn't ask."

I bit my lip, trying to hold on to the last vestiges of my resolve. "Tell me, Captain. I need to know. I need to understand."

For a long moment, the fire crackled between us, the air heavy with the weight of his silence. And then, finally, he spoke.

"There were people. People who thought they could control it. Control the fires, control everything. I didn't know it then, but I was part of it. Part of something bigger than just a fire or a village. And when I tried to stop it... when I tried to warn people, I became a target. A pawn. The fires weren't just flames. They were messages. And I was the one who couldn't stop them."

My stomach twisted. My mind raced, trying to put together the pieces. "So you... you were involved?"

He nodded, his eyes darkening further. "In the worst possible way. But I didn't know what they were doing until it was too late. And by then, it was already a part of me. A scar I could never get rid of."

I swallowed hard. I didn't know how to respond. How could I? How could I possibly understand a man who had carried such a burden alone for so long? The truth was too raw, too jagged. But I couldn't look away. I wasn't sure I even wanted to. Because in that moment, as he spoke of regrets and ghosts that had haunted him for years, something inside me shifted. I wasn't just hearing his story—I was living it with him. And maybe, just maybe, I was beginning to fall for him. Despite every warning sign that flashed in my mind, I couldn't stop myself. I was falling, deeper than I could have ever imagined.

The fire between us flickered, casting long, twisted shadows that seemed to stretch toward the edges of the camp like reaching hands, desperate to pull us deeper into whatever darkness he'd just let slip into the air. I wanted to press him further, to make him finish the story, to put the pieces together like a puzzle, but something about his silence held me captive, as though the truth was a force more dangerous than any fire he had ever fought.

I leaned back, my legs sore from standing too long, but I couldn't bring myself to sit. I needed to stay on my feet, ready to move at the first sign of danger—or maybe it was just because sitting felt too intimate, too close to what was between us now. Whatever it was, I felt something shifting inside me, like an earthquake that didn't show on the surface, but made everything feel just a little bit off-balance.

"You can't just leave it at that," I said, trying to keep my voice steady, even though it trembled slightly, betraying me. "You can't drop this bombshell and then... what? Expect me to walk away like nothing happened?"

He met my gaze, his eyes dark and unreadable, as though trying to decide if he should say more, or if he should simply shut me down completely. For a second, I thought he might turn and walk away. I would have understood if he did. But instead, he stared at me in silence, a kind of battle going on behind his eyes—something between wanting to share and wanting to keep me as far away from the truth as possible.

Finally, he spoke, his voice low, almost to himself. "There's a reason I don't let anyone get too close, Sol."

I didn't flinch, even though his words landed like a slap. "And I'm supposed to just respect that, huh? Stay in my lane while you carry your burden alone?"

He let out a small, bitter laugh, the sound almost drowned by the crackle of the fire. "You think you understand? You think I want your pity? I've made peace with it. With them." His words hung heavy in the air, and the way he said them made me realize this wasn't just a single mistake. No, this was something deeper, something far darker.

"You don't know anything about peace," I retorted, my own frustration bubbling to the surface now. "You just keep running from it. That's the problem with people like you. You never face it head-on. You bury it. And it'll keep haunting you until it breaks you."

His gaze was hard, unyielding, but there was something else there—something I had never seen before. A crack. A flicker of vulnerability that disappeared just as quickly as it appeared, swallowed by his carefully crafted walls.

"I don't need your help," he said, his voice a little sharper now, the walls rising back up. "And I certainly don't need your judgment."

"You don't get to tell me how I should feel about this, Baird," I snapped, stepping closer, the space between us feeling like an electric current. "I don't know everything about you, but I know enough to see the lies you're telling. You've been running from this for years. But you can't outrun the truth. It'll find you."

I don't know what I was expecting, but when he stood up, his body stiff and tense, I wasn't ready for the tension in the air to snap like a wire. He didn't back down, didn't retreat into his usual commanding self. Instead, he stood there, his jaw clenched tight, fists at his sides as though he was holding back from saying something that might shatter us both.

"Sometimes," he began, the words slow and deliberate, "the truth isn't something you want to face. You think you know it all, but you don't. You have no idea what I've done, what I've been through. I didn't choose this life, Sol. I didn't choose any of it. But I did what I thought I had to do."

There was a rawness in his tone that I hadn't expected, and I saw it then—the weariness, the regret, the scars that ran deeper than any fire could ever burn. He wasn't just a soldier. He was a man who had been molded by the very thing he fought against, someone who had been burned by the flames he had once thought he could control.

"You didn't have to make those choices," I said, my voice quieter now, but no less insistent. "You could have walked away. You could have chosen differently."

But instead of answering, he turned his back to me, walking toward the edge of the camp, the flickering light of the fire casting long shadows behind him. I knew then that he wasn't running away from me. He was running from himself, from the ghosts that had followed him for so long. And I didn't know how to help him face them. But I couldn't just stand by and watch him drown in his own guilt either.

I took a deep breath, steeling myself for whatever came next. "Baird," I said, taking a step closer, my voice firm. "If you think I'm going to leave you alone now, you're wrong. I'm not going anywhere."

He didn't answer right away, but I saw his shoulders tense. He wasn't used to being challenged, not by anyone. But I wasn't backing down. Not this time.

"You think I'm just going to let you push me away?" I continued, my voice rising with each word. "I know you don't want me here, but I'm not going to let you do this alone. You don't get to keep carrying this weight by yourself."

There was a long pause before he spoke again, his voice so low it was almost a whisper. "I never asked you to stay. But you're already too deep, Sol. You don't understand what you're getting into."

I was too close now, too tangled in this mess to walk away. But the air between us was shifting again, and I didn't know what it meant. And just as I opened my mouth to respond, I heard a rustling sound behind me, and then the unmistakable crackle of a twig snapping in the woods. Something—someone—was out there.

I turned my head sharply, my heart skipping a beat. "Did you hear that?"

Baird's expression changed in an instant, his body going rigid as he scanned the darkness.

And that's when we both heard it—a low, guttural growl, rising from the trees just beyond the camp's edge.

Before either of us could react, the shadow in the trees moved, and I realized we weren't alone anymore.

Chapter 21: Broken Trust

The crackling sound of the fire seemed almost eager, like it was alive, stretching its limbs toward the night sky. The heat licked my skin in waves, making me feel as though the air itself was suffocating me. I should have been focused, should have been prioritizing the safety of the camp and everyone in it, but my mind kept drifting back to the shadows that had slipped under my skin, the ones I couldn't shake, no matter how hard I tried. There was a fire on the horizon—one that felt much too deliberate, too calculated. It wasn't just a coincidence, not this time. It was like the flames were beckoning us, daring us to come closer.

"Are you listening?" Evan's voice sliced through my thoughts, sharp and urgent.

I blinked, focusing on his face as he pulled me toward the nearest bucket of water. His expression was tight, eyes darting between the inferno and the camp. He didn't need to say anything more. We both knew it was too close for comfort, and we didn't have time for whatever internal drama was playing out in my mind.

My hands shook as I grabbed a bucket, the cold metal biting into my palms. The fire didn't wait for us, didn't care about our plans or fears. It raged with a life of its own, consuming the dry brush in a frenzy of reds and oranges that danced wildly in the night. The smell of smoke burned my nostrils, and I could taste the acrid sting of it at the back of my throat.

"We need to move faster," Evan muttered, his voice hoarse. His gaze never left the fire, and I could see the tightness in his jaw, the way his shoulders were drawn up in preparation for a fight—against the flames, against whatever was coming next.

But my heart wasn't in the fire anymore. It was somewhere else—somewhere between the words I'd overheard earlier, the ones that had crawled into my thoughts like a parasite, leaving me with nothing but confusion and suspicion. They said he knew more about the fires than he let on. That he had something to do with them.

And I couldn't stop thinking about it.

I didn't know when it started, this gnawing doubt, but it had grown. Every time he smiled that crooked smile, every time his hand brushed against mine in passing, I couldn't help but wonder if I was seeing the truth—or if he was hiding behind that mask of charm he wore so effortlessly. It wasn't just about the fires, either. There were whispers, too, whispers that painted him in a dangerous light, a man who could charm the world and then destroy it in the blink of an eye.

And now, with the fire dangerously close, my mind wouldn't let me forget those whispers.

"Are you sure we're not making it worse?" I asked, my voice trembling with a mixture of doubt and fear, my eyes never leaving the blaze as it crept ever closer.

Evan gave me a quick, sharp glance before dousing the flames with a well-aimed splash of water. The heat was unbearable now, and my skin felt like it was being pressed against a hot iron, the sweat trickling down my back, making my clothes stick to me. But I didn't care about that. I cared about the knot in my chest, the one that had tightened ever since the rumor had spread.

"I'm sure," he said, but his voice lacked its usual certainty. It was more strained now, like he was trying to convince both of us.

We worked in silence for what felt like hours, our bodies aching from the exertion, the weight of the fire pressing down on us, threatening to swallow us whole. The flames were unpredictable, shifting in the wind, and no matter how much water we threw at them, they seemed to multiply, faster and fiercer. Every time I thought we were getting a handle on it, another flare would shoot up, and we'd be scrambling again, hearts pounding in our chests.

Finally, when the fire seemed to retreat, just enough for us to catch our breath, we stumbled back toward the camp, covered in ash, our faces streaked with soot. The air smelled like burnt wood, and I could taste the bitterness in my mouth, but it wasn't the fire that lingered—it was the feeling in my gut, the one that wouldn't let me breathe easy.

The camp was buzzing when we returned, voices rising in alarm, hushed conversations that I couldn't quite make out. It wasn't until we reached the center of the camp that I heard the whispers clearly. They were sharper now, more pointed, filled with suspicion.

"It was him. I swear, I saw him near the woods before the fire started. He knew something was coming."

The words hit me like a punch to the stomach. They had already started—rumors, accusations. The very same ones I'd overheard before.

My heart slammed against my ribs, and for a moment, I couldn't breathe. There were no concrete answers, no clear evidence, just these swirling doubts. But then, I saw him. Evan, standing off to the side, his face drawn in that way I knew too well—guarded, distant, like he was already preparing for something worse than the fire we'd just fought.

I made my way over to him, my feet heavy, each step more reluctant than the last. When I reached him, he didn't look at me. His eyes were focused on the ground, his posture tense, as if he knew what was coming.

"I didn't start the fire," he said, his voice barely above a whisper. But the way he said it—flat, resigned—was all wrong.

I opened my mouth to respond, but nothing came out. What could I say? The doubts had already taken root, and I could feel them twisting in my chest, suffocating me. I wanted to believe him. I really did. But with every passing second, the truth seemed further out of reach.

"Then why were you out there?" I asked, my voice cracking, but I couldn't help it. The questions spilled out before I could stop them.

Evan's gaze flicked up to mine, but there was no warmth, no spark of the man I thought I knew. Only coldness, and something darker behind his eyes that I couldn't quite place.

"I don't owe you an explanation," he said, his voice hardening. "Not anymore."

And just like that, the world tilted. The fire, the rumors—they all seemed to pale in comparison to the weight of those words.

The night had settled in like a cold hand pressing against my skin, and the chill only deepened the knots in my stomach. I didn't know how long I had been standing there, staring at the space where Evan had stood just moments before. His absence weighed heavier than the fire we had just fought, heavier than the smoke that still lingered in the air. He hadn't even said goodbye. He'd just walked away, his back stiff and his steps quick, as if he was running from something he couldn't outrun.

I tried to shake off the chill creeping into my bones, but it wasn't the night air making me cold. It was the silence that had stretched between us, the space that had opened up where trust used to be. I wanted to chase him down, ask him to explain, to give me something—anything—to help me make sense of the growing distance between us. But I couldn't. Every time I thought I could, I found myself frozen, paralyzed by the weight of his words. "I don't owe you an explanation."

The thought of it made my stomach churn. The same man who had once looked at me with warmth, with hope in his eyes, had just stripped me of everything we had. I wasn't sure if it was the fire that had scorched him, or if it had been something darker, something deeper, that had been festering for far longer than I could have known.

I forced myself to walk, to move, but my feet seemed to drag with every step, as though the weight of my thoughts was pulling me down. I passed the campfires where people sat in tight-knit circles, their faces flickering in the shadows. The sound of laughter mixed with the crackling of the flames, but it was all distant, muffled, as if I were standing outside of it all. I wasn't part of it anymore. Not tonight. Not with the way things had shifted between me and Evan.

I found a spot by the edge of camp, away from the bustling chatter, and sank down onto a fallen log, wrapping my arms around my knees. My thoughts were too loud, spinning in circles, each one tangling with the last. I closed my eyes, letting the cool night air wash over me, but even that felt like a lie—like I was suffocating in the silence, in the space he had left behind.

A soft sound interrupted my thoughts—a rustle of leaves, followed by the crunch of boots on the ground. I didn't have to look to know who it was. I could feel him before I saw him, a presence that was all too familiar and all too distant now.

"I thought you might be here." Evan's voice was low, guarded, and I didn't dare turn around. I wasn't sure if I was ready to see him yet, not with the way his absence felt like a bruise on my soul.

"You were right, you know," I said, the words slipping out before I could stop them. "You don't owe me anything. I should have figured that out a long time ago." My voice cracked at the end, and I cursed myself for it, but the damage was already done.

There was a long pause, the kind that stretched on for far too long, as if he were trying to decide whether to stay or leave, whether to apologize or walk away. Finally, I heard his footsteps come closer, slow but steady. I didn't open my eyes, but I could feel the weight of his gaze, the heat of it burning through the space between us.

"I never wanted you to think that," he said quietly, his voice rough. "I didn't want to hurt you. But I don't have answers. Not right now. Not for this."

I let out a humorless laugh, shaking my head. "Not for this? Not for everything?"

There was a tremor in his voice when he spoke again, a rawness that I hadn't expected. "I don't even know where to begin. But I won't lie to you. Not about that. Not anymore."

The honesty in his voice was like a slap, but it was a wake-up call I needed, even if I wasn't ready to hear it. I turned my head slowly, just enough to catch a glimpse of him. His eyes were shadowed, distant, but there was something there—something buried deep behind that impenetrable wall he had put up between us.

"I don't even know who you are anymore, Evan," I said, the words tasting like ash in my mouth. "You keep telling me the truth, but I don't know what the truth is anymore. I don't know what's real and what's... what's just a lie I've been too blind to see."

His expression faltered, but he didn't look away. Instead, he stepped closer, closing the distance between us, but not enough to touch. There was a hesitation in his movements, a wariness that only added to the tension between us.

"You're not the only one who's confused," he said quietly. "I'm not the same person I was when you first met me. And I don't know how to fix that. I don't know how to make you understand... or forgive me."

I swallowed hard, trying to fight the wave of emotion threatening to overtake me. "Then maybe we shouldn't try to fix anything. Maybe we're better off leaving it broken." I didn't mean it. Not really. But it was easier to say than face whatever was left between us.

A flicker of pain crossed his face, but it disappeared so quickly that I almost doubted I'd seen it at all. He looked at me, his eyes flickering with something indecipherable before he exhaled, the sound heavy in the still night air.

"I don't want to let you go," he whispered, more to himself than to me.

I closed my eyes, a single tear slipping free despite my best efforts to hold it back. "Then why are you pushing me away?"

"I'm not pushing you away. I'm trying to protect you."

I laughed, but it was bitter, the sound jagged as it left my mouth. "Protect me? From what? From you?"

"Yes," he said, his voice quiet but firm. "From me."

For a moment, the world held its breath, and in the silence that followed, I realized there was nothing left to say. The fire between us had burned too hot, too quickly, and all that was left was the smoldering wreckage.

The night felt thicker now, the air pressing down on me like a weight I couldn't shake, no matter how hard I tried to breathe through it. Evan's words were still hanging in the air, the finality of them like a stone lodged in my chest. "From me." It was the way he'd said it, his voice so quiet yet so resolute, that made everything inside of me freeze. As if the only way to protect me was to turn away, to let go before I could get any closer.

I wanted to shout. To demand he explain himself, but the words tangled in my throat. I wasn't even sure what I was angry about. Maybe it was the fact that I couldn't untangle the mess he had made of my emotions. Or maybe it was the way I had let myself be swept into his world without seeing the dangers lurking beneath the surface.

I stayed quiet, too. My chest tight with the things I didn't want to say, the things I couldn't. I was angry at him, but I was angrier at myself for feeling this way. For caring so much when everything felt so fragile, so broken.

The fire had consumed more of my thoughts than I wanted to admit, but it wasn't the only thing threatening to burn me alive. It was what lay beneath it—the questions, the doubt—that gnawed at me relentlessly. The fires weren't just natural occurrences. Someone was behind them. And if I was honest, I couldn't shake the feeling that Evan knew more than he was letting on.

"I need to understand," I said finally, the words forced and heavy as they left my lips. "I need to know what's going on. Not just with the fires... with you."

Evan's expression darkened. He turned his head slightly, his jaw tightening. The distance between us stretched, but not just physically. It was something in the air, a tension that had grown too thick to ignore.

"I can't give you answers, not right now." His voice was low, almost weary. "And you don't need to be involved in this. It's not your fight."

My laugh was bitter, the sound more to myself than to him. "Not my fight? Evan, it's already my fight. It's all of our fight."

He didn't argue, didn't even look at me. Instead, he rubbed his face with both hands, as if trying to scrub away the remnants of the truth he couldn't—or wouldn't—say. "I never meant for you to get pulled into it. You were supposed to stay out of it. You were supposed to be safe."

The words hit me like a slap. "Safe?" I scoffed, shaking my head. "From what? From you? You think I'm better off not knowing the truth?"

"No," he said sharply. "I think you're better off not being a part of this mess."

I felt my breath catch in my throat, something icy spreading through my veins. I hadn't realized how much I had needed to hear the truth from him until now. Even if it broke me, even if it was the last thing I wanted to hear. "So that's it? You're just going to walk away and pretend like nothing happened?"

His eyes, when they met mine, were stormy, guarded. "I don't have a choice anymore."

The crack in his voice wasn't lost on me, but it wasn't enough to make me step back, either. I felt my frustration surge, sharp and cutting. "You always have a choice, Evan. You just don't want to make it."

He flinched at that, but there was something else in his eyes now, something raw. Something that made my stomach flip. He opened his mouth to say something, but then closed it again, as if the words had gotten stuck somewhere deep inside him.

"I can't do this right now," he said, voice barely audible.

"Then when, Evan?" I shot back. "When will you be ready to do it? When it's too late?"

But he didn't respond. Instead, he turned and walked away, his back stiff, his pace quickening as he left me standing there, the weight of his silence suffocating me.

I stood there for a long time, my hands clenched into fists at my sides, my heart pounding in my chest. The camp was quiet now, the sounds of the fire and the crackling of the dying embers filling the void between us. I wanted to go after him, wanted to drag the truth out of him, but I didn't know if I could. Not when the distance between us felt like a chasm I couldn't cross.

What was I supposed to do now? Trust him? Doubt him? The fire wasn't the only thing consuming me. It was everything he had said and everything he had left unsaid. I didn't know where I stood anymore.

My thoughts were spinning, too many questions and no answers, when the sharp sound of footsteps interrupted my spiraling thoughts. I looked up quickly, my heart skipping a beat, but it wasn't Evan.

It was Leo.

He had a hard look in his eyes, something unfamiliar and calculating. I hadn't seen him since before the fire started, and the way he was walking toward me now sent an icy chill down my spine.

"Is everything okay?" he asked, his voice careful, almost too careful, as if he were measuring every word.

I didn't answer immediately, just stared at him, trying to decipher the look on his face. He was too calm. And there was something in the way he was holding himself, a tension in his shoulders that hadn't been there before.

"I'm fine," I said, my voice sharp. It wasn't entirely true, but it was all I could give. "Why?"

Leo didn't respond right away. He just looked at me for a long moment, his eyes narrowed, calculating. Then he spoke, his words slow and deliberate. "I think you should know something. About Evan."

My stomach dropped, and my throat went dry. It was the last thing I wanted to hear, but something in Leo's expression made it impossible to look away.

"What about him?" I asked, though I wasn't sure I was ready for the answer.

Leo took a step closer, his voice dropping to a whisper. "The fire wasn't an accident. And Evan... he's hiding something. Something big."

My heart skipped a beat, and for the second time that night, the ground felt like it was slipping out from under me.

"Don't," I started, my voice thick with the weight of fear, "What are you talking about?"

Leo looked around, checking if anyone was nearby, then stepped closer, his words barely audible, "You're not the only one wondering if you ever really knew him."

I froze, every nerve on edge, as my mind raced. What had I missed? What was Leo trying to tell me? But before I could push him for more, I heard something—footsteps approaching from behind, a voice cutting through the tension.

"Is everything alright here?"

It was Evan's voice, smooth and calm, but there was something in the way it cut through the silence that made every muscle in my body tighten.

And that's when I realized: Whatever was happening—whatever I had started to understand about Evan—was only the tip of the iceberg.

Chapter 22: Into the Smoke

The air is thick with the scent of damp earth and pine, the kind of smell that clings to your clothes and refuses to be shaken off, no matter how many times you bathe. The forest is quiet tonight, almost unnaturally so, as if it's holding its breath. The moon, a thin sliver in the sky, doesn't offer much light, but enough to catch the shimmer of the river's surface, broken only by the occasional ripple from an unseen fish or the faintest current. I should have felt safe here, in this remote place where no one would find us. But instead, I felt exposed, as though every crack in the earth and every whisper of the wind was part of some grand design to expose the uncertainty between us.

I should have been used to the silence by now. The way it wrapped itself around us, a tangible thing. But tonight, it felt different—heavier, almost suffocating. My steps on the forest floor, soft as they were, felt too loud, like I was trying to break the stillness with every footfall. As I drew closer to the river's edge, I saw him. His broad shoulders were hunched slightly, the fabric of his coat pulled tight against the cold air, his eyes fixed on the water as though he was searching for answers in its depths.

I paused, my heart doing that strange little flip it always did when I saw him, that little spark of something I couldn't quite name. The man was a mystery to me, layers upon layers that I couldn't quite peel back, no matter how hard I tried. His face—chiseled, angular—always held an expression that was difficult to read. Was it because he was so guarded, or because I was too afraid to look closely enough to see the truth? I never knew. But tonight, something was different. His posture, his stillness—it spoke of something unspoken, a grief that weighed heavier than the silence between us. He wasn't the stoic figure he always portrayed. No, tonight, he was someone else. Vulnerable, lost, even.

My feet moved on their own then, as if they had a mind separate from mine, guiding me toward him, toward the stillness we could never quite escape. He didn't turn when I approached, but the space between us was charged with the tension of unsaid things, things we both knew but hadn't yet acknowledged. When I was close enough, I hesitated, unsure of the next step. My mouth went dry, and I had to fight the urge to say something—anything. To break the silence.

Instead, I stood there, watching him as he stood there, alone in his thoughts. The moonlight glinted off the river, casting a soft glow around him, making him seem almost ethereal. It felt like the world had come to a standstill, the river frozen in its slow dance, the forest holding its breath. He exhaled deeply, his chest rising and falling under the weight of it all. His jaw was set tight, and for a moment, I wondered if he even knew I was there.

I wasn't sure what to say. There were a thousand words I could have spoken, a hundred things I could have asked. But none of them seemed right. The questions burned in my throat, begging for release, but I swallowed them down. What was the point? We weren't ready for those answers yet.

Finally, he broke the silence. His voice, low and rough, made the air around me feel heavier, as if it too were straining to hold his words.

"You've been avoiding me."

It wasn't an accusation. It wasn't a plea. It was a simple fact, stated as if it were something so obvious he barely needed to say it out loud. But the weight of it hit me like a physical blow. I swallowed, the taste of regret bitter in my mouth. I had been avoiding him. The reasons were tangled up inside of me, impossible to sort out.

I could feel the space between us widening, stretching out in ways I didn't know how to fill. I could sense his gaze on me now, sharp, waiting for something. The silence settled around us once again, but this time, it was different. It wasn't the same heavy, suffocating silence. It felt like a pause. A breath before something changed.

I took a small step forward. Just one. It wasn't enough to close the gap entirely, but it was a start. I could feel the thud of my heart in my chest, the nerves rising in my throat like a knot that wouldn't untangle. But there was something about this moment, something about the way he was standing there, staring at the river, waiting for me, that made me want to try.

"You're right," I said, my voice softer than I meant it to be, but it was the truth. I had been avoiding him. But how could I not? I couldn't explain it—what we were, what we weren't—but I could feel it in the way he looked at me. The way his presence filled the space between us. There was too much there, too much I didn't understand.

I watched as his expression softened, his hand twitching at his side as though he wanted to reach for something but wasn't sure what. Finally, he let out a breath, low and slow, and for the first time in what felt like forever, his gaze lifted from the river to meet mine. There was no anger there, no judgment, just a quiet understanding.

And then, before I could think better of it, I reached for him, my fingers brushing his hand, tentative at first. His skin was warm, the touch electric, and when he didn't pull away, when he didn't flinch, I felt something shift. Something small, but significant. He turned his hand so that his fingers were curled around mine, a soft, simple gesture that spoke volumes.

In that instant, the world felt just a little less uncertain. Just a little more bearable. It wasn't everything, but it was something. And that, somehow, was enough.

His hand is warmer than I expect, like a gentle flame, yet there's a tension beneath the touch, an unspoken wariness that stirs something deep within me. I tell myself I shouldn't read too much into it, but it's hard not to. His fingers, so steady, so sure, don't tremble, don't shift away. He just holds on, as though he knows this moment matters more than either of us are willing to admit.

The river's murmurs have changed. The rhythm of the water seems to slow, as though even the current is watching us, curious about what we might do next. The moon's reflection flickers on the surface, shifting like it's caught between worlds, uncertain of where it belongs. I glance back at him, his profile now familiar, but still an enigma. There's a sharpness to the line of his jaw, like the harsh angles of a cliffside, and a dark smudge of something unspoken in his eyes. His breath comes in shallow intervals, controlled, though I can hear the soft rasp of it, betraying him in the silence.

"What's wrong with you?" I ask before I can stop myself. The words tumble out, almost accusing, but I don't mean them that way. I just can't shake the feeling that there's something he's not telling me. It sits between us, thick as the mist rising from the river.

He doesn't flinch, doesn't move, but I feel the slight shift in the air, like he's bracing for something. "I don't know," he answers finally, and his voice is quieter than I expect, rough around the edges. "Maybe I don't know what's wrong with me, either."

I stare at him, the vulnerability in his words pricking at something in my chest. For all his stoic demeanor, for all the walls he builds around himself, there are moments like this, moments when the cracks in his armor appear, and I wonder how long they've been there—how long he's been hiding behind them.

"Could've fooled me," I mutter, more to myself than to him, and there's a bitterness in my own tone that surprises me. Why does it bother me so much?

He shifts slightly, his thumb tracing the back of my hand, grounding me, and for a moment, I forget what I was going to say.

"You think I'm fooling you?" he asks, his voice softer now, almost too gentle.

I turn to face him fully, searching his eyes. There's something about the way he looks at me now that makes my stomach tighten, like a trap closing in slowly, surely. "I think I'm fooling myself," I reply honestly, the words slipping out before I can think them through. I laugh, a short, dry sound that doesn't sound like me. "I'm not exactly sure what's happening here, but it's definitely not simple."

He doesn't respond right away, and I wonder if I've pushed him too far, too fast. But then he does something that surprises me even more than his quiet answer. He laughs. Not loud, not boisterous, but a real laugh, the kind that slips out when you can't quite hold it in anymore. It's soft, but there's a rawness to it that makes my heart ache in ways I can't explain.

"You've got that right," he says, his lips curling into a smile that's fleeting but genuine. "Nothing about this is simple. But that's probably what makes it... interesting." He doesn't look at me as he says this, his gaze drifting back to the water, but there's a flicker in his eyes, a challenge I can't quite place.

I try to keep my voice steady, but I know it trembles a little when I speak. "Interesting isn't always a good thing."

He turns to face me, his expression softening, and for a moment, I wonder if he's going to say something that will change everything. But instead, he leans a little closer, the movement slow, deliberate, and then his breath is warm on my cheek, his hand still holding mine.

"You're right," he murmurs. "Interesting isn't always good. But it doesn't have to be bad, either."

The air between us thickens again, charged with something unspoken. I could lean in, let the distance collapse, let the tension in my chest dissolve into something else entirely. But the fear keeps me still, the same fear that's kept me locked away for so long. What if I'm wrong about him? What if all this is just another game, another way to distract myself from something I can't quite name?

I pull my hand back slightly, and the space between us feels much larger now, much emptier. "I don't know what you want from me," I say, trying to keep my voice steady, but failing miserably.

His eyes flicker, almost imperceptibly, but it's enough to make my breath catch in my throat. "I want nothing from you," he says, his voice low, even. "I never have. But that doesn't mean this"—he gestures between us with his free hand—"isn't real."

The words hang in the air like a promise and a threat, both at once. My mind spins, trying to make sense of them, but I can't. It's as if the ground beneath me has shifted without warning, and I'm standing on something I don't understand.

Real. What does that even mean?

The question lingers in my mind, sharp and demanding. But when I look at him again, really look at him, I see something else. Something I wasn't expecting. Something that makes my heart skip a beat.

It's not an answer, not a clear one. But it's something. Something that feels like the beginning of something else. The beginning of whatever this is.

There's a new wariness in the air, an unfamiliar pulse of tension that we both know too well but have never fully acknowledged. It hums between us like a string pulled taut, a breath held too long. His hand, still warm in mine, is steady, yet I can feel the slight tremor in his fingertips as though he's waiting for something—anything—to disrupt the moment. And as much as I want to believe this is some kind of breakthrough, a new chapter where the silence between us could be replaced with understanding, I can't help but wonder if we're both too damaged to ever truly bridge the gap.

The river in front of us has lost its sparkle under the dim light of the moon. The surface is a flat, glassy mirror, reflecting only the shadows of the trees, the darkness swallowing everything else. It's eerie, like the stillness before a storm, and I find myself scanning the water, as though looking for something to focus on to avoid meeting his gaze. But when I do look up, there's a sharpness to his eyes, like he's been reading my every thought and doesn't particularly care to see the truth reflected in mine.

"Don't," he says, his voice low, tight. There's a bitterness there, just under the surface. I don't ask him what he means. I already know. He's asking me not to pull away, not to shut him out. But can I really stay here, feet planted firmly in the present, when everything inside me is screaming to retreat?

"I'm not..." My voice falters, and I swallow, trying to steady the tremor in my chest. "I'm not pulling away."

His jaw tightens, the muscle flicking beneath his skin. "No. But you are. You always do." His words are like a lash, but they're not unfair. He's right. I've been slipping away ever since the first time I felt the pull of this—whatever this is between us—and every time it's gotten too real, too much, I've stepped back. One small retreat after another, like walking away from a fire that's too hot to touch.

I step back now, unconsciously, my fingers loosening from his as if on cue. The moment stretches between us, that single breath hanging in the air like the sharp edge of a blade. He doesn't try to stop me, doesn't reach for me again. He simply watches, his eyes dark and unreadable, as though the truth he's been holding back is still something he's not willing to let me see.

I wish I had the strength to stand my ground. But I don't. Not yet. Maybe not ever.

"I don't know how to do this," I admit, the words tumbling out before I can stop them. They feel raw, too exposed. But it's the truth. And maybe for once, the truth is all I have. "I don't know how to trust anyone. Not after everything."

His lips press together, a thin line. He doesn't speak immediately, and for a long, drawn-out moment, I wonder if I've said too much. But when he finally does speak, it's quieter, softer—almost too gentle.

"You're not the only one with scars," he says, and I catch the edge of something in his voice, something that makes me feel like he's peeled back a layer, just for a second, to let me see the rawness beneath. But then it's gone, swallowed back down. "But maybe we both need to stop pretending we can heal alone."

I want to argue, want to tell him I've been alone for so long, I wouldn't know how to start healing with anyone else. But the words die on my tongue. Because deep down, I know that's the lie I've been telling myself. Maybe it's not about healing at all. Maybe it's just about not being alone anymore. And maybe, just maybe, I'm afraid that letting him in will mean losing myself.

I shake my head, the words too tangled in my mind to form into anything that makes sense. But I can feel the silence between us thickening again, suffocating both of us, and I know we're standing on the edge of something we can't ignore.

The tension is unbearable now, the need to say something—to do something—spilling out of me in fits and starts. So I move closer again, against every instinct that tells me not to. Maybe it's the pull of his presence, maybe it's the weariness that has settled into my bones like a deep ache, but I take a step forward.

I wish I could say it's intentional, but it isn't. I don't know what I want from him, from this moment. I just know I need to bridge the gap. I need to prove to myself that I'm not as afraid as I've always been.

But then, just as I'm within arm's reach, he steps back, his expression shifting to something unreadable, almost calculating.

His hand falls to his side, and I feel the distance between us, once again, stretching farther than I can bear.

"Don't get any closer," he says, his voice low and rough, and there's a finality to it.

I freeze, confused, hurt. "Why?" I ask, the word sharp, though I don't mean it to be.

"Because you won't like what happens next."

The words hit me like a punch to the gut, and for a moment, I stand there, blinking, trying to make sense of what he's just said. The pull toward him that I've been fighting for so long seems to dissipate in an instant, replaced by a flicker of fear. The kind of fear that settles low in your stomach, the kind that makes your spine go rigid and your hands clammy.

"What do you mean?" I ask, and my voice comes out quieter than I intend.

He doesn't answer immediately, but the look in his eyes tells me everything I need to know.

Something is coming. And I'm not sure either of us is ready for it.

Chapter 23: Ashes of the Past

The sun hung low, casting long shadows over the small town. It had been a restless night, the kind where sleep doesn't come easily, where the mind churns through a thousand unanswered questions, turning each one over, seeking the truth beneath the surface. I had spent the hours after midnight pacing in my apartment, staring at the glowing neon of my phone as if it could somehow provide the clarity I desperately needed. The sound of the waves crashing against the rocky shore outside was a constant hum, but it couldn't drown out the nagging feeling in my chest—the sense that I was standing on the edge of something, but unsure whether I was about to fall or fly.

I grabbed my coffee cup, the chipped ceramic worn smooth from years of use, and took a long sip. The bitter heat burned my throat, and I let out a breath. The world outside was still waking up, the streets quiet but for the occasional car or early riser. It was the kind of morning where everything felt like it was holding its breath. But for me, the moment I had been waiting for had arrived: the lead I'd gotten last night.

His name was Elias Davenport, and I'd been hearing whispers about him for months. Most people knew him as a quiet, brooding figure—someone who had a way of fading into the background, unnoticed. But there was something about him that didn't quite fit the usual small-town mold. I'd heard stories of his past, of the way he carried himself with a kind of defiance, like he was running from something, or maybe running toward it.

There were rumors that the fires, the ones that had been tearing through the town for weeks now, were more than just random acts of destruction. People were starting to talk, and the threads were beginning to pull together in a way that made sense—at least, a dark, twisted kind of sense. Elias had been the one who was always just a little too close to the action, his presence like a shadow, lurking in the background whenever the flames reared their ugly heads. I had tried to ignore it, to chalk it up to coincidence, but today, the pieces of the puzzle were beginning to snap into place.

I pushed myself out the door, the fresh morning air hitting me like a wave. The smell of saltwater clung to the wind, and I could taste it on my tongue as I made my way down the narrow street. The world felt different today—sharper, as if everything had been placed under a microscope. I wasn't sure whether that was because I was about to uncover the truth or because I was simply too tired to keep pretending I didn't already know it.

Elias's cabin was on the far edge of town, perched just outside the reach of the busy streets, where the trees grew thick and the fog hung low like a shroud. His place was as mysterious as the man himself—rustic, weather-beaten, and tucked away as though he had gone to great lengths to keep the world from seeing inside. As I approached the cabin, the air seemed to thicken, the silence pressing in on me. I could almost hear his voice in my head, that deep, gravelly tone, warning me not to go any further.

But I wasn't here to heed warnings. I was here for answers.

The door creaked open as I knocked, and I stepped inside without waiting for an invitation. Elias was sitting at his kitchen table, his broad shoulders hunched over a stack of papers. His eyes, usually cold and guarded, flicked up to meet mine with a flash of something—a mix of surprise, annoyance, maybe even a bit of relief. I couldn't quite tell. His jaw tightened as he pushed a few stray strands of hair behind his ear, his lips curling into something that was close enough to a smile to make me question whether I was imagining things.

"I wasn't expecting company," he said, his voice low, as though the very idea of having someone in his space disturbed the fragile peace he'd managed to create here.

"Guess I don't care about expectations," I replied, setting my bag down on the counter. "I need answers."

Elias didn't flinch, though I could see the muscles in his neck tense. He didn't like being challenged—not by me, not by anyone. But there was something different in the way he carried himself today. He was on edge, like a man who had been waiting for the inevitable to catch up with him. The room was thick with an unspoken tension, and I felt it in the pit of my stomach. Something was coming, something neither of us could avoid.

"I know you're involved in these fires," I said, cutting straight to the heart of the matter. His eyes locked onto mine, and for a moment, there was no sound but the rhythmic tick of a clock on the wall. His expression didn't change, but there was a flicker in his gaze—a shift, almost imperceptible, but it was enough to tell me that I had struck a nerve.

"You don't know anything," Elias said, his voice strained.

"I know more than you think," I countered. "I know about the accident, the one from years ago. The one that's been eating you up inside."

The air between us seemed to freeze, and for the first time, I saw the mask slip. His hand trembled slightly as he reached for his coffee mug, and the crack in his stoic exterior became unmistakable. He wasn't just guilty—he was broken. The man who had spent years hiding from the past was now trapped by it, and I could feel the weight of his history pressing down on both of us.

He didn't speak for a long moment. And when he did, his voice was barely above a whisper, carrying the weight of things he had kept buried for far too long.

"You have no idea what it's like to live with that kind of guilt," he muttered, his words so raw, they cut through me. "You think you know someone because of the choices they make, but you don't. Not really. You never see the things they've lost, the ghosts they carry."

It wasn't just guilt, though. It was a desperate need for redemption, one that had driven him to the edge—and perhaps beyond it. As the truth settled over me, I realized that Elias hadn't set those fires to destroy the town. He'd set them to burn away the past. And as much as it pained me to see him like this, a part of me couldn't help but pity him.

The question now was: how far would he go to bury the truth before it consumed him completely?

The silence between us stretched, and though the wind outside was fierce, tearing at the branches of the trees with a ferocity that matched the tension in the room, neither of us moved. Elias had retreated into himself, his hands wrapped tightly around the edges of his mug, as though it could anchor him to something solid in this storm of his past. His gaze was distant, unfocused, like a man caught between two worlds. I waited, unwilling to let him slink back into the shadows, but uncertain of how to coax him out. I had the distinct feeling that if I pushed too hard, I might shatter whatever fragile grip he had on his resolve.

"You think you're the only one who's lost something?" I said, trying to keep the bitterness from my voice. "You think you're the only one who's been buried by the weight of regret? Let me tell you something, Elias—you're not alone in that."

His eyes finally met mine, raw with a fury that wasn't directed at me, but at the cruel hand life had dealt him. "You don't get it," he said, his voice low, dangerous in its quietness. "You don't know what it's like to watch someone burn and know you could've stopped it."

I flinched, the words slicing through the air with a precision that left a mark. The pain in his voice wasn't an act. This wasn't some tortured hero complex. This was a man who had lived through something unspeakable and had chosen, for reasons I still didn't fully understand, to bear it alone. The fires weren't just flames to him. They were a manifestation of the guilt he had been running from for years, a way of burning down the ghosts that haunted him.

I wanted to ask him about it. I wanted to demand the details—the incident, the fire, the one that had started this whole mess—but I knew that pushing him too hard would do more harm than good. He wasn't ready to talk. Maybe he never would be. But that didn't mean I couldn't offer him something, some small crack in his defenses.

"You don't have to carry it by yourself, you know," I said, my voice softer now, like I was handling something fragile. "It doesn't have to be this way."

He looked at me, and for the briefest moment, I thought I saw something in his eyes—something that was almost hope. But it vanished just as quickly, smothered by the walls he had erected around himself. He shook his head, a bitter laugh escaping his lips. "You don't get it," he repeated, as though the words could shield him from the truth.

I wasn't sure what made me do it—whether it was the exhaustion, or the quiet ache that had settled in my chest after everything we'd uncovered—but I reached for the chair across from him and sat down. "Tell me about it," I said, my voice quiet, but firm. "Tell me about the fire, Elias. Maybe if you just talk about it, it won't hurt so much."

His eyes narrowed, the wariness creeping back in. He was testing me now, watching, waiting for me to flinch. I didn't. I wouldn't. I wasn't leaving until I had answers, no matter how difficult they were to hear.

He sighed, a long, heavy exhale like he was carrying the weight of the world on his shoulders. "It's not that simple," he muttered, his voice thick with the words he didn't want to say. "Some things can't be undone."

"Some things can't," I agreed. "But others, well, they can. But only if you let them."

He stared at me, and for a moment, I thought he might say something—anything—but then he turned his gaze away. The silence stretched again, but this time, I refused to let it consume us. I was here, and I was staying, no matter how hard he tried to push me away.

When he spoke again, it was with a strange calmness, like he had resigned himself to the fact that I wouldn't leave until I had the whole story. "There was a girl," he began, his voice rough, like he hadn't used it in years. "We were... close. Too close. And one night, we got caught in a fire. It wasn't supposed to happen. I tried to save her. I swear to God, I did. But..." His voice faltered, and I saw something in his eyes—a crack, like a dam breaking under pressure. "She didn't make it. I... I couldn't get her out in time."

The words hung in the air between us, heavy and suffocating, as though they had weight enough to crush both of us under their burden. His face twisted, the memory of that night clearly still etched in his features. "I could've done more," he said, his voice barely a whisper. "But I didn't. And now it's too late."

There was nothing I could say to ease that pain, nothing that could take away the guilt he was drowning in. But I wasn't here to fix him. I was here to understand. And maybe, just maybe, to show him that it didn't have to end this way.

"You're not to blame for the fire," I said, my voice steady despite the rush of emotions inside me. "People die. Sometimes, it's no one's fault. But you can't keep punishing yourself for something that wasn't in your control."

He looked at me then, really looked at me, and I saw the conflict warring in his eyes. He was torn—torn between the man he thought he should be and the man I was offering him the chance to become. A man who could finally let go of the past, of the ghosts that had kept him chained.

"How do you let it go?" he asked, his voice raw, filled with a pain so deep it made my chest ache for him.

I didn't have an answer. Not the kind that could fix him, at least. But maybe, just maybe, the first step was letting him see that he wasn't alone in his suffering. That maybe, together, we could untangle the mess of guilt, regret, and rage that had trapped him here for so long.

And I wasn't sure where this journey would take us—if we were even headed in the right direction—but I knew one thing for sure: I wasn't backing down. Not now, not ever. Because whatever this was, this connection between us, it was the only thing standing between Elias and the darkness he was so desperately trying to outrun.

The room was so still that I could hear the soft hum of the refrigerator in the corner, an almost soothing sound in the midst of the tension that crackled between us. Elias was staring out the window now, his arms folded across his chest, his back rigid. He looked like a man at war with himself, and in some ways, he was. The battles he fought weren't visible to the outside world, but I knew they were there, lurking beneath the surface, just waiting for the right moment to break free. The question was, how long could he keep them contained?

"You don't have to carry this alone," I said again, my voice steady but quiet. "You don't have to keep punishing yourself for something that wasn't your fault."

He didn't respond at first, his gaze locked on the dense trees outside, as though he could will the past to stay buried there, just out of reach. I could almost hear him thinking, weighing the cost of what I was asking. To open up, to let go of that burden—it was a hell of a thing to ask of someone, especially someone like Elias, who had spent years building walls around himself. But the fire, the guilt, it had burned him from the inside out. It wasn't going to stop until he let it out.

"I didn't deserve to live," he muttered finally, his voice barely above a whisper. "Not after what happened. Not after I... didn't save her."

I felt a pang in my chest. His words hit me like a fist, but I didn't flinch. I knew better than to react to his self-inflicted wounds. His guilt wasn't something I could fix, but it was something I could listen to. And sometimes, listening was the first step toward healing.

"Elias, I know you're carrying more than anyone should have to bear," I said, my voice soft, but resolute. "But you don't get to decide who deserves to live or die. That's not your choice to make."

He finally turned to face me, his expression hard, the lines of his face etched with years of struggle. "You don't get it," he said, his voice rough with something more than anger. "You don't know what it's like to watch someone burn and know you could've stopped it."

I stood up then, walking across the room until I was standing in front of him. "You're wrong," I said, meeting his gaze head-on. "I do get it. I've seen the way people can destroy themselves over one mistake, one moment they can never take back. But it doesn't have to be the end, Elias. You're still here. You still have a chance to make things right."

He stared at me, and for a long moment, I wasn't sure if he would break down or push me away. But in the end, he did neither. Instead, he just let out a harsh breath, like a man resigned to his fate.

"I don't know how to make it right," he admitted, his voice a little less certain now. "I don't know if I even deserve to."

"You're wrong about that," I said, shaking my head. "Everyone deserves a chance to make amends. Even you."

There was a beat of silence. I could see the walls in his eyes starting to crumble, just a little, and I wondered if I was getting through to him. I had to believe that I was. I wasn't sure how much longer I could keep this up if I didn't.

But before he could say anything else, there was a sharp knock on the door. It was loud, insistent—too loud, too late in the evening to be casual. My heart skipped a beat, and I turned to Elias, who was already moving toward the door. I don't know what made me step back from him in that moment, but I did. There was something about his movements, his tense posture, that made me feel like I was suddenly intruding on something far darker than I'd realized.

Elias hesitated just a moment before pulling open the door, revealing a figure standing on the threshold.

The man was tall, dressed in a dark jacket, his face hidden beneath the brim of a baseball cap. His eyes, though, were sharp—sharp enough to send a shiver down my spine as they flicked from Elias to me. His gaze lingered a moment too long on my face, like he was weighing something—danger, perhaps, or a warning. Either way, it didn't sit right with me.

"Elias," the man said, his voice low but commanding, "we need to talk."

There was a cold edge to his tone, one that made my heart race, even as Elias stiffened beside me. I could see the way his jaw clenched, the way his fists tightened at his sides. Whoever this was, he wasn't someone Elias wanted to deal with. That much was clear.

"I told you," Elias began, his voice strained, like he was trying to keep his composure in the face of something far more volatile than I had expected. "I'm not interested. Not anymore."

The man didn't flinch at Elias's words, but he did step closer, the faintest smirk playing at the edges of his lips. "You think you can just walk away from this?" he said, his voice almost a growl. "You're in deeper than you realize, Elias. You've been hiding long enough. It's time to pay up."

The atmosphere in the room shifted, the tension now a palpable thing, thickening the air. I couldn't tell what was happening here, but I knew it wasn't good. Elias's past—his guilt, his secrets—they were coming back to him in ways neither of us were prepared for.

"You don't want to do this," Elias said, his voice quieter now, more controlled. But I could hear the faint tremor in it, and I knew he wasn't as calm as he was pretending to be.

The man's smirk only deepened. "Too late for that."

Before I could react, the man took a step forward, pushing past Elias into the room. The air was suddenly too thin, too suffocating, and I knew without a doubt that whatever was about to unfold in this small, dimly lit cabin, we weren't going to come out of it unscathed.

Then, as the man's gaze flicked to me, I saw something shift in his expression—a flash of recognition, followed by a dangerous smile.

"Well, well," he said, his tone cold and calculating. "Looks like we have a guest. This just got interesting."

Chapter 24: Blazing Confrontation

The air in the captain's office was thick with the scent of smoke and stale coffee, the kind of place where secrets festered and the walls whispered of old betrayals. The captain's desk, cluttered with half-empty mugs and scattered papers, stood like a fortress between us and him, a symbol of power, control, and something darker I couldn't quite place.

His eyes locked on mine as we entered, cold and calculating. There was no warmth, no hint of recognition in his gaze, only the stark, unblinking stare of a man used to command. I could feel the pulse of tension that crackled between us, humming in the space like a live wire. Every step we took felt too loud, too heavy, as if the world was holding its breath, waiting for something to shatter.

"You've come to accuse me," he said, his voice low, steady, each word deliberate. "But you have nothing."

I clenched the folder in my hand, the one that had cost us weeks of digging and piecing together. The evidence was irrefutable, but I could see it in his face—the confidence, the knowing smirk that danced at the edges of his lips. He wasn't afraid. He wasn't worried. He was playing a game, and I was a mere pawn.

"We have everything we need," I shot back, trying to steady the tremor in my voice. "The documents, the messages, the testimonies. You can't deny it."

For a moment, his gaze flickered, just a fraction of a second, but I caught it—an unspoken admission, a crack in his armor. But then it was gone, replaced by that same cold composure that made my stomach churn.

"You're delusional," he said, leaning back in his chair, steepling his fingers in front of his face like some twisted king surveying his kingdom. "I suggest you leave this office. Before things get... unpleasant."

There was a subtle warning in his voice, the kind that made the hairs on the back of my neck stand up. It wasn't just a threat. It was a promise. And for a moment, I wondered if this was it—the point where we had gone too far.

But beside me, I could feel him, his presence solid and unyielding. His hand brushed mine, just the faintest touch, a silent reminder that we were in this together. The cool, steady weight of his hand against mine brought a rush of warmth, grounding me in the midst of the storm that was brewing. I glanced at him, just for a moment, and saw the fire in his eyes—the same fire that had gotten us into this mess in the first place. But it wasn't just anger. There was something deeper, more primal. A need for justice that matched my own.

"We're not going anywhere," he said, his voice cutting through the captain's condescension like a knife through silk. "You can't intimidate us. Not anymore."

The captain's lips curled into a tight smile, but there was no humor in it. He leaned forward, the chair creaking under his weight, his eyes narrowing as he studied us. "You think you're the first to challenge me?" he asked, his tone dripping with menace. "You're nothing. You have no idea who you're dealing with."

I felt a chill creep up my spine. His words were a warning, yes, but it wasn't just the threat of what he could do to us that made my pulse quicken. It was the certainty in his voice, the confidence that came with a man who had made a habit of crushing those who dared stand in his way.

I swallowed, but the lump in my throat wouldn't budge. The files in my hand suddenly felt heavy, as if they were going to crumble under the weight of the moment.

"You're wrong," I said, my voice barely above a whisper. But the words were there, and I knew they were true. "We're not afraid of you."

The captain's eyes flicked to the door for just a second, and I could almost hear the wheels turning in his head. He was weighing his options, calculating how far he could push, how much he could threaten before we'd break. I could see it all—his mind working in the background, like a predator sizing up its prey.

"You should be," he said, his voice now icy cold, all pretense of civility gone. "I've ruined people for less. You're already in too deep, and you can't walk away now. You're tangled in something far beyond your understanding."

I felt the air grow thicker, pressing in around me, suffocating, as his words sank into my bones. But then I heard it—the faintest shift, the creak of a chair. His hand on mine, warm and steady, squeezing just enough to remind me that I wasn't alone. That I wasn't facing this monster by myself.

"We'll take our chances," he said, his voice firm, his eyes never leaving the captain's.

The captain's lips tightened, and for a moment, I thought he might actually do something—his fingers twitched, the knuckles white with tension. But then, just as quickly as it had appeared, the anger melted away, replaced by that cold, calculating demeanor.

"Leave," he said, his voice as smooth as glass, but sharp enough to cut. "Now."

The door slammed behind us as we stepped into the hallway, the silence of the office suddenly deafening. I felt the weight of what we'd just done settle in. We had made an enemy today, and not just any enemy—one who would not back down easily. But there was something in the way he had looked at us, in the way his eyes had flashed with barely contained rage, that told me we had touched something important. Something dangerous.

As we walked down the hall, I couldn't help but glance at him again. His jaw was clenched, his eyes dark with the promise of whatever came next. He was unwavering, his resolve as solid as stone, but beneath that was a flicker of something—something that made my heart race. We had crossed a line, and there was no going back now.

I wasn't sure whether to be terrified or exhilarated by that thought, but I knew one thing for sure—we were in this together, for better or worse. And that, at least, was a comfort.

The hallway felt too quiet as we moved through it, the clack of our shoes against the cold floor echoing louder than it should have. I could feel the captain's presence lingering behind us like a shadow, his voice still ringing in my ears, even though I knew we were well out of earshot. I didn't want to look back—didn't want to see if he was watching us, if he was plotting his next move. It was as though the very air around us was thick with the weight of everything that had just happened.

His hand, warm and reassuring on mine, kept me tethered to the present. To him. I could almost hear his thoughts, though, in the way he kept his gaze straight ahead, jaw set, his every step deliberate. I'd never seen him like this—so focused, so determined. It wasn't just the captain that had him this way; it was something deeper, something more personal. We had crossed a line today, and the price of this war would be steep.

"Do you think he'll really come after us?" I asked, my voice almost a whisper, as though the walls might have ears.

He didn't answer right away, his grip tightening for just a second, like he was sorting through his own thoughts. I could see the tension in his back, the way his shoulders were pulled tight, like he was preparing for something, though I wasn't sure what.

"Doesn't matter," he finally said, his voice low, but there was a sharp edge to it. "We've already committed. We can't turn back now."

I swallowed hard, the realization of what that meant settling into my bones. We had committed. No backing down, no retreating to safer ground. We were in this fight together, and that, for better or worse, was the only thing I could trust.

The elevator doors slid open in front of us with a soft chime, and we stepped inside. The air in the small space was stifling, the faint scent of cheap cologne mingling with the sterile tang of metal and concrete. My heartbeat was louder than the hum of the elevator, and I could feel the weight of the world pressing in on me, tighter and tighter.

He stood beside me, his eyes fixed ahead, but I could tell his mind was elsewhere. He was calculating, like the captain, but in a different way. I knew he wasn't just thinking about what we'd done; he was thinking about what we'd have to do next. What was at stake.

"I'm not afraid of him," I said, though my voice wavered slightly, betraying the lie. I wasn't afraid of the captain—not exactly. But there was something about the way he'd looked at us, the way he'd dismissed us so easily, that set my nerves on edge. "But I'm not stupid either."

He glanced at me then, a quick flick of his eyes, the faintest smile playing at the corners of his mouth. "No, you're definitely not stupid," he said, the teasing note in his voice a welcome distraction. But even in his attempt at levity, I could see the tension still radiating off him, sharp and raw.

The elevator jerked to a stop on the ground floor, and the doors slid open. We stepped into the lobby, the bright fluorescent lights overhead casting harsh shadows across the polished floors. The room was quieter than it had been when we arrived, the usual hum of activity stilled, as if the building itself was holding its breath. I could feel the prickle of eyes on us as we walked past the receptionist's desk, but I didn't dare look up.

"Where to now?" I asked, my voice barely above a whisper, even though I knew there was no one close enough to hear.

He didn't answer right away, and I could feel the wheels turning in his head. "We need to regroup," he said after a beat, his tone grave. "But first... we need to make sure we're not being followed."

A rush of adrenaline surged through me at the thought, and I felt my pulse quicken. We had made a lot of noise today. A lot of waves, and the kind of ripples that couldn't be unseen. It wasn't just the captain we had to worry about now—it was everyone who had ever been part of his empire, those who would stop at nothing to protect their own interests. And the people who wanted him gone. Who might just want us gone, too.

We made our way through the building with quick, purposeful steps, taking the back staircase to avoid the main exit. I kept my eyes on the floor, on his back, trying not to let my imagination run wild. If we were being followed, I wanted to see it before it was too late.

By the time we reached the alleyway behind the building, I could feel the weight of my heart pounding against my ribs. It wasn't fear. Not exactly. But it was something close, a sense of urgency that clawed at my chest. I wanted to run, but I knew better.

He stopped just before we rounded the corner, his hand resting lightly on my arm. I looked up at him, meeting his gaze, and for the first time today, I saw something different. It wasn't just resolve that burned in his eyes—it was the fire of someone who had been pushed to the edge, someone who was about to take things further than they ever had before.

"We have to be careful," he said, his voice low, almost a growl. "This isn't just about us anymore. It's about everyone we care about."

I nodded, feeling the weight of his words settle over me like a shroud. The game had changed. We had made our choice, and now, we were going to live with the consequences. Whatever came next, I knew one thing for certain—we would face it together. There was no going back. Not now. Not after everything that had happened.

As the night air cooled the sweat on the back of my neck, I realized just how much I was willing to sacrifice to see this through. And just how far he was willing to go.

The night felt like a different world entirely—a world far removed from the sterile lights and sharp edges of the captain's office. Out here, the city hummed with life, the air thick with the scent of street vendors and the soft murmur of people moving about their lives, unaware of the storm that was brewing just a few blocks away. The kind of storm that would leave everyone in its wake wondering where it had come from.

We hadn't spoken since we left the alley, but the silence between us felt like the unspoken understanding of two people who had seen the edge and decided to step off it together. There was no going back now. And I think, deep down, we both knew that.

His hand was still wrapped around mine, a constant reminder that, despite everything, we weren't alone. The warmth of his touch was the only thing that kept me from falling apart entirely. Because, truth be told, I didn't know what came next. I didn't know how deep the rabbit hole went or how far we'd be willing to go to pull ourselves out of it.

We turned the corner and found the car waiting for us. A sleek black sedan, the kind that blended into the night, practically made for disappearing into the shadows. He opened the door for me, and I slid into the passenger seat, my breath catching in my chest.

"Where are we going?" I asked, my voice barely audible over the sound of the engine starting.

He didn't answer immediately, his eyes focused on the rearview mirror as he pulled away from the curb. His knuckles were white against the steering wheel, the tension in his body evident as he drove through the winding streets, weaving in and out of traffic like a man who had done this a thousand times before. It felt like we were moving in a dream—fast, too fast, with no clear destination, and no real map to guide us.

"The safe house," he said finally, his voice tight but controlled.

I nodded, though the words didn't bring the comfort I thought they might. The safe house. The very idea of it felt like a lifetime ago, a place where we could hide from whatever the world was throwing at us. But now? I didn't know if hiding was going to be enough. It wasn't just the captain anymore. It was everyone who had ever backed him, everyone who stood to lose something if the truth came to light. And truth, it seemed, was a dangerous thing.

As we drove through the city, the streets growing darker, the buildings more imposing, I could feel the weight of the decision we'd made bearing down on us. We weren't just risking our own lives anymore. We were gambling with the lives of everyone who had ever been a part of our world. Everyone who had trusted us.

I couldn't help but glance over at him. He was still driving with that same focused determination, his jaw set, his eyes trained on the road ahead. But there was something else there, too. A crack, a vulnerability that had slipped into his expression when he thought I wasn't looking. I wanted to reach out to him, to comfort him, but I didn't know how.

"We'll be okay," I said, my voice barely a whisper. It was a lie, but it was the kind of lie we needed right now.

He didn't respond immediately, but I felt his gaze flicker to me, a brief flash of something I couldn't name. Then he turned his eyes back to the road, as if he couldn't afford to let anything distract him. I wanted to believe him. But I knew the stakes had grown higher than either of us had ever imagined.

The safe house was a small, nondescript building tucked away in a quiet neighborhood, the kind of place that no one would look twice at. It was supposed to be a place of refuge, but tonight, it felt more like a prison. We hadn't spoken since we parked the car, but the silence between us felt heavy, laden with unspoken fears and questions that neither of us knew how to ask.

As we entered the building, I couldn't shake the feeling that something was off. The air inside was stale, like it hadn't been disturbed in days, and the faint hum of the lights overhead did little to ease the tension that clung to the walls. He led me through the narrow hallway to a room at the back, where a single lamp burned low, casting long shadows across the floor.

He locked the door behind us and turned to face me, his expression unreadable.

"Do you trust me?" he asked suddenly, his voice low, almost too soft to hear.

I hesitated, the weight of the question pressing against my chest. It wasn't that I didn't trust him—I did, with every fiber of my being. But in this world we were now part of, trust was a fragile thing, easily broken by the smallest crack.

"I do," I said, my voice steady despite the storm raging inside me. "But I need to know we have a plan."

He didn't answer right away. Instead, he walked over to a table in the corner of the room, where a stack of files sat waiting. The papers looked innocuous enough, but I knew better. I knew they held the answers to everything we had been fighting for. And everything we had been fighting against.

"There's always a plan," he said finally, turning to face me. His eyes were darker now, filled with something I couldn't quite place. "But sometimes, plans go sideways. And when they do, we'll have to adapt."

I frowned, the unease creeping back into my chest. "Adapt how?"

His lips curved into a wry smile, but it didn't reach his eyes. "By making sure we're the ones who control the outcome."

Before I could respond, there was a sharp knock at the door. A pause. Then, another. This time, it was more insistent, more urgent.

His expression shifted, the warmth in his eyes replaced by something colder, more dangerous. He motioned for me to stay quiet, his finger pressed to his lips in a silent warning. I held my breath, every muscle in my body tense, as he moved toward the door.

The knock came again, louder this time.

And then I heard the voice, muffled but unmistakable:

"I know you're in there."

Chapter 25: Inferno of Redemption

The fire didn't roar at first. It whispered, a quiet creak in the bones of the building, a tentative flicker of smoke curling up toward the ceiling. But by the time I realized what was happening, the world had already been swallowed. The flames were like something alive, reaching, twisting, consuming everything in its path with the hunger of a thing that knew no end.

I could feel the heat even through the thick walls of the hallway, the air thick and heavy with that sharp, acrid scent that burns the lungs. My fingers tightened around the cold metal of the fire axe, the steel biting into my palm as if reminding me of the weight of what I was about to face. "Ready?" I asked, though the words were barely audible over the sound of chaos around us.

Dante didn't answer immediately. But I didn't need him to. His presence beside me was like the steady pulse of a heartbeat in the chaos, a calm in the storm, a constant that grounded me. His eyes, usually so dark and unreadable, were alive with something fierce tonight—a spark of purpose in them that I recognized all too well. And I wasn't sure if it was the fire or him, but everything inside me felt like it was unraveling.

"Don't let go," he finally said, his voice a gravelly whisper, almost drowned out by the crackling flames.

The heat was unbearable as we pushed forward, the fire now swallowing the hallway in great, unforgiving tongues of red and orange. The air was thick with smoke, and my lungs screamed for air, every breath an agonizing drag of burning fumes. Sweat beaded down my face, stinging my eyes, but I didn't dare wipe it away. There was no time for that.

The building felt alive, groaning under the weight of the flames. The walls seemed to bend, to shift as the fire tore through it, each crackle of the inferno a cruel reminder of how fragile everything we had built was.

I could barely make out the shapes of the others in the distance, their forms flickering like shadows in the haze, but Dante never let go of my side. Every now and then, his hand brushed against mine, a silent assurance that he was still there.

And then, in a moment that felt like it stretched on for eternity, something shifted. The fire that had been in front of us suddenly surged in a wave of violent heat, pushing us back, forcing us apart. The ground beneath my feet shook, the air grew even hotter, and I felt the unmistakable tremor of panic clawing at my chest.

"No!" I shouted, but my voice was lost in the roar of the flames. Dante's eyes locked onto mine, his face suddenly pale beneath the layer of soot that marked him. His lips parted as though to speak, but no words came.

"Get to the exit!" he yelled, his voice cracking with urgency.

But I couldn't. Not without him. Not like this.

My body moved of its own accord, my heart racing in my chest as I fought my way through the smoke, the heat, the surging wall of fire that seemed to want to keep us apart. But I couldn't get to him. Every step I took felt like wading through a sea of molten lava, the air thickening, suffocating.

The heat in the hallway intensified, but my eyes were fixed on Dante. He was closer now, his body moving toward me in the same frantic rush, as if we were tethered by something more than the destruction around us.

And then, suddenly, there was a voice—a voice that came from the very depths of him, raw and exposed. His hand found mine in the chaos, our fingers locking together in a desperate, tight grip. The intensity of the touch sent a tremor through me, but it was his words that broke me.

"I love you," he said, his voice hoarse with emotion. "I've loved you for so damn long, and I never—"

But the words trailed off as the fire surged between us, forcing him back. I couldn't breathe. I couldn't think. The flames between us were a wall, a thing that could separate us even as the weight of his confession settled deep in my chest.

"I love you too," I shouted, though I wasn't sure if he heard me. The fire was too loud. The heat too consuming. But I didn't need him to hear it. Not right now. I needed to get to him.

But before I could take another step, the ceiling above us cracked with an explosion of sound, and a heavy chunk of debris crashed down between us, forcing us apart. I gasped, a terrible, hollow feeling flooding my chest as I watched the dust and smoke cloud the space between us. My heart stopped as I called his name, but my voice was drowned by the sound of the fire's fury.

I couldn't lose him. Not now. Not after everything we'd been through. The fire, the danger, everything—it all seemed to lead to this moment. I didn't know what it meant, but I knew this: I wasn't ready to let him go.

Not when he had just given me everything. Not when I had just given him everything.

The seconds between us stretched into hours. I reached out, desperate, my fingers brushing the smoldering air where he had been just moments before. The smoke clung to my skin, thick and acrid, and every breath I sucked in only served to burn my lungs more. My eyes stung from the ash that hung like a fog, and in the chaos of the fire, I couldn't tell where he was, only where he had been.

I knew he wouldn't leave me. Not like this. But in the same breath, I feared that the flames would take him, that they would consume him as they had consumed so many before us. My heart hammered in my chest, frantic and wild, as if it could somehow bridge the gap the fire had formed between us.

"Dante!" The word was ripped from me, a jagged scream lost in the fury of the inferno. My voice was swallowed whole by the crackling heat, the hissing sound of flames clawing at anything in its path. I could feel my heart dropping lower and lower with each passing moment, the panic threatening to suffocate me.

And then—out of nowhere—there was a hand. A familiar, strong hand reaching through the smoke, grasping mine like a lifeline.

I didn't question it. I didn't wait to make sure. I just held on, with every ounce of strength I had left.

Dante's face emerged from the smoke, his features darkened by soot, eyes wide with something wild and sharp that I recognized instantly. The kind of panic I had felt when we were separated. But there was also something else there, something deeper—relief, raw and unfiltered, that we had found each other again in this madness.

"You think you can get rid of me that easily?" he muttered, a smirk curving his lips despite the circumstances, despite the fire that still raged around us. His voice was a little rougher, a little more desperate, but it was him.

I laughed, a shaky, disbelieving sound that felt foreign to my own ears. "You're a stubborn son of a—"

Before I could finish the sentence, the building groaned, a low, terrifying sound that echoed through the flames. There was no time to finish what I was saying, no time for anything but the present moment, the burning walls and the perilous world collapsing around us. Dante's hand tightened on mine, pulling me forward with a surge of determination. His grip was unrelenting, like a promise, like a force that could withstand anything.

"Stay close," he urged, his voice barely audible over the roar of the fire. I wanted to argue, to remind him that I was perfectly capable of standing on my own two feet, but my feet had already betrayed me once tonight. My legs felt like they might give way at any second.

I nodded, wordless, as we pressed on. The fire was everywhere now—up the walls, across the floor, like a beast with no appetite for mercy. We fought our way through the smoke and the flames, our breath shallow and ragged, desperate for something resembling oxygen. I couldn't think, couldn't plan, couldn't do anything but follow the path Dante was carving, his hand like a tether, dragging me forward through this nightmare.

And yet, even in the midst of everything, there was a part of me that couldn't ignore the ache in my chest—the unanswered confession he had given me. The weight of those three words hung in the air between us, thick as the smoke, heavier than the fire, but there was no time to give them space. No time to make sense of them. Not when the building was on the brink of collapse.

The temperature was rising with every step, the heat threatening to suffocate us. We rounded a corner, and I saw it—an exit, a light at the end of the tunnel. But there was no relief in sight. Not yet. Not with the fire closing in behind us, not with the doorway so far, the smoke so thick. The exit was so close, and yet it felt as though it was miles away.

"We're almost there," Dante said, as if he could read my thoughts. His eyes locked onto mine, something soft flickering in the depths of them—something that had been buried beneath the ashes of our time together. I wondered if, in this madness, he could see it too: the unspoken truth we had been dancing around for far too long.

I nodded, my throat tight, words useless. But the truth had already been spoken. The confession wasn't just in his words; it was in his actions. In the way he held my hand like it was the only thing keeping him alive. In the way he didn't let go, even when everything around us threatened to break apart.

We were almost there.

But the fire had other plans.

The ground trembled beneath us as another burst of heat ripped through the hallway. I barely had time to react before a section of the ceiling collapsed, the debris crashing down between us and the exit. The force of it knocked me to the ground, the air knocked from my lungs in a brutal rush.

I gasped for air, my vision blurred by the smoke, my head pounding from the impact. My fingers scraped against the floor, trying to find something, anything to hold onto. I could hear Dante's voice through the ringing in my ears, but it was distant, as if I were underwater.

"Stay with me," he called, and I clung to his voice like a lifeline.

But the world was spinning. The fire was everywhere.

The last thing I saw before the darkness claimed me was Dante's face, his brow furrowed in concentration, his eyes locked on mine with an intensity that made my heart stutter.

And then, nothing.

The next thing I knew, I was drowning in silence. The kind that's so thick, so heavy, it presses against your chest until breathing feels like a crime. My body ached, a dull throb that hummed in every bone, every muscle. I opened my eyes slowly, wincing against the sharp stab of light that cut through the haze. The world around me was soft at the edges, like I was looking at it through a fogged window, and everything felt distant, disconnected.

But the heat still lingered in my skin, a phantom burn from the fire that hadn't yet let go of me.

"Hey, hey, look at me." Dante's voice was there—familiar, grounding—and yet it made my heart stutter, that lingering edge of panic still thick in his tone. "Stay with me. You're gonna be fine, just breathe."

I tried to respond, but my throat was raw, my mouth too dry. I managed a weak blink, but even that felt like too much effort. My body wasn't ready to move yet, wasn't ready to fight its way out of whatever this was. I could feel the pull of sleep, the numbness threatening to swallow me whole, but I couldn't let go. Not when his voice was there, not when the weight of his presence was the only thing tethering me to the world.

The heat, the fire, it all felt like a dream now. Like something I had left behind in another life.

"Come on, you've made it through worse," he muttered under his breath, though I wasn't sure if he meant it for me or for himself. His fingers were warm against my cheek, brushing the sweat from my skin in a tender gesture. His touch was like fire in its own right, hot, desperate, but still holding something soft behind it.

I blinked again, forcing my eyes to focus, forcing the world back into sharper lines. He was kneeling beside me, his face pale, streaked with soot and ash. His usual unreadable expression had cracked, revealing something raw beneath. Fear? Relief? I couldn't tell. His hand was still on me, his thumb moving in slow circles against my skin, a silent promise I wasn't sure I could trust.

"You're here," I whispered, surprised at how thin my voice sounded.

"I'm here," he replied, though his words felt hollow, not entirely convincing. He swallowed hard, glancing around as though the fire might still be lurking, waiting to strike again. But I knew better. It was more than the flames that had him looking over his shoulder.

The walls of the building groaned, a sound that rumbled deep under my skin, reminding me that the danger wasn't over. The fire might have been contained, but the wreckage was still settling around us, pieces of a crumbling world that didn't seem to want to leave us behind. There was no safety in the air, no security in the walls of the room that had become our sanctuary for only a moment.

"We need to move," I managed, my voice a little stronger this time, though still uncertain. My body protested, every inch of me still wanting to collapse, but the adrenaline was beginning to take over, pushing me forward in spite of it.

Dante hesitated, his eyes searching mine as if he was looking for some sign, some piece of hope in the wreckage we'd left behind. "We'll move when you're ready. We've survived worse."

I shook my head, trying to push away the fog in my mind. "I'm not talking about that." I tried to sit up, but my legs wobbled beneath me, a cruel reminder of how close the fire had brought me to the edge. "I'm talking about us, Dante. We're—"

"I know," he interrupted, his jaw tight. The distance between us seemed to grow with each word he didn't speak. He was pulling away, even as he hovered closer. His voice cracked when he spoke again. "I know exactly what we are. But now is not the time for this."

I was quiet for a moment, the truth of it sitting between us, heavy and undeniable. There was something unspoken, a thing that had always been there but never really surfaced. But I wasn't sure I was ready for it to surface, not in the middle of this mess. Not when the world outside the room still felt like it was burning to the ground.

"Dante," I started again, but the words felt like they were slipping away from me. It was as if the fire had taken them, consumed them with everything else.

His hand found mine again, squeezing tight. "Don't say it, okay? Just... just give it a second."

I wanted to argue. I wanted to scream. To demand that we address what was between us. But there was a part of me that knew he was right. The fire was still too close, the danger still too real.

A sound—soft at first, a distant tremor in the ground beneath us—pulled both our attention. Dante's gaze snapped to the door, his muscles tensing as if the air itself was thick with the threat of something far worse.

I followed his gaze, but I couldn't see what he saw. All I felt was the subtle shift in the atmosphere, the dread that settled in the pit of my stomach. I couldn't explain it, but I knew. I knew we weren't done. That we hadn't escaped yet.

"What the hell was that?" I whispered, my voice barely more than a breath.

"I don't know," Dante said, his expression darkening as he stood, pulling me to my feet with surprising strength. He didn't look at me when he spoke again, his eyes locked on the door. "Stay close. We're not safe yet."

Before I could protest, the sound came again—louder this time, closer. The door splintered, a violent crack splitting the air as something—or someone—began to force their way inside.

"Dante," I breathed, the fear suddenly sharp and raw, seeping through every crack in my resolve.

He turned to face me, his grip firm on my wrist, his voice steady but with a warning I couldn't ignore. "Whatever happens, don't let go."

The door gave way with a final, terrifying crack, and everything went still.

Chapter 26: Phoenix Rising

The smoke stung my eyes, the acrid scent of burning wood and earth curling into my nostrils like a cruel reminder that nothing here was sacred, nothing was safe. The fire crackled and hissed, a beast of fury, its orange tendrils licking the air as it devoured everything in its wake. Trees, homes, the lives of anyone foolish enough to believe they could outrun it. I had seen this kind of destruction before—on the news, in the tales told by survivors, but nothing could have prepared me for the raw, primal devastation of standing in its path.

We didn't have much time.

My heart pounded in my chest, the rhythm frantic but steady, a strange comfort in the chaos that surrounded me. It was almost laughable how the world seemed to slow down in these moments, like the fire had a mind of its own and knew how to savor every burning second. Each breath was an act of defiance. Each step forward felt like a betrayal of reason, but we had no other choice.

As I stumbled through the charred underbrush, I heard his voice behind me, low and rasping but clear. "Keep moving, Ellie. Don't stop."

I didn't need to be told twice. If I stopped now, if I hesitated, the fire would claim me, just like it had claimed so many others. There were no second chances in this world. Only forward. And forward was exactly where I intended to go.

The wind howled, a cruel whistle through the trees, scattering embers like confetti in a nightmare parade. Every gust carried with it the heat of a thousand burning suns, and my skin prickled with the sensation of being close to something far too dangerous to comprehend. The air was thick, suffocating, but I pushed it aside, clutching my water bottle like it was my only tether to reality. My fingers were slick with sweat, but I held on. I had to. For him.

For us.

His hand found mine again, cool and steady, as he pulled me up over a ridge, his grip never wavering. He was stronger than he looked, despite the exhaustion dragging at both of us. When we reached the clearing, the devastation was even worse than I had imagined—blackened earth stretching for miles, the sky above a deep, bruised purple that made the world feel like it had forgotten how to breathe. And yet, amidst the ruin, I could feel a strange pulse in the air, a heartbeat of resilience. Maybe it was the fire itself, or maybe it was us. I wasn't sure.

His voice was softer now, barely a whisper. "We made it. You—"

I didn't let him finish. "We're not out of the woods yet." It was more of a warning than anything else, but I didn't have time for pleasantries. Not now. Not when the world still felt like it was on the edge of unraveling.

He nodded, his jaw tight. I could see the familiar wariness in his eyes—always calculating, always assessing. But for once, there was something else there too. Something softer. Something that had been buried for far too long beneath the layers of anger and fear.

"I didn't think we'd make it," he muttered, almost to himself. His voice was rough, as if it had been strained by the smoke, but I knew better than to think it was the fire that had broken him. It was the years—the things he'd seen, the things he'd done—that had left him hollow. But I could see it now. That hollow space was slowly filling with something else. Something I didn't have a name for yet.

I took a deep breath, savoring the coolness of the air for the first time in what felt like hours. It was hard to imagine, after all this destruction, that life could still exist in such a place. And yet, it did.

I was alive. He was alive. And that, in its own way, was something to be thankful for.

The silence between us stretched, thick and heavy, as we both stared at the horizon. The sky was no longer burning, but the remnants of the fire still smoldered in the distance, and I felt a strange sense of peace in the ashes. Perhaps it was the realization that the worst had passed. Or maybe it was just the weight of surviving something so impossible that made the world seem oddly still.

Finally, I turned to him, my voice quiet but firm. "We can't stay here. We have to keep moving."

His eyes flicked over to mine, then back to the horizon. He didn't argue, didn't question. Instead, he simply nodded and started walking again. This time, his hand brushed mine, a soft, barely perceptible gesture, but it was enough. I didn't need him to say anything. He was here. I was here. And for the first time in as long as I could remember, I didn't feel like I was just surviving—I felt like I was living.

And maybe, just maybe, there was a future after the fire. One we could build together.

The silence was oddly loud, almost deafening, like the world had taken a collective breath, unsure of what to do with the aftermath. The fire had left its mark, the scorched earth a mute testament to its fury. The trees, once lush and proud, were now nothing more than brittle skeletons, their branches reaching toward the heavens like desperate pleas for mercy. I should have felt more—something deeper than this strange sense of calm that had settled over me—but there was only the weight of what we'd just survived.

His hand still clasped mine, firm and unyielding. I hadn't expected him to hold on, but he did, as though he, too, knew something had changed between us, something irrevocable. The world around us had burned, but in the space between our fingers, something new was taking shape, fragile and uncertain, but real.

"Do you ever wonder," I said, breaking the silence, my voice quieter than usual, "how we make it out of something like this? The fire's not just in the trees, it's in us, too."

He didn't answer right away. His eyes scanned the horizon, the darkened sky a canvas of swirling purples and deep reds, remnants of the chaos that had just unfolded. His jaw was tight, a muscle twitching in that way I'd come to recognize as his version of stress. But then he exhaled, a long, slow breath, and looked at me. The edges of his mouth curved slightly upward.

"You fight it," he said, his voice rough like gravel, but there was a softness to it now. "You just... keep fighting. It's what you do. You survive, no matter what."

I snorted, half in disbelief, half in amusement. "You make it sound so simple."

He raised an eyebrow, a hint of mischief now in his gaze. "It's not. But you wouldn't know that from looking at you. You're tougher than most people I've met. I don't think you give yourself enough credit."

I scoffed, trying not to let the compliment take me by surprise. "That's the nicest thing anyone's ever said to me. Honestly, I was expecting a 'We should never speak of this again' type of comment."

He chuckled, the sound low and real. "Maybe that comes later." His hand tightened around mine for just a moment, grounding me in the moment, in him.

I leaned back against a fallen log, the rough bark pressing into my spine, a solid reminder of everything we had just walked through. The heat of the fire still lingered in the air, even though the worst had passed, leaving a faint burn in my lungs, like the remnants of a dream you couldn't quite shake. I couldn't help but wonder how long it would take to forget the sound of the flames cracking and snapping, the way they seemed to mock us as we fought to stay ahead of them, as if daring us to outlast their rage.

"I never imagined it would feel like this," I said, more to myself than to him. "Quiet. Empty."

"You've been running on adrenaline for so long, you didn't stop to think what happens when it's all over. It's like... falling off a cliff, I guess. You expect to land hard, but you just—float."

"Float," I repeated, laughing despite myself. "That's one way to put it. It feels more like sinking."

He didn't respond right away, but I could see his mind working, piecing together something from the chaos, something he hadn't quite figured out yet. "You think you're sinking, but really, you're just waiting for the next wave."

I turned to him, a flash of curiosity sparking in my chest. "And when does that next wave hit?"

His eyes locked onto mine, a flicker of something in their depths, something that felt almost like a promise, but I wasn't sure what kind. "Soon," he said, his voice low, almost too soft. "But for now, we breathe."

We stayed there for a while, not saying much, just breathing in the air that, while heavy with the scent of smoke and ash, was still somehow sweeter than it had been just hours before. It was as if the world was holding its breath, unsure of what came next, and we were just waiting with it, suspended in time.

I finally stood, stretching out the tension in my body, feeling the tightness in my muscles after all the running, the sprinting from danger. There was a moment where the weight of everything—the fear, the loss, the exhaustion—seemed almost too much to bear. But when I turned back to look at him, I found his eyes on me, steady and sure, and I knew that whatever came next, we would face it together.

"Ready?" I asked, trying to make my voice sound more confident than I felt.

He gave me a slow smile, the kind that made my heart skip in a way I wasn't prepared for. "Ready."

I didn't know what the future held, not really. But for the first time, I wasn't afraid to find out. The fire had changed us, but maybe it had also given us something we hadn't expected. A second chance. And maybe that was enough.

We walked together, side by side, into the unknown. No longer haunted by the past, no longer running from the flames. Just two people, ready to rise.

We didn't talk much as we walked, each step taking us farther from the flames and closer to some uncertain future. The air, once thick and oppressive, was beginning to clear, though the taste of soot still lingered on my tongue, a reminder of what we'd just survived. The world felt muted, washed out, as if the colors of the earth had been burned away along with the trees. Yet despite it all, I couldn't shake the feeling that something else was simmering beneath the surface, something that I hadn't quite figured out yet.

"You're quiet," he said after a long stretch of silence. His voice was low but threaded with curiosity, as though he was trying to piece together whatever was running through my mind.

I glanced at him, surprised at how naturally his presence had come to feel—steady, like an anchor, even when the world around us was shifting in ways we couldn't control. His shirt was singed at the edges, his hair a little wild, but there was something oddly comforting about the way he looked now, despite the chaos. He wasn't just the man who had faced the fire with me; he was also the one who had somehow found a way into my thoughts without me even realizing it.

"I was just thinking," I said, slowing my pace as I tried to find the right words. "About how we get to keep going after all this.

Like, how do we make it through something so—" I searched for the word, finally settling on the only one that made sense. "So raw?"

He didn't answer immediately, and for a moment, I wondered if I'd said something wrong. But then he slowed down too, his footsteps matching mine as we wandered through the ash-coated landscape. It felt like we were tiptoeing on the edge of something new, something delicate, and I wasn't sure if it was the aftermath of the fire or something more that had begun to unfurl between us.

"I don't know," he said, his tone thoughtful, like he was still wrestling with the same question. "I think you just... keep moving. You don't get to stand still when the world's burning around you."

I nodded, even though I wasn't entirely sure I understood. It was like we were both trying to make sense of the unspeakable—trying to reconcile the parts of us that had been torn apart by the flames with the parts that still managed to survive, against all odds.

We continued walking, our shadows long and stretched across the ground, the eerie stillness of the world pressing in on us. Every now and then, I'd glance at him, catching a glimpse of the man who had been there through every moment of the fire. The weight of what we'd survived sat heavy between us, but there was something more, something that I hadn't anticipated. It wasn't just the fire that had brought us together, it was everything that came after it—the quiet moments, the shared understanding, the fact that we had managed to find a rhythm in the chaos.

He reached over and tugged a branch out of my way, a simple gesture, but one that made me realize just how little I'd seen him as a man with his own burdens. Before, he'd been a soldier, a survivor, someone who carried his pain in ways that had felt unapproachable. But now, as the dust settled, as the air cleared, I saw him in a different light. There was vulnerability in the way he moved, a fragility that matched my own.

"I guess," I said, my voice quieter now, "we're not really the same people we were when this all started, are we?"

He didn't hesitate before answering. "No, we're not. But maybe that's the point. Maybe you can't go through something like that without being changed." He looked at me, his gaze holding mine for a beat longer than usual. "I don't know if that's a bad thing."

I swallowed, the words tasting strange on my tongue. "No. I don't think it is."

But as I said it, something inside of me twisted. I couldn't help but wonder—what if the change wasn't just about surviving the fire? What if it was something deeper, something that we weren't yet ready to face?

The wind picked up again, stirring the ashes around us, and I let the sound of it fill the space between us, trying to chase away the sudden chill in my bones. We kept walking, our steps syncing in a rhythm that felt more natural with each passing minute. The world had been irrevocably altered, but I couldn't stop thinking that maybe, just maybe, we had a chance at something more than just survival.

Then, without warning, the faintest sound reached my ears—a crackling, like something breaking in the distance. I froze, my heart leaping into my throat. For a moment, I thought it was just the wind, playing tricks on me, but then I heard it again. Louder this time. Closer.

"Did you hear that?" I whispered, my voice thin with anxiety.

He stopped beside me, his body going still, every muscle taut with the same tension that was suddenly coursing through me. "Yeah. I heard it."

Before I could ask him what he thought it was, the ground beneath our feet seemed to shift, as though the earth itself was groaning under the pressure of something heavy, something fast approaching. My pulse quickened, and I instinctively took a step closer to him.

"Ellie—" he started, his voice tight, but then there was no time for words. The sound grew louder still, a rumble that vibrated in my chest. It was unmistakable now. Something was coming.

And then, as if the earth had cracked wide open, a shadow loomed in front of us, dark and terrifying.

I didn't have time to react. My breath caught in my throat, my eyes wide with the kind of fear I hadn't allowed myself to feel since the fire. But this—whatever this was—it wasn't just the aftermath of flames. This was something new. Something we hadn't seen coming.

And it was heading straight for us.

Chapter 27: The Smoldering Lie

The heat of the fire still clung to my skin, an invisible burn that wouldn't fade no matter how many deep breaths I took. I leaned against the cool stone of the alleyway, my hands gripping the edges of the worn bricks. The darkened sky above, thick with smoke from the wreckage that had once been our sanctuary, felt suffocating. I should have been glad that we escaped, that the threat of those flames no longer pressed on my chest like a weight I couldn't shrug off. But all I could feel was the tension crawling beneath my skin, prickling like tiny shards of glass working their way in, deeper and deeper.

I turned to him—always him. The one who insisted he was my savior, the one whose presence had become so familiar that it almost felt like breathing. But as I looked at his face, dimly lit by the flickering embers, something stirred in my gut. A faint unease, like a shadow lurking in the back of my mind, refusing to be ignored. There was something wrong. Something he wasn't saying.

"I should have known," I muttered, more to myself than to him. My voice cracked at the edges, a bitter sound in the cold air.

He stiffened beside me, his broad shoulders tensing, but he didn't speak, didn't offer the comforting words I'd grown used to hearing. Instead, he stared into the distance, as if the flames that once had raged had somehow become a mirror, reflecting his thoughts back to him.

"Do you want to tell me what's really going on?" I finally asked, the words coming out too harsh, too desperate. I didn't want to sound like this, like a woman on the verge of a breakdown, but there it was—ugly, raw, and exposed. My voice cracked again, and I hated it. I wanted to be steady. I wanted him to say everything I needed to hear and somehow make this all okay.

But he didn't answer immediately. Instead, he ran a hand through his disheveled hair, letting out a low, frustrated breath. His eyes locked with mine, the weight of them suffocating.

"You're right," he said quietly. "I should've told you sooner."

My stomach dropped, and my pulse quickened. I knew. I knew this wasn't going to end with any easy answers.

"Tell me," I said, my voice softer now, less demanding. There was no point in pushing him, not now. If he wasn't ready to come clean, I couldn't force it out of him. But I needed the truth. I needed it more than I needed anything else.

He exhaled, the breath thick with tension, and turned away, his gaze tracing the path of a glowing ember as it floated toward the sky. "I wasn't always—" He stopped himself, rubbing his fingers over his temples like they ached. "I wasn't always the man you think I am."

The words hung in the air, unfinished, like an open wound I wasn't sure I wanted to touch.

"Who are you?" The question slipped out before I could stop it. But the moment I asked it, I regretted it. The vulnerability in his eyes wasn't something I was prepared to handle. The truth, whatever it was, would be jagged, sharp, and painful. And yet I had to know. I had to see if this—we—could be salvaged, or if I had been living a lie this whole time.

His voice was quieter this time, almost a whisper. "I wasn't just a part of the crew. I was... involved in things, things I thought I could walk away from. I thought it was behind me."

A bitter laugh escaped me, unbidden. "And now you're telling me it's not?"

"I'm not proud of what I've done," he said, finally meeting my eyes. "But I never meant for you to be a part of any of it. You were never supposed to know."

"You didn't think I'd notice?" The words left my lips sharper than I intended, but I couldn't stop them. This wasn't the time for tact. It wasn't the time for pretending. "You didn't think I'd notice the lies, the inconsistencies, the little things you left out?"

He didn't flinch. That was one of the things I hated about him, his ability to remain unshaken. It was like nothing could touch him, like he could hide the truth behind a mask of indifference.

"Look, I was trying to protect you," he said, his voice low. "But I can't keep doing that. It's not fair to either of us."

I crossed my arms, unable to suppress the bitter laugh that bubbled in my chest. "Oh, so now you're the hero?" The sarcasm was thick, but I couldn't help myself. This whole situation felt like a game I wasn't prepared to play. A game where I was left behind, left to pick up the pieces of whatever broken truth he decided to share.

His jaw tightened, his eyes darkening. "I never said I was. I'm not a hero, and I never was. But I swear to you, I would've kept you out of it if I could."

I couldn't shake the feeling that there was something more. Something deeper. I pushed, because I had to. "What aren't you telling me? What did you do?"

His gaze shifted away, and I saw a flicker of something—guilt, maybe, or regret. I wasn't sure. But whatever it was, it made my stomach twist in knots.

"I wasn't just one of them," he said, his voice barely above a murmur. "I was the one who betrayed them."

And just like that, the world tilted beneath my feet.

His confession landed like a weight in the pit of my stomach, heavy and unexpected, and for a moment, I forgot how to breathe. The air was still thick with the scent of smoke, the remnants of the fire clinging to everything. It should have been a moment of clarity, but instead, I felt the ground beneath me crack, the distance between us widening with every second he stayed silent.

"You betrayed them?" I repeated, my voice a little too high, a little too strained. "How do you go from one of them to... that? What—what were you thinking?"

I couldn't wrap my head around it. The man standing in front of me, the man who had held me close when I trembled, who had whispered in my ear that everything would be alright, had once been the very thing he swore he would never become. A traitor. A betrayer. How could someone shift so violently? How could someone play both sides without losing their soul in the process?

His hands clenched at his sides, his knuckles going white. The dim light of the alleyway illuminated the sharp planes of his face, but it did little to ease the storm swirling in his eyes. "I didn't have a choice," he said through gritted teeth, the words so strained it felt like he was speaking through the tightness in his chest.

"Really?" I laughed, though there was no humor in it, just bitterness, like the remnants of a dream I once had, now shattered and sharp. "No choice? You're telling me you just... walked away from all of it, from them, because there was no other option?"

He met my gaze, but it wasn't the look of a man who was sorry. It was the look of someone who had long made peace with his decisions, a person resigned to the choices he had made, whether they had been the right ones or not. The indifference in his eyes made my blood boil.

"I didn't walk away," he said finally, his voice low but unmistakable in its finality. "I ran. From the things I had done, from the things I was still capable of doing. I knew it was a matter of time before they found out."

My mind raced, but nothing about this felt like the man I thought I knew. Nothing about this made sense. "Why didn't you tell me?" The words were out before I could stop them, a desperate plea for some kind of truth that made sense, that fit neatly into the narrative of us I had constructed in my head.

He stepped forward then, closing the distance between us, his eyes softening for just a moment. "Because I didn't want you to see me the way they did," he whispered. "I didn't want you to look at me like I was broken."

I laughed again, this time more softly, the sound like a shudder in my throat. "Well, you've certainly broken something." I raised my hand, as if to stop him from responding, from explaining further. "You think I don't see it? That I don't see the cracks in your story? The holes in your answers?"

His face fell, and for the briefest moment, I wondered if I had gone too far. But no, something in me told me this was the only way—this brutal honesty, this unrelenting truth, even if it broke me.

"You're right," he said finally, his voice soft but heavy. "You deserve to know everything. I've been hiding it from you, and for that, I'm sorry. But the truth is..." He paused, as if weighing each word. "The truth is that I didn't just leave them. I destroyed them."

I stiffened, my heart thumping in my chest, an uncomfortable thud that echoed in my ears. "Destroyed them? What does that even mean?"

"I betrayed their trust. I sold them out. And when I did, I signed my own death sentence. That's why they're after me. That's why I can't ever go back."

The admission was like a slap across my face. I felt the heat of it sting my cheeks, the sting of betrayal, of shattered trust. The man I had leaned on for support, the man I had trusted to be my anchor in this mess of a world, was now the very thing I feared the most. A liar. A manipulator. A danger.

"But why?" The question left me breathless, raw. "Why would you do something like that? You knew what it would cost you."

"I didn't think it would cost me you," he murmured, the words so soft, so quiet, that they almost sounded like an apology.

That hurt. That hurt more than I cared to admit.

"Is that supposed to make it better?" I asked, barely holding myself together. "Are you telling me you're the victim here? That you betrayed everyone and ruined everything, but it's okay because you didn't think it would cost me?"

He looked away then, his jaw clenched, his fists tightening at his sides like he was trying to hold himself together. The silence between us was thick, suffocating, pressing in on my lungs.

"I'm not asking for forgiveness," he said, his voice low and strained. "I'm not even asking you to understand. I just—I don't know what to say anymore, except that I never meant to drag you into this."

I stared at him, the words hanging heavy in the air. "You've already dragged me into it. You've already made me a part of this mess. And now, all I have is the wreckage of what I thought we had."

His eyes softened, but the sorrow in them was something I wasn't sure I could bear. "I didn't want this for us. I never wanted this. But everything's falling apart, and there's nothing left to do but watch it burn."

The words, the weight of them, hit me harder than anything else. He had taken so much from me, without even meaning to. And yet, as I looked at him, my heart ached with something I couldn't quite explain. Something that felt dangerous, something that felt like I was still tethered to him, no matter how hard I tried to pull away.

For better or worse, I wasn't sure where the lines between truth and lies blurred anymore.

The ache in my chest twisted as I watched him shift, as if the weight of his past was settling once more around his shoulders, threatening to break him under its pressure. It wasn't just the words; it was the way he said them, like he was giving pieces of himself to me—pieces he hadn't ever intended to share, pieces he was certain would shatter whatever I thought we were.

"You can't expect me to just forgive you, can you?" I asked, though the question hung in the air, more an expression of disbelief than anything else. His silence was answer enough.

"You're asking too much," I added, the words sharp, like broken glass. "You've lied to me, for how long now? You've kept secrets from me, made me believe in something that never existed."

He took a step toward me, slow, deliberate, as if afraid any sudden movement might break the fragile thread of conversation between us. "I didn't lie to you," he said, his voice rougher now, but there was something else underneath—the weight of regret, the same weight that had crushed his expression the moment he spoke of the betrayal. "I never lied to you. I just... omitted the truth. I thought it was the best thing. For you. For us."

The bitterness in his words clung to the air between us, and I couldn't help but laugh, the sound too hollow, too empty to be real. "For us," I repeated, almost mockingly. "You thought it was for us? If you thought it was for us, why are we here now? Why is everything burning? What's left of us, after you've destroyed everything that held us together?"

He flinched as if the words had struck deeper than any physical blow. His lips pressed into a thin line, his hands flexing at his sides as though he were fighting some internal war. I could see it in his eyes—he wanted to reach out, to explain, to make everything right, but the more he spoke, the more tangled his words became.

"I never wanted this," he said quietly, the rawness in his voice making me pause, if only for a second. "You have to understand, I didn't think it would turn out this way. I thought I could fix it. I thought I could get away before it all came crashing down."

A tight laugh escaped me, bitter and cutting. "Well, it crashed down, didn't it? Just not in the way you expected."

His gaze flickered away, and I saw the shame in the way he held himself, the way he couldn't meet my eyes. It wasn't enough. It wasn't enough to make me feel pity for him, not after everything that had been destroyed. Not after everything that had been taken from us without warning.

"You think you're the only one who's suffered?" I bit out, my voice a dangerous whisper. "You think I haven't seen the cracks in you, the lies you keep telling, trying to make this into something it was never meant to be? You've kept me in the dark, and for what? To protect me from the truth?" My chest tightened as I spoke, a pressure that had been building for days, for weeks, finally exploding out of me in a rush of anger and hurt.

He opened his mouth to speak, but I silenced him with a gesture, holding my palm up between us. "Don't," I snapped. "Don't try to make it sound noble. Don't try to make it sound like you were some kind of martyr. Because you weren't. You were selfish. And now we're both paying for it."

There was a heavy silence that stretched between us, thick and suffocating, as though the very air had turned stale with the weight of everything unspoken. I could feel my heart pounding in my chest, the sound too loud, too present, like it was beating against my ribs in protest, wanting to break free, wanting to escape the wreckage of everything that had gone wrong.

Finally, he spoke again, his voice low, almost hoarse. "I never meant to hurt you."

The sincerity in his words made my insides twist, but I couldn't trust it. Not now. Not after everything. "You never meant to hurt me?" I shook my head, the laugh that came out of me sharp and hollow. "You hurt me the moment you decided to lie. The moment you decided that the truth wasn't something I deserved. So don't stand there and tell me you never meant to hurt me. Because you did."

He winced, and it was like a physical blow to see the man I had trusted in so much pain, even if that pain was self-inflicted. I wanted to feel sorry for him. I did, a little. But it wasn't enough. The damage had been done, and there was no undoing it now.

"We can't go back from this," I whispered, the words more to myself than to him. It was the truth, undeniable and final. We were standing on the edge of something—something fragile, something that felt like it could crumble into dust at the slightest misstep.

He shook his head slowly, a look of desperation creeping into his expression, but I couldn't bring myself to offer him any reassurance. There was no comfort left for either of us. "Maybe we can't," he said, his voice small, as if he too was realizing the weight of what had been lost. "But we don't have to let it end here."

I stepped back, the space between us growing, my heart aching with the distance I had to put between us. "And how do you suggest we do that? How do we go forward, after everything?"

The words seemed to hang in the air, a question that had no answer, a question that felt impossible to face. And yet, despite everything—the lies, the pain, the betrayal—I could still feel the remnants of what we had, buried deep inside. As much as I wanted to hate him, as much as I wanted to walk away and never look back, something in me refused to let go.

And then, just as I was about to speak, to tell him everything I had been holding back, the sharp sound of footsteps echoed in the alleyway, followed by the unmistakable creak of a door opening. My stomach dropped. I knew that sound. I knew who it belonged to.

A figure stepped into view, shadowed by the dim light, and everything inside me went cold.

"Did you really think you were safe?" The voice was familiar, but it wasn't his. And that was the moment everything shifted again.

Chapter 28: Bound by Flame

The note was barely more than a whisper of paper, folded crisply into a corner of my cot where his warmth had still lingered. It might as well have been a piece of ash, the way it seared me with its sharp simplicity. "Gone. Don't follow." His handwriting, all jagged angles and urgency, scraped at the edge of my mind like a familiar, painful song. It was enough to make my breath hitch in my throat, the lump forming so swiftly that I almost couldn't swallow past it.

Of course, he was gone. Of course, he thought he could handle this on his own. He always had, hadn't he? Ever since we first locked eyes across a crowded room, drawn together by some force we couldn't understand, yet felt in our bones like a promise. A promise I was certain he hadn't realized had long since become an unspoken bond—something thicker than blood, forged through fire and sacrifice. I had never asked for it. I hadn't even wanted it, but it was ours, whether we liked it or not. And there was no way in hell I was letting him run off to face danger alone.

I pulled myself up from the cot, the rustle of the note falling to the floor as I moved. My heart pounded in my chest, but the anger was hotter than the fear—blazing, scalding. He hadn't even said goodbye. No, he had simply slipped away in the middle of the night, thinking he could spare me the pain of seeing what he had to do. As if I hadn't already seen him do the impossible—time and time again, risking it all for those he loved.

"You're damn right I'm following you," I muttered to myself, grabbing my coat from the peg by the door. The leather felt heavy in my hands, almost like a shield. I could feel the weight of the decision settling in my bones, making each movement feel deliberate, purposeful. I wasn't going to let him shoulder this alone. We had both chosen this path, for better or worse, and he didn't get to back out now. Not without me.

The others would need to know. I didn't even hesitate before I pulled the door open, letting the cold of the early morning air rush in to slap my face. They were already starting to stir as the first light of dawn began to stretch across the horizon, pale pinks and oranges mixing in the sky like an artist's hasty brushstrokes. The camp was quiet, the kind of quiet that made your skin prickle, like something was about to happen, and you couldn't quite decide if it was the calm before the storm or the calm after it.

I found them by the fire—Nia sitting cross-legged, the flickering flames casting shadows across her face, while Dorian cleaned his blades with the sort of precision only a man like him could manage. And Ben, leaning against the post, staring out at the woods like he already knew what was coming.

"He's gone." I wasn't sure if it was a question or a statement. But it didn't matter, because they all looked up at me in unison, their faces already wearing that expression—the one that said they knew this was coming, but they hadn't wanted to acknowledge it. They had seen it in my eyes last night. They had known the moment I had realized he was slipping away that there would be no keeping me behind.

"We're going after him," I said, the words coming out like a decree. It wasn't negotiable.

Ben's lips twisted into something between a smile and a grimace. "Figured you would." He stood, not waiting for any further explanation, the gravel under his boots crunching as he moved toward the horses.

Dorian didn't speak, but his eyes met mine—sharp, calculating, the kind of gaze that told me he was already mapping out the best route, assessing every risk, every danger. Nia, ever the quiet one, simply nodded, her dark eyes flickering with something I couldn't quite name. She didn't question my decision, but the concern in her eyes said more than words ever could.

They weren't my team. Not in the way we were a team. I had joined them out of necessity, out of the need for survival. But they had become something else—something I didn't expect, and now it seemed as though I couldn't live without. They were family in a way that went beyond anything blood could have made. They were the ones I turned to when things grew darker than I could stand alone. And, God help me, I wasn't going to leave them behind, even if it meant risking my own neck.

We gathered our things in silence, the weight of our shared understanding pressing down on us as we saddled up and set out. The horses' hooves clattered against the stone path, the sound hollow in the cool morning air. I kept my gaze fixed ahead, heart thudding in my chest as the trees of the forest loomed larger, darker. It was easy to pretend the world hadn't been turned upside down in the past few weeks, that the dangers weren't closing in on us with every step. But as we neared the edge of the woods, I felt it—a tugging sensation, pulling at the back of my mind, making my instincts flare. Something was wrong.

I wasn't sure what it was at first, but the hairs on the back of my neck stood up. The usual sounds of the forest were muted, dampened, like it was holding its breath. A cold breeze stirred the leaves, and for a fleeting moment, I thought I saw shadows dart between the trees—too fast to be natural, too deliberate to be an accident. My heart stuttered.

And that's when I saw him. He was standing at the clearing's edge, his back to me, framed by the trees. My chest tightened, relief and fury both crashing over me in waves. He hadn't gotten far, but he had already walked into the trap. The ambush was well-set—too well-set. He was already surrounded.

"Shit," I muttered, before urging my horse into a gallop.

The moment my horse's hooves hit the dirt of the clearing, I could see it all—too clearly. The trees around us stood like silent sentinels, heavy with shadows, their gnarled branches stretching toward the sky like twisted fingers. The air was thick, unnatural, as though the forest itself had taken a deep breath and was holding it. I didn't have time to think about the uneasy stillness or the strange prickling sensation in my skin. I focused on the man at the center of it all, the one who had once whispered promises of safety into my ear, only to disappear into the dark without so much as a backward glance.

His back was to me, but even from behind, I could see the tension in his frame. He knew something was coming, knew the trap had already been sprung. I wasn't sure whether it was the sharpness in his posture or the fact that he hadn't turned around to greet me that hit me hardest. His presence was unmistakable, but there was a hollowness to it, an emptiness that made my heart ache. He wasn't just facing down the threat—it was clear he was already preparing for the worst.

I reined my horse in with a sharp pull on the reins, the animal's hooves sliding in the loose dirt as I brought it to a stop a few paces behind him.

"You always did have a way of making things complicated." The words slipped out before I could stop them, sharp, tinged with a bite that I wasn't sure I was fully prepared to own. But it didn't matter. He turned, his face lighting up with surprise, though it quickly shifted into something else—something I couldn't quite decipher.

"What the hell are you doing here?" His voice was low, dangerous even, but there was no mistaking the way his eyes softened when they found mine. That was the thing with him—he could be cold and distant one moment, and then, in an instant, a look from him would shatter all that and remind me of the man beneath the layers of armor he'd built around himself.

I laughed, but there was no humor in it. "What do you think I'm doing here? You really thought I'd let you march off into the woods, into danger, alone? After everything?"

His eyes narrowed, but there was no real anger there, only something that felt too much like regret.

"I didn't want you to get caught up in this. It's too dangerous. It's—"

"Too dangerous for me? You really think I haven't seen danger before?" I cut him off, my voice rising as I spoke, the frustration boiling over now that I was standing in front of him, trying to untangle the mess he'd made.

His gaze shifted from mine to the shadowed edges of the clearing, and I followed his line of sight, but there was nothing there—nothing except the feeling of being watched. The faint rustle of leaves was the only sound in the otherwise suffocating silence. And that, I realized with a sick feeling in my stomach, was exactly what they wanted. They were waiting.

"God, you don't get it." His hands balled into fists at his sides, the muscles in his jaw ticking as if he were trying to hold something back. "I can't let you—"

But he didn't finish the sentence. Instead, there was a sudden crackle of movement in the trees, and I was already halfway to drawing my knife before I even realized it. The air seemed to pulse with the intensity of it, the tension thickening around us like a storm cloud, and I knew, without a doubt, that this was the moment they'd been waiting for.

There was no time for anything else.

"Move!" I shouted at him, pushing my horse into a swift gallop as figures emerged from the shadows. More of them than I had expected—too many. My heart hammered in my chest as I reached for my bow, eyes scanning the trees for any hint of their movements. But they were clever, their steps too quiet, their faces hidden in the darkness. The only thing I could count on was the sharpness of my instincts, honed by years of running, hiding, and fighting.

"Dorian!" I shouted, though I didn't know if he could hear me. There was no time to wait for him to catch up, no time to do anything but fight. The first wave came from the left, charging out from the brush like a pack of wolves, and I was already meeting them halfway, arrows whistling through the air.

One went down, then another, but the rest surged forward, their eyes glowing with a dangerous intensity. I didn't have to look to know that the others were at my back, that they would cover me if I needed it, but the truth was, I didn't want to need it. I didn't want to rely on anyone else. Not anymore.

I swung my bow around, drawing another arrow with practiced speed, my heart in my throat as I let it fly. It found its mark, and another one of them crumpled to the ground. But that was only the beginning. The figures in the shadows were spreading out, coming at us from every angle, and I had to move faster. I had to be smarter.

Through the chaos, I caught a glimpse of him—Dorian, standing by the trees, his sword in hand, but his gaze fixed on me. There was no fear in his eyes now, just a kind of grim determination. He was here, by my side, fighting. He hadn't abandoned me after all, despite the way he had tried to push me away.

"Get moving!" I shouted at him, though the words were more a plea than an order.

He didn't respond, but he didn't need to. The moment the call went out, he was already charging in, taking down one of the attackers with a single, fluid strike. And suddenly, everything seemed to snap into focus. We were no longer two separate entities—no longer one person running to save the other—but one single force, moving in tandem, instinctively connected by something stronger than the danger surrounding us. We didn't have time to think. We had only time to fight.

But even as we fought, I couldn't shake the feeling that something was off. This wasn't just a skirmish. It was too well orchestrated. Someone was pulling the strings, watching from the shadows. And when the dust settled, I wasn't sure if we were walking out of this alive.

The clash of steel on steel echoed through the trees, reverberating like the drumbeats of a war drum, stirring the very air with its urgency. Sweat dripped into my eyes as I fought my way through the chaos, the metallic scent of blood thickening the air. Dorian was a blur of motion beside me, his sword slicing through the air with deadly precision, and I couldn't help but be reminded of how we had once fought together, in sync, without even thinking. But this time—this time, everything felt different. The weight of it all, of all the secrets, the lies, the things unsaid, hung heavily between us.

I caught a flash of movement to my right, too quick to react at first, but just as my instincts kicked in, something sharp bit into my side, a searing pain that stole my breath. I barely had time to register the shock of it before the world tilted. The ground rose up to meet me, but my vision blurred, and all I could see was the outline of Dorian, his face drawn tight in fury and disbelief as he made his way toward me through the tangle of bodies.

"Damn it, don't do this," he muttered under his breath, as if I hadn't just heard the sharp intake of his breath, the panic beneath it that he tried so hard to mask. But it was there, beneath the calm facade he tried to uphold. The sight of me in pain, of me struggling, was enough to unravel everything he thought he'd kept tightly bound in his chest.

"Don't worry about me," I gritted out, pushing myself upright despite the waves of dizziness crashing over me. "You're the one who's going to need saving in a second."

He shot me a look—half exasperation, half disbelief. It was clear he had no intention of letting me take the brunt of this fight. "Stop being so damn stubborn," he growled, just as another attacker lunged forward, a dark figure too swift, too vicious.

I saw it before he did. The glint of steel from the corner of my eye, the flash of a weapon just behind his back, aimed straight for his throat. Without thinking, I reacted, my legs moving before my brain could catch up, throwing myself into the path of danger, my body crashing into his with an impact that knocked both of us to the ground.

The world spun, and the air whooshed out of my lungs as we hit the forest floor. My head cracked against the hard earth, a sharp burst of pain exploding in my skull, but I could still hear him, still feel the heat of his body pressed against mine as I shoved him further out of the way.

"Stay down," I rasped, even as my body screamed for release, for rest. But there was no time for that.

Dorian, his breath ragged, grabbed my wrist and yanked me to my feet, his grip tighter than I'd ever felt it before, almost like he was trying to hold onto me—not just physically, but something deeper, something I couldn't put into words. His eyes met mine, but there was no soft glow, no warmth. Only fire and fear, the fear of losing me, of failing me in the face of this insurmountable odds.

"We need to get out of here," he said, his voice tight, but it wasn't a question. It was a command wrapped in desperation, the kind of command that made my chest ache because I knew—he knew—he couldn't keep me safe forever.

But I wasn't going anywhere without him. Not now. Not ever.

We broke apart, our swords flashing as we turned back to face the oncoming tide of attackers. The ground beneath our feet was slick with mud and blood, the remnants of lives lost too soon, too senselessly. I could hear the ringing of metal and the breathless cries of the men and women who fought beside us, but there was something more—something lurking, something beneath the surface that made my skin crawl.

"Dorian," I called out, my voice sharp, my breath ragged as I scanned the trees for any sign of movement. "We're not alone. Not just these idiots. There's someone watching us."

He didn't look surprised. In fact, his eyes narrowed as he surveyed the surrounding forest, his instincts aligning with mine. But there was no one to be seen. Nothing but the shifting shadows between the trees, the rustling of leaves in the wind, like the forest itself was alive—alive with secrets, alive with death.

"Damn it," he muttered under his breath, clearly considering how best to deal with this new threat, but he wasn't fast enough. The realization that we were not just fighting the enemy before us, but someone orchestrating this entire disaster, settled in. And with it came the crushing weight of dread.

"Look out!"

I didn't need to turn to know what he meant. I saw the glint of a hidden blade just as it aimed for me—too close, too fast—but Dorian's arm was already around me, pulling me backward, out of the path of the strike. My heart stuttered, a shudder of panic rippling through my body as I realized how close we were to losing it all.

"Dorian, we need to—"

But before I could finish, the ground shook beneath us. A loud crack filled the air, and the entire clearing seemed to tremble. I whirled toward the sound, my pulse racing, my mind struggling to process what had just happened. Then I saw it—a figure stepping out from the trees.

At first, I couldn't make out much, just a silhouette in the fog of the forest, but as the figure stepped forward, a strange chill crept down my spine. It wasn't just the leader of this band of attackers. No, this was someone else—someone more dangerous. Someone who had been pulling the strings all along.

"Dorian," I whispered, my voice barely audible, as I took a step back. "This is it."

His eyes flicked toward me, understanding settling over his face like a heavy fog. "I knew it wouldn't be over this easily."

Before either of us could react, a voice cut through the clearing, cold and smooth, like velvet wrapped around a blade.

"Did you really think you could run from me forever?"

Chapter 29: The Silent Burn

The camp was still when we returned, the flickering fire casting erratic shadows across the ground. A quiet hum seemed to hang in the air, as though the world was holding its breath, waiting for something that neither of us could name. I glanced over at him, my heart twisting at the sight of his slumped shoulders, the way he moved with such deliberation, as if every step carried a weight he was too tired to bear. His jaw was tight, his face unreadable, and I knew better than to ask what was wrong. There was nothing more exhausting than trying to get a man to talk when he didn't want to, especially one like him.

The night wrapped itself around us, thick and unyielding, but the fire was a small, warm reprieve, flickering and crackling as it clung to its last breath. I sat down on the log near the edge of the camp, the rough bark pressing against my legs. I could see his back, rigid as he stared into the fire, his expression so closed off that it felt like a brick wall had been built between us.

"Hey," I ventured, trying to sound casual, though I knew my voice came out softer than I'd intended. "You good?"

He didn't answer, not at first. The silence stretched out, punctuated only by the occasional hiss of embers collapsing into ash. My fingers toyed with a loose thread on my sleeve, a nervous habit I couldn't shake.

"I'm fine," he said finally, his voice low, rough like gravel. He didn't turn to look at me, didn't make any move to show that he was even aware of my presence, beyond the fact that I had spoken. But I could feel the distance, the way it hung between us like a cloud, thick and oppressive.

I sighed, sinking further into the log, wishing the ground would just swallow me whole. He was always like this when something was bothering him, a silent fortress that nothing could penetrate. But tonight was different. Tonight, there was something in the air—something in him—that made it feel like the walls were higher than ever before. And though I couldn't place my finger on it, I had a sinking feeling that whatever was troubling him had nothing to do with me.

The wind picked up, rustling the leaves, making the fire flicker as if it was about to go out. I couldn't just let it be, not when there was a part of him I knew he was keeping hidden. I had seen too many sides of him by now to pretend I didn't understand that look in his eyes, that heavy, faraway stare. It wasn't just the weight of the past—it was something deeper, something that clung to him like smoke.

I leaned forward, resting my elbows on my knees, feeling the faint warmth of the fire against my skin. "You don't have to tell me if you don't want to. But I can tell when something's eating at you."

The silence that followed felt heavier than the moments before. The only sound now was the faint crackle of the fire, but even that seemed too loud in the thick quiet.

I should have let it go, let him retreat into himself, but the stubbornness I'd inherited from my mother kicked in, and I found myself inching closer, my heart pounding in a way that had nothing to do with the cold. "Look, I'm here, okay? For whatever it is. I don't need you to explain everything right now, but I can't help if you don't let me in."

His head tilted slightly, as if he were trying to decipher my words, but still, he said nothing. His hand clenched at his side, his fingers twitching like they were fighting against some invisible restraint. I noticed then, for the first time, the way his hand looked—rough, callused, like it had been through things that left scars deeper than skin.

And then, just as I was about to give up, when my patience was on the verge of fraying, he reached for me. His fingers brushed mine, tentative, as though afraid I might pull away. But I didn't. Instead, I let my palm rest in his, fingers curling around his, the warmth of his skin sinking into mine. It was a small thing, a touch, but it felt like everything in that moment.

"I've lost people," he said, the words coming out in a whisper, as if they were too painful to speak any louder. His eyes closed, and I could see the muscles in his jaw working, the strain of it tightening his face.

I waited, letting him find the words at his own pace. The wind picked up again, tugging at the flames, and I shivered, though I wasn't sure if it was the cold or the weight of his confession that did it.

"Not just lost them. I've... left them. Let them down. And I can't shake the feeling that I'm always one step away from doing it again." He ran a hand over his face, a frustrated motion that tugged at something inside me. "I'm not a hero, you know? I don't even know what the hell I'm doing half the time. I just—I just keep moving forward because I don't know what else to do."

I held onto his hand, the silent promise between us growing stronger, unspoken but clear. I didn't know what he had been through, what losses haunted him, but I could feel the ghosts swirling around him, just out of sight, just out of reach.

"I don't need you to be a hero," I said softly, my voice steady despite the way my heart was hammering in my chest. "I just need you to be here. With me. Whatever happened, whatever you think you've done... you're not doing it alone anymore."

For a long moment, neither of us spoke. The fire had died down to embers now, glowing faintly in the darkness. But his hand, wrapped around mine, was warmer than any flame. And in that silence, something shifted between us—something fragile, something real.

I leaned in, my forehead resting against his shoulder, the steady rhythm of his breathing grounding me in a way nothing else could. "You're not alone," I repeated, my voice barely a whisper. "I'm not going anywhere."

The air felt denser now, heavy with the weight of unspoken things. I could still feel the warmth of his hand in mine, but it wasn't the comfort I had hoped for. His fingers were trembling slightly, and though he didn't pull away, there was an unmistakable tension in the way he held onto me, as if he wasn't sure whether to let go or pull me closer. I waited for him to speak again, my own thoughts swirling, dizzy from the intimacy of the moment, the quiet urgency that had seeped into the space between us. But words—his words—seemed trapped somewhere just beyond his reach.

The fire flickered again, its orange glow sending shadows dancing across his face, making him seem far away, as though the man I thought I knew was somehow slipping into a version of himself I couldn't understand. His jaw clenched. His eyes flicked to the side, to the treeline, where the black silhouettes of the trees loomed like silent sentinels.

I shifted slightly, leaning into him, letting my breath come slower, more deliberate. "It's okay, you know," I murmured, careful not to break the fragile spell we had cast around us. "You don't have to carry this alone."

He didn't respond right away. The only sound was the crackling of the fire, a soft pop of a log breaking in half. His gaze remained fixed on the darkness, unfocused, as though he were searching for something—someone—in the shadows of his own mind.

"I wasn't always like this," he said after what felt like an eternity. His voice was rougher now, but still faint, like the distant rumble of thunder on the horizon, the kind you can't ignore, but can't quite grasp either. "I used to think... that I had it figured out. What I was meant to do. Who I was meant to be."

His words hung in the air, and I held my breath, leaning forward, my hand still caught in his. I had never seen him this vulnerable before, and as much as I wanted to press him for more, I knew better than to push. The silence between us had its own weight now, but I didn't want to break it just yet. Not when he seemed to be struggling with something so much bigger than the two of us.

"I thought I was strong," he continued, his voice growing quieter, "That nothing could break me. But then the walls... they started cracking. First slowly, then all at once." His eyes found mine then, and I saw something raw in them, something dark and haunted. "And I didn't know who I was anymore."

It was as though the world had shifted in an instant, the ground beneath me tilting, but I stayed steady. He didn't say anything else for a long while, and I let the silence stretch, allowing him the space to gather his thoughts. I knew better than to rush him, to fill the space with empty words. This was the kind of thing that took time, and in some strange way, I knew that our connection was deepening, folding in on itself like the slow, deliberate swirl of an ocean tide. It didn't need to be rushed, not now.

"You're not broken," I said softly, the words slipping out before I could stop them. "No matter how many cracks you think there are, they don't define you."

He didn't reply immediately, but when he did, his voice was strained. "You don't understand. You can't."

"I don't need to understand," I answered, my thumb tracing small circles along the back of his hand. "I'm not trying to fix you. I'm just here. And I'll be here, even when it gets hard. Even when you don't know what's next."

For a long time, he said nothing, and I almost thought I'd said too much. But then, just as the last of the fire seemed to sputter out, his body seemed to relax ever so slightly. It wasn't a dramatic shift, but it was enough for me to notice. His grip on my hand loosened, the tension easing from his fingers like a breath finally let go.

"You're not like anyone else," he said, and his voice carried an edge of something—I couldn't quite place it, but it felt like both gratitude and regret all tangled up together. "I've never met anyone like you."

I wasn't sure how to respond to that. Part of me wanted to say something clever, to deflect it with a joke or a teasing comment, but I held back. There was no need to hide behind sarcasm when something real was finally starting to take shape between us. So, I just smiled—soft and gentle—and gave his hand another reassuring squeeze.

"You'll get through this," I whispered. "Whatever it is, you're not doing it alone."

The air shifted again, the cold creeping in around us as the fire burned lower, but somehow, I felt warmer. As if the space between us, once filled with unsaid things, was slowly being filled with something else. Something I couldn't quite put my finger on, but something that felt right.

He inhaled sharply, like he was about to say something else, but then stopped. Instead, he shifted slightly, pulling his knees up and wrapping his arms around them. The moment passed, but it wasn't lost on me. I knew that whatever walls he had put up, whatever armor he'd worn for so long, were starting to crack. It wasn't an easy process, and it wouldn't be a fast one, but it was a start.

"I've done some things," he muttered, his voice dropping again, a shadow crossing his features. "Things I wish I could undo. Things that make me question... everything. Every choice I made. Every person I left behind."

His words made my stomach tighten, but I wasn't about to shy away. "You're not defined by your past," I said quietly, my heart aching for the man I was slowly getting to know. "You're not the mistakes you've made."

The fire crackled one last time, sending a few sparks into the night air before it finally settled into embers, leaving only the faintest glow. But for the first time that night, the silence didn't feel so suffocating.

The air around us was thick with unspoken words, hanging like a veil between us. The embers flickered, casting a ghostly light on the ground, and for a moment, the world outside our small camp felt far away. I could hear the wind stirring the trees, the soft murmur of the night itself, but all that existed in that moment was the quiet pulse of his presence next to mine.

I didn't know what to say next, and I couldn't help but wonder if he even knew. The man sitting beside me, his face shadowed by the firelight, was a stranger in ways I hadn't expected. All this time, I'd thought I understood him—his strength, his resolve. But now, as I looked at him, I realized there were so many layers I had yet to see, so many pieces of him I'd never even known to ask about.

He shifted slightly, his hand slipping from mine for a fraction of a second, before he settled back again. It was a small movement, almost imperceptible, but I felt the loss of his touch like a sharp pang in my chest. I wanted to reach for him again, to hold him close, but I could sense that this—whatever this was—needed to be on his terms.

"I didn't ask for any of this," he muttered, his words coming out in a low, gravelly tone that made my heart tighten. "I didn't ask to be... to be this way." He glanced at me briefly, his eyes dark, searching. "I didn't want to be someone who had to keep running. Someone who couldn't look back, couldn't stop moving, even when he had no idea where he was going."

I didn't answer at first, unsure how to reassure him without sounding like I was minimizing the weight of what he was carrying. So instead, I just nodded. Sometimes, the best thing you can offer isn't a solution—it's just the act of being there.

"You've been through a lot," I said quietly, my voice barely above a whisper. "I can't pretend to know what it's like, but I know that you're not alone in it anymore."

He let out a bitter laugh, shaking his head. "You don't know the half of it. There's so much... darkness in my past. Things I've done, people I've lost. And every time I think I'm over it, it comes back. It follows me."

I could feel the heaviness in his words, like they were dragging him down, pulling him back to something I couldn't see but could almost feel in the air. There was a depth to his pain that was impossible to ignore, a silent scream buried deep within him, and I knew he wasn't ready to share it all—not yet, anyway.

But still, I pressed on, trying to break through the wall he'd built around himself. "You don't have to talk about it if you're not ready. But I need you to know that whatever it is, you're not the only one carrying it. We all have our demons. They might look different, but they're all just as real."

He didn't answer, but I could see the tension in his jaw, the way his fingers twitched, like he was holding back something, something he wasn't sure he was ready to let out. I waited, my own thoughts racing, as I wondered just how much of himself he was willing to reveal to me. The silence stretched on, heavier now, like the weight of his words was sinking into the ground beneath us.

And then, just when I thought he would retreat back into his shell, he spoke again, his voice softer this time, almost hesitant.

"Do you ever wonder if you were meant to be something else? Like... if the person you are now isn't the person you were supposed to be?"

His question caught me off guard, and I looked at him, trying to make sense of what he was asking. His eyes were intense, focused on me, but there was a flicker of something—a vulnerability—that made me feel like I was seeing a side of him he hadn't shown to anyone in a long time.

"I don't know," I replied slowly, my voice steady despite the rush of emotions tumbling through me. "I think about it sometimes. But I've learned that I don't have to have everything figured out. Life doesn't always go the way we expect. Sometimes we just have to make peace with who we are, even if it's not the version we imagined."

He seemed to consider this, his gaze drifting back to the dying fire. "I'm not sure I can do that," he said after a moment, his tone darkening again. "I don't know if I can ever make peace with what I've become."

There was a long pause, one that seemed to stretch across miles of unspoken thoughts. I could feel the air growing colder, the shadows of the trees wrapping around us like a shroud. And still, there was something about the way he was looking at me that made me feel like I had to keep holding on. That I had to keep fighting for him, even when he wasn't sure he was worth it.

"I think you're stronger than you give yourself credit for," I said quietly, my voice unwavering. "Strength doesn't always look like what we expect. Sometimes it's just about keeping going. Even when it feels like you're falling apart, even when it feels like you're lost."

He was quiet again, his eyes narrowing as though my words had triggered something deep inside him. For a second, I thought I'd said the wrong thing. But then, without warning, he stood up, his movements abrupt, as though he couldn't stay seated any longer.

"Maybe you're right," he muttered, his voice taut with frustration. "Maybe I am stronger than I think. But you don't know what it's like to be this... this broken. To carry the weight of everything and feel like you're never going to be whole again."

I stood too, trying to close the distance between us, but before I could reach him, there was a sudden crack in the silence. A sharp snap—like the breaking of a twig underfoot—followed by a low, ominous growl from the trees behind us. My heart skipped a beat, and I froze, my eyes widening.

For a split second, I thought my mind was playing tricks on me. But then the growl came again, louder this time, unmistakable, and I felt a chill run down my spine.

He turned to face me, his expression unreadable, but there was a flicker of something in his eyes—a warning, maybe. Or fear.

"Stay behind me," he whispered urgently. "Now."

And then, before I could respond, he was already moving, stepping forward with the kind of purpose I knew meant trouble. And I didn't hesitate. Not for a second.

I followed him, my heart pounding, the sound of footsteps echoing in the darkened forest around us. But the growl was growing louder, closer, and I knew whatever was lurking in the shadows wasn't going to wait much longer.

Chapter 30: Edge of the Flame

The fire had left its mark on everything—the charred bones of trees that once whispered in the wind, the ground, still warm and soft beneath my boots, and the air, thick with the scent of scorched earth. There was something sinister about it, something that felt deliberate. The investigator's arrival only cemented that nagging suspicion.

He was tall, too tall, with a presence that seemed to make the shadows shift around him. The flicker of the firelight bounced off his dark coat as he stepped into our camp, the snap of branches under his boots an oddly jarring sound against the stillness. I didn't trust him, and something about the way he glanced at the people around me—those I considered family—made my skin crawl. It wasn't just his eyes, which were an unsettling shade of grey, too cold for any warmth to linger, but the deliberate way he moved, as if measuring every step, every word, every glance.

I had been standing by the fire, absentmindedly poking the embers with a stick, when he approached. The others were too busy with the aftermath, sorting through the remnants of tents, securing the perimeter, but I noticed him immediately, his sharp gaze cutting through the haze of smoke.

"Are you in charge here?" His voice was low, edged with something I couldn't quite place.

I straightened, stepping away from the fire, watching his every move. I should have known the question was coming, but it still felt like a trap, his words hanging in the air like a slow poison. "Depends on your definition of in charge," I replied, my tone light, a little too light, as I wiped my hands on the sides of my jeans.

He didn't smile. Not even a flicker. Instead, he stared at me like I was a puzzle he was trying to solve. "This isn't the first time you've had to deal with fires, is it?"

I flinched, the question cutting deeper than I'd expected. "We've had some issues with lightning strikes before, but nothing like this."

He nodded slowly, as if cataloging my response, and then took a step closer. I wanted to back up, but something kept my feet rooted to the ground. The others were watching now, their gazes flicking between us, unsure if they should intervene. I was the one who had to take control, whether I wanted to or not.

His next question came out like a blade slicing through the air. "How do you know you weren't involved?"

The accusation hit me like a slap. I could feel my heart rate spike, my mouth going dry. I glanced over at the others, catching their eyes, but none of them seemed as shocked as I was. Had they heard this before? Had they expected it? I forced a smile, though it felt brittle on my lips. "I don't know what you're insinuating, but I've been too busy trying to save people to have any part in starting fires."

His expression didn't change. He didn't blink, didn't seem to take a breath. Just those cold eyes, watching me, waiting for a crack. "And the man you're with?" His voice dropped lower, the words a challenge. "You've known him how long?"

I stiffened. The man he referred to, the one who had come into my life with as much disruption as a thunderstorm, was my ally, my protector, my something more. The thought of anyone questioning his loyalty—his honesty—was enough to make my pulse race with a fury I couldn't hide. "Long enough," I bit out. "And long enough to know he's not the kind of person who sets fires. Not to people. Not to anything."

His lips twitched into something that might have been a smile, but it didn't reach his eyes. "Is that so? And yet you're here, surrounded by the remnants of one. Do you ever wonder if you're trusting the wrong person?"

There it was again—the implication. The cold, steady way he was framing every question like a noose tightening around my neck. He didn't care what he was insinuating. The man had his own agenda. I could feel it. Could almost taste it in the air—sharp and bitter.

I wanted to lash out, to tell him where to shove his suspicions, but instead, I stood firm, all the while my mind spinning, my heart pounding. "I don't have to wonder. I've seen enough to know where my loyalty lies."

His eyes flicked to the others, measuring them. "And they? Are they all so sure?"

A muscle in my jaw tightened. He didn't know them. He didn't know what they'd been through, what they'd sacrificed to get here, to survive this world. My eyes narrowed as I met his gaze. "You're asking the wrong questions," I said, my voice steadier than I felt. "You're asking about things you don't understand."

His smile was sharp, cold. "Maybe. But I'll get the answers I need." He turned, his coat swishing behind him, the momentary heat of the fire flickering in his wake.

I stayed rooted to the spot, my heart still hammering, my thoughts tangled in a web of doubt. As he walked away, I felt the weight of his words pressing on me, the uncertainty lingering in the air long after he was gone.

It wasn't just about the fires anymore. It was about the man who had walked into my life, the one whose secrets were becoming as much a part of me as the ones I carried myself. The investigator had been here for more than just answers. He was looking for someone to blame. And, for the first time, I wasn't sure if he was wrong.

The air had grown heavier, the scent of charred wood clinging to everything like a second skin, as if the fire had left its essence in the very molecules around us. The investigator's departure did nothing to ease the tension—it only thickened it, like the heat of a storm just before the first drop of rain. I could feel the weight of his words hanging around us, even after he was gone. The way he'd looked at me, his questions too sharp, too pointed. It wasn't just an interrogation; it was an accusation, and no matter how much I wanted to shake it off, I couldn't. It lingered.

I paced the perimeter of the camp, my boots sinking slightly into the earth, the light of the dying fire flickering across the edges of my vision. The others had fallen into their usual rhythm after the chaos, but there was an edge to everything now. Their eyes flicked toward me more often, as if waiting for me to say something, to give them some kind of reassurance that everything was fine. But I couldn't. How could I when the very air seemed to pulse with the question that had followed the investigator's departure: What if I had been wrong?

I found him by the river's edge, where the water still churned from the fire's wake, catching the reflection of the pale moon overhead. His back was to me, his broad shoulders tense beneath the weight of unspoken thoughts. I knew this man. Knew the way his eyes softened when he looked at me, how his smile could cut through any storm, how his laugh had once made the world feel smaller, safer. But tonight, there was none of that. Just the same taut silence that had filled the space between us since the investigator left.

"Is it true?" I asked, my voice barely a whisper as I approached, as if the words themselves might crack the fragile tension.

He stiffened but didn't turn. His jaw tightened, and I could see the muscles in his neck strain under the effort to keep still. "What do you mean?"

I swallowed hard, not sure how to push through this without sounding accusatory, without unraveling everything we had built. "The investigator thinks—" I cut myself off, not wanting to repeat the words aloud. It felt like betrayal, like giving power to something that didn't belong to us.

He turned then, slowly, as if the effort required was too much for him to make a sudden move. His eyes were dark, unreadable, but I could still see the tension in his face, the way his brows pulled together, the faint line around his mouth. "The investigator's job is to suspect. To question. That's all."

I shook my head. "You know that's not it. He's not just asking questions. He's making accusations. And I—" I paused, trying to steady myself before I said something I couldn't take back. "I don't know if I can keep defending you."

His expression softened for the briefest moment, but the vulnerability disappeared as quickly as it had come. "Then don't," he said, his voice like gravel underfoot. "Don't defend me. Defend what you believe in. What you know."

I wanted to argue, to say that I wasn't sure what I knew anymore. That his presence here was more complicated than it had been a few weeks ago, that the weight of his secrets was starting to press too hard against the boundaries of what I could accept. But I didn't. Instead, I stared at him, watching the way his chest rose and fell with each breath, steady, controlled, as if nothing could touch him.

"You're asking me to trust you when the whole world's turning against us," I whispered, stepping closer, the distance between us closing as the night crept around us. "How am I supposed to do that?"

He met my gaze then, his eyes fierce, intense. "Because you have no other choice."

The finality in his tone hit me harder than any accusation. It was a cold slap, but it carried a weight of truth I couldn't deny. He was right. I had chosen to stand by him. I had placed my trust in him, in his silence, in his strength, even when everything else seemed to unravel.

I stepped back, suddenly aware of how close we had come. The firelight cast long shadows between us, and the world felt smaller, quieter, as if it were holding its breath. The tension was almost unbearable, the unspoken words heavier than the air around us.

"You think the investigator's wrong?" I asked, breaking the silence that had stretched between us.

He exhaled sharply, the sound filled with frustration, but there was no malice behind it. Just exhaustion. "I think the investigator's looking for something that's not there. And maybe I don't blame him. Maybe I'd do the same if I didn't know the truth."

"And what's the truth?" I asked, unable to keep the sharp edge from my voice. I knew what I wanted to hear, but I wasn't sure if I was ready to hear it.

He hesitated, his gaze flicking to the ground before it returned to mine. "The truth is that I'm not your enemy. The truth is that I'm trying to keep us all alive. The rest of it... it doesn't matter. It's just noise."

For a moment, I stood there, my breath coming in uneven bursts, wondering if I had enough left in me to fight for him, to fight for us. But then, as if sensing my hesitation, he stepped forward, his voice low and urgent.

"You can't keep second-guessing everything," he said, his words cutting through the doubt like a hot knife. "You'll break under the pressure. And if you break, we all do."

I opened my mouth to argue, but no words came. Instead, I let the silence wrap around us, the weight of his words sinking deep into my bones. What had we become? What had I allowed to happen between us? This wasn't just about fire anymore. This was about survival. And survival, it seemed, came at a much higher price than either of us had realized.

The moon hung low in the sky, its pale light barely cutting through the thick, damp fog that had rolled in from the mountains. The stillness of the night felt oppressive, as if the world were holding its breath, waiting for something to shatter the silence. I was restless, every nerve in my body tingling with the unsettled energy that had taken hold since the investigator left. The questions he'd planted in my mind had grown like weeds, twisting through every thought, and no matter how much I tried to shake them off, they kept coming back, sharper, louder.

I couldn't stay in the camp any longer. Not like this. Not when everything was slipping through my fingers, and I could feel the walls closing in. The air was thick with smoke, even hours after the fire had been contained, and the familiar scent of pine had been replaced with something acrid and bitter. I needed to clear my head, to push away the weight of the decisions I had made, even as they gnawed at my insides.

I walked toward the trees, my footsteps muted by the soft ground, the weight of the night pressing down on me. The shadows seemed to stretch unnaturally, twisting in ways they shouldn't, and I found myself instinctively glancing over my shoulder. It was too quiet, too empty, like the world itself had been abandoned. And then I heard it—a faint rustling, like the crackle of dried leaves underfoot, followed by the soft snap of a twig.

My heart skipped a beat. Instinctively, my hand moved toward the knife I kept at my side, the cold steel offering a brief sense of comfort. But the noise stopped as suddenly as it had started, leaving behind only the chirp of crickets and the far-off hoot of an owl. I told myself it was nothing. The wind. An animal. Something benign. But the nagging unease refused to let go.

I pushed through the trees, the rough bark scraping my palms as I passed. The camp was a distant memory now, swallowed up by the vastness of the wilderness. The deeper I went, the more it felt like the forest itself was alive, breathing with me, wrapping me in its heavy embrace. It had always been a safe place, the trees standing tall like sentinels, watching over us. But tonight, they seemed to hold secrets of their own, secrets that I wasn't sure I wanted to uncover.

The sound came again, louder this time, closer. I froze, every muscle in my body locked in place, the hairs on the back of my neck standing up. Slowly, I turned, my eyes scanning the dark underbrush. And that's when I saw him.

His face was barely visible, his outline barely more than a shadow against the darkness. But I knew who it was before he even spoke.

"You shouldn't be out here alone," his voice was low, rough, carrying the weight of the same tension I'd felt since the investigator left. His gaze, dark and intent, locked onto mine, and for a moment, neither of us moved.

I felt the sudden urge to step back, to put distance between us, but my feet stayed planted. "I could say the same to you," I muttered, my voice barely above a whisper. "You've been following me."

He didn't deny it. Instead, his lips pressed into a thin line, the muscles in his jaw working under the strain. I could see the way his body was poised, ready to move at a moment's notice, like he was anticipating danger—or perhaps preparing to cause it.

"What do you want?" I asked, my tone sharper than I intended. I hated the way the questions I hadn't asked were still hanging in the air between us.

He didn't answer immediately. Instead, he took a step closer, his boots crunching softly on the ground, and I instinctively reached for the hilt of the knife at my waist. But he stopped, his hands raised in a gesture of peace. "I need to know if you're with me," he said, his voice low but insistent. "I need to know if I can trust you."

The words hit me harder than I expected. A strange mix of relief and fear washed over me, and I could feel my breath quicken, the reality of the situation settling in like a heavy weight on my chest.

"Trust me?" I repeated, a bitter laugh escaping my lips. "You want trust? After everything? After what the investigator said? After you—"

"I don't care what the investigator said," he interrupted, his voice rising with the frustration I had heard simmering beneath the surface for days. "What matters is where you stand. Do you trust me, or do you trust him?"

I opened my mouth to reply, but the words caught in my throat. The question was simple enough, but the answer wasn't.

"I don't know," I said quietly, my voice cracking under the weight of it. "I don't know anymore."

The silence that followed felt heavy, suffocating. I could feel the distance growing between us, the space between us wide and impossible to cross. He stepped back, his hands dropping to his sides, and I watched as his shoulders slumped, the rigid tension that had held him so tightly now unraveling before me.

"You have to decide," he said, his voice softer now, as if the storm inside him had passed. "And you have to decide soon. Because if you don't, everything we've fought for, everything we've built here—it's going to fall apart. The investigator won't stop. He'll keep digging, keep looking for someone to blame, someone to take the fall. And if we don't make a stand, we'll be the ones who pay the price."

I felt the weight of his words sink into me, like stones sinking into a still pond. His gaze was steady, unwavering, and I could feel the urgency in his voice, the desperation that had become familiar in his eyes. But it wasn't just his desperation I felt. It was mine too, mingling with his, twisting into something darker.

"Are you asking me to choose between you and him?" I asked, barely recognizing the shakiness in my own voice.

He nodded once, sharply, his gaze never leaving mine. "That's exactly what I'm asking. And you need to do it now, before it's too late."

I stared at him, my thoughts spinning in circles, my mind trapped in a place I couldn't escape. And then I heard it—a rustle in the bushes behind him. A sound so small, so quiet, yet it was enough to snap me out of the spiral I was falling into.

I didn't know what it meant. But I knew I wasn't alone. And neither was he.

Chapter 31: Fuel to the Fire

The air is thick with smoke, acrid and suffocating, clinging to my skin like a second, unwanted layer. It tastes like rust and ash. My breath comes in shallow, ragged gasps, each inhale a struggle against the fiery beast that rages in front of us. The world is bathed in a chaotic orange glow, every flicker of flame casting long, monstrous shadows across the ground. It's not a fire; it's a creature. A wild, ferocious thing that moves and breathes, and right now, it's hungry. It devours everything in its path, as if the earth itself has become its feast.

There's a scream in the distance, distant but unmistakable, a raw sound that cuts through the roar of the flames. My heart stutters. I don't know who it is, but I know what it means: someone is out there, someone needs help. The weight of that realization settles like lead in my chest. I reach for the walkie-talkie strapped to my shoulder, my fingers fumbling for a moment before the static crackles to life.

"Shannon, get in position, we've got a life in danger!" I snap, voice tight with urgency.

The response is immediate, but the panic I hear in Shannon's voice sends a ripple of dread through me. "I can't get through! The fire's too thick. We're gonna lose them!"

I bite my lip, fighting the rising panic clawing at the back of my throat. That's not an option. Not tonight. Not on my watch.

Beside me, Jake's voice is a calm anchor in the storm. He's not panicking. He's never panicked, not in the years I've known him. He moves with purpose, eyes scanning the area, his body taut, ready to spring into action. He's always been the steady force in this chaotic world of flames and danger. But tonight—tonight, his jaw is clenched so tight it looks like it might break.

"Head toward the east exit, we need to evacuate anyone left," he says, voice low and steady, but the tension is there, hidden beneath the calm exterior. I can see it in the way his brow furrows, in the tight line of his lips.

I nod, though I'm not sure if he's talking to me or to himself. Either way, I'm already moving, pushing forward into the firestorm, the flames licking the air around me as if trying to burn everything in their path. The heat is unbearable, but I don't falter. Not now.

I can feel Jake at my side, his presence like a shield, though the world around us is disintegrating. His gloved hand brushes mine for a moment, a touch so brief it almost isn't there, but it's enough to send a jolt through me. His proximity has always been a comfort, even when everything else seems to be crumbling. And yet, tonight, something's different. The weight in his eyes is heavy, laden with unspoken words, with thoughts I can't read. It gnaws at me, that invisible barrier between us, but I don't have time to dwell on it. Not now.

I push forward, my body aching with every step, but my focus is sharp, unwavering. The team is scattered, each one maneuvering through the fire, working in harmony like the well-oiled machine we've become over the years. But there's something off tonight, a sense of unease that I can't shake. The fire is different. It's darker, more violent. As if it's not just nature at work, but something else, something... deliberate.

"We're close," Jake says, his voice suddenly quiet. "Stay sharp."

I glance at him, but he's staring ahead, eyes narrowing against the blaze. There's a weight to his words, something that makes my skin prickle with unease. I know what he means. The fire's been building, but now it feels like it's going to consume everything in its path. It's more than just a fire; it's something else. Something malicious.

I feel it then, a shift in the air. The temperature rises, the wind picks up, and the flames roar louder, angrier, as if reacting to our presence. The ground beneath my boots vibrates with a low hum, like a pulse, a heartbeat of the fire itself. It's not normal.

I turn to Jake, the words tumbling out of me before I can stop them. "Do you think... do you think someone set it?"

His eyes meet mine, and for a moment, the world around us seems to freeze. There's a flicker of something in his gaze—an emotion I can't name. But before I can process it, he shakes his head, muttering, "We're not sure yet, but we'll figure it out."

I want to press further, but I know better. I can see it in his face—the things he's not saying. The fear. The realization. We might be facing something more dangerous than we thought.

Suddenly, the roar of the flames shifts, growing louder, more intense. The fire seems to twist, funneling in on itself, forming a vortex of heat and destruction. My heart skips a beat. This isn't just a fire. It's something else entirely.

I don't wait for Jake's command. I run toward the epicenter of the chaos, my breath coming in harsh bursts as I push through the flames. The heat is so intense I can feel my skin singeing beneath my suit, but I don't stop. Not now.

And then I see it—a figure, silhouetted against the orange glow, stumbling toward me. A child.

My heart slams in my chest, the blood roaring in my ears. Without thinking, I spring into action, my arms outstretched as I move toward them, the heat pushing against me like a wall.

The heat crashes into me, waves of suffocating fire curling around every corner, every crevice, trying to choke the life from everything it touches. I can feel my suit pressing against my skin, damp with sweat and clinging uncomfortably, but it's the suffocating weight of the smoke that gets to me the most, seeping into my lungs, stinging my eyes, threatening to pull me under. It's hard to think clearly, but I push it aside, focusing only on the task at hand: saving whoever's still alive in this inferno.

The child.

I can still see her through the flames, her tiny frame stumbling toward me like a ghost, her movements erratic, as though she's not entirely sure where she is or how she got here. Her face is streaked with soot and tears, her little hands reaching out for something—anything—to grasp, to hold on to.

"Stay with me!" I yell, my voice barely cutting through the roar of the fire. I reach for her, my fingers brushing against the heat. The flames lick at my face, but I ignore the burn. I ignore everything but the child.

She stumbles again, and my heart catches. The smoke makes it hard to see, harder to breathe, but I can't stop now. I can't fail her. Not when she's this close. My arms stretch out, and just as my fingers graze her, she looks up at me, her wide, terrified eyes locking with mine.

I scoop her up without thinking, her body light and fragile in my arms, her weight nothing compared to the urgency that grips me. I turn, my boots slipping on the charred earth, the heat a suffocating wave crashing into me from every side. The fire is everywhere, and I can feel its fury, its hunger, behind me. But right now, there's only her—only her desperate, trembling little body against mine.

The radio crackles to life, and Jake's voice filters through, the urgency threading through every syllable. "Get out of there now! We don't have much time!"

I don't need any more encouragement. I turn, sprinting toward the direction I know will lead to safety, pushing through the smoke, my lungs burning with each labored breath. The fire snarls at my back, a beast snapping at my heels, but the girl in my arms is steady, her small fingers clutching at the front of my suit as if she knows I'm her lifeline.

But it's not enough. Not this time.

The ground beneath me shifts, the earth groaning with the weight of the fire's wrath. A low rumble shakes the air, and for a split second, I freeze, uncertainty flashing through me like a bolt of lightning. My heart skips a beat, my breath catching. Something isn't right. The rumble intensifies, and I feel it in my bones. It's not the ground—it's the fire, responding to something.

"Shannon, move! Now!" Jake's voice booms in my ear, sharp with panic. His tone, usually calm, now frays at the edges, betraying his own fear.

I force myself forward, clutching the child tighter, my legs pushing me faster. I can hear her soft cries, muffled against the inferno's roar, and it spurs me on. Every muscle in my body is screaming, the heat searing through my suit, but I have to keep moving. I won't let this child become another victim of this raging beast.

And then, it happens. A sharp, guttural crack rips through the air. The trees around us—what's left of them—sway violently, their trunks snapping with the sound of breaking bones. The fire isn't just creeping; it's tearing through the landscape like a savage animal, and the shift in the air—the pressure—warns me just before the world around me collapses.

The ground trembles beneath my boots, and then, in an instant, the earth gives way. I don't have time to react, don't have time to do anything except brace for the impact. My body lurches forward, and for a heart-stopping moment, I feel weightless. Then I'm falling, hurtling downward, the ground swallowing me whole.

I scream.

But there's no time for panic. I squeeze my eyes shut, pulling the child tighter against me, willing myself to absorb the fall, to protect her. The world spins as I plummet, and then—darkness.

I wake to a crushing pressure on my chest, the taste of dirt and ash in my mouth. My head throbs with an ache I can barely register, and the heat has grown even more oppressive, burning through my suit, through my skin. I blink, trying to clear my vision, and the first thing I see is the sky—shattered with smoke, a sickly orange hue spreading across the horizon. I lift my head, gasping, only to find myself pinned under a twisted mess of debris.

For a moment, I can't feel the child. My heart stutters, my pulse thundering in my ears, until I hear her small whimper, muffled beneath the rubble.

"Hey, hey, it's okay," I whisper, my voice barely a rasp. I force my hands beneath the debris, using every ounce of strength I have left to push the twisted metal and charred wood away. "I'm here. You're safe."

My fingers find her first, the warmth of her skin like a shock against the cold of the wreckage. She's trembling, her tiny body pressed into the dirt, but she's alive. Thank God, she's alive.

I pull her into my arms, her face streaked with dirt and fear, and I press my lips to the top of her head, holding her as tightly as I dare. We're not out of danger yet. We're far from it. But I don't care. Not anymore.

"Hang on, kid. We're gonna get out of here," I say, though I don't know if it's me or her I'm trying to convince.

My radio crackles again, and I hear Jake's voice, clear and sharp this time. "Where are you? What's your status?"

"I'm alive. We're alive," I say, my voice rough but firm. "Get the team here. We're trapped. But we're not done yet."

I glance up at the smoke-filled sky, my heart pounding. We've survived this far, but something tells me this fire is far from finished with us. And as I sit there, cradling the child in my arms, with the weight of the flames pressing down on us, I realize I'm not the only one caught in this fight.

It's not just the fire anymore. It's whatever's controlling it. Something worse than just flame. Something that feels far too deliberate.

Chapter 32: Burned Bridges

The sky is still scorched with the remnants of the afternoon heat, the air thick with the lingering scent of smoke, as I sit on the old log by the fire. My fingers trace the rough bark absentmindedly, eyes fixed on the embers that crackle and spit in the dwindling flames. The forest is quieter than usual tonight, as if even nature itself is holding its breath. Or maybe it's just me. My chest tightens with every passing minute, the weight of everything pressing down like a second skin. The arguments, the doubts, the fear that has settled deep in my bones. I wonder if I can really shake it off this time.

A rustling sound breaks the silence, and I tense instinctively, every muscle in my body alert. But when I glance over, it's just him. The last person I expected—or wanted—to see right now.

He stands there for a moment, his eyes flicking from the fire to me, his jaw set tight, hands shoved in the pockets of his jacket. The shadows seem to swallow him whole, leaving only the outline of his figure in the dim glow of the dying flames. It's the first time we've been in the same space since the explosion of anger this afternoon. My heart beats faster, a furious, erratic rhythm that doesn't belong here, not in this place where the air smells like ash and regret.

"Should've known I'd find you here," he says, his voice gravelly and low, rough from days of strained silence between us.

I don't answer. There's nothing to say, at least not anything that wouldn't make it worse. So, I focus on the fire, watching the sparks jump into the night like tiny, fleeting stars that will burn out as quickly as they appeared.

"You're still mad," he adds, his tone resigned, almost wistful. Like he knows something that I don't.

"Maybe," I mutter, but I don't look up. Because the truth is, I'm not just mad. I'm hurt. And more than that, I'm scared.

The fight this afternoon, the one that has been smoldering ever since we arrived here, still feels like a freshly opened wound. The words we threw at each other—sharp, cutting things—still echo in my head. The accusation that I was being reckless, the suggestion that I wasn't taking this seriously. And then the way he turned on me, his face like a stone wall, his trust splintering in front of me. How could he not see the sacrifices I've made? How could he not understand how much this all means to me?

"You should've said something sooner," I finally say, my voice quieter than I intended. It comes out more like a confession than an accusation, and I hate how vulnerable it makes me feel. "You should've said something before we got here. Before everything went to hell."

His expression tightens, his gaze flicking away from me for a fraction of a second, but it's enough to make me catch it. I know that look. It's the same one he gets when he's trying to hide something, when he's too busy wrestling with his own demons to see what's in front of him.

"I didn't think it would come to this," he admits, his voice barely above a whisper, and for a moment, the rawness in his tone cuts through the tension like a blade.

I exhale, a sound full of frustration and exhaustion, and finally, I look at him. Really look at him. There's nothing soft about the way he stands, shoulders tense, fists clenched, but his eyes? There's something in them that betrays him—something that says he regrets what was said. I don't know if it's guilt, or fear, or maybe both, but it's enough to make my heart twist painfully in my chest.

"I didn't think we'd end up here, either," I say, the words thick with all the things I haven't been able to say. All the things I've held back. I want to tell him that I've tried to make this work. That I've given everything I have, not just to this mission, but to us. "But here we are, and I don't know how to fix it."

There's a long, charged silence between us, the kind that makes my skin crawl, like the air before a storm.

"I don't know if we can," he says finally, and the bluntness of it feels like a slap in the face. "We've both been lying to ourselves about a lot of things."

I swallow hard, trying to hold back the sudden sting in my eyes, but it's no use. The tears burn at the back of my throat, and I hate myself for it. I hate the vulnerability I can't seem to escape. I hate that, despite everything, I still want this to work. But I don't know if I can keep fighting, not if he's already given up.

"I never lied to you," I say, my voice tight with the effort of holding everything in. "But you? You've been hiding behind that wall of yours, pretending like you don't care. Like it's easier to just shut me out than to deal with the mess we've made."

For a split second, his expression falters. His hand twitches, like he wants to reach for me, but then he pulls back. "Maybe it's easier this way," he says quietly. "Maybe it's better that way. Maybe we're better off... apart."

The words hit me like a cold wave, sweeping over me, and for the first time, I wonder if this is really it. If there's nothing left to salvage. Maybe I've been fooling myself this whole time, believing we could make it work. But deep down, I know something's broken between us, and no amount of words or apologies will fix it.

The fire crackles again, louder this time, but I don't hear it. I'm too busy trying to hold myself together, watching him turn away from me. The space between us, once filled with understanding and camaraderie, is now a chasm, dark and deep and insurmountable.

And as he walks away into the shadows, the words hang in the air between us, thick and heavy.

I can't sleep. It's not the usual tossing and turning, the kind of restless energy that keeps you shifting between dreams and reality. No, this is different. This is the kind of sleeplessness that crawls under your skin, makes your bones ache, and turns every flicker of thought into an argument you can't escape. I've been staring at the ceiling for what feels like hours, the darkness around me pressing in like a suffocating weight. The fire outside, once a comforting blaze, now flickers weakly in the distance, and I can hear the occasional crack of dry wood snapping under the night's cool breath.

I haven't heard him since he walked off, and somehow, that's worse than the shouting. Worse than the words we exchanged, because in silence, there's a space where regrets grow wild. That's the kind of space you don't want to acknowledge, because once it takes root, it's a lot harder to pull up than a moment of sharp words.

I roll over, burying my face in the pillow, but it only muffles the thoughts a little, not enough to block them entirely. It's not just the fight. It's everything else—the way we used to fit together so effortlessly, the way we seemed to understand each other without needing words. The kind of connection that makes you believe nothing could pull you apart. But tonight, I wonder if I've been fooling myself all along.

The wind stirs, sending a low moan through the trees, and for a split second, I imagine I hear his voice calling my name. But I know it's not him. It's just the wind. I pull the blanket tighter around my shoulders, trying to feel a semblance of warmth, but it doesn't help. The hollow feeling in my chest lingers, sharper now than it was hours ago.

I glance over at the dark corner of the tent where I know his gear lies—his pack, his boots, the rifle slung across the fabric. For a moment, it's almost as if I can feel his presence there, even though he's not. Not physically. But he's still here, isn't he? Even if we've shredded the last remnants of whatever was between us, I can't seem to push him away completely.

When the rustling of a figure outside the tent breaks through my thoughts, I sit up so quickly I nearly knock over the lantern on the table. My pulse spikes, and I tell myself it's nothing. Probably just one of the others coming to check on the camp after the fire.

But then the figure stops, just outside the entrance, and I freeze. It's him. I can tell by the way he shifts, the subtle tension in the air around him. There's a hesitation there that wasn't there before, a gap between his movements, like he's waiting for something. Maybe me. Maybe the right words. But the silence grows louder with every second.

Finally, he speaks, his voice low but still carrying that rough edge from earlier. "You awake?"

I don't answer immediately. I want to say something, anything, but the weight of the day keeps my tongue tied. The fight between us still feels like an open wound, and I'm not sure I'm ready to bleed all over again just yet.

After a beat, he speaks again, the sound of his voice almost too soft to hear, "I don't know how to fix this." He's not asking for forgiveness, not yet, but there's something in his tone that catches me off guard. It's raw, vulnerable, and for the first time tonight, I don't hear an accusation in his voice.

I take a steadying breath, my fingers clutching the edge of the blanket, and finally manage to speak. "You can't just... throw words at me and then walk away like nothing happened. It's not that easy."

The words feel heavy, but they're also freeing. There's a certain power in acknowledging the hurt, even if it doesn't feel like it's going to change anything.

He steps closer to the entrance, the movement slow, like he's carefully testing the ground beneath him. "I know. I didn't want to hurt you."

I scoff, the bitterness that's been swirling around me all night making itself known. "You think that matters? You think saying you didn't mean to do it changes anything?" I hate how sharp my voice is, how it trembles with frustration and fear. "You can't take back what you said. You can't just erase it. It's there now. Between us."

There's a long pause, a stretch of silence that makes the space between us feel vast and cold, and then he speaks again, quieter this time. "I didn't mean to push you away, but I guess I did. I don't know how to—"

"How to what?" I interrupt, more sharply than I intend. My heart races, not just with anger but with something else, something that feels like the last thread of connection pulling tight between us. "How to trust me? How to make this work? You don't get to just walk in here and—"

But I stop. Because that's the thing, isn't it? He's not walking in here, not yet. He's standing outside, waiting for me to make the first move, and I can feel the weight of that expectation. He's waiting for me to forgive him, to fix everything. But I don't know if I can. Not tonight. Not when it feels like he's asking for a piece of me that I don't have to give right now.

Instead of finishing my sentence, I stand up. My legs feel unsteady, like they've forgotten how to move, but I push past the tremor, my steps heavy as I cross the tent to the flap. I pull it open just enough to look at him, standing there in the half-light, his eyes unreadable in the dark. For a moment, neither of us says anything.

Finally, I let the silence linger, letting it stretch out longer than either of us probably wants it to. Then, I say, quietly, "Maybe we're just too broken."

His eyes flicker, and for the first time in what feels like days, I see a flash of something in them. Regret? Desperation? I don't know. I wish I did. But the words I've said hang between us, and I wonder if they're the truth. Or if they're just the only thing left to say.

I never thought I'd find myself standing in the middle of this camp, where everything once felt solid, now swaying on a razor-thin edge. The sun has barely risen, and yet, the weight of the night still hangs in the air—heavy, almost oppressive. I sit at the edge of the firepit, watching the flickering embers die out as the world around me begins to wake up. The others are stirring, their movements stiff with the tension that has been building for days. They've all felt it, too. The uneasy quiet that lingers in the space between us.

I want to say something, to break the silence, but the words catch in my throat. I want to explain how I feel, but I'm not even sure I understand it myself. The fight we had yesterday—words that can't be unsaid, accusations thrown like knives—are still raw, still so sharp. And the worst part? I can't shake the feeling that I'm losing him. That everything I thought we had, everything I believed we were building toward, is slipping through my fingers like sand.

I glance over at the others, who are busy packing up their gear, avoiding eye contact, each of them too wrapped up in their own fears to acknowledge what's really happening between us. But then my gaze lands on him.

He's standing apart from the group, his back to me, focusing on something in the distance. Even from here, I can see the tension in his shoulders, the way his hands flex and unflex at his sides. He looks like a man at war with himself. He doesn't turn around when I stand, but I can feel his awareness, his sense that I'm moving closer, that something is about to change.

When I reach him, I hesitate. I'm not sure what I'm hoping for—a confrontation, a resolution, or simply the courage to walk away for good. But I can't seem to tear myself away. We're locked in this moment, the space between us tight and fraught with unspoken words.

"Are you going to ignore me all day?" I ask, my voice lighter than I feel, trying to sound casual even though my stomach is twisted in knots.

His shoulders stiffen, and for a moment, I think he might ignore me entirely, retreat into his silence once again. But then, finally, he turns. His face is set, eyes guarded, like he's bracing for an impact.

"I don't know what you want me to say," he admits, his voice low but sharp. "I don't know how to fix this."

The honesty in his words takes me by surprise. I thought I would be the one to say that, the one to admit I don't know how to make it better. But it's him, standing there, as vulnerable as I feel. It's almost enough to break me. Almost.

"I don't know either," I reply quietly, my voice trembling slightly despite my efforts to hold it together. "I don't know what happens now."

For a moment, we just stand there, staring at each other, the distance between us almost too much to bear. Then, he takes a step forward. Just one, but it's enough to close the gap. My breath catches in my throat, a flicker of hope sparking, then dying before it can catch fire.

"We keep moving forward," he says, his words carrying a weight that goes beyond simple direction. It's more of an answer than I expect, a quiet promise that maybe we're not too far gone. Maybe we can salvage whatever we've lost.

But I don't respond. I want to. I want to tell him that I'll follow him, that we can figure this out, that the wreckage of our last few days won't define us. But the truth is, I'm not sure if I can. Not anymore.

"I can't keep doing this," I finally say, my voice cracking with the honesty of it. "I can't keep pretending that everything is okay when it's not."

The words hit him like a punch, and I can see the shock on his face, the way his breath catches in his chest. For a second, I wonder if he'll walk away, leave me here to deal with the aftermath.

But instead, he stays. He looks at me with something like understanding in his eyes.

"I'm not asking you to pretend," he replies, his voice quieter now, more tentative. "I just... I don't know how to make it right. I don't know how to fix what we've broken."

I swallow hard, the weight of his words pressing down on me, and I realize, with sudden clarity, that this isn't just about us. It's not just about the words we said or the trust we lost. It's about everything else—everything we've been running from. And I don't know if I can keep running anymore.

"Maybe we don't fix it," I say, my voice barely above a whisper. "Maybe we just... let it go."

For a moment, he stands there, his face unreadable, and I'm not sure if he'll agree with me or if he'll argue, try to convince me that it's not over. But then, to my surprise, he nods. A slow, reluctant motion, like he's finally accepting what we've both been too afraid to admit.

"I guess that's it, then," he says softly. "We let it go."

And just like that, the last thread between us snaps. The silence that falls is thick with finality, and I can feel the weight of it, pressing down on me, heavier than anything I've ever felt. It's done. We're done.

But before I can move, before I can walk away and try to find something—anything—else to hold on to, a loud crack echoes from somewhere behind me, followed by a shout.

I turn quickly, heart hammering in my chest, but the scene unfolding before me is something I never could've anticipated.

Chapter 33: Kindling Hope

I hadn't expected the knock at the door. I'd been staring at the same patch of wall for what felt like hours, nursing a cup of cold coffee and a growing sense of dread that had settled into my bones like a second skin. The case had turned into a labyrinth, twisting back on itself in such a way that I was beginning to doubt whether there was a way out, let alone a culprit to pin it on. Every lead had been a dead end, every clue an unsolvable riddle. The firestorms were more than just arson—they were the beating heart of something darker, something far more insidious. And I was the one who was supposed to stop it. But I couldn't even find a foothold.

I heard the knock again, sharper this time, like a warning. I wasn't in the mood for visitors, least of all him.

When I opened the door, there he was. Michael. Of course, it had to be him. The man who seemed to embody every contradiction I'd ever known—impossible to trust, yet somehow impossible to turn away from. His broad shoulders and confident stance didn't soften the tension in his jaw. He looked tired, like the kind of tired that didn't go away after a good night's sleep but lingered in the corners of your eyes, in the line of your spine.

"I didn't know where else to go," he said, his voice quieter than usual, stripped of the bravado I was so used to hearing.

I swallowed hard, the words I wanted to say stuck somewhere deep in my throat. He didn't wait for me to invite him in. He stepped over the threshold without hesitation, as if he were entitled to be there, as if he were home.

"Don't." I held up a hand, stopping him before he could say anything more. "I don't need your apologies. Not now."

Michael's face hardened for a moment, then softened, as if he'd expected that much. "We're not here for apologies. We're here for answers."

There was something about the way he said it—steady, deliberate—that made me pause. My gut clenched. He had a lead. I knew it before he even said it. His lips pressed into a thin line as he dropped the file onto the small table between us. The man had learned something, and he was about to drag me through it, whether I was ready or not.

"Why the sudden change of heart?" I asked, though I already knew the answer. We didn't get this far without a few grudging concessions. We'd never been friends, but after everything that had gone down, I was beginning to wonder if we might be able to be something else. Something new, something we could build on.

He met my gaze, eyes searching mine like he was looking for a way to unravel whatever I'd hidden under all the walls I'd carefully constructed. But I was done hiding. At least, for now. I let out a slow breath. "You didn't exactly leave me with a lot of options."

Michael's lips twitched at the corners, something close to a smile pulling at the edges of his usually stoic features. He seemed to sense my reluctance and mirrored it, almost as if he was trying to force some understanding between us—something more than just professional respect.

"I don't expect you to trust me," he said, sitting down on the chair opposite mine. He leaned forward, tapping the file in front of me. "But you should at least hear me out."

I looked at the file, the weight of it suddenly real. I had no time to waste. Whatever this was, whatever he was about to lay at my feet, it could be the key to unraveling the mess we'd been stuck in for weeks. Every fire, every accusation, every broken lead. They'd all started to blur into one. But this—this was different.

I flipped open the file. It was filled with photos, notes, and a few printed reports. Nothing too groundbreaking at first glance, but the handwriting on the corner of one particular photo caught my eye. It was scrawled in black ink, sloppy but unmistakable.

"Who's this?" I pointed to the name next to the photo.

Michael sighed, a long, drawn-out sound that spoke of frustration and familiarity. "Someone I thought I could trust."

"Thought you could trust?" I echoed, my brow furrowing. "What, you're not friends anymore?"

He looked at me, his expression unreadable. "Not since he started playing both sides."

I leaned back in my chair, processing the information. So, there it was. The first real lead that might actually mean something. We were finally on the right trail. I could feel my pulse quicken, the cold dread that had settled in my gut for weeks easing just a fraction. It wasn't much, but it was enough to light a small flame of hope. A hope that had almost been extinguished.

"Alright," I said, glancing at Michael. "Let's see where this goes."

The words hung in the air between us, charged with something unfamiliar, something like mutual understanding. There was no grand gesture, no moment of clarity where everything fell into place, but it was a start. A tentative beginning. And as much as I hated to admit it, I needed him just as much as he needed me.

As we stood up to leave, I felt a strange sense of balance, like we had both been holding our breath and, for just a moment, we'd both exhaled. Together.

The city was quiet when we stepped outside. Not the kind of quiet that follows a storm—when the air still crackles with the remnants of thunder—but a heavy, expectant kind of quiet. It hung around us like the smoke that always lingered long after the fire had been put out. I couldn't help but notice the difference in Michael's posture, the way he moved now. Before, he had been all sharp edges and barely contained urgency. But now? He was more measured, like he'd figured out how to pace himself—like he knew he was in this for the long haul.

We didn't speak as we walked to the car. The kind of silence that passed between us was familiar, though not in a comforting way. More like the silence that follows an argument, the kind where both of you know there's more to say, but neither of you wants to be the one to say it. The air crackled with the possibility of something unspoken, something uncharted, and I wasn't sure whether that scared me or made me want to chase it.

He opened the door for me—just as he had so many times before—and I slipped into the passenger seat, noting the faint scent of coffee and leather that seemed to permanently settle in the vehicle. Not an unpleasant smell, but it made me wonder how long it had been since he'd actually driven anywhere without a deadline or a phone call waiting to pull him back into whatever this was. Whatever we were.

"You've done this before, right?" I asked, more to break the silence than anything else.

Michael's eyes flickered to me, then back to the road as he turned the ignition. "What, follow a trail of lies and half-truths? Yeah, a few times."

His voice was dry, almost too dry, like the words were pulling themselves out of him rather than being spoken.

I raised an eyebrow, ignoring the tightness in my chest that came with that. "Well, let's hope your experience counts for something then."

There was a pause. The kind of pause where, if this were anyone else, they'd throw in a joke, a playful quip to deflect. But it wasn't anyone else, and he didn't. Instead, the muscle in his jaw twitched—a habit he had when he was thinking too hard about something—and when he spoke again, his voice was softer.

"We'll get to the bottom of this. Whatever it takes."

I turned my head toward him, my mouth opening to speak, but the words got caught in my throat. There was a sincerity there, buried under the layers of cynicism and armor he wore, but it was there all the same. For the first time since this whole mess started, I believed him.

It was a dangerous thing, that belief. It settled into me like a slow-burning ember, one that might catch fire if I wasn't careful. I wasn't sure what was scarier—the idea that Michael might be right, or the idea that we might actually work together.

The rest of the drive passed in a blur of city lights and the rhythmic hum of the tires on asphalt. The streets became less familiar the farther we went, transitioning from bustling neighborhoods to quieter, more industrial areas. The kind of places that looked like they'd been left behind, forgotten in favor of something shinier and more convenient. It didn't take much for me to guess where we were headed—there was only one lead we'd been chasing lately, and it had led us to a set of warehouses on the edge of town.

The parking lot was nearly empty when we arrived. Only one other car was parked off to the side, an old sedan that looked like it hadn't been washed in years.

I hesitated, the weight of the file in my hands suddenly heavier than it had been back at my apartment. "This is it, huh?" I said, trying to keep my voice steady.

Michael didn't answer right away. He stepped out of the car and circled around to my side, his boots thudding against the concrete with a heaviness that seemed to echo off the surrounding buildings.

"We're not leaving without answers," he said simply, as if that should have been enough.

And maybe it should have been. But as I followed him across the lot, the hairs on the back of my neck stood up. The quiet of the place felt wrong—too still, too empty. It wasn't the kind of silence that spoke of peace or safety. It was the kind of silence that made you wonder if someone was waiting, just beyond the shadows, ready to make their move.

I glanced over at Michael, but he was already focused on the task ahead, his eyes scanning the perimeter with the kind of intensity that said he wasn't expecting anyone to come out of those darkened windows to greet us. We weren't here for a friendly chat. We were here to drag out secrets, and I had a sinking feeling they'd been buried deeper than we thought.

As we approached the door of the first warehouse, Michael stopped, turning to me with a look that could've been interpreted as cautious—or maybe I was just projecting my own nerves onto him.

"You ready?" he asked, his voice low.

I nodded, but the answer felt more like a lie than anything else. Ready for what, exactly? A confrontation I wasn't prepared for? A revelation that could turn everything I thought I knew on its head?

But it didn't matter. I was in it now, and there was no turning back.

We stepped inside, the door creaking on its hinges, the scent of dust and old metal filling the air. The space was cavernous, filled with nothing but the hum of the fluorescent lights overhead.

And then, from the shadows, came a voice I didn't expect. "You're too late."

It was like the floor dropped out from under me. The voice was too familiar, too full of disdain. And I knew, without a doubt, that we had walked straight into something far bigger than either of us had anticipated.

The voice that emerged from the shadows hit me like a punch to the gut. It was low, mocking, and filled with a venom that I recognized all too well. I froze, Michael's sharp intake of breath beside me the only sign that he'd heard it too. I didn't need to see him to know his expression mirrored mine—surprised, but not entirely shocked. We both knew that the road we were on had been leading us straight into dangerous territory. We'd just hoped it wouldn't be this dangerous.

"Too late for what?" I managed to croak, my words feeling small in the cavernous space around us. I hadn't realized how tightly I'd been holding my breath until it escaped in a rush.

From the shadows emerged a figure, but I already knew who it was before they fully stepped into the light. His silhouette was unmistakable—broad shoulders, sharp angles, and that damn smirk that always made me want to slap it off. Gabriel Dempsey. The same Dempsey who had crossed every line I had ever drawn in this town, and whose name I had cursed in private more times than I cared to admit.

"You've been chasing ghosts," Gabriel said, his voice laced with an almost eerie calmness as he strolled toward us. "And I'm afraid they've already moved on."

Michael tensed beside me, but I didn't flinch. I didn't give him the satisfaction. My jaw tightened instead, a familiar surge of anger stirring beneath my skin. Every time Gabriel spoke, every time he showed up like this, it was like he was reminding me of every failure, every setback. He thrived on it.

"Not a ghost," Michael said, his voice low, but the challenge was unmistakable. "You've been playing both sides of this game. And it's about to catch up with you."

Gabriel chuckled, the sound too smooth, too controlled. "Oh, I think you'll find I'm playing it much better than you think."

I forced my hands to uncurl from the fists they'd become. This was it—the confrontation we'd been circling for weeks. But instead of feeling triumphant, I felt a pit of dread open up in my stomach. I wasn't sure why—maybe it was the certainty in Gabriel's voice, or maybe it was because every step we took, every piece of the puzzle we pieced together, had led us straight to this moment.

"Tell me you didn't think you could just walk in here and make everything right," Gabriel continued, his eyes gleaming with a satisfaction that made my skin crawl. "You've been playing catch-up, haven't you? Just like everyone else."

The arrogance in his voice was enough to make me snap, but I held it together, reminding myself that getting emotional now would only make me look weak. I took a step forward, my heels clicking sharply against the cold concrete floor. "What exactly are you trying to say, Gabriel?"

For a moment, I thought I saw something flicker in his eyes—a brief flash of something. Regret? Fear? It was gone in an instant, replaced by that familiar mask of superiority.

"I'm saying you've been following the wrong trail," he replied smoothly. "And I'm saying you're too late to stop what's already in motion."

"Stop what's in motion?" Michael's voice was deadly calm, but I could hear the edge in it. The edge I'd been waiting for. "You think we're just going to walk away from this? Let you destroy everything we've worked for?"

Gabriel took a deliberate step toward Michael, his eyes narrowing in a way that made the hairs on my neck stand on end. "It's not destruction if it's already gone," he said, each word dripping with malice. "You're too late to save this town. Too late to save yourselves. Too late for everything."

I wanted to shout something—anything—to cut through the tension, to break through the haze of his taunts. But I didn't. Instead, I moved my hand slowly toward my waistband, fingers brushing the cool metal of my gun. Gabriel didn't seem to notice. He was still fixated on Michael, watching him with a kind of twisted amusement.

"You don't scare me, Gabriel," I said, my voice steady. I wasn't sure whether that was a lie or not.

"Good," he replied, his smirk widening. "You're going to need every ounce of courage you have when the truth comes out."

Before I could respond, there was a sound—distant at first, then growing louder. Footsteps, purposeful and quick. I felt my pulse quicken, a sudden alarm ringing through my veins.

"We've got company," I muttered, my eyes darting toward the far end of the warehouse. There were at least three shadows moving, their shapes ominous and quick. Gabriel, however, didn't seem concerned.

"You think you've got time to play hero?" he sneered. "You're not in control here. You never were."

I turned to Michael, catching his eyes for a split second. His gaze was sharp, calculating. He had a plan. He always had a plan. But we weren't just up against Gabriel anymore. We weren't just up against his manipulation. Whatever had been set in motion was bigger, darker, and more dangerous than we had ever realized.

The footsteps were closer now, and I knew we didn't have much time. I felt the weight of the situation—the weight of everything—crushing in on me. Every decision I had made had led me here, to this moment, and now it was too late to turn back.

Before I could react, a figure stepped into the dim light, and I froze. A gunshot rang out.

Chapter 34: The Final Blaze

The forest was quieter than I'd ever remembered, as if it was holding its breath, waiting for the storm we were about to unleash. The trees, thick and gnarled, seemed to huddle together like old men gossiping about things better left unsaid. The air smelled of wet earth, pine needles, and something else—something metallic that clung to the back of my throat, a promise of danger that I could taste on my tongue. I pushed through the underbrush, the thick ferns and tangled vines scraping at my legs as the damp cold seeped into my boots. But it wasn't the cold that made my skin prickle. It was the tension that clung to me, the gnawing sense of something breaking. It was him. I could feel him ahead, hidden in the wilderness, waiting for us.

I wasn't sure what to expect when we found him. If I'm being honest, a part of me had been trying to avoid this moment. Maybe I thought I could change things, fix it somehow, but now I knew better. No matter how much we had fought side by side in the past, no matter how much history weighed between us, betrayal had a way of cutting through everything. Even the strongest bonds couldn't withstand the weight of lies.

Seth was by my side, his breath coming fast as he tried to match my pace. His hands were steady, but I could see the muscle in his jaw flexing, the vein pulsing at his temple, as if the same gut-wrenching realization was sinking into him too. He didn't need to say it aloud, but I could feel the words hanging between us like a stormcloud. It's him, isn't it?

I didn't want to answer that question. I couldn't. Because the truth was already smoldering in the pit of my stomach, a fire that had been slowly building since the first ember of suspicion had flickered to life. As much as I had tried to push the thought aside, the evidence had been undeniable, each piece falling into place with a sickening precision. And now we were here, at the cabin that had once seemed like a sanctuary. Now it felt like a tomb.

The house loomed ahead, a broken silhouette against the darkening sky. I could almost see the echoes of the past in the way the shadows clung to its weathered walls. There had been nights we sat on that porch, sipping whiskey and talking about everything and nothing. Nights where everything felt so... easy. I don't know when it started to change. When the cracks began to form beneath the surface, but now they were wide open, threatening to swallow us whole.

I took a deep breath, the air bitter and sharp. The wind tugged at my hair, pulling strands loose from the braid I had tied hastily before leaving the safety of the town. I wiped the sweat from my palms onto the front of my jacket. My heart hammered against my ribs. I wasn't afraid, not exactly. But I wasn't sure what would happen when we crossed that threshold, and that uncertainty gnawed at me like a hungry animal.

Seth shifted beside me, a grim determination in his eyes as he pressed his hand to the small of my back. "You ready for this?" he asked, his voice low, rough with emotion.

I didn't look at him. Couldn't. "I don't think anyone ever is," I replied, my words harsh, cutting through the stillness like a blade. I felt him flinch, but I didn't have the energy to soften them. Not now.

We moved forward, each step heavy with the weight of our shared history, of the things we had trusted in, and the things that had betrayed us. The door was slightly ajar, hanging crooked on its hinges, as though the cabin itself was too tired to keep up the pretense of safety. I stepped over the threshold first, my boots creaking on the old wood floor, the smell of stale smoke and something sharp and sour drifting in the air.

"Is it really you?" I asked, the question aimed at the darkness that filled the small room.

The figure in the far corner stirred, and for a moment, I thought I saw a flicker of recognition, something human beneath the cold exterior. But then his head lifted, and I felt my stomach drop. The man who had once been my ally, my friend—stood there, his face half-illuminated by the faint glow of the dying fire in the hearth. His eyes were dark, hollow, the shadows under them deep enough to hide the truth that had been eating him alive.

"Did you think I wouldn't find out?" My voice cracked, and I hated myself for it.

He didn't answer at first. Instead, he just watched us, as if the weight of our presence was something he'd grown accustomed to, something he didn't have to fight anymore. Then, slowly, his lips twisted into a smile, but it wasn't the kind of smile I remembered. It was cruel, jagged, like something that had been stitched together out of desperation.

"I didn't think you'd figure it out so soon," he said, his voice calm, unnervingly so. "But I knew you would. Eventually."

Seth stepped forward, his fists clenched at his sides, the anger radiating off him like heat from an open flame. "Why, Mark?" he spat, each word a challenge. "Why the hell would you—"

Mark held up a hand, cutting him off. "You never asked the right questions, Seth. Neither of you did."

The realization hit me like a slap across the face. The betrayal wasn't just about the fires. It was about everything. The lies. The deceit. The manipulation. And now, in the quiet aftershock of that understanding, I felt the suffocating weight of it all settle on my shoulders.

"Did you ever really trust me?" he asked, his voice softer now, the edges of it curling into something almost sad. "Or did you just need to believe I was on your side?"

I didn't have an answer for that. Because the truth was, I had trusted him. Trusted him more than anyone. And now I knew that trust had been nothing but a facade.

The fight that followed was wild, frantic, a blur of fists, adrenaline, and raw emotion. Mark fought like someone who had nothing left to lose. But together, Seth and I pushed back. We had nothing left to say to each other, not anymore. Only the fire between us—the blaze of anger and betrayal—could fill the silence that had grown too loud to ignore.

Finally, it was over. We stood, panting, bloodied, the smoky scent of burnt wood and sweat thick in the air. The silence that followed was deafening. And even as we stood victorious, the victory felt hollow.

It was done. But the damage? That was just beginning.

The smoke that clung to the air wasn't just from the fires, but from something deeper, something that had settled between us like a thick fog. The silence that hung after the fight, after Mark had crumpled to the ground, was not the kind of silence that comes after victory. It was the kind that makes you realize the world has shifted beneath your feet, that nothing would ever be the same again.

Seth was the first to move. He stepped over to where Mark lay, the light from the fireplace dancing across his blood-spattered face, but he didn't touch him. Instead, his eyes traced every detail—the subtle rise and fall of Mark's chest, the bruise already darkening on his cheek, the way his hands twitched as though struggling to remember how to be human. For a moment, it was like Seth was waiting for some kind of apology, some kind of explanation that would make sense of the chaos that had just unfolded.

But Mark was done with words. The battle was over, but the war inside him had been fought long before we ever arrived. And we were only ever going to be the aftermath.

I watched the back of Seth's head, the tension in his shoulders, the way his fists were still clenched. I could practically hear the question he was dying to ask—Why? But it wouldn't change anything. It wouldn't bring us back to what we had, to what we'd lost.

I wanted to speak, to fill the silence with something, anything. But all I could do was stand there, my feet rooted to the floor, my fingers gripping the edge of the doorframe like it was the only thing that could keep me upright.

"Why, Mark?" I finally heard myself say. It wasn't much, but it was enough to make him raise his head. There was no fear in his eyes—no remorse either. There was only the shadow of something old, something ugly, buried deep inside him.

"Why?" he repeated, his voice hoarse from the struggle. "Because I had to. You never saw it, did you?" He exhaled a bitter laugh that sounded like broken glass. "You and Seth, you were always so busy fighting the fire that you didn't notice the sparks you were leaving behind. I was the one picking up the pieces. I was the one cleaning up after your mess."

I recoiled. Not from the physical threat, but from the words. There was nothing else to say. Nothing that would make sense of what he was claiming.

"You think you're the only one who's been carrying the weight of this whole thing?" Seth finally spoke, his voice hard. "You think you're the only one who's been playing the martyr? That's rich, Mark. So damn rich."

Mark's lips twisted into a smile that didn't belong on the face of someone who was supposed to be our friend. "You really think it was easy? Do you think I enjoyed watching you both burn out, chasing ghosts while everything crumbled around you?" He lifted his hand as if to wipe away the years, but his fingers hovered in the air, unwilling to touch the past. "I've been the one keeping the flames alive. Someone had to do it. Someone had to finish what you couldn't."

Seth's jaw tightened so much I thought it might crack. "You were behind the fires?" he asked, though I already knew the answer.

Mark let out a short, bitter chuckle. "You really thought they were just accidents? Fires of opportunity? That's cute." His voice softened, eyes narrowing. "But I guess you don't understand. I'm not the villain here. You're the heroes, remember?" The last word came out like a sarcastic sneer.

I stepped forward, my boots creaking on the floorboards. "You're the one who turned this into a game of smoke and mirrors, Mark. And for what? Power? Control?"

He laughed again, a hollow sound that didn't reach his eyes. "Control, power, whatever you want to call it. It's survival, not some crusade. You never understood, did you? How fragile everything is. How easily it can all go up in flames. But you will. You're going to see. You already have. The world doesn't care about your plans or your good intentions. It only cares about the fire, and who can control it."

I shook my head, suddenly too tired to stand. Too tired of trying to make sense of him. The world he'd created, the lies he'd built his life on, it was all unraveling in front of me, and there was no coming back from it.

I reached for the edge of my coat, pulling the collar tighter around my neck, trying to shield myself from the chill that had nothing to do with the cold. "And now what, Mark?" I whispered, more to myself than to him. "Now we burn?"

He didn't respond. Instead, he closed his eyes as though the very act of answering was beneath him. That's when I realized—I was done. Done with trying to salvage something from the wreckage, done with questioning the choices we'd made that led us here.

Seth finally moved. He knelt beside Mark, his face hard as stone. His hand hovered for a moment over the gun strapped to his waist, but he didn't take it out. He didn't need to. Mark was already a ghost, already lost in the flames he'd started.

"You think this is over?" Seth said softly, almost as if speaking to himself. "You think you've won?"

Mark's lips twitched, but the bitterness was gone. Instead, something else lingered there—something tired. "I've already won," he said, almost kindly. "You just don't know it yet."

And for the first time, I saw it—the real Mark. Not the one who'd once been our friend, but the one who had been hollowed out by his own fire. The one who had been consumed by the flames until all that was left was ash.

The cabin was still as we stood there, neither of us sure of what to say next, but both of us knowing that the fire was never really about the flames. It was about what we were willing to burn away in order to survive.

I couldn't remember the last time I felt so much weight in the air. It clung to everything—the smoke that had been left behind, the silent void between us, the old house that now felt like a mausoleum rather than the place where we'd once laughed and drank away the hours. Mark's confession still hung there, an invisible rope pulling tighter with each passing second, a reminder that we had crossed a line that could never be uncrossed.

The realization hit me like a physical blow, my chest tight, my breath shallow. The fire had been his doing all along, not an accident, not something beyond our control. Every time we had rushed to extinguish the blaze, we had been playing into his hands, dancing to a rhythm he had orchestrated from the start.

Seth hadn't moved since Mark spoke last. His gaze never left him, but I could see the tension in the muscles of his neck, the way his fingers flexed as if to steady himself. He was waiting for something—maybe an apology, maybe an explanation. But Mark wasn't going to give him that. No, Mark was done with the pretense. Done with us.

"What happens now?" I asked quietly, but the question didn't really have an answer. Not when the past had already burned itself out in front of us, leaving only smoldering remnants.

Seth's voice was hoarse when he finally spoke, his words thick with something that sounded like disbelief. "We finish it. We take him in."

I nodded, but I could feel the hesitation. The bitterness. I didn't need to look at Seth to know that the man we had once trusted was no longer the person we needed to take in—he was the one who had to be stopped. And it was clear from Mark's stance that he wasn't going to make it easy.

Mark pushed himself up, moving slowly, deliberately, like someone who had all the time in the world. His eyes never left Seth. There was no fear in them. Not anymore. "You think this is how it ends?" His voice was a low murmur, a challenge rather than a plea. "That you can just walk away from this?"

"I don't know how this ends," I said, my voice breaking into the space between us. "But it's over, Mark. You're done."

He gave a hollow laugh, and the sound of it made my stomach twist. It was like listening to a stranger mock everything you thought you knew about the world. "You're wrong. This is just the beginning. You think I'm the mastermind, but you don't see it. You never saw it." His gaze flicked to Seth, and then to me, before resting back on the bloodied floor. "You're so caught up in your own little story that you missed the bigger picture."

The words hit me harder than I expected. The bigger picture? What was he talking about? Everything had led us here. Every fire, every chase, every misstep had pointed to Mark. The puzzle pieces were so perfectly aligned that it felt foolish to even entertain the idea that there was something more.

"You're wrong," Seth said again, but it was quieter now, like he wasn't so sure anymore. His fists clenched and unclenched by his sides, the fight gone out of him for a split second. The doubt in his voice made my stomach churn, because I was starting to feel it too.

Mark straightened, ignoring the blood staining his shirt, the exhaustion in his eyes. He almost looked relieved, as though he had been waiting for this moment—waiting for us to question everything we thought we knew. "You two are cute, you know that?" His voice took on a mocking tone, but there was no real malice there, only weariness. "You think you're the heroes, the ones with the answers, but you're just as trapped in your own game as I am. We all are."

I stepped forward, a sharp, jagged breath escaping me. "What game, Mark? What are you talking about?"

He didn't answer right away. Instead, he glanced over his shoulder, at the dark windows of the cabin, his eyes flickering between Seth and me, like he was measuring us, considering the endgame. "You ever wonder why it always seemed like the fires were one step ahead of you?" he asked, his voice soft but cutting. "Why you couldn't catch the person responsible? You were chasing shadows, and shadows don't leave tracks. But I—" He stopped himself mid-sentence, eyes narrowing. "No, it's not just me. There's someone else. Someone you never thought to look at."

The hairs on the back of my neck stood up. "Someone else?" I echoed, my pulse quickening. "Who?"

Mark's lips parted, but instead of answering, he gave a small shake of his head, like he was weighing whether to tell us or not. Then he smiled, that same crooked, broken smile, and shrugged. "You'll see. You always do, don't you? When it's too late."

Seth and I exchanged a glance, but neither of us spoke. The air between us was thick with confusion and suspicion. There was something more. Something darker at play, and the twist in my gut told me it wasn't over.

Suddenly, the sound of footsteps echoed from outside, slow and deliberate, but unmistakable. I froze. I didn't have to look to know that we weren't alone anymore.

Mark's eyes flicked toward the door, a look of something approaching resignation flickering across his face. "Told you," he said with a knowing tone. "You think it's me, but it's never been just me. Not really."

The door creaked open, the chill of the night air spilling into the room like it was invited. Someone stepped through the doorway, a figure cloaked in shadows, their face half-hidden by the low brim of a wide hat.

For a split second, I thought I recognized the silhouette, but it was gone before I could make sense of it. And then they spoke, their voice cold, cutting through the tension like a blade.

"Did you really think it was Mark behind all of this?" the voice asked, the words hanging in the air like a question too dangerous to answer.

And for the first time in what felt like forever, I realized we had been wrong. Dead wrong.

The darkness had only just begun.

Chapter 35: Rising From the Ashes

The fire had left its mark on the landscape, but not on us—not this time. The smoke still clung to the air like a memory, as if trying to remind us of the chaos we'd just escaped. But in the clearing, where we stood beneath the brittle branches of trees now stripped of their excess, there was a soft hum of quiet. It was the kind of peace that settles into the bones, tender and unfamiliar, like a lover's touch after a long, aching absence.

I found myself leaning against the rough bark of a cedar, taking in the darkened sky, the remnants of stars just beginning to pierce through the ash-ridden haze. It was the silence I'd longed for, that strange serenity that comes after surviving something you thought would break you. The night was still, too still, and the weight of what we'd just endured hung between us like the fragile thread of an old song, waiting to be sung again.

"Are we really done?" The voice, low and uncertain, sliced through the stillness. It was his voice—familiar, yet hesitant.

I turned to find him standing a few feet away, a figure of uncertainty in the moonlight. His shoulders were slumped, but there was no escaping the way his eyes darted toward me—searching, probing, like he was trying to piece together some new reality, something neither of us had quite figured out yet.

"We're done with that," I said softly, my gaze drifting past him to the camp, where the others were tending to their wounds, their spirits visibly soothed by the absence of the danger that had stalked us for so long. The fire might have gone out, but its echoes lingered in the air, crackling with the promise of new beginnings.

He nodded, but the movement seemed automatic, as if he wasn't entirely sure whether to believe me.

"I think I'm afraid of what comes after." His voice dropped, barely audible, as if the words were more of a confession than a statement.

I stepped closer, the weight of his vulnerability wrapping around me like a blanket, warm and heavy. He never wore his fears like this—never exposed himself so plainly—but here, in the cold quiet of the forest, he couldn't hide them, and it felt like we were standing at the edge of something neither of us understood.

"You're afraid of the future?" I asked, the words coming out with a sharpness I hadn't meant. It was just… it was just that I hadn't expected this. I hadn't expected him to be the one pulling away now, after everything we'd been through.

He met my gaze then, his expression pained. "Not the future. You." His words landed like stones at my feet. "You, and what happens after all of this. You're so… so much more than this fight. And I'm not sure what to do with that."

The confession settled between us, leaving an aching silence in its wake. The words were simple, almost too simple for the weight they carried. But I knew what he meant. I knew that the life we'd been living, surrounded by fire and fear, had somehow become the only reality we could cling to. It was familiar, predictable in its chaos. The future, however, the one that didn't have firestorms and running for cover, was a terrifying unknown.

I exhaled, a steadying breath. "You don't have to do anything with it," I said, my voice steady even though I was trembling inside. I reached out for him then, my hand sliding into his, the heat of him familiar and grounding. "You're not alone in this. I'm here. Whatever comes next, I'm here."

He took my hand, his grip tight but unsure, like he was testing the waters of something he'd never quite dared to touch before. His eyes—those eyes that had seen so much, and yet had remained soft, vulnerable beneath it all—locked with mine, and for the first time in a long while, I didn't see fear in them. I saw something else. Something closer to hope.

"I don't know how to do this," he whispered, and I smiled, a quick, wry curve of my lips.

"Neither do I," I said. "But I'm willing to try. For once, I'm ready to see what comes next."

The silence between us now felt different, more comforting. No longer tense, but accepting—an invitation.

Behind us, the others were settling in for the night, their laughter muffled by the distance, and I felt the tug of that shared camaraderie, the familiar comfort of belonging to a tribe, to something larger than myself. But right now, in this moment, it was just us. And for the first time since I could remember, I didn't feel like the world was closing in. Instead, it felt as though it was opening up, revealing an expanse of possibility I hadn't dared to dream about.

"I think we should get some rest," I said, my voice low, pulling myself from the edge of that thought. There was something important about being grounded in the present, about not letting the future be a storm that threatened to undo us before we'd even arrived there.

He nodded, but before we could move, his hand tightened on mine, an unspoken question lingering between us.

"Promise me something," he said, his voice a whisper in the dark.

I turned to face him fully, letting my heart catch up to the words I knew were coming. "What?"

"That we won't let fear win. Not now. Not after all of this."

I held his gaze, my fingers threading through his with more certainty than I'd ever known. "I promise. We won't let fear win."

I couldn't stop looking at him, even as we stood there, the silence stretching like an invitation neither of us had the courage to fully accept. The stillness of the night was almost unsettling, a calm that seemed to suffocate instead of soothe. I wanted to say something, anything, to fill the space between us, but the words felt too fragile to speak aloud.

His hand was still in mine, the heat of it a reminder that this, whatever it was, was real. He wasn't going anywhere, not yet, and neither was I. For the first time, the weight of the world felt lighter—just enough for me to take a breath without feeling like I was suffocating under the pressure of everything that had come before.

I let my gaze drift past him to the campfire, where the others were starting to settle in. The flames flickered, casting shadows over their tired faces, each of them carrying their own burdens, their own unspoken fears. But for the first time in a long time, they looked at peace. Even Olivia, who rarely let anything break her stoic exterior, was smiling—soft, genuine, the kind of smile you only saw when the world had stopped its relentless pursuit of you.

I wanted to hold onto this moment. Wanted to bottle it up and keep it safe in the palm of my hand, because I wasn't sure how long it would last.

"Do you ever wonder," he said, breaking the silence with a question I didn't see coming, "if we're just pretending to be okay?"

I raised an eyebrow at him, half amused, half frustrated that he could read me so well, even in the darkness. "Pretending to be okay?" I asked, a laugh escaping me before I could stop it. "I'm not pretending. Are you?"

His lips quirked, a hesitant smile tugging at the corners of his mouth, but it didn't quite reach his eyes. "I don't know. Maybe I am."

"Because you think that when the dust settles, when the fighting stops, we'll just... what? Go back to the way things were?"

His gaze flicked to the campfire before returning to me. "I don't know what I'm supposed to feel. We've been at war for so long. Now that it's over—what does that even mean?"

I stepped closer, not sure what compelled me to do it, but the urge to close the distance between us was too strong to ignore. I put my other hand on his arm, just a light touch, but it seemed to ground him, if only for a moment. "It means we get to decide what comes next. We don't have to go back to anything. We can choose."

He looked at me then, really looked at me, like he was seeing me for the first time—or maybe like I was seeing him for the first time. There was a vulnerability in his eyes that made my heart ache.

"You're right," he said slowly, like he was testing the idea. "I'm not used to that. To not having a plan."

"I know," I said softly. "I'm not used to it either."

The air between us felt charged now, thick with the things we hadn't said but somehow both understood. He was right—there was no plan, not anymore. There had been one once, but it had crumbled the moment we realized the fire was bigger than us. The war had always been about survival. About getting through each day, each moment.

But now... now there was a different kind of survival. It was about rebuilding, about finding something worth fighting for that wasn't just about escaping. And I could see it in him—he didn't know how to live without the battle, without the urgency of danger. And I wasn't sure I did, either.

"I'm scared," he admitted, his voice barely above a whisper.

I tilted my head, studying him for a moment, unsure what to say. I had always been the strong one, the one who kept her head down and got things done, but I didn't feel strong anymore. I felt tired. And I felt like I'd been holding my breath for years, not knowing when or if I could ever exhale. But somehow, I didn't want to let go of him—not yet.

"Me too," I finally said, the words surprising even me.

He blinked, clearly taken aback. "You? Scared? I thought—"

"I know," I cut him off with a small laugh, the kind that didn't quite reach my eyes. "I thought I was invincible too. Turns out, I'm just human."

He smiled at that, a crooked, bittersweet grin, and I felt the tension ease between us, just a little. "You always act like you're in control."

"I like to pretend I am," I replied, a glimmer of my old self breaking through. "But pretending doesn't get you very far, does it?"

"No," he said, the smile lingering in his voice. "It doesn't."

We both fell silent again, but this time it didn't feel like the silence of something broken. It felt like the kind of silence you find when two people stop pretending and start being real.

The wind picked up, rustling the leaves of the trees above us, and I shivered, wishing I had a jacket or something to wrap around myself. He noticed, of course—he always noticed—and before I could stop him, he pulled off his outer layer and draped it over my shoulders.

"Better?" he asked, his voice soft with something I couldn't quite place.

"Much," I said, pulling the fabric tighter around me.

He stood there for a moment, watching me, and I could feel the weight of his gaze, like it was drawing something out of me. "I guess we'll figure this out," he said, the words heavy with unspoken promise.

"I guess we will," I agreed, not sure what that meant, but for the first time in a long time, I wasn't as afraid of what might come.

The firelight flickered in the distance, casting shadows over our small corner of the world. It felt strange, almost absurd, how quiet everything had become. No more sirens of danger. No more urgent whispers, hurried footsteps, the thrum of battle keeping us on edge. Instead, there was this peculiar peace—like the world had hit pause, but no one had bothered to press play again.

He didn't let go of my hand. I couldn't blame him for that; I wasn't in any rush to pull away either. The softness between us was palpable, but underneath it, there was something darker—something that wasn't going to disappear just because we stood here, watching the embers die.

"I never thought it would be like this," he said, his voice low, almost to himself.

"What, peaceful?" I asked, the word tasting strange on my tongue. Peace was the last thing I'd expected, too.

He exhaled sharply, a soft laugh mixed with a hint of disbelief. "No. I mean... us. Together. After everything."

I looked at him then, really looked at him. I wanted to say something flippant, something that would ease the tension building between us. But the truth of it was, I didn't know what to say. What did you say when everything had shifted, when the air between you was suddenly filled with so much more than it had been before? I wasn't ready for this—wasn't sure if I ever would be.

"We're still here," I said after a beat, the words heavier than I'd intended. "We made it through. And now... we figure out the rest."

His eyes softened, the guarded edge slipping just a little. He nodded, though the wariness didn't completely leave his gaze. "It's just hard to believe after all that. I mean, do you think we can really... start over?"

I bit my lip, trying to figure out how to frame the answer, as though this wasn't something both of us were grappling with. There were days when I'd sworn there was no such thing as starting over—just trudging through, surviving the way we always had. And yet... now there was the space for something different. Something more.

"Maybe we don't start over," I said, my words slipping out with more certainty than I felt. "Maybe we just begin. We've been through the worst of it. Everything else is just... the rest."

He was quiet for a long moment, but I could see the way his brow furrowed, his mind spinning with a thousand questions that he didn't have the answers to. He wanted to believe it. I could tell. But he was afraid, too afraid to let himself hope just yet.

"I never thought I could want something like this," he murmured, his voice barely audible in the stillness.

I wasn't sure what he meant by "this"—whether he was talking about us, or the sense of calm, or maybe the life we hadn't yet begun to live. But something in his voice made my chest tighten, a subtle ache that I couldn't ignore.

"I think I've spent so much of my life being afraid of what I might want, that I never realized what I already have." My voice came out softer than I intended, more raw, more vulnerable than I liked.

He turned to face me then, eyes scanning mine like he was trying to uncover some hidden truth buried there. But I wasn't ready to expose everything just yet. Not when I was still trying to figure it out myself.

Before I could say anything else, a sharp sound—like a branch snapping—crackled through the air. The peace shattered instantly, replaced by the familiar tension I'd been running from.

We both stiffened at the same time, instinctively reaching for weapons that weren't there anymore. For a moment, it felt like everything we'd just fought for had unraveled in a single breath.

"What the hell was that?" I whispered, my heart racing as my senses spiked.

His face darkened, the light from the fire reflecting in his eyes as they darted toward the trees.

"I don't know," he said quietly, a touch of disbelief in his voice. "But I don't like it."

The sound had come from deeper in the woods—beyond the camp, past the trees where the shadows seemed to take on a life of their own. A rustling followed, followed by something that sounded like a low growl. It wasn't human. And whatever it was, it wasn't just a passing animal.

"We should check it out," he said, his tone almost matter-of-fact, like he was already bracing for whatever we were about to walk into.

"You're insane," I snapped, barely keeping my voice steady. "We just fought a damn war. We're not walking into any more trouble."

But he was already moving, not waiting for me to change my mind, not even sparing a glance to see if I was following. I cursed under my breath, grabbing for a makeshift weapon—a jagged piece of metal that had been lying discarded nearby.

"Don't walk away from me," I hissed, taking off after him.

He didn't respond, but the tension in his back was enough of an answer. He was just as uneasy as I was, but his instincts, always sharp, had him on edge, ready for anything. The ground beneath our feet was soft with the residue of the storm, and the smell of wet earth mixed with the smoke that still hung in the air. Every step felt heavier, more ominous, as though the forest itself was holding its breath, waiting to see what we'd do next.

Then, as we crept deeper into the trees, I saw it—a flash of movement in the shadows. It was quick, too quick to identify, but it was there. And it was big.

We froze. The hairs on the back of my neck stood on end, and the quiet was suddenly too loud. The air thickened with something I couldn't quite name, an unease settling into the pit of my stomach.

Another growl—closer this time.

I didn't have time to react. The sound was deafening, and before I could process what was happening, a massive shape lunged from the darkness.

Chapter 36: Embers of a New Beginning

The mornings are quieter now, the sun creeping through the trees with an ease that doesn't feel earned, as if the world is tired of fighting. I sip my coffee, the bitter warmth soothing against my throat as I let the sounds of the camp become part of me—low murmurs of conversations, the occasional rustle of wind through leaves, the distant laughter of children still unaware of all they've lost. It's a false sense of peace, one that only comes when the chaos has had its fill, when everyone pretends they aren't holding their breath, waiting for something—anything—to knock them off course again. But for now, the air feels still, and I'm willing to pretend with them.

I look over to where he's sitting, his back against the old oak tree, legs stretched out in front of him, one booted foot tapping a rhythm only he can hear. His face is unreadable, as always, but today there's a softness in the lines of his jaw, in the way his eyes linger on the horizon, as if he's seeing something I can't. I want to ask, but the words are caught in my throat, tangled with my own questions about the future, about us. What could we possibly have when everything we've known has been burned to the ground? What is left to build on?

He catches my eye then, and I swear I feel the earth shift beneath me, just slightly, like it remembers the weight of us together and shifts to accommodate it. The tiniest of smiles plays at the corners of his lips, and my heart stutters in its usual dance. "You've been quiet today," he says, his voice rough, still carrying that edge of something unspoken, something buried. I've always loved the sound of his voice—deep, almost too smooth, like it could lull you into forgetting everything but the moment you're sharing with him.

"I've been thinking," I reply, leaning back against the log beside him, wrapping my fingers around the coffee mug like a lifeline.

He raises an eyebrow, and I can see the way his curiosity flares, just for a second, before he schools his features again. "About what?"

I want to tell him everything—the storm that's still brewing in my chest, the way his presence is a comfort I didn't know I needed, the way I find myself dreaming of a future I hadn't thought I could want. But none of it feels real enough, not when we've only just come out of the wreckage, not when the world still holds its breath. I can't be that fragile, that raw, just yet. Not when there are too many things still unsaid.

"Just... wondering what comes next, I guess." I keep my voice light, as if it doesn't matter, as if I haven't been spinning this same question in my head for days.

"Next?" he repeats, his tone careful now.

I nod. The fire that has been burning inside me for what feels like a lifetime isn't fully extinguished, but it's quiet now, glowing in the background like embers waiting to catch again. "After all this, what do we do now? Do we rebuild? Do we start over? Or do we just... wait?" I'm surprised at how easily the words slip out. It feels like I've been holding them in forever, keeping them tucked away like fragile things.

His gaze sharpens, the familiar walls creeping back into place. But just for a moment. His lips press together, and I watch as his fingers flex, as if trying to hold on to something that isn't there. "What do you want to do?" he asks quietly, the question hanging in the space between us like a dare.

It's a challenge I hadn't expected, and yet, somehow, it feels like the only one that matters. What do I want? The answer should be easy—clear, a direct path I've been walking toward without even knowing it. But the truth is, I don't know. Not really. Not when so much has already been lost, when so many pieces are still shifting in ways I can't control.

"I don't know," I admit, my voice barely above a whisper.

He nods, as though my uncertainty is something he understands all too well. "Maybe that's okay," he says after a moment, his eyes softening as they meet mine again. "Maybe not knowing is where we start."

The words settle between us, and for the first time in days, I feel like I can breathe again. Not fully, but enough. Enough to remember that there's still time. Enough to remember that there's still a chance to build something out of this mess. Something good, something real.

His hand brushes against mine, just a fleeting touch, but it's enough to send a ripple of warmth through me. I turn my hand, letting our fingers entwine, the gesture so simple, so quiet, but it feels like a promise. I don't know what the future holds. I don't know what any of this means, or what I'm supposed to do with it. But I do know this: I'm not ready to walk away from it. From him. Not yet.

"Maybe we'll figure it out," I say, my voice steadier now. "One step at a time."

He smiles then, a slow, quiet thing that spreads warmth through me like sunlight breaking through clouds. "One step at a time," he repeats, his grip tightening just slightly, as if holding on to the same fragile hope I'm clutching with everything I have left.

The mornings have become a ritual now, something steady in the midst of this quiet chaos. I find myself waking just before the sun stretches its fingers over the horizon, the first light trickling through the canopy above. There's something about those early moments—when the world is still half asleep, and only the brave dare to stir—that feels like mine. The air is cool but not cold, the scent of dew and earth filling my lungs with every breath I take. For a few minutes, I can forget about the weight of what we've survived, the scars that still mar us, and just exist in the moment.

Today, as always, I'm waiting for him. He's not far—just out of sight, somewhere in the camp, but it feels like an eternity before he finally steps into view. He's always late. Always has been. But somehow, it's become part of the rhythm of us. I tease him about it, of course, because someone has to. But there's a tenderness in the way I say it now, a quiet understanding that I've grown into this version of us, just as he's grown into me.

"You know," I start, when he finally appears, wiping his hands on his pants, looking far too innocent for someone who's spent the last few hours doing something that could only be described as laborious, "If you're trying to make a habit of being late, you're doing a fantastic job."

He raises an eyebrow, the corners of his mouth tugging up just enough to show he's amused. He doesn't even bother responding at first, just leans against the wooden post, watching me with that steady gaze of his. I like it, the way he watches, like he's studying me even when I'm not trying to be studied. It makes me feel seen in a way I didn't know I needed. "You're the one who's early, as always," he says, his voice low and gravelly. "What's wrong with you?"

"Nothing," I reply quickly, with a grin, "I'm just... efficient. Punctual. A shining example of what anyone should aspire to be."

He chuckles softly, the sound warm and familiar. "We all can't be like you."

"Clearly," I quip, my voice dripping with mock indignation. "But you should try."

It's easy, this back-and-forth, easier than I've ever allowed it to be with anyone else. The banter, the teasing, the way we make each other laugh without even trying. It feels like I've been waiting for this—this kind of simplicity, this kind of connection—for longer than I realized. And yet, there's still a heaviness that follows us. A shadow that lingers, just out of reach, never far enough to let us forget.

"So," I say, trying to steer the conversation away from the playful but too familiar, "what's next?"

He stares at me, then looks out toward the edge of the camp. The sky is starting to blush with the first hints of pink and gold, and the morning birds have already begun their songs, an endless chorus. There's something about the way he watches the world that makes me feel like he's seeing it through a different lens, one that I'll never fully understand. "Next?" he asks, almost to himself. "You really want to know?"

"Of course I do," I answer without hesitation. "It's not like we can just... sit here forever."

I'm watching him now, trying to catch any hint of emotion behind that stoic expression. And for a moment, I swear I can see it—the briefest flicker of something in his eyes, something that's too complex to name. "You think we're going back to normal?" he asks, and I feel my heart skip a beat. It's an innocent question, or at least it sounds that way, but there's an undercurrent to it. A tension that I hadn't expected, one that takes me off guard.

"Normal?" I echo, my voice a little softer than I intended. "What's normal anymore?"

The question lingers between us, heavier now, but neither of us makes a move to resolve it. I know he's right, that "normal" is a word we've lost the right to use. After everything—after all we've been through, the things we've done and the things we've seen—nothing will ever be what it was. We can only hope to rebuild something new from the ashes.

"You know," I say finally, breaking the silence, "I used to think I had all the answers. That I knew what I wanted and where I was headed. But now?" I shake my head, offering a small, rueful smile. "I have no idea."

He looks at me then, really looks at me, and for the first time in what feels like forever, I feel like we're seeing each other clearly. Not through the lens of the past, not through the weight of expectations or fear. Just us. "I don't know either," he admits, his voice almost a whisper. "But I think maybe... maybe that's enough."

I blink, surprised at how much those words hit me, how they land in a place I didn't know was empty. Maybe that's enough. It's simple. It's quiet. But there's truth in it—truth in the way we can only move forward by accepting the unknown, by letting go of the past that doesn't serve us anymore.

"I think you're right," I say softly, the words slipping out before I can stop them. And when he smiles, it's like the world shifts just slightly, like everything finds a place it was meant to be.

It's a beginning, I realize. Not just for us, but for everything we've yet to build. A new kind of normal, one where we can hold on to each other, to this moment, and let the future unfold in whatever way it's meant to. And maybe that's all we need.

It's late afternoon when the air changes. It's subtle at first, a shift so slight you'd almost miss it if you weren't paying attention. The light slants at a different angle, the breeze picks up, a whisper of something urgent weaving through the trees. I'm on the edge of the camp, watching the horizon as if I can will the world to reveal something—anything—before I have to look away.

I hear his footsteps before I see him. The soft crunch of gravel, the unmistakable rhythm of his walk. It's become one of those small things that feels like home to me now. I turn, but the words die in my throat when I see the expression on his face. It's not the guarded look I've grown used to; this is different. His jaw is tight, his eyes narrowed in that way that makes me wonder if he's been holding something back.

"Is everything okay?" I ask before I can stop myself, the question slipping out like an instinct.

He stops a few paces away from me, not quite close enough to touch, but just enough to fill the space between us with something heavy. "Yeah," he says, but the word doesn't quite reach his eyes. "Just... thinking."

I cross my arms, instinctively creating a small barrier between us, though I'm not sure why. "About what?" I ask, despite already knowing the answer. It's always something with him, isn't it?

He runs a hand through his hair, pushing it back from his forehead in that frustrated way he does when he's trying to work through something. "About the future, I guess." The words hang in the air for a beat too long.

I can't help it. I take a step closer, unable to resist. "What about it?"

"You know," he says, glancing around as if the trees might somehow provide him with the answers he's looking for, "I've been wondering what happens when all this is over. When we're not just trying to survive anymore."

I nod slowly, the question making something inside me tighten. Because I've been wondering that too, even though I'm not sure I'm ready for the answers. The truth is, I've been pretending not to think about it, hiding behind moments of calm like this one. But the truth is there, under the surface, waiting for me to face it. "I think we'll have to figure it out," I reply, and I'm not sure if I'm trying to convince him or myself. "One step at a time."

He shifts his weight, eyes flicking to mine with that intensity that always makes me feel like I'm the only one in the world. "But what if one step isn't enough?" His voice is low, the words carrying a weight I wasn't expecting. "What if we've been pretending this whole time? Pretending that when everything settles, we'll be fine."

I feel my chest tighten. "You think we're not fine?"

He doesn't answer immediately, and I watch as the quiet stretches between us, thick with something I can't quite name. There's no easy way to navigate this, no clear path that leads to an answer I want. "Maybe not. Not yet."

I swallow, my throat suddenly dry. "Then what do we do?"

He steps closer, just enough so that I can feel the heat of his presence without touching, and I find myself holding my breath, waiting for him to say something that will change everything. But instead, he just looks at me, searching my face like he's trying to find something buried beneath the surface.

"I don't know," he says finally, his voice almost a whisper. "But I think we have to stop pretending."

I open my mouth, but no words come out. I want to say something, anything, that will make this make sense, that will pull us back from the edge of something I'm not sure I'm ready for. But before I can, there's a sudden noise—sharp and out of place. The crackle of a branch snapping, too close for comfort.

His hand shoots out, grabbing my wrist with surprising strength, and in an instant, everything I thought I knew is thrown into chaos. His eyes meet mine, wide and alert now, every muscle in his body coiled with tension. "Stay behind me," he commands, low and urgent.

I don't argue, even though my heart is thudding in my chest, the adrenaline already rushing through my veins. This is different. This isn't the world we've been learning to navigate in the quiet moments; this is the world we've been running from.

Another snap of a branch. Then a voice. A low, gravelly sound that makes my blood run cold.

"Thought you'd get away, did you?" The voice drips with malice, and I can feel the hair on the back of my neck stand on end.

I freeze, not out of fear, but in disbelief. I know that voice. I know it in my bones, in the places I've tried to bury. The last person I ever thought I'd see again. The one person who's made me question everything I've fought for.

And then, like the world itself is taking a breath, everything shifts. The trees seem to close in around us, the sky darkening, and I know, with a sinking feeling, that we've just crossed into something we can't undo.

I turn to him, my voice shaky. "Is it really him?"

He doesn't answer, but the way his grip tightens on my wrist tells me everything I need to know.

And just as the first figure steps into view, the ground beneath us shakes with a sound that is far too familiar. A sound I've heard once before.

A bomb.

Chapter 37: The Heart's Inferno

The café smelled of fresh espresso and burnt sugar, the air thick with the rich aroma of pastries and idle chatter. I took a sip of my cappuccino, watching the steam curl above the rim of my mug, the warmth spreading through my fingers. It was a quiet morning—too quiet, perhaps. Or maybe it was just me, a side effect of living in a space between past and present, where nothing felt entirely real, and everything felt like it was being held together by the faintest thread. But I couldn't let myself think that way. Not when the last few weeks had been filled with more than I ever thought I'd deserve.

Luke walked into the café like he owned the place, his presence filling the room even before his eyes found mine. There was no hesitation in his steps, no second-guessing. He had a way of making you believe that everything was exactly as it should be when he walked in—like the sun had just decided to shine brighter, the world a little warmer. He smiled when he saw me, a smile that made my heart skip the way it always did, no matter how many times I saw it. It was the kind of smile that made you feel like maybe—just maybe—you had found the one thing in life that wasn't going to slip through your fingers.

I set my cup down, smoothing the napkin beneath it, suddenly aware of the way my fingers were trembling. It was stupid, really. The whole situation was stupid. I'd spent so much time hiding from the truth, from the real me, and now I was here, sitting across from him, no walls, no secrets. Well, almost none. There was still the matter of how I felt. But somehow, I didn't want to think about it. Didn't want to ruin the moment by pulling at the thread of my own fear. Not when everything else between us had been so easy. Not when the weight of the world felt just a little lighter with him beside me.

"You look distracted," Luke said, settling into the chair across from me with a relaxed ease that somehow only made me more tense. He didn't lean back, didn't make any attempt to relax. He sat there, his eyes locking with mine, watching me carefully, like he could see right through my skin.

"I'm not distracted," I said, raising an eyebrow in an attempt to match his playful tone. "Just... thinking."

"About what?" He tilted his head, his smile shifting into something warmer, more inviting, and I couldn't help but soften at the sight of it. God, he was good at this. At making me feel like the most important person in the room, no matter where we were.

"I was just thinking about how we ended up here." The words slipped out before I could stop them, and immediately, I regretted them. It wasn't the time to dissect things. Not yet.

He didn't respond immediately, instead taking a moment to study my face. It was the same look he'd given me the night we stayed up talking about everything that had happened. The fires, the secrets, the pain that had settled between us like a stubborn stain we couldn't scrub out. And yet, we had. We had somehow managed to scrub it away, piece by piece, until the stains were nothing but faint memories, hovering on the edges of our minds. The truth was out there now, nothing left to hide, and for the first time, it felt like we were standing on solid ground.

"I never thought I'd get here," Luke said, his voice low, almost as if he were admitting something to himself as much as to me. "I never thought I'd find someone who could see me for who I really am, all of it. The good, the bad... everything in between."

I swallowed, feeling the weight of his words settle over me. "You're not as bad as you think," I said, my voice softer than I intended. The way he spoke about himself—it always made me want to reach out and wrap him in something safe, even though I wasn't sure I had anything safe left to offer.

He chuckled, but it wasn't his usual easy laugh. It was deeper, tinged with something I couldn't quite place. "You really think that?"

"I know it." The words were sure, even if I wasn't. There were too many things we had yet to say, too many spaces left between us that I wasn't sure how to fill. But in that moment, with him sitting across from me, with the quiet hum of the café surrounding us, I realized something. Maybe we didn't need to fill every silence. Maybe some things were better left unspoken, just allowed to be, to grow into something that didn't need words to be understood.

Luke shifted in his chair, his gaze drifting down to his coffee. He took a long sip, then set the cup down with a gentle thud. "I used to think love was something you had to earn. Something you had to prove you were worthy of. But... you changed that. You made me see that maybe it's just something you get to be a part of, no matter who you are."

My heart skipped a beat, and I found myself frozen, the weight of his words almost too much to bear. I wanted to say something, to respond in kind, but the truth was, I wasn't sure I knew how. There had been too much distance between us before this, too much hesitation. And now that I was finally here, finally in this place where everything felt right, I didn't want to risk shattering it with the wrong thing.

So instead, I reached across the table, my hand hovering just above his, the space between us like a thin veil of air, too fragile to break. He met my gaze, and in that instant, I felt it—the same fire that had burned between us, the same heat that could both destroy and rebuild. The kind of fire that left nothing untouched, nothing unchanged. But in that fire, I saw a future, a possibility. And maybe, just maybe, that was enough for now.

He reached for my hand then, his fingers brushing mine, and the world fell away, leaving only the two of us, caught in the quiet, unspoken understanding that no matter where we went from here, we'd do it together.

There are moments when life slows down just enough for you to notice the things you've been ignoring, the tiny details that are easy to overlook when you're too busy running from one thing to the next. I caught myself staring at Luke's hands one afternoon, the way his fingers flexed around his coffee cup as though the weight of the world could be held there if need be. He always had that sense about him—the ability to carry more than anyone should have to, and yet, he never seemed to buckle under it. I, on the other hand, felt like I was one wrong step away from collapsing into a heap of emotions that didn't know how to exist in the same space.

"I was thinking we should go away," I blurted out one evening, the words hanging awkwardly between us. It was one of those moments where I had no idea if I'd just proposed something wildly romantic or come off as a lunatic who was too desperate for a break from the chaos.

Luke didn't miss a beat. He didn't frown, or look skeptical. Instead, he raised an eyebrow, his lips curling into that mischievous grin of his, the one that made my heart race. "Away?" he repeated, almost like a dare. "What do you have in mind?"

I shrugged, trying to appear nonchalant, but the truth was, I had no idea. Maybe I just wanted the world to pause. "Somewhere quiet. Peaceful. I don't know, the beach maybe? Or a cabin in the woods." I let out a laugh that was probably too high-pitched for someone pretending not to care. "I just... I need a place where I can breathe without hearing my own thoughts for a while."

He studied me, a glint of understanding in his eyes, and for a brief second, I thought I might have pushed too hard. But then he set his cup down and stood, moving across the room with that effortless grace I'd come to adore. "The beach sounds good," he said quietly. "I think we both could use the kind of quiet that comes from crashing waves, don't you?"

I nodded, suddenly lighter than I had been in weeks. There was something about the way he spoke that made it feel like the decision had been made before the words even left his mouth. Like we were already there, toes buried in sand, the world falling away behind us. I wasn't ready for anything permanent yet—God, I wasn't even sure what permanent meant—but in that moment, with the sound of the city outside and the warmth of his gaze, it felt like the only thing that mattered was right here. Right now.

A few days later, we found ourselves in a small coastal town, tucked between jagged cliffs and a wide stretch of beach that looked like something out of a postcard. The air was salty and crisp, with just the faintest hint of something wild—seaweed and brine and the occasional gust of wind that made the palm trees sway in protest. Luke didn't talk much on the drive down, which was unusual. He usually had something to say about everything, whether it was the scenery or the latest headlines, or even a ridiculous story from his childhood. But that day, he was quiet. Not in a brooding way—more like he was gathering thoughts, maybe letting everything settle before letting it out.

We checked into a small, weathered inn by the shore, the kind of place you didn't expect much from, but somehow, it ended up being perfect. The room was cozy, with a fireplace crackling softly in the corner, the scent of pine and sea air filling every corner. The bed was oversized, inviting, with linens that felt like they belonged in some luxurious resort, but the view from the window—wide and open, stretching toward the endless horizon—was the only thing that mattered.

I leaned against the windowsill, watching the waves crash against the shore, the rhythmic sound a perfect counterpoint to the turmoil that had been spinning inside me for months. The fire in my chest had settled, though not entirely gone, and I wasn't sure if it was the waves or Luke's presence that made everything feel a little clearer.

Luke joined me at the window, his shoulder brushing mine as he looked out at the ocean. There was a certain quiet strength about him, an energy that seemed to emanate from him without effort, as though he were constantly grounded in something deeper than I could understand. But I didn't need to understand it—not yet. Not if this was how things were going to be.

"I've never really done this," I said, my voice almost lost to the wind. "Gone away, I mean. With someone. Just... taken the time to be somewhere that wasn't weighed down by everything else."

He nodded, his gaze still on the ocean, but his hand moved slowly toward mine. When he finally touched it, I felt the jolt of electricity—no less powerful than the first time he'd reached for me—and I didn't pull away. "We're both learning, aren't we?" he said, his voice low and warm, a little rough from the salt in the air. "How to let go, how to take the time we need. It's strange, isn't it? To feel like you're standing on solid ground for the first time, but not know how to hold it together."

I smiled, the edges of my lips turning up despite the weight of his words. "Strange doesn't begin to cover it."

There was something so raw, so honest about the way we were speaking now, as though the space between us had shrunk down to something manageable. The fires were behind us, yes, but that didn't mean the burn wasn't still there. It was quieter now, more manageable, but it was still there. And somehow, I felt like that was okay. That maybe this—whatever this was—was enough to survive it. Enough to make something better from the ashes.

Luke squeezed my hand, then leaned down, brushing his lips against the side of my head in that way he always did, a soft gesture that felt more intimate than anything else. "Maybe we don't need to figure everything out all at once," he murmured. "Maybe we can just let it be for now."

I closed my eyes, the weight of his words settling over me like a blanket. Let it be. Maybe that was the key. Maybe, for once, I didn't have to try so hard to make everything make sense. Maybe, in that moment, just being here was enough.

The night wrapped itself around us like a velvet blanket, soft and heavy, as the stars above flickered in a way that felt almost deliberate—too perfect to be accidental. Luke and I sat on the edge of the dock, our legs dangling over the water, the sound of the waves mingling with the occasional rustle of the palms behind us. The air was cooler now, the heat of the day giving way to something calmer, something that felt like a promise.

"You ever think about what happens next?" I asked, my voice barely above a whisper. I wasn't sure why I'd asked it; maybe I just needed to know where this was going, or maybe I just wanted to hear him say it out loud, as if putting it into words could make it real. But I wasn't prepared for the way the question felt when it left my lips, as though I'd just opened a door that I hadn't realized was locked.

Luke shifted next to me, his eyes following the dark horizon. "I think about it. More than I probably should." He turned to face me then, his gaze steady, unfaltering, as if he was trying to measure how much of himself I was willing to let in. "But thinking about it doesn't always make it clearer, does it?"

I shook my head, the uncertainty knotting itself in my chest. "No. It's like staring into the fog. You know there's something ahead, but it's too blurry to really figure out."

He nodded slowly, but there was a smile tugging at the corner of his mouth, something reassuring in his expression. "Maybe that's the point. Maybe it's not about figuring it out. Maybe it's about seeing where it takes us."

His words settled in the space between us, hanging there in the cool night air. And for a moment, I thought I understood—understood how he could make everything sound simple, even when I knew nothing about what was really ahead. But that simplicity, that trust, was exactly what I'd been craving all along. The notion that we didn't have to have all the answers—that we could just be.

"I think I'm tired of thinking," I said, the words slipping out before I could second-guess them. "Tired of analyzing everything and worrying about how it'll all work out. I just... I just want to be with you. Here. Now."

The shift in Luke was subtle, but I felt it. His shoulders relaxed, and the air between us seemed to shimmer, as if some invisible weight had been lifted. He reached for my hand, his fingers cool against my skin, and his touch grounded me in a way that felt almost primal.

"I get that," he said, his voice a low murmur, the sincerity behind it unmistakable. "But sometimes, being in the moment doesn't mean ignoring what comes after. It's not about controlling it, but about knowing it'll come when it does."

I let out a short laugh, but there was no humor behind it. "You sound like you've been reading self-help books."

He gave me a mock-serious look, the corner of his mouth twitching. "Maybe I have. Couldn't hurt, right?"

I laughed then, a genuine chuckle that felt like it had been waiting to escape for days. "You're insufferable."

"Would you prefer brooding, silent Luke? Because I can do that too, if you like." His voice had an edge of humor, but there was something else there too—something darker, something I couldn't quite place.

I turned toward him, my eyes narrowing slightly. "Why does it feel like you're holding something back?"

Luke hesitated, his gaze flitting away for a moment before settling on the water again. The way he said nothing made my chest tighten with the kind of unease I hadn't expected. "Not everything needs to be said all at once," he said quietly, almost to himself. "Some things take time to figure out."

I felt a sharp pang of discomfort, but I pushed it aside. Not everything needed to be said. Not yet, anyway. Instead, I forced a smile, pretending I hadn't heard the unspoken weight in his voice. "Fine. But don't expect me to just sit here and pretend everything's perfect when I know you're hiding something from me."

He glanced at me again, and this time, the expression on his face was far less playful. There was a seriousness in his eyes, a storm I hadn't anticipated. "Maybe it's not about hiding anything," he said, his voice low but controlled. "Maybe it's just not the right time for everything."

The silence that followed was thick, almost oppressive. I could feel the tension between us, like an electric charge building, ready to crack the calm in an instant. For a moment, I wasn't sure if we were on the verge of something new, or if we were about to face something that might break us both apart.

But just as I opened my mouth to say something—anything—Luke's phone buzzed in his pocket. He cursed under his breath and pulled it out, his eyes scanning the screen with a sudden sharpness that had me leaning forward.

"What is it?" I asked, though I already knew.

Luke didn't answer right away. His jaw clenched, his fingers hovering over the phone, and then, without a word, he stood up, pacing to the edge of the dock, his posture tense. I watched him, a sense of dread creeping up my spine.

"Luke?" I called, my voice smaller than I meant it to be.

He turned, his face drawn, his expression unreadable. "It's my brother. Something's happened."

I felt the world shift, the reality of the situation coming crashing down on me like a wave. The stillness, the peace we'd found—everything I thought we'd been working toward—seemed suddenly fragile, like it was all going to unravel at any moment.

"Is it... bad?" I managed to ask, though I already knew the answer.

Luke didn't answer, his eyes darkening with a pain I couldn't quite decipher. And then, in one swift motion, he turned and started toward the truck, his footsteps heavy on the wooden boards.

"Luke, wait!" I called after him, but he didn't stop. The only thing that followed him was the hollow sound of his retreating footsteps, and a deep sense of dread that settled in my chest. Something had changed. Something I hadn't seen coming.

And just like that, everything I thought I knew—everything I thought was solid—started to slip away.

Chapter 38: Blaze of Passion

I hadn't intended for it to happen this way. The whole thing, every last moment of it, was entirely unplanned. Life's little messes don't care for plans. They sweep you off your feet, leave you dazed and wondering if you've missed something along the way, like a crucial turn or an inconvenient lesson on how to keep your heart in check. I certainly hadn't been prepared for him.

It started off harmless enough—an accidental brush of the hand, a shared glance that lingered a bit too long, a conversation that didn't quite know how to end. We both acted like we didn't notice, but we did. And from that moment, I was tangled in him. Not the obvious kind of tangled, the swooning kind of tangled, but the kind that creeps up on you, subtle, almost a whisper, until you wake up one day and realize you can't breathe without thinking of them. It's intoxicating, really. The slow burn, the way it eats away at your composure, little by little, until you're nothing more than a mess of desire and uncertainty.

That was us. A fire, carefully kindled, never meant to catch. But we did. It started in the quiet spaces between words, in the silences where we didn't need to speak to understand each other. There was something about the way he moved, the effortless ease with which he carried himself, like he knew the secret to navigating life without ever really breaking a sweat. It didn't matter that I couldn't put my finger on it. It didn't matter that every rational part of me screamed that this wasn't how things were supposed to go. I ignored it. I always did when it came to him.

The first night we really touched, really let the heat of it all rise between us, I couldn't remember if the world had always been this vivid. It was as if every color, every sound, had intensified. I felt the weight of him, the press of his lips on mine, the warmth of his hand as it slid around my waist, pulling me close. There was no hesitation, no holding back. He was a man who didn't ask for permission, didn't wait for signals that things were "right." He simply moved, and I followed, falling headfirst into the abyss of him.

Afterwards, when the storm of it had passed, I lay there, tangled in sheets and thoughts. The world outside our little bubble continued on, indifferent. But inside, it felt like time had stopped. There was no rush to speak, no need to put a name to what we were. I could hear his steady breathing next to me, feel his body just inches away, the air thick with unsaid words.

"I didn't expect that," he murmured, his voice a little hoarse.

I smiled without opening my eyes, savoring the moment. "You never do."

It was dangerous, this. I knew that. The way he made me feel like I could fly and crash in the same breath. The way his touch lingered long after he left. It was intoxicating, this pull between us, and I had the sneaking suspicion I'd never get enough.

We spent the days that followed in a constant loop of stolen moments, each one more intense than the last. There was no need for grand gestures. He didn't need to say the words, didn't need to declare anything to the world. It wasn't about that. It was about the way he made me feel, about the moments when he looked at me like I was the only person in the room, like everything else was just noise.

I'd been cynical about love for so long, convinced that it was nothing more than a clever trick the universe played to keep people off balance. But with him, it was different. There was no trick. He didn't need to pull me in with promises or pretty lies. He just was, and somehow, that was enough. And it scared the hell out of me.

I knew I was falling—no, I had already fallen. The pieces of me that I'd guarded for so long, the little parts that had been hidden and protected, were exposed. Vulnerable. It felt like standing on the edge of a cliff, the wind at my back, and no idea whether I'd fly or fall. The only thing I knew for certain was that I wasn't ready to stop.

Then came the moment when the world shifted again, when it became undeniable that something had changed, had deepened. We were sitting at his kitchen table, sipping wine, the evening light spilling in through the window, painting everything gold. He reached across the table, his fingers brushing mine, a touch so simple, so ordinary, yet it felt like a promise.

"I'm not good at this," he said quietly, his eyes not meeting mine.

I could feel the tension in the air, the weight of whatever he was about to say. But I didn't want to hear it. Not then, not now.

"At what?"

He hesitated. "At... caring too much. At letting someone in." His voice dropped to a murmur, as if the admission alone would crack him open. "I've always been better at pushing people away."

I wanted to laugh. How ridiculous was that? I was the queen of keeping people at arm's length, the expert at building walls around my heart. And yet, here I was, with him—so close, I could almost touch everything that had been hidden away. The pieces of him he didn't show to just anyone. And I was ready to catch every shard.

"You're not as good as you think," I said softly, meeting his gaze, and for the first time, I wasn't afraid of what I saw there. "Neither am I."

The air between us shifted, thickened, but in a way that felt like a release. Something had clicked. It wasn't perfect, and it wasn't smooth, but it was real. And that was enough for me.

The days drifted by in a blur of warmth and words that never seemed to be enough. It was the kind of time that stretched, but never quite long enough to satisfy the hunger between us. Every glance, every smile felt like a promise we hadn't made aloud but understood all the same. We moved through each day as if it were an unspoken agreement that nothing would come between us, nothing would disturb the careful balance we had begun to cultivate.

But there was always something lurking at the edges. A tension I couldn't shake, not even when his hand was warm in mine, when his laughter vibrated through me like a melody I wanted to play on repeat. There was always the nagging feeling that I was waiting for something to slip, for a moment where the ground would shift beneath us and the perfect symmetry we'd built would fracture. I told myself I was being paranoid. He had been honest with me, I was sure of that. But there was always a little voice in the back of my mind reminding me that nothing perfect lasts. And that was something I was far too familiar with.

One evening, as the sky painted itself in hues of soft lavender and orange, he pulled me close, his lips barely brushing against my ear. "Stay with me tonight," he said, his voice a low rumble that made my stomach flutter in the best possible way.

I froze, not because I hadn't imagined this moment before, but because it was so much more than what I'd envisioned. It was one thing to be tangled in his arms, to let the passion carry us through the night. It was another to stay. To allow myself to be part of something that extended beyond the chemistry between us. To know that tomorrow wouldn't come with an end, that the absence of him wouldn't return with the light of the morning.

"I always stay with you," I said, forcing a casualness I didn't quite feel.

His grin was slow, knowing, as if he could see right through me, to the parts I was trying to keep hidden. "Not like this," he murmured, his fingers sliding into my hair. He didn't ask for permission, never had, and somehow that made everything about him seem that much more inevitable. "You don't have to say anything. Just be here. With me."

I didn't need convincing. What he offered wasn't just a night together—it was the sense of belonging, of being anchored. He was offering me more than his bed; he was offering his space in this world, a place where I could come and rest without the need to explain myself. He didn't need to be anything more than what he was, and somehow, that felt like the truest form of intimacy.

The night stretched on, weaving between the comfort of quiet touches and the deep, rhythmic intimacy of shared space. The weight of the world outside seemed so far away, as if it had been suspended by the warmth of our silence. When he pulled me closer, his lips grazing my forehead, I realized something that hadn't fully dawned on me before—he was giving me all of him, with no hesitation, no second thoughts, and I wasn't sure if I was ready for that.

But then, maybe that was the point. It wasn't about being ready. It was about letting go. Letting go of the things I had held onto for so long—the walls, the self-protection, the doubt. With him, I was learning to trust again, in ways I hadn't allowed myself to for years. He was a safe space, but in the most unexpected way, because it wasn't about being perfect. It was about being real.

Morning came too quickly, as it always did. He was already awake when I stirred, watching me with an intensity that sent a rush of heat through my chest.

"Good morning," he whispered, his fingers tracing patterns on the back of my hand, the simplest of gestures that somehow felt like the most profound.

I stretched, still tangled in the sheets, the sunlight streaming through the windows like a quiet invitation. "It's too early for this kind of sweetness," I mumbled, half-sleepy, half-aware of how everything about this felt a little too perfect to trust.

"I don't care what time it is," he said, his grin playing at the edges of his words. "It's always the right time with you."

I smirked, rolling onto my side to face him. "You know, you're dangerously close to becoming a cliché."

He laughed, the sound low and warm, filling the space between us in a way that felt too personal, too real. "If this is a cliché, then I'm glad I'm the one living it."

For a moment, everything was easy. There was no tension, no hidden fears. Just two people, in the warmth of morning light, and a sense that we were on the verge of something—something more than I had anticipated.

But then, as if the universe had decided that we needed a reminder of life's chaos, his phone rang, the sudden sound of it breaking the fragile bubble of contentment we'd created. I saw the shift in his expression, the way his smile tightened at the edges, the subtle pull of his jaw as he reached for the phone.

"Hello?" he answered, his voice losing its easy warmth. It was a different side of him, one I wasn't used to seeing. Professional, detached.

I could hear the sharpness in his tone, the abrupt way he spoke. I sat up, suddenly aware of the change, the way it shifted the air in the room. The moment between us had fractured, just like that. One call, and everything seemed to tip, the weight of his attention now focused elsewhere, on something outside of us.

I watched him, the man I had come to know, now suddenly distant, his mind clearly elsewhere. And in that moment, the doubts I'd pushed aside—the ones that whispered that maybe I wasn't enough, that maybe this wasn't as perfect as it seemed—came rushing back.

When he ended the call, his eyes met mine, but the distance was there now, not just physical, but emotional. "Sorry about that," he said, his voice a little strained. "I'll be back later. Things to take care of."

I nodded, even as the knot in my stomach tightened. Things to take care of. Of course, there were always things.

The silence between us grew heavier as the minutes passed, thick with unsaid things. He had left hours ago, the soft click of the door closing behind him echoing in the stillness of the apartment. And yet, I couldn't shake the feeling that something had shifted, that the space between us had become... fragile. I sat on the edge of the bed, my fingers brushing the worn fabric of the sheets, still warm from where he had been. The faint smell of his cologne lingered in the air, and for a moment, I almost let myself believe everything was still the same.

But it wasn't. It couldn't be. Not after the phone call.

I didn't mean to eavesdrop. Honestly, I didn't. But when you've spent so much time in someone's world, when their habits become yours, it's hard not to notice the cracks when they form. I had seen the shift in his expression, heard the subtle change in his tone when the phone rang. He hadn't even looked at me before he picked it up, his movements sharp, businesslike. The warmth that had always been there, the ease of us just existing together, evaporated in the split second it took for him to answer.

And then, of course, there was the line he had used—"I'll be back later. Things to take care of."

Things. I wasn't sure if it was the word itself or the way he said it, flat and dismissive, but it didn't sit right with me. Because it wasn't just business; I knew it wasn't. He didn't let me into those parts of his life, not really. And I had never asked. Maybe I should have, but the fear of what I might find held me back, kept me in this place where everything was simple and easy. Where everything felt like it had a future.

I stood up abruptly, pacing the room, the walls pressing in with every step I took. This wasn't me. I wasn't the kind of person to overthink, to dissect every little moment like a lawyer pulling apart a case. I was spontaneous, impulsive, the girl who dove headfirst into anything and everything. I had always believed in feeling things, in trusting that gut instinct that led me toward people, toward places, toward moments.

But this? This uncertainty, this nagging feeling of being kept at arm's length—it was new. And I hated it.

The sound of the doorbell broke through the haze of my thoughts, sharp and demanding. I froze, momentarily paralyzed by the suddenness of it. When I reached the door and opened it, I didn't expect to see him. Not after everything. Not after he had just left. But there he was, standing in the hallway, his hand still hovering over the doorframe, as though he hadn't quite made the decision to knock.

"What are you doing here?" The words were out before I could stop them, my voice carrying more edge than I intended.

He looked at me for a beat, his expression unreadable. "I... I needed to talk," he said, stepping forward without waiting for an invitation.

There it was again—the weight of the words that didn't match the reality. Talk? Now? After hours of silence, after a phone call that left me more confused than before, now he wanted to talk?

I stepped back, allowing him inside, though I didn't quite know why. Maybe I was still in denial, still clinging to the version of him that had once seemed so clear, so steady. Or maybe I just didn't want to be alone with the thoughts that had started to crowd in.

He didn't waste time. "I didn't mean to make things weird," he said, his voice tense, like he was walking on a tightrope, unsure of whether he'd make it across. "But you're right to feel... off. I've been keeping things from you, things that I should've told you a long time ago."

I could feel the air shift with the weight of his words, his admission hanging between us like a heavy fog. This wasn't the man I had known, the man who had whispered my name like it was the only thing he cared about, the man who had made me feel seen, cherished, and loved.

"I don't want to hide things from you," he continued, his eyes never leaving mine, a flicker of something—guilt, maybe—darting across his gaze. "But sometimes, it's easier to keep people at a distance, especially when they start to matter."

I swallowed hard, the lump in my throat threatening to choke me. I didn't know what I expected, but it certainly wasn't this. I had trusted him. I had let myself believe that maybe—just maybe—there was a future for us, one that didn't come with complications, one where we could just exist in the chaos of each other without needing to explain everything.

"And what is it you've been keeping from me?" I asked, my voice soft, but the ache in it was unmistakable.

He took a step toward me, his face etched with a raw vulnerability I wasn't used to seeing. It felt like a confession was coming, something that would strip us both bare, make us more than just two people lost in the fire of desire. He exhaled, like the weight of it all was too much to bear. "I'm not who you think I am," he said, the words low, barely audible, but piercing all the same. "I've been lying to you, in ways that go deeper than you could ever imagine."

My heart hammered in my chest, the sudden fear creeping up my spine like a cold rush of air. This was it. The moment I had been dreading. But even then, I couldn't bring myself to pull away, to shut him out completely. I was too far gone, too tangled in him to even consider the option of running.

"What do you mean?" I whispered, my voice shaking despite my best efforts to remain calm.

His eyes darkened, a storm brewing behind them, and for the first time since I'd met him, I saw something I hadn't expected—regret.

"I've been working with people who have their own agendas," he confessed, his voice thick with the weight of the truth. "Dangerous people. And I've kept you in the dark because I thought it would keep you safe."

The words hit me like a punch to the stomach, and for a moment, I couldn't breathe. My entire world had just been turned upside down. This wasn't just some misunderstanding, some small lie. This was something bigger, something dangerous—and I was caught in the middle of it.

Chapter 39: Ash and Bone

The autumn air was sharp with the promise of winter, an invigorating chill that seemed to cut through the bones and right down to the marrow. The horizon stretched before me, pale gold and tinged with a darker, foreboding hue as the last of the leaves danced and twirled in the breeze, surrendering their hold on the branches. I stood at the edge of the forest, where the dense woods met the clearing, the air filled with the scent of damp earth and pine. It was a place that had once felt foreign to me, a place I had wandered through like a ghost, unsure of who I was or where I was going.

But now, standing here in the fading light of day, it felt different. Home, in the quietest sense of the word. The kind of place that doesn't demand a grand entrance but simply welcomes you with open arms, unspoken. And at the center of it all—of everything that had brought me here—was him.

Elliot.

He was standing a few feet away, leaning against a low stone wall, his profile cast in shadows, but even in the dimming light, I could see the firm set of his jaw, the slight tilt of his head as he surveyed the land, as if the world itself were his to command. I had watched him for days, at times from a distance, and sometimes from right beside him, trying to make sense of the choice that loomed over me.

I could go back to the life I had before. The one that had been so neatly packaged, so predictable, though it had never been truly mine. It was a life I had worn like a coat that no longer fit, the edges frayed and torn, leaving me cold and exposed. I had always known, deep down, that it wasn't the life I was meant to live. But it was the life I had always known, and walking away from it meant leaving behind everything that had shaped me, everything that had held me together.

But then there was Elliot. And the quiet life we had begun to build here, on the cusp of winter, under the weight of the mountains that seemed to cradle us in their ancient arms. His presence was a constant now, steady and unwavering, like the ground beneath my feet. With him, I was more than just a girl running from a life she didn't want. I was someone with purpose, with direction. And the thought of leaving him behind was an ache that settled deep in my chest, gnawing at my heart until I couldn't ignore it.

I felt his gaze before I saw him turn. It was like a thread pulling me back to him, a silent pull that I had never quite understood but had always felt. He smiled—half a smile, as if he knew exactly what I was thinking, what was tearing me apart inside.

"You're overthinking it," he said, the words slipping out of him like he had been waiting for them. He was always waiting for me, in a way that felt both comforting and terrifying. "Come here."

I didn't hesitate, didn't think to argue or try to find some clever retort. Instead, I moved toward him, my boots crunching on the frost-covered ground, the faint sound like the only thing that mattered in the world. When I reached him, he held out his hand, a simple gesture, but one that made my chest tighten.

His palm was warm, the callouses rough under my fingertips, the skin a map of the life he had lived. The warmth of him spread through me, an anchor in the storm of my thoughts. I slipped my fingers into his, feeling the weight of his presence, his steady breath, the rhythm of his heart.

"I don't want you to go," he murmured, his voice low, rough in a way that made my insides tighten. "But I won't make you stay. I never will."

His words settled around me like a blanket, soft but heavy with meaning. I couldn't bring myself to say anything, not yet. What could I say? The decision, the weight of it, still pressed on me like a weight I couldn't shake. There was no simple answer, no easy road to follow. Staying meant giving up the past, a past that had been my life, my identity. Leaving meant leaving him, the only person who had ever truly seen me.

The wind picked up again, sending a flurry of dead leaves swirling around us, spinning in a dance of their own, just as I felt caught in the whirlwind of my own indecision. I could feel the pull of the past, the life I had once known, tugging at me, as if it were a rope pulling me back into the fog of what was familiar. But there was another pull, one that was softer, more gentle, yet no less powerful. It was him. It was the life we had started to build here, the quiet moments between us, the shared silence that spoke louder than any words.

Elliot's thumb brushed lightly across my knuckles, a slow, deliberate movement, and in that simple touch, I felt everything fall into place. The decision was there, waiting for me to recognize it, to admit what I had known all along.

I took a deep breath, the cool air filling my lungs, the scent of pine and wood smoke mixing together, and for the first time in weeks, I felt the weight lift. It wasn't a perfect answer, and it wasn't without sacrifice. But when I looked up at him, my heart steady in my chest, I knew there was no other choice.

"I'm staying," I whispered, and when I saw the way his eyes softened, the hint of a smile curling at the corners of his mouth, I knew I had made the right one.

This was home.

The night settled in slowly, creeping over the land like a blanket of thick, inky velvet. The stars above blinked lazily, barely catching the last flicker of fading daylight. I leaned against the edge of the porch, letting the cool air rush past me, carrying with it the scent of distant pine and the damp undertones of earth that had been softened by the rain earlier in the day. The warmth of the cabin was just inside, but the space between here and there—the pause, the quiet moments before entering the familiar—had become my sanctuary.

Elliot had slipped inside hours ago, his quiet presence lingering like a shadow even though the room was empty. I had watched him, studied the way his shoulders relaxed as the tension of the day slipped away. But something had changed, a shift, something that gnawed at the back of my mind. It was as if we had come to the edge of something unspoken, both of us waiting for the other to make a move, to confirm the choice that had been made for us without words.

I couldn't understand it—how something as simple as being near him, breathing the same air, could feel like standing at the edge of a cliff. We had built something here, something fragile but real, and now there was the question of whether it would shatter under the weight of my past or hold steady, like the old stones that lined the trails around the property.

The wind gusted, tugging at my hair, and for a moment, I felt like I might fall off that edge, lost to the dark world beneath me. The past called to me in ways that I couldn't ignore. I'd built my life with certain truths—certain rules, expectations. But here, in the shadow of this place, under the vastness of the sky that stretched in ways I had never understood, those rules didn't seem to apply. And neither did the person I thought I was.

There was a weight to it all, heavy and pressing, but at the same time, it felt like a release. The pull was subtle, as though the mountains themselves were exhaling, and I was drawn into the rhythm of their breath. It had been months since I had been able to think clearly, to see beyond the sharp edges of my decisions, but tonight it was as though the world had softened just enough to allow me to breathe.

I pushed myself off the porch, my boots scraping against the weathered wood, and made my way toward the small grove of birch trees that bordered the cabin's yard. The crisp leaves crunched beneath my feet as I walked, my breath visible in the sharp night air. There was something comforting about the solitude, about the stillness of the night that felt almost like a private conversation. I didn't need to speak, not yet. I just needed to feel the quiet hum of the world as it turned around me.

Somewhere in the distance, the sound of hooves caught my attention. I froze, listening intently. At first, I thought it was the echo of my own thoughts, but then it came again, sharper this time, a rhythmic pounding that grew louder by the second. My heart raced in anticipation, but it wasn't fear that gripped me—just a sense of something imminent, something I had been waiting for but hadn't quite realized until now.

The silhouette of a rider emerged from the fog of trees, their figure cloaked in the haze of night, the horse's breath visible in clouds of mist. I hadn't expected anyone, let alone this. My stomach churned, and before I could move, the rider approached, pulling the reins with a sharp tug, the horse snorting as it slowed to a halt.

It was strange, this sense of recognition I felt despite not knowing the rider. But there was something about the way they sat, their posture rigid, the familiar worn cloak they wore, that stirred an uncomfortable knot in my chest.

"Evening," the figure called out, their voice low, a trace of familiarity laced with something else—a warning, maybe.

I hesitated, caught off guard by the sudden appearance, and yet, I felt as though I had been waiting for them, like this moment had been written in the stars long before I had walked out the door.

"You're far from the road," I said, finally finding my voice. I knew I was speaking to no one in particular, just a reminder to myself, maybe.

The rider gave a small, dry chuckle. "Thought I might find you here."

The words hung in the air between us, thick with unspoken meaning. It wasn't just coincidence that had brought them here. I could sense it, the invisible thread that tied us together, as though they had been tracking my every move for longer than I had known.

I took a cautious step forward, my eyes scanning the figure. The cloak was pulled tightly around them, and though I couldn't see their face clearly, the faint outline of their jaw seemed oddly familiar.

"Who are you?" The question was blunt, more demand than inquiry, and it echoed in the air like an accusation.

They sighed, the sound carrying a weight of its own. "Someone who has been waiting for you to make your choice."

I felt the ground shift beneath me, an unnerving sensation, as if the earth itself were preparing to swallow me whole. The words were simple, but the implications were not.

"You've been waiting?" I echoed, incredulous, my heart thundering in my chest. "For what?"

The rider shifted on their horse, their gaze now piercing, unwavering. "For you to decide whether to stay or go."

The wind picked up again, but it was no longer comforting. It seemed to carry with it the weight of my past, the one I thought I had left behind, rushing back with the force of a storm. I opened my mouth to say something, anything, but found the words caught in my throat.

And then, as if on cue, the rider leaned forward, the faintest glimmer of recognition crossing their face. "You've been running long enough," they said, their voice softer now, like an old friend offering a truth I wasn't yet ready to hear. "But running doesn't always lead you to freedom."

I felt the knot tighten in my chest, my pulse quickening. Freedom. The word seemed impossible here, tied as I was to the land, to him, to everything that had led me to this moment.

And yet, the rider's words held a strange kind of gravity, pulling me further into the night.

I took another step closer to the rider, my boots sinking into the soft, damp earth beneath me. My heart was thudding erratically, as if I could feel the rhythm of some ancient drum, beating in time with the tension that crackled in the space between us. The words, those simple truths they had dropped, were like stones in a pond—ripples expanding, touching everything.

"You think running leads to freedom?" I asked, my voice sharper now, tinged with the frustration that had built up over days, weeks, months of indecision. "What if it leads me straight back to the cage I'm trying to escape?"

The rider didn't flinch at my outburst. If anything, they seemed to lean into it, as if my anger were just another part of the game they were playing—another piece in the puzzle that I wasn't sure I was ready to solve.

"I don't think you understand the cage you're talking about," they said softly, their voice like velvet, smooth but heavy. "You think you're free, but you're already trapped. Just not by what you think."

I frowned, a rush of confusion clouding my thoughts. "What does that even mean?"

The rider remained silent for a long moment, their gaze unwavering, as if the answer to my question was written in the space between us, and I just had to figure it out for myself. The horse shifted, restless beneath them, the dark creature's breath misting in the cool air. I could feel my own breath catch in my chest as I waited, not sure whether I was more curious or terrified of what might come next.

"You've been running from yourself, haven't you?" The question was so quiet, so simple, that it almost didn't make sense. But it landed with the force of something far heavier. "You've convinced yourself that leaving the life you knew would be your salvation, but you can't outrun what's inside you."

I opened my mouth to argue, to tell them that they didn't know me, that they didn't know the things I had done, the life I had chosen to leave behind. But the words stuck in my throat, heavy and foreign. Because somewhere deep inside, I knew they were right. I hadn't left the life behind. I had only run from the fear that haunted me, the same fear that clung to me even now, out here in the open. The fear of facing what I had become.

"And now you're asking yourself if you can really build something here," the rider continued, their words weaving around me, pulling me deeper into the truth I didn't want to see. "If you can be the person he believes you are, or if you'll break and become the person you fear."

A sudden gust of wind swept through the grove, pulling at my hair, the cold snapping me out of the fog their words had left in my mind. I shook my head, as though the action could clear the haze that had settled there. The rider's words held power, and that power was terrifying in its simplicity.

I couldn't stay here in this limbo, couldn't continue this dance of uncertainty. I needed to go back inside, to feel the warmth of the cabin, the warmth of him, but part of me was tethered to the rider. To the truth they carried.

"I don't know what you want from me," I said, my voice quiet now, almost a whisper, as though saying the words aloud might make them real. "I'm not asking for salvation. I'm not asking for anything but a chance to breathe."

The rider shifted in the saddle, their eyes narrowing slightly as they surveyed me. "Then breathe," they said simply, as though it were the simplest thing in the world. "But stop running."

I wanted to argue. To snap back, to shout that it wasn't that easy. But I couldn't. The truth of their words hit too close, too hard. My breath came in shallow bursts, my chest tight, as I tried to push away the suffocating feeling that gripped me. The choice I had been avoiding, the one that had seemed so distant and unattainable, was suddenly here, on my doorstep.

Before I could process it, the rider turned their horse sharply, the creature snorting as it moved, and with a soft click of their tongue, they urged it forward, moving quickly, retreating into the trees without another word. I stood frozen in place, watching the fading silhouette as the sounds of hooves became distant, swallowed by the night.

It was only then that I realized the rider hadn't given me the one thing I had expected from them: an answer. An easy resolution, a way out. Instead, they had left me with more questions than I could handle, and the unsettling sensation that I was standing on the edge of something I wasn't prepared to face.

I turned back toward the cabin, my feet heavy with the weight of uncertainty, but when I reached the porch, the door creaked open, and there he was—Elliot. His figure framed in the warm, golden light spilling from the doorway. The moment our eyes met, my breath caught in my throat, and I felt everything I had been running from—the fear, the guilt, the love—rush toward me in a wave that nearly knocked me off my feet.

"You okay?" he asked, his voice low, the concern in his eyes clear, but it was the way he looked at me—like he saw me, truly saw me—that nearly undid me.

I opened my mouth to speak, but the words wouldn't come. Instead, I took a step toward him, then another, until I was standing before him, so close I could feel the heat of his body, the steady rhythm of his heartbeat against mine. My heart was beating wildly, but it wasn't from fear anymore. It was the pull of everything that had been left unsaid between us.

"Elliot," I whispered, reaching up to touch his cheek, feeling the warmth of his skin beneath my fingertips. "I—I don't know if I'm strong enough for this."

He cupped my hand with his, his touch warm and steady. His eyes locked onto mine, searching, as if trying to read the storm raging inside me.

"You don't have to be strong enough for anything," he said, his voice soft but firm, like a promise I wasn't sure I could trust. "Not for me."

I opened my mouth to respond, but then a sharp crack echoed through the night—the unmistakable sound of breaking wood, followed by a sudden, guttural shout.

And then—silence.

Chapter 40: Flickers of Forever

The sky was impossibly blue, the kind of blue that feels like it's been brushed with hope. Camp had always been a place where the world seemed smaller, like time itself had slowed its relentless pace just for us. But now, as the last days melted away like summer's fading heat, I could feel the shift, the closing of one chapter and the hesitant opening of another. The air around me was alive with the chatter of goodbyes—loud, jubilant, and tinged with the same sadness that curled in my chest.

I stood at the edge of the clearing, where the lake stretched out before us like a mirror, its surface shimmering under the dappled sunlight that filtered through the towering trees. The smell of pine and campfire lingered in the air, a scent that I knew would cling to my memories long after I left. My fingers intertwined with his, and I could feel the pulse of his hand beneath mine—steady, unwavering, as though he could keep me anchored in this moment for just a little longer.

"You're quiet," he said, his voice low, teasing in that way I'd come to love. I looked up at him, catching the soft curve of his smile, the one that always made my heart stutter in a way I still couldn't explain.

"I'm just... thinking," I murmured, shifting my weight to my other foot, the crunch of gravel beneath me somehow louder in the silence between us.

"About what?" He tilted his head, his dark eyes searching mine with that intensity that could make me feel like I was the only person in the world who mattered.

"About how we're supposed to just... leave," I said, my voice barely above a whisper. I didn't want to admit it, but there was a pit in my stomach, a gnawing ache that seemed to grow the closer we came to the end of this place. "How we're supposed to walk away from this—this, us—and everything will just go back to normal."

"Normal?" He raised an eyebrow, his lips quirking in that way that suggested he was trying to make light of it, but I saw the underlying seriousness in his expression. "I don't think there's a 'normal' anymore, not for us."

His words settled over me like a weight I wasn't prepared to carry. I wanted to believe that the world we had built here—between the stolen moments, the shared laughter, the way we made each other feel like we belonged—would somehow follow us back into the real world. But I wasn't sure. The real world was never kind to people like us, not with its endless obligations, its sharp edges, its expectations that always seemed to break you down, piece by piece.

"Do you think this... this is just a summer thing?" I asked, the question hanging between us, fragile and uncertain. My heart thudded against my ribs, as if it already knew the answer.

He let out a soft laugh, the sound so familiar, so comfortable, that it almost lulled me into believing everything would be okay. "No. I don't think this is just a summer thing. Not for me." His thumb brushed over the back of my hand, a simple gesture that made everything feel right again. "But what happens next? That's something we have to figure out."

I turned my gaze back to the lake, watching the ripples that danced across its surface as if trying to outrun the breeze. It was so beautiful, so endless, and I wondered if the stillness I saw on the water was an illusion—if beneath the surface, there were currents I couldn't see, pulling everything in different directions.

"I'm scared," I admitted, my voice a little shaky as I turned back to face him. He'd always been my rock, the one constant in this whirlwind of emotions that summer had thrown at us. I trusted him more than I'd trusted anyone in my life, and yet, standing here with him, I couldn't shake the gnawing doubt that maybe the world was bigger than either of us knew. That maybe, despite how deeply we felt for each other, the universe had other plans.

He cupped my cheek, his touch warm and reassuring, and for a moment, the world seemed to pause, holding its breath. "You don't have to be scared," he said, his voice a promise, even though I knew he didn't have all the answers either. "We'll figure this out together."

I leaned into his touch, closing my eyes for a moment to savor the feeling of being here, with him. The hum of camp life around us faded as I let myself bask in the quiet certainty that for now, in this moment, we had everything we needed. I wasn't ready to let go, not of him, not of this place that had somehow felt like home.

But as the sun dipped lower in the sky, casting long shadows across the ground, I knew that we would have to. The time would come when we would have to leave this sanctuary behind, return to the world outside, where things weren't so simple. And in that moment, the weight of the world seemed heavier than I could bear.

He kissed the top of my head, his lips soft against my hair. "No matter what happens," he said, his words a steady rhythm that seemed to align with my own heartbeat, "we'll always have this. We'll always have us."

The warmth of his breath lingered in the air between us, and I wanted to believe him. Wanted to believe that no matter how far apart life tried to pull us, we would always find a way back to this. To each other.

And maybe, just maybe, that was enough for now.

It's strange, how you can be standing in the middle of something so familiar, and yet, at the same time, feel as though you're seeing it all for the first time. The camp was still the same—the same crackling fires, the same laughter echoing off the walls of the mess hall, the same clumsy games that made us all look like kids again. But it was as though everything had shifted in the briefest of moments. The heavy weight of goodbye hung in the air, and suddenly, nothing was permanent. The sun-kissed faces of friends who had become family seemed more fragile, more fleeting. And as much as I wanted to memorize every last detail—every laugh, every touch, every shared secret—I knew I couldn't hold onto it all. Time, like water, always finds a way to slip through your fingers.

I tugged at the hem of my shirt, the fabric soft but worn in places from too many days spent under the hot sun. The camp's usual rhythm had settled into a lull, a quiet before the storm of departure. My fingers were still threaded through his, but now the air felt thick with unspoken words. As the days stretched out, I could feel the pull of uncertainty, like an invisible thread tugging me toward something I couldn't quite see.

"So, what happens when we leave?" I asked, my voice cutting through the stillness between us. He glanced down at me, his brow furrowing slightly, as if he was trying to gauge if I was asking a simple question or something much more complicated.

"I don't know," he said after a beat, his lips twisting into a half-smile that didn't quite reach his eyes. "But I'm not worried about it. Not yet."

"I think I'm more worried about it than you," I admitted, my shoulders stiffening slightly as I forced myself to meet his gaze. There it was again—the weight of the future hanging over us, casting a shadow I couldn't shake. "I can't help it. We're not kids anymore, and I'm not sure we're ready for what happens after."

He shrugged, his thumb brushing over the back of my hand in that familiar, calming way. "We'll be fine. You and me. We always figure it out."

I wanted to believe him. I wanted to take those words and tuck them into my heart like a secret promise. But part of me knew better. The world outside wasn't as forgiving as the camp had been.

Out there, everything moved faster, louder, and far less forgiving. Relationships weren't forged in the quiet solitude of pine forests or late-night confessions over marshmallows. They were messy and complicated and prone to falling apart when you least expected it.

"I hope so," I muttered, more to myself than to him. "I hope you're right."

The sound of footsteps crunching in the gravel behind us made me glance over my shoulder. One of our friends, Casey, was making her way toward us, her face flushed from a run, a wide grin spreading across her face as she saw us.

"Hey," she said, her voice breathless but somehow still full of that unmistakable energy. "You two planning on just standing here all day?"

I laughed, a little too sharply, and stepped away from him, as if the distance could somehow lessen the pressure that had been building up between us. "I was just thinking," I said, the words slipping out before I could stop them. "About what comes next. After this place."

Casey's grin faded, her eyes narrowing slightly as she studied me. "Are you worried?" she asked, her voice quieter now, more serious. "Because I've been trying not to think about it, but I kind of figured you would be."

"Worried?" I shook my head, trying to laugh it off. "Of course not. I'm not worried. Why would I be?"

She raised an eyebrow, clearly not buying it. "You know," she said slowly, glancing between the two of us, "I don't think you realize how rare what you guys have is. I mean, we've all seen it. The way you two look at each other, like you're the only two people in the world."

I felt my stomach twist at her words, because for all the moments we'd shared, the quiet understanding, the warmth in his gaze, I hadn't realized just how fragile it all felt. "We're just...

figuring it out," I said, my voice trailing off as I turned my eyes back to the lake.

Casey, sensing the shift, dropped the teasing tone, her expression softening. "You'll figure it out," she said with certainty, and then, as if to lighten the mood, added, "And if not, you can always come back here. We'll build a camp for grown-ups. I'll even run the concession stand."

Her attempt at humor was the kind of thing that should've made me laugh, but all I could manage was a half-smile. The truth was, I wasn't sure what would happen when I left. Whether we would remain tangled in this quiet, perfect connection, or if the weight of the outside world would pull us apart. I wanted to think we could survive it, that the distance wouldn't matter. But the truth always felt more complicated than the simplicity of hope.

"Thanks, Casey," I said, swallowing the lump in my throat. "I think we'll need more than just a camp."

Casey shot me a look, her usual grin returning. "Hey, I'll take care of the camp. You just handle the love story." With that, she turned and jogged away, her laughter ringing out behind her, leaving me standing there, still holding his hand, still feeling the weight of everything left unsaid.

And as the sun began its slow descent behind the trees, casting the camp in a warm, amber glow, I found myself wishing I could just freeze time—hold onto this moment forever. But life wasn't like that. Life didn't wait, and neither did love. We had to move forward, step by uncertain step, and hope that whatever came next would be enough to hold us together.

The last night felt like something pulled straight out of a dream—beautiful, fragile, and fading all too quickly. The fire crackled in the center of the clearing, sending sparks into the inky black sky like little whispers of everything that had passed. I should've been caught up in the joy of one last campfire sing-along, but instead, I couldn't shake the feeling that I was standing at the edge of something I couldn't control, like trying to hold onto a tide that was already pulling away from me.

He sat beside me, his hand still resting in mine, but there was a tension in the way his thumb moved over my skin, a nervous energy in the small motions, as if he, too, could feel the weight of this moment.

"You're quiet," he said, his voice low but laced with the playful edge I knew so well.

I glanced up at him, forcing a smile. "I'm just trying to soak this all in," I said, trying to sound casual, like the lump in my throat wasn't threatening to choke me.

"You've been 'soaking it in' all week," he teased, nudging me with his shoulder. "What is it really?"

I took a deep breath, pulling my knees up to my chest as I stared at the flames. "It's... I don't know. It's everything. Everything we've built here, all of us, all these memories." I turned to look at him, meeting his gaze, the familiar warmth in his eyes doing little to ease the tightening knot in my chest. "It feels like it's slipping away, like it'll never be real again once we leave. And I'm not ready to say goodbye to this. To you."

He didn't say anything for a moment, just looked at me with an intensity that made my breath hitch in my throat. He was the kind of person who could make you feel like the whole world was just the two of you, no barriers, no distance. And now, standing on the precipice of the unknown, that feeling had never felt more fragile.

"We don't have to say goodbye," he finally said, his voice almost too soft, too careful, as if he was testing the waters of something bigger than either of us were ready for.

"I wish it were that simple," I replied, my voice cracking despite my best efforts to hold it together. "You and I both know it's not. We're going back to real life. Back to... everything that's out there."

The fire shifted, sending another shower of sparks into the air, and I watched them fade, one by one, until the night was left in its deep, unyielding quiet. The world outside camp was waiting for us, as if it had been holding its breath for us to return. And that was the part I couldn't shake—the way the real world had a way of demanding more than you had to give. Camp had been an oasis, a space where I could breathe, where we could just exist without the weight of expectations crushing down on us. But the moment we stepped outside those boundaries, it was like we were back in the race, lost in the hustle of everything that could pull us apart.

"You don't have to go back to it, you know," he said, his voice steady, insistent.

I raised an eyebrow at him, glancing sidelong as I let out a laugh that held no humor. "And what exactly do you think I'll do? Just run away from everything? You know that's not how life works."

"I don't know," he said, leaning in just enough that I could feel his breath warm against my ear. "Maybe it should be."

His words held a weight to them, something deeper than we'd ever talked about. It felt like something was shifting, like the space between us had narrowed, making every word feel more like an ultimatum than a suggestion.

"I can't just leave," I whispered, the admission slipping out before I could stop it. "I can't leave everything behind... you behind."

His hand tightened around mine, and for a moment, I could have sworn I felt the pulse of his heart echo mine. "Then don't."

My chest constricted at his words, a sharp pang in my throat that made it hard to breathe. "And if I can't stay? What if everything falls apart when we leave? I won't have this, and I won't have you."

"We don't know that yet," he said, and this time his voice was firm, resolute. "We don't know what comes next. But I do know this—this, us, is real. And whatever happens, we'll figure it out."

I looked at him, really looked at him, as if seeing him for the first time again. His jaw was set, his eyes wide and unyielding, as if he was already willing to fight for whatever we were. The realization hit me like a wave—he wasn't just holding my hand; he was holding onto us, to something we'd built out of nothing but trust and moments that seemed too fleeting to last. But here he was, offering me the same promise I'd been desperately craving: we were real, and maybe that was enough.

"I wish I could believe you," I murmured, my voice barely above a whisper.

"You don't have to believe it," he said, his thumb brushing over my knuckles in that soothing motion. "You just have to let it be true."

I closed my eyes, letting his words settle over me like a blanket, something warm, something steady. But just as I thought I might be able to breathe again, the sharp crack of a twig snapping broke through the moment, and I turned, heart leaping in my chest.

In the distance, barely visible in the shadows of the trees, a figure emerged—someone I hadn't expected to see tonight, someone I hadn't expected to see ever again. And in that moment, the air between us turned heavy, thick with something unspoken, something I hadn't been prepared for.

My breath caught in my throat as I locked eyes with the newcomer, a chill running down my spine. Because standing there, silhouetted against the fading light of the fire, was someone who had no business being here at all.

Chapter 41: Beyond the Flame

The sun hadn't quite risen, but the air already tasted of salt, thick with the scent of earth and the sea's endless murmur. I shifted my weight from one foot to the other, the rough canvas of my pack digging into my shoulders, but I didn't mind. It was a comfort now—this weight, this small, familiar burden. Behind me, the remnants of the camp smoldered faintly in the morning light, the last of the embers giving way to the crisp wind that swept through the clearing. I was free, and it felt like I had never truly understood what that word meant until this very moment.

The distant cry of seagulls seemed to echo the stirrings in my chest, an invitation to something more, something I wasn't entirely ready for but knew would be impossible to resist. The future stretched before me, an unmarked trail with no guarantees. For once, that didn't scare me. I had been afraid for so long, long enough to make uncertainty feel like home, but I was done with it. With every step I took away from the past, the weight of my old life grew lighter. Even the air seemed cleaner, as if the winds had swept away the ghosts of my doubts, leaving only space for what was to come.

Beside me, Rowan adjusted the straps on his own pack, his movements steady and precise. I caught the slight grimace of discomfort as the weight shifted, but he never once complained. The man was a mystery wrapped in muscle and restraint, a paradox I hadn't even begun to unravel. There were nights, when the fire was low, when I could see the shadows in his eyes, the quiet battles he fought in silence. He wore his past like an old coat, something he never spoke of but always carried. And yet, for all his silence, his presence was a balm, a steadying force in a world that had once threatened to swallow me whole.

I glanced at him as we began walking, the soft scrape of our boots against the ground the only sound between us for a while. His eyes were distant, fixed on the horizon. I'd learned that Rowan, in moments like this, was always thinking three steps ahead, plotting paths only he could see. Sometimes, I felt like an intruder in the workings of his mind, a guest in a world he barely shared with anyone. But today, as the first rays of light caught in his dark hair, I couldn't help but wonder if he was thinking of me—of the new life we were building together, the one that started the moment we decided to leave the camp behind.

The landscape around us was changing, the forest giving way to more open land. The path we walked on was barely a trail, overgrown with wild grasses that brushed against our legs with every step. I welcomed the uneven ground, the unpredictability of it, just like the future. In the distance, the sound of waves crashing against jagged rocks reached my ears, reminding me that the sea was never far from us. Its vastness, its endless horizon, felt like a reflection of everything that lay ahead.

Rowan finally spoke, his voice low and rich like the earth itself. "You're quiet."

I glanced over at him, catching the corner of his lips curling into something that almost resembled a smile. "I'm thinking," I replied, a little too defensive. "And sometimes, thinking requires silence."

He raised an eyebrow, his gaze flickering over to me. "If it's a choice between silence and conversation, I'll take the latter."

I laughed, shaking my head. "Of course you would. It's easier for you to talk, isn't it? Always so sure of what to say." I paused, then added with a smirk, "I wouldn't be surprised if you've got a whole list of charming lines stored up for moments like this."

He chuckled, the sound low and pleasant, like the rumble of thunder in the distance. "You've got me figured out, haven't you?"

His tone was playful, but there was something deeper in it, something I couldn't place. A vulnerability, maybe, carefully masked by his dry humor.

"Not quite," I said, daring to reach out and nudge him with my shoulder. "You're more than just your charm, you know."

His eyes met mine for a moment, something soft flickering there before he looked away again. "I hope so."

I felt the weight of his words settle between us, an unspoken acknowledgment of everything we had been through, everything that had brought us to this point. There were things I still didn't know about him, things he had yet to share, but I wasn't afraid. Not anymore. We had made it through the worst of it, hadn't we? There was nothing that could stand in our way now—not with him by my side.

The path began to incline, the land rising gently toward a small hill. I could see the distant outline of a village, the smoke from chimneys rising into the sky, but it felt far away, like something from another life. A life I was done living. What mattered now was what lay ahead. The horizon beckoned, and with it, the promise of a future we would carve out together, one day at a time.

Rowan's hand brushed against mine, a fleeting touch that left my skin tingling. It was subtle, but unmistakable. He wasn't saying anything, but the simple gesture said enough. We were in this together. The past was behind us, and the future was ours to claim. We were no longer bound by secrets or fear. Our love, however wild and uncontainable it had been, had become the very thing that anchored us, that kept us grounded in the face of the unknown.

I didn't know where the road would lead, or what awaited us beyond the next bend. But I did know one thing for sure: with Rowan by my side, there was nothing I couldn't face. Nothing we couldn't face together.

The village came into view more quickly than I had expected, the crooked rooftops and winding streets spread out before us like a map I hadn't yet learned to read. As we walked, I noticed how different it felt to be moving toward something, rather than running from it. The heavy thrum of uncertainty that had once vibrated through my veins now seemed to pulse in sync with the rhythm of our steps, steady and sure. I glanced over at Rowan, whose silence, for once, felt comfortable, like the quiet before a storm, where you knew something wild was coming, but you weren't quite sure what it would look like. It was the kind of silence I'd come to trust.

The town was small but bustling, filled with the rich scent of baking bread and the tang of salt that clung to the air. It reminded me of everything I had longed for but never allowed myself to dream of—peace, simplicity, a place where the only thing that mattered was what you made of your days. I hadn't realized how starved I'd been for something so basic, so elemental. And yet, as we walked through the town's modest square, I could feel the stirrings of something more between us, something that was beginning to feel real in a way that neither of us had expected. Rowan had been quiet, too quiet, but not in the brooding way he sometimes got when something was weighing on him. No, this was different. He was waiting, watching, perhaps even expecting something from me, though what, I wasn't sure.

A street vendor with a wide-brimmed hat and a shirt that looked like it had seen better days waved us over. "Fresh fruit!" he called, his grin wide and inviting. "The best in the whole town, guaranteed!" He pulled a wrinkled apple from his basket and offered it to me. The bright red of the fruit against the dull gray of the cobbled street seemed like a small miracle.

I smiled, feeling suddenly lighter. "I'll take two," I said, reaching into my bag for some coins.

Rowan stood beside me, his gaze fixed on the vendor's wares, but his expression was unreadable. He wasn't much for small talk, but there was something about this place, about the simplicity of it, that made even he seem more at ease. I handed the vendor the coins and took the apples, feeling the coolness of them in my palm.

He leaned over as we started walking again. "Do you ever stop and think that this is real?" he asked, his voice soft but steady. "That it's happening?"

I looked over at him, his words catching me off guard. I hadn't expected him to voice the question that had been swirling in my mind ever since we'd started walking this morning. "Isn't it?" I said, my mouth suddenly dry. I took a bite of the apple, the sweetness cutting through the tension in my throat. "What do you mean? It's real. We're here, aren't we?"

He chuckled, a sound that made my pulse race in a way that had nothing to do with the walk or the destination. "I mean," he paused, his voice trailing off for a moment, like he was trying to choose his words carefully, "I thought it would feel different, you know? I thought we'd feel... I don't know, like we were pretending." His gaze flickered to the side, as though he was embarrassed to admit it.

It was my turn to laugh, but it came out in a soft, relieved sort of exhale. "We're pretending nothing. We're living, Rowan. For the first time in a long time, we're really living." I paused, studying his face. "Maybe it's not about the destination, but how we get there."

He didn't answer right away, but his hand brushed mine as we walked, the contact barely there but enough to make me forget how to breathe for a beat. I felt the intensity of his unspoken thoughts, like he was weighing them against something too heavy to voice aloud. I wanted to ask him what was bothering him, but I also knew that I had to let him come to it in his own time. For all the ways we were alike, there were still parts of him that were entirely his own, and I wasn't going to rush him into sharing them with me.

"Do you think they'll take us in?" he asked, changing the subject. His eyes flickered toward the inn up ahead, its sign swaying gently in the wind.

I turned my head, scanning the building. It was modest, nothing flashy, but it had a warmth to it that seemed to promise comfort. "If they don't, we'll find somewhere else," I said with a grin, pretending to be braver than I felt. "And if we don't find anywhere else, we'll figure something out. Together."

Rowan's lips quirked in the faintest of smiles. "Always 'together,' huh?"

I nodded. "Always."

The innkeeper was a broad-shouldered woman with hair the color of chestnuts, streaked with silver, and a welcoming smile that felt like home in an unexpected way. Her hands were calloused, her nails short and practical, but her eyes were sharp as she sized us up. It didn't take much, just a moment of silence, before she seemed to make up her mind.

"You two look like you've been on the road a while," she said, brushing her hands off on her apron. "I've got a room for the night, if you need it."

I wasn't sure what I expected—perhaps a warmer reception, a kinder inquiry into our story—but her matter-of-fact tone was like a balm for the raw edge of vulnerability that had been gnawing at my nerves. It was exactly what we needed: no questions asked, no pitying looks, just a place to rest.

"We'll take it," I said, and Rowan nodded his agreement, his gaze still on the innkeeper but with a new softness in his eyes. Maybe, just maybe, we weren't the strangers we had once thought ourselves to be.

The room was small, the bed tucked neatly against one wall, a fireplace crackling softly in the corner, its warmth spreading across the wooden floor. There was a faded tapestry hanging above the mantle, depicting a scene that seemed almost too perfect—rolling hills, a sky that stretched on forever, the sort of thing you could only dream about when the weight of the world was pressing on your shoulders. It felt like a promise, a glimpse of the life that could be ours if we were brave enough to take it.

Rowan set his pack down by the door with a muted thud and turned to me, his gaze thoughtful. I couldn't tell if it was the flickering light from the fire casting shadows across his face or if something was truly shifting in him, but there was an intensity in his eyes that made me want to hold my breath. He didn't speak right away, just moved to the window, where the soft glow of the evening sun painted the town below in hues of orange and gold.

I watched him, feeling the quiet stretch between us. It was a comfortable silence, but one that felt heavy with unspoken things—things I wasn't sure I was ready to address. The past had a way of creeping into moments like this, no matter how far you thought you'd run from it. But I wasn't going to let it define us anymore.

Rowan finally broke the silence, his voice soft, as if testing the weight of his words. "Do you think it'll be enough?"

I turned to face him, the question catching me off guard. It wasn't the kind of thing you asked when you were standing on the edge of something new, something exciting. But there it was, hanging in the air between us, the vulnerability in his question laid bare.

"Enough?" I repeated, my brow furrowing as I searched his face for the meaning behind it. "Enough for what?"

He turned toward me, his gaze unwavering. "For the life we want. For everything we've been through and everything that's ahead of us. Do you think we can really leave it all behind?"

My chest tightened at the rawness in his voice. I knew what he meant. The ghosts of our past, the things we couldn't outrun, they had a way of catching up to us, no matter how much distance we put between them. But it wasn't the past that I was focused on. It was the present, the here and now.

"I think we can," I said, my voice steady. "We already have."

He was silent for a moment, and I could see the tension ease from his shoulders, though the storm behind his eyes didn't completely subside. I wanted to say more, to offer him some comfort, but I wasn't sure what words would do. Some things were too deep, too tangled for simple answers.

Instead, I walked over to the small table by the window, where a pitcher of water and two glasses sat, waiting. The act of moving, of doing something, felt like the right answer, even if it was only temporary. I poured the water into the glasses, my hands steady, and handed one to him.

"Thank you," he murmured, his voice softer now, the weight of his question still lingering in the air, unspoken but understood. I didn't ask him to clarify. I didn't need to.

The room seemed to shrink around us, the walls closing in, the fire crackling with an almost too eager energy, as if it could feel the weight of our shared uncertainty. I wasn't sure where we were headed, not really. It was hard to imagine the future when all you had was the present, but I knew one thing with certainty: we were in this together.

We sat in silence for a while, the low hum of the town drifting in from the street below, the quiet comfort of the moment wrapping itself around us like a blanket. There was no urgency now, no need to rush. We had time, at least for tonight.

I leaned back against the chair, my eyes drifting over the room, the firelight dancing on the walls, the scent of woodsmoke filling the space. But even in the midst of such calm, I couldn't shake the feeling that something was coming, something that would shift everything we thought we knew. Rowan had a way of looking at me sometimes, like he could see right through the layers I had carefully built. And as much as I hated to admit it, I couldn't always do the same with him.

The knock on the door startled both of us, the sound sharp and unexpected, slicing through the quiet like a blade. Rowan stood immediately, his instincts alert, and I followed suit, my heart pounding a little faster than it should have. Who could it be at this hour?

Rowan crossed the room quickly, his hand on the door, his body tense, ready for whatever lay on the other side. I stood behind him, my breath caught in my throat, unsure if I should be afraid or curious. The moment stretched out, thick with anticipation, before the door finally creaked open.

The man standing in the doorway was unfamiliar, tall and broad-shouldered, with a face that was weathered but handsome in an untamed way. His eyes were a sharp, steely blue, and they locked onto Rowan's immediately, a flicker of recognition passing between them. I noticed the way his hand hovered near the hilt of a knife at his belt, the subtle tension in his posture. Whatever this was, it wasn't a friendly visit.

"I need to speak with you," the man said, his voice rough but urgent. His gaze shifted to me, assessing me quickly before returning to Rowan. "Alone."

Rowan's posture stiffened, his jaw tightening, but he didn't move to close the door. Instead, he gave a slight nod, his eyes never leaving the stranger's face. "Come in," he said, his voice low, measured.

As the door swung wide, I took a step back, my instincts screaming that whatever was about to unfold would change everything. The stranger stepped inside, his boots clicking softly against the wooden floor. The air in the room shifted, and I knew, with a cold certainty, that our new life—the one we'd barely begun to build—was already under threat.

The sun had barely stretched its arms over the horizon when I pulled into the parking lot of the little café on the corner. The air smelled of saltwater and something like rain, though the sky was still clear, the deep blue of the early morning sun almost making the ocean look too perfect to be real. My fingers tightened around the steering wheel as I parked, the leather of the seat squeaking under me as I shifted my weight. It had been one of those nights—when you lie awake, staring at the ceiling, fighting the pull of a thousand half-formed thoughts that dance in your head like fireflies, teasing and never quite landing long enough to make sense of them.

I wasn't entirely sure why I was here. Maybe it was the familiar hum of this place, or the way the café seemed to have forgotten time. I'd come here a hundred times before, but this morning felt different, like the universe had shifted and I was just catching up. The doorbell above the entrance jingled as I stepped inside, and I inhaled deeply, letting the scent of brewing coffee and baked goods settle into my bones.

"Morning," Sam called from behind the counter, his voice low and warm, like the sound of distant thunder. I waved, offering the briefest of smiles before slipping onto one of the worn stools that lined the counter. There was a kind of comfort in the routine of it all—the clink of ceramic mugs, the low murmur of other patrons, the steady drip of coffee from the machine. It was all background noise to the quiet that buzzed in my own mind.

"You look like you could use something strong today," Sam said, arching an eyebrow as he poured me a cup of coffee, black as midnight, thick and inviting. I didn't respond immediately, just wrapped my hands around the mug, feeling the warmth seep into my skin. A second passed, and then another. Sam didn't push. He'd learned a long time ago that when I was quiet, it was best to leave me to my thoughts.

"Still waiting for the world to make sense?" he asked after a moment, leaning on the counter in a way that was too casual to be entirely innocent. I let out a soft laugh, the sound almost foreign coming from my lips.

"You make it sound like I'm waiting for a miracle," I replied, letting the steam from the coffee fog up my glasses before wiping them off absently. The question I didn't ask hung between us like an invisible weight. I could feel it. He could feel it. But neither of us was quite ready to confront it.

He poured a little more coffee into my mug, and I watched, entranced by the way the liquid darkened, swirling around the edges before settling into a steady pool. There was something about the motion that made everything else feel still. Maybe that's what I needed—stillness, the kind that let me untangle the knot in my chest.

I glanced around the room. The café was mostly empty, save for a woman sitting at a table near the window, her face hidden behind a stack of books. The shelves lining the walls were cluttered with old novels and dusty trinkets, a world all their own. Every piece of the place was familiar—too familiar, maybe. But the familiarity was like a hug I didn't realize I needed until I was wrapped in it.

"You ever think we're all just..." I trailed off, not sure how to finish the thought, but Sam picked it up anyway, as though he'd known exactly where I was going.

"Waiting for something that never shows up?" he finished for me, and I nodded, the weight of his words settling heavily on me.

Sam had a way of making everything sound simple, even when it was anything but.

"Yeah. That," I said, my voice softer this time, almost as if saying the words out loud could make them disappear. "Except sometimes I wonder if I'm not waiting for something at all, but just for the moment to be... over. The waiting. The wondering."

"You mean, like we're all just biding time until we finally figure out how to move on?" Sam asked, and I met his gaze, seeing something in his eyes that I hadn't expected. Understanding. It was like he'd peeled back a layer of himself I hadn't known was there.

I shifted in my seat, avoiding the intensity of his look. "Maybe that's what it is. Or maybe we're just too afraid to look too closely at what's right in front of us." My fingers tapped lightly on the edge of the mug, a nervous habit I hadn't even realized I had until now.

"Or maybe," Sam said, his voice suddenly quieter, "we're all just scared of realizing that we're the ones standing in the way of our own happiness."

The words hung in the air between us, heavy and sharp. I couldn't quite shake the feeling that he was speaking from somewhere deep, some place where truth lived but never quite found its way into daylight. His eyes never left mine as I processed the weight of what he'd said. Sam had a way of cutting straight to the heart of things without even trying.

I took a sip of my coffee, the heat burning my tongue, and forced my thoughts back to the present. "I'm not sure what it is," I said finally, the words tasting bittersweet as they left my mouth. "But I think maybe... just maybe, I'm ready to find out."

Sam didn't answer right away. Instead, he smiled, just the smallest, knowing curve of his lips, and I knew he wasn't expecting an answer from me just then. Maybe he didn't need one. Maybe I didn't either. All I knew was that for the first time in a long while, I didn't feel entirely lost.

It was easy to pretend that nothing had changed in the last few days, especially with Sam standing there behind the counter, wearing that faint, enigmatic smile that seemed to be a permanent feature of his. He always knew when I was skating around something, and worse, he had this uncanny ability to wait me out. It was like he had a stopwatch in his head that started ticking the second I walked in, counting down the exact moment it would all spill out of me. And today, I could feel it coming. The thing I'd been trying to avoid, the thing that had lodged itself right in my chest.

I took another sip of coffee, the bitterness grounding me, but it didn't quite stop the tremble in my hands. It had been two days since I'd seen Jacob—two days of pretending I could just let everything go back to normal. But normal was a broken thing. A cracked, splintered version of what it used to be. And I wasn't sure I could fix it, or if I even wanted to.

The door opened with a soft jingle, and a gust of fresh air swirled inside, carrying with it the scent of rain from the horizon. A man in a navy jacket stepped in, shaking droplets from his hair. For a moment, my gaze lingered on him, the starkness of his presence cutting through the haze of my thoughts. He caught my eye as he entered, and for the briefest second, I could have sworn I saw something flicker in his expression. But then he blinked, and it was gone.

He approached the counter with purposeful steps, his boots tapping against the worn floor, and I shifted, trying to look like I wasn't overly aware of him. I didn't know who he was, but I couldn't deny the sharp pull of curiosity that tugged at me. Sam slid a mug in his direction, and the man gave a polite nod.

"Thanks," he said, his voice low, a roughness to it that suggested long nights spent talking or yelling, or maybe both.

"No problem," Sam answered, returning to the back with the sort of quiet efficiency that made you feel like the whole café operated in perfect rhythm without you even noticing.

I leaned back, staring at the space between me and the stranger. For some reason, it felt like he was waiting for something—waiting for me to do something. As if I owed him a reaction.

I blinked, and my mind snapped back into focus, trying to shake off the absurdity of it. I wasn't exactly in the habit of making eye contact with strangers—especially not ones who seemed so... present. The kind of presence that demanded acknowledgment, like the weight of their gaze could actually make you move.

"So," I said, forcing a bit of humor into my voice, "we're all waiting for the rain, huh?"

The man's lips twitched, and for the briefest second, I thought he might actually laugh. But instead, he looked out the window, at the grey sky pressing down like a blanket, threatening to swallow the sun. "Seems that way," he said, his tone even, measured.

"Yeah," I replied, my fingers tapping idly on the rim of my cup. "It's like it's always just about to rain, but never quite does."

The silence that followed felt too heavy for casual conversation. I shifted on my stool, feeling like I was too close to some unspoken edge, teetering right at the brink.

"I'm Abby," I said, because it seemed like the right thing to do. Introduce myself. A small gesture. Something that would make the air feel less thick. But as soon as the words left my mouth, I knew it hadn't done anything at all.

He glanced at me then, a flicker of something I couldn't quite name in his eyes. "Drew," he said. Just one word, but it was enough.

I nodded and returned to my coffee, trying to ignore the prickling feeling that had settled along my spine. But Drew didn't leave. He stood there, sipping his drink, the occasional glance flicking back to me, his gaze almost... calculating? My chest tightened again. This wasn't the sort of encounter I was in the mood for. I wasn't ready for anything that wasn't comfortable, and this guy—this man with the storm in his eyes—had made things anything but comfortable.

I fumbled with the handle of my mug, the motion a little too sharp, too quick. "So, you from around here?" I asked, not sure why I even cared. The words felt empty, hollow, like I was going through the motions of conversation without actually feeling it.

"Not exactly," Drew replied, his voice still holding that quiet strength, as if each word was deliberate, like he was weighing it before it left his lips. "Just passing through."

"Passing through, huh?" I chuckled, but there was no humor behind it, only the sudden sensation that I had wandered into something I wasn't supposed to. My palms began to sweat, a flush rising on my cheeks that had nothing to do with the warmth of the coffee in front of me.

The air in the café had shifted, the very space feeling thicker, more charged. I glanced toward Sam, hoping for an escape, but he was busy with a tray of pastries, his back turned. As if he knew I didn't need saving. I was going to have to deal with this myself.

"So, what brings you to town?" I tried again, because what else could I do? When you're uncomfortable, you ask questions to fill the silence. You keep the small talk going, pretending you're in control of the moment. Pretending like you aren't just waiting for the storm to break.

Drew met my gaze, his eyes darkened now, like they had come alive under some unspoken weight. "Just looking for something," he said, his voice lowering. "Not sure what yet, but maybe I'll find it here."

My heart stuttered, the words landing like a punch I hadn't been ready for. I swallowed hard, my throat dry. There was something in his look now—something I hadn't anticipated. Like he was speaking to me and not just about his passing through town. I couldn't quite pin it, but I knew one thing: whatever this was, it wasn't about coffee anymore.

The tension between us hung there like a thread, barely visible but enough to make the air feel too thick to breathe. Drew hadn't said anything else since his cryptic comment, but the silence had become its own kind of noise, filling the space with something unspoken. My heart beat a little too fast, my fingers gripping the edge of my mug just to steady myself. I hadn't signed up for this—not today, not in this quiet corner of a place that was supposed to be my refuge.

"So," I said, my voice a little sharper than I meant it to be, "looking for something, huh?" I smiled, though it felt more like a mask than a genuine expression. "And what exactly is it that you're hoping to find?"

Drew's gaze lingered on me for a moment too long, as though he were trying to decide how much to reveal. The man was a puzzle, and I wasn't sure if I was intrigued or just unsettled by the mystery of him. He took another sip of his coffee, the cup in his hands almost looking too small for the size of his grip. He set it down slowly, as though weighing his words before letting them slip free.

"Maybe it's not about finding something specific," he said finally, his voice low, like he was talking to himself as much as to me. "Maybe it's about finding a place where you can stop running for a minute." He met my eyes again, the weight of his words making them feel too heavy. "A place where you don't have to pretend anymore."

I blinked, the unexpected depth of his answer taking me off guard. For a moment, I forgot to breathe. My gaze shifted to the rain that had started to fall against the windows, the soft patter of it a distant background to the conversation that had suddenly veered into something far more personal than I was prepared for.

"I'm not sure I know what you mean," I said, not sure whether I was deflecting or genuinely confused.

Drew chuckled softly, but there was no humor in it. It was more like he was amused by how much I was trying to play it off. "You don't have to pretend with me," he said, his voice carrying that same raw honesty from before. "You can stop running."

And there it was. That shift. The thing that made me stiffen, the thing that made me want to get up and walk away from this whole conversation. He was looking right through me, wasn't he? Like he could see the parts of me I didn't want anyone to see.

I swallowed hard, staring at the surface of my coffee as if the swirling dark liquid could somehow absorb the weight of his words. My mouth went dry, and I felt a flutter of panic clawing at my chest. I couldn't let him know. Not now. Not ever. It was easier to keep up the walls, to hide behind the bright, sarcastic smile that I'd perfected over the years.

"You don't know anything about me," I said, my voice coming out sharper than I intended, the edges of my words cutting into the space between us. "You're just passing through, remember?"

His eyes narrowed, but there was no anger in them—just a quiet understanding that made my insides twist. "Maybe," he said, his voice dipping lower, "but sometimes we meet people for a reason, even if we don't know what it is yet."

I wanted to argue with him, to tell him he was wrong. But the truth was, I couldn't remember the last time I'd had a conversation that felt this... real. Most of my interactions were filtered through layers of fake politeness or meaningless small talk. I couldn't remember the last time someone had looked at me like they saw past the surface, like they knew the mess of things I tried so desperately to keep hidden.

I shifted on my stool, uncomfortable with the sudden shift in the dynamic, unsure if I was ready to navigate whatever this was.

But before I could say anything else, the door opened again, this time with the force of a wind gust, and a woman stepped inside, shaking the rain from her coat. She had that look about her—the kind of woman who was used to getting what she wanted, and who could do it with a smile that could melt glass.

I didn't recognize her, but there was something about her presence that felt almost... predatory. She scanned the room, her gaze flicking from Drew to me, and then back to Drew again. A moment passed, just a fraction of a second, before she moved toward the counter, her heels clicking on the floor like the ticking of a clock.

"Excuse me," she said, her voice smooth and practiced. "I'm looking for Drew Turner. Is he here?"

The name hit me like a slap in the face, and I froze. Drew's head jerked up at the mention of his name, his entire posture shifting in an instant. The woman, her lips curving slightly, stepped closer to the counter, her gaze not leaving Drew's face.

Drew's jaw clenched, and for the first time since I'd met him, I saw a flicker of something darker in his eyes—something I couldn't quite place. He didn't answer immediately, and the woman didn't seem to mind the silence. Instead, she smiled, but it wasn't warm. It was sharp, calculating.

"I've been looking for you," she said, each word slow, deliberate. "We need to talk."

I watched Drew for a long moment, searching his face for some clue as to what was going on, but his expression had gone completely still, like someone who was trying very hard not to react. The air in the café seemed to thicken once again, a quiet hum filling the space between us.

I didn't know who this woman was or what she wanted, but I could feel the weight of her presence pressing down on Drew, on me, on everything.

"Do you know her?" I asked, the words slipping out before I could stop them, my voice barely above a whisper.

Drew's eyes flicked to me briefly before he stood, slowly, his movements deliberate. He didn't answer me right away. Instead, he looked at the woman and then back at me, his gaze filled with something unreadable.

And then, without a word, he walked toward the door.